The Chill of Night

JAMES HAYMAN

PENGUIN BOOKS

PENGUIN BOOKS

Published by the Penguin Group
Penguin Books Ltd, 80 Strand, London WC2R ORL, England
Penguin Group (USA) Inc., 375 Hudson Street, New York, New York 10014, USA
Penguin Group (Canada), 90 Eglinton Avenue East, Suite 700, Toronto, Ontario,
Canada M4P 2Y3 (a division of Pearson Penguin Canada Inc.)
Penguin Ireland, 25 St Stephen's Green, Dublin 2, Ireland (a division of Penguin Books Ltd)
Penguin Group (Australia), 250 Camberwell Road, Camberwell, Victoria 3124, Australia
(a division of Pearson Australia Group Pty Ltd)
Penguin Books India Pvt Ltd, 11 Community Centre, Panchsheel Park, New Delhi – 110 017, India
Penguin Group (NZ), 67 Apollo Drive, Rosedale, Auckland 0632, New Zealand
(a division of Pearson New Zealand Ltd)
Penguin Books (South Africa) (Pty) Ltd, 24 Sturdee Avenue, Rosebank,
Johannesburg 2196, South Africa

Penguin Books Ltd, Registered Offices: 80 Strand, London WC2R ORL, England

www.penguin.com

First published in the United States of America by St Martin's Press 2010
First published in Great Britain by Penguin Books 2012

1

Copyright © James Hayman 2010
All rights reserved

The moral right of the author has been asserted

Set in Garamond MT Std 12.5/14.75 pt
Typeset by Jouve (UK), Milton Keynes
Printed in England by Clays Ltd, St Ives plc

ISBN: 978-0-141-04730-0

www.greenpenguin.co.uk

To Kate and Ben
for your love and constant support

Acknowledgments

Once again there are many people I want to thank for their help and insights in writing this book. They include:

Detective Sergeant Tom Joyce, who once held McCabe's job as head of the Crimes Against People unit of the Portland Police Department and who now teaches Criminal Justice at Southern Maine Community College. Tom was always ready, willing, and able to answer my many questions, both big and small, about the Portland PD in particular and police procedure in general.

Lieutenant Tony Ward and Officer Cindy Taylor, also of the Portland Police Department.

Dr Ted McCarthy, head of the Department of Psychiatry at Mercy Hospital in Portland, for offering his insights into schizophrenia, and to emergency physician Dr George 'Bud' Higgins of Maine Medical Center for his help with ER procedures. Dr S. Erin Presnell, Associate Professor of Pathology and Director of Medical and Forensic Autopsy at the Medical University of South Carolina for her generosity in helping me in these areas.

Cynthia Thayer, Kate Sullivan, Brenda Buchanan, Jane Sloven, and Richard Bilodeau, who were all kind enough to read and reread the manuscript and offer suggestions that improved it enormously.

Charlie Spicer, Yaniv Soha, and Andy Martin of Minotaur Books and my agent, Meg Ruley.

I'd also like to thank the authors of two remarkable memoirs that were invaluable in helping me understand, in a very personal way, the experience of schizophrenia. Both books should be required reading for anyone interested in learning about this terrible disease: *The Quiet Room: A Journey Out of the Torment of Madness* by Lori Schiller and Amanda Bennett and *The Center Cannot Hold: My Journey Through Madness* by Elyn R. Saks.

Finally, thanks to my wife, Jeanne, and to our children, Ben and Kate, for their love and unstinting support from the very beginning.

The Chill of Night

One

Portland, Maine
Friday, December 23

Had Number Ten Monument Square been set among the skyscrapers of New York, or even Boston, no one would have noticed it. In a town like Portland it stood as one of the defining features of the skyline. Twelve stories of reddish brown granite with black windows set between vertical piers, Number Ten towered arrogantly over the east side of the square, a big player in a small town. At its top, large white letters proclaimed to anyone who cared to look that the building was the headquarters of Palmer Milliken, the city's largest and most prestigious law firm. It was also, according to Palmer Milliken's partners, one of the best anywhere in New England, including, they insisted, Boston. The firm's 192 lawyers plus appropriate support staff occupied all but two of the building's twelve floors.

At seven forty-two in the evening, on the Friday before the long Christmas weekend, a young woman stood at the window of her modest office on the seventh floor, gazing down at the activity in the square. Elaine Elizabeth Goff, Lainie to those who knew her well, was one of Palmer Milliken's senior associate attorneys. She'd already finished her work reviewing terms of a pending merger agreement between two small Maine banks. She'd pored over the documents half a dozen times, made a few changes, and sent in her recommendations an hour ago. Now she was ready to begin her winter vacation, a two-week jaunt, away from the bone-numbing cold of Portland, to the small, elegant Bacuba Spa and Resort on the southwest side of Aruba. Only two last things remained. A FedEx envelope on her desk that needed to go out tonight, and a phone call that should have come twelve minutes ago. Its lateness was making her edgy.

Six years out of Cornell Law, Lainie was still in her twenties, though, as she recently and frequently began reminding herself, just barely. But even as the dreaded thirtieth approached, she took pride in her conviction that she, Lainie Goff, the scholarship kid from Rockland, Maine, was about to become one of the youngest partners in Palmer Milliken's fifty-seven-year history. The offer, though not certain, was now so close she could almost taste it. She hoped word of the lucrative partnership would come tonight with the call she was waiting for. If only the damned phone would ring. She'd planned her life around that happening. Begun spending money she didn't have. The $500 Jimmy Choo shoes that were a torture to wear. The gleaming $40,000 BMW 325i convertible waiting in the garage downstairs. Not the bright red she really wanted but the platinum bronze metallic she thought more lawyerly. And now the expensive vacation on Aruba. All that money ponied up in anticipation of greater rewards lying just around the corner.

It wasn't that Lainie was such an exceptional lawyer. Her intellectual and legal skills, while formidable, ranked her no higher than half a dozen others among Palmer Milliken's ambitious pack of associates. But in the race for the top, Lainie enjoyed a key advantage not shared by any of her eager competitors. She was not only an able lawyer, she was also an exceptionally beautiful woman with shoulder-length dark hair, a slim athletic figure, and penetrating blue eyes that most people, but men in particular, found impossible to forget. And she was sleeping with her boss.

Lainie glanced at the old-fashioned electric sign atop the Time & Temperature Building. Seven forty-six. Four minutes since the last time she looked. The temperature was fourteen degrees. Down five in the last hour. The cold that had gripped the city for the better part of the past four weeks was showing no signs of letting up. It was a good time to be taking off for the sunshine. A good time to celebrate. Or would be if only Hank would get off his ass and call. Henry C. 'Hank' Ogden, managing partner in charge of Palmer Milliken's lucrative M&A practice. Her mentor. Her boss. Her lover. Elegant, rich, fifty-three years old, and very, very married.

Hank told her he'd call at seven thirty. She didn't know why the call was late, but she didn't like it. The Partnership Committee meeting should have been over hours ago. She strummed her long nails on the sill in front of her. Maybe Hank was just stuck in another meeting. He'd call as soon as he got out. Maybe. That was the charitable assumption. The best of three possibilities. The second was that he was keeping her waiting just for the hell of it. To provoke a little extra anxiety. One of the power games Hank liked playing. His way of letting her know who was in charge. Stupid and pointless, like a little boy poking a stick at a hamster in a cage. Well, she could handle his games, she told herself. She was tougher than that. The third possibility, the disaster scenario, was the one she wasn't sure she could handle – that, in spite of Hank's promised sponsorship and strong support, the partners, in their infinite wisdom, had decided not to extend an offer. If that was the case, then Hank wasn't calling because he'd be nervous about her reaction. He hated scenes, public or private, and knew there'd be one. She took a deep breath. She'd give him ten more minutes. Then she'd call him.

She pushed fears about the Partnership Committee from her mind and decided to think, instead, about her upcoming vacation. Far more pleasant to think about that. Two weeks of being pampered in the sunshine. Two weeks to either celebrate her triumph or salve her pride. Massages. Facials. Mud baths. Hanging out on the beach by herself with a bunch of trashy paperbacks. Well, to be honest, not *all* by herself. She'd find someone to play with. Someone with no connection to Maine or to Palmer Milliken. Someone European might be fun. Maybe she'd have a chance to practice her French. Patti LaBelle's rendition of 'Lady Marmalade' riffed through her brain.

Voulez-vous coucher avec moi ce soir?
Voulez-vous coucher avec moi?

If the news was good, she supposed, Hank would want a 'performance review.' He'd probably want one anyway. He found the term amusing. *Ms Goff, could you stop by, oh, at five thirty or so? We need to do a performance review. Thank you very much. We'll see you then.* Not an elaborate review either. Just forty minutes of snatch-and-grope on the red leather couch in his office. That was really all there was to this so-called affair. That and the occasional 'nooner' back at her apartment or a rare business trip to some out-of-the-way hotel. Lainie wanted more. She wanted a real relationship. If it was with Hank, fine. If not, that was fine, too. There were others she found interesting. One in particular she occasionally spent time with. Either way, she wasn't sure how much longer she could keep this bullshit going.

It started a year ago as a one-night stand after a few drinks on an overnight trip to East Millinocket to do due diligence on the sale of a paper mill, but it had long since become a regular thing. For him, she knew, it was totally casual. For her, things were more complicated. Sleeping with Hank as a means to an end was fine. She'd always been attracted to older men, powerful men, and, when they had enough time, Hank could be a skilled and attentive lover. Intelligent. Charming. Attractive. She knew he liked her. She toyed with the idea that she could somehow close the deal. Wouldn't that be a hoot? Lainie Goff as the second Mrs Henry Ogden. Elaine Elizabeth Goff Ogden. The trophy wife. It was a role she could play to a fare-thee-well and one she would thoroughly enjoy.

Deep down Lainie knew it would never happen. Divorce for Hank wasn't an option. He was married for good or ill, till death do them part, to the plain, plump, immensely wealthy Barbara Milliken Ogden, the only granddaughter of Edward A. Milliken, one of the firm's founders. Once the partnership was safely tucked away, it would be time to think of a good way to end the relationship without damaging her career. The idea of being free to pursue new adventures pleased her.

Lainie watched the activity below her window. Banks of dirty snow were pushed to the side, and the center of Monument Square was filled with people. Small groups, mostly twos and fours, scurried in and out of the shops and restaurants that lined the pedestrian plaza on the south side of the square. On this last Friday before Christmas, they were open late and busy. In the middle, near the monument, a brilliantly lit, sixty-foot blue spruce commemorated the season. A big, beautiful decorated tree. Not a Christmas tree, though. Lainie remembered reading that in the *Press Herald*. These days calling a Christmas tree a Christmas tree wasn't done. A city spokeswoman told the reporter that Portland was calling it a *holiday* tree. 'We want it to sound denominationally neutral,' she said. 'We don't want to offend anybody.' Lainie snorted. She hated such PC stupidity.

At the base of the tree, a troupe of carolers in faux Victorian garb sang. A few dozen people gathered around to listen and sing along. Most were bundled up against the cold and looked, from where Lainie stood, like little round Michelin men and women. Some held the mittened hands of even smaller Michelin children. Down near the entrance to Longfellow Books, she spotted Kyle, the hot-dog man, tending his pushcart, his trademark white apron wrapped tightly around a heavy woolen jacket. On his head he wore a leather aviator's cap with the earflaps pulled down over his gray hair. He seemed to be doing a brisk business selling the gyros, hot dogs, and Italian sausages he grilled over an open charcoal fire.

Lainie smiled. Kyle was her buddy. He always asked how she was doing, when they were going to make her a partner, and, with a wink and a smile, when she was going to go out on his boat with him. He talked about his boat a lot. A twenty-eight-foot Chris-Craft. He'd have to sell a hell of a lot of hot dogs to be able to afford a thing like that. Then again, Lainie knew, because she was a customer, Kyle sold merchandise more profitable than snacks. *Need a little happiness? Need a little joy? Go see the hot-dog man.* Either way, she enjoyed his flirting, enjoyed his easy Irish charm. Sometimes, when she was making a buy, she caught him looking at her a little too directly. Sometimes he looked away. Sometimes he didn't. Once or twice he said with that wry little smile of his that he might let her have a bag or two for free. God, what a thought. Lainie and the hot-dog man. There was no way in hell she would ever let *that* happen. Not now. Not ever. Still, he wasn't bad-looking.

She wasn't sure how old Kyle was but guessed somewhere in his early fifties. It was an age she found attractive. The same age as Hank. The same age as her Contracts professor at Cornell, the one who gave her the A she needed to make *Law Review*. About the same age, she calculated, her stepfather would be today.

Lainie had been thinking a lot about Albright lately, though she hadn't seen him in years. Her mind went back, once again, to that time in their old house in Rockport. A year or so before his career started taking off. Two years before he divorced her mother and moved out. Without his income her mother couldn't afford the old place. She sold it, used part of the money

7

to buy the smaller, crummier place in Rockland, and invested the rest.

She could see that bastard's face now. The handsome, brilliant Wallace Stevens Albright. A lawyer whose parents named him for a poet, though she'd never known a man with less poetry in his soul. He never let anyone call him Walt or Wally or any other nickname. It was always Wallace. Or Mr Albright. Lainie was seven when he married her mother and they went to live with him. He wanted her to call him Daddy. She never would, though she knew it made him angry. He wasn't her father. He even wanted her to change her name from Goff to Albright. She didn't want to do that either. Thank God, her mother said no and made it stick. Otherwise Lainie might be carrying that bastard's name even now.

A strict disciplinarian and a stubborn perfectionist, Wallace Stevens Albright held himself, he said, to a higher standard. Lainie smiled bitterly at the memory. Yeah, right. A higher standard. Like pulling down her pants and spanking her when she was little for the slightest infraction. Bastard was getting off on it. But, oh, did he ever put on a righteous show. She was never able to please him or earn his praise, no matter how hard she tried – and, though she hated him, she did try. It seemed important to win him over, to impress him. Important but impossible. She remembered how once in ninth grade, she got a ninety-five on an algebra exam. It was an exam half the class flunked, even a lot of the smart kids. When she told him about it, proudly, he mocked her. *Oh, really? A ninety-five? What happened to the other five points?* She went to bed that night feeling like she had failed. Again. Fuck him.

She was fifteen when the really bad shit started. The day of the Belfast soccer game. Lainie closed her eyes and it all came flooding back, immediate and real. Her sophomore year in high school. Camden Regional, not Rockland, where she had to go after the divorce. It was an afternoon in late October. One of those cold, rainy fall days that in Maine presage the coming of winter. It was an away game, and it had rained on and off all day long. The field was a sea of mud. All the girls were slipping and sliding, and by the end of the game their skin and hair were covered in drying brown gunk. Lainie scored two goals and just missed a third when the ball hit the left upright and bounced back onto the field. She knew, if she told him, Wallace would focus on the one she missed. *Maybe if you'd worked a little harder you would have made it, Lainie. You can always improve. You can always strive to be better.* Yeah. Just like you, Daddy Dearest.

After the game, Annie Jesperson's mom offered Lainie and another friend, Maddie Mitchell, a ride home. Both girls accepted. It was a lot more comfortable than riding in the team bus, and they wouldn't have to stop at school and catch a ride home from there.

'Get in,' Mrs Jesperson told the girls, throwing a tarp across the backseat. 'Just try not to get any mud on the upholstery. This car's brand-new, and we'd like to keep it looking that way.'

'We won't,' they promised and climbed in, shoving Dudley, Annie's dopey golden retriever, over the seat top and into the cargo area. The girls giggled all the way home, pulling monster faces and rubbing mud balls into each other's hair and fending off Dudley's eager efforts to join in the fun. Mrs Jesperson dropped Lainie off first, in front of her house. The big white colonial with the wraparound porch and black shutters on Mabern Street in Rockport. The house they lived in when they still had money.

It was almost dark when they got there. There were no lights on in the house. That meant her mother and Wallace were still at work. Her mother managing her antiques shop in Camden, Albright tending his growing law practice. He stayed late at the office almost every night. *You'll never achieve anything, Lainie, never amount to anything. Not unless you're ready to put in the hours.* She fetched the key from where it hung under the back steps and let herself in. She pulled off her shoes at the door, stripped down, and tossed her muddy uniform onto the laundry room floor. She walked naked across the semidarkened front hall and climbed the stairs, heading for the bathroom on the second floor.

About halfway down the corridor, the door to her mother and stepfather's room opened, and Albright stepped out. Lainie gasped. She threw her right arm across her breasts and her left hand over her thatch of pubic hair. He'd never seen her naked before, not even as a little kid, and she wasn't sure which way to run. Albright just stood there looking at her, surprise on his face. He was blocking her way to the bathroom door. Blocking her way to her own room as well. She turned and thought about running back down the stairs – but where could she go stark naked? She turned back and saw his expression change, morphing from surprise to something very different. She heard his breathing quicken. She knew she'd made that happen. Not to some boy in sophomore class. To *him*. To Wallace Stevens Albright. The perfectionist. The man guided by a higher standard. For the first time since he'd come into their lives, Lainie felt a sense of power. It was amazing. Intoxicating. It lasted less than a second.

In the instant it took for Albright's mouth to close, for his lips to draw back into a thin, ugly smile, power turned to fear. And then to panic. She darted for her bedroom door, blindly hoping she could get there before him. Hoping she could somehow slip inside. Slam the door. Lock him out.

She never had a chance. As she reached for the knob, he grabbed an arm, turned her around, and wrapped his arms around her waist, pulling her into him, her back against his body. She could feel his erection through the fabric of his pants, pushing, probing at her butt. She tried pulling away but couldn't. He lifted her off the floor and carried her, flailing and kicking and screaming, into her room. Across the oval knotted rug Grammy Horton made for her. He threw her down among the stuffed bears and bunnies that still populated the head of her bed. She tried a sudden bolt for the door. He grabbed her and pushed her down again. She screamed. He slapped her hard across the face. The pain was explosive, shocking. 'Don't try that again.' He spat out the words in a quiet voice that was, for all its quietness, full of threat. 'This is your fault, Lainie. All your fault. You asked for it, and you're going to get what you deserve.' He slapped her again. She felt a thin line of blood trickle from her nose.

She closed her eyes and retreated into the corner, more frightened than she'd ever been in her life. She pulled her muddy knees up, wrapped both arms around them, hugged them tight against her chest. When she dared open her eyes, he was unzipping his pants, pulling them down over his high black socks. Her mind froze. This couldn't be happening. Not in her own room. Not on her own bed. He pulled down his underpants. He folded the suit pants along the creases and hung them neatly over the back of her desk chair. She supposed he was thinking he'd have to wear them to the office the next day. He left his underpants on the floor. He didn't bother taking off his shirt or black socks.

From a distance of fifteen years, the adult Lainie could still see Wallace Stevens Albright's hard little cock poking out, peekaboo fashion, from between the flaps of his blue-striped Brooks Brothers shirt. She was crying now. Sobbing quietly. She could still feel his soft white hands grabbing her ankles, pulling her out of the corner, pulling her legs apart. Then he pushed her knees up and apart and knelt between them. He lowered his chest so all she could see was shirt. She remembered that shirt so well. The feel of the starched cotton, the smell of it. All his shirts had a little blue monogram on the pocket. A *W* and an *S* on either side. A big blue *A* in the middle. It was all she could see. She felt him open her with his fingers and push himself up and in. It still amazed her such a little prick could inflict such pain.

Afterward, he smiled and spoke gently. Told her she'd done very well. It was the first time, maybe the only time, he ever praised her. He told her if her eye turned black where he hit her, she had to tell people she'd been hit in the face with a soccer ball. Then he made her go to the bathroom and wash herself out. He stood at the open door and watched as she did. Finally he told her in the same gentle voice that if she ever breathed a word about what happened, either to her mother or to anyone else, he'd kill them both. 'That's a promise,' he said. She never doubted he would keep his word.

That night and many nights after that, he came back to her room for 'a visit.' Each time it was the same. Except sometimes, instead of fucking her, he'd make her get down on her knees and give him a blow job. Each time, before he left, he told her it was her fault. He did what he did because she was a dirty girl who tempted him. Then he would again threaten to kill her and her mother. She sometimes wondered if her mother knew where he was going when he left their bed in the middle of the night. Downstairs for a snack? To read a book? No. Her mother knew – she must have known – but she never had the courage to say or do anything about it. Never wanted to talk about Wallace at all. And Lainie never asked. Finally, two years later, Wallace left her mother. He found a younger woman who was rich and beautiful, and he filed for divorce. He gave her the white house in Rockport as part of the settlement. She sold it, and she and Lainie moved to the little Cape Cod in Rockland. It was over. But the stain stayed with her. It could never be washed away. Her mother was dead now. She committed suicide two years after Lainie graduated high school and went off to Colby. Swallowed a handful of Xanax tablets to still her anxiety and slit her wrists in the tub. But Wallace Stevens Albright was still out there. Still married. With two little girls of his own. Respected attorney. Oft-mentioned candidate for the federal bench. Child fucker. Bastard.

*

13

Lainie glanced again at the Time & Temperature Building. Seven fifty-five and still Hank hadn't called. She hadn't eaten since breakfast, and she was hungry. Despite, or maybe because of her usual regimen of plain grilled fish or chicken and garden salads, she found herself lusting after one of Kyle's plump garlicky Italian sausages, covered with sautéed onions and Kyle's own special sauce. She couldn't actually see the sausages cooking from her seventh-floor perch, but she could sure as hell picture them, crackling away in the frosty air on their bed of hot coals. She could almost taste that first spray of hot fat bursting into her mouth as she popped the skin with her teeth.

Lainie realized her mouth was watering. For a brief, tempting moment, she thought about running downstairs and getting herself one of the damnable but delicious things. Maybe score a little coke at the same time. A twofer. A dumb idea, she supposed. But it would only take a minute. No longer than going to the ladies' room. She might miss Hank's call. But then he'd leave a message. Of course, meeting Hank, literally face-to-face, with onions and garlic on her breath might just turn him off. So what if it did? He couldn't take away a partnership on grounds of bad breath, could he? And it might just spare her a session on the red leather couch. Of course, in less than twenty-four hours, she'd be sunning in a skimpy bikini on a beautiful beach where she wouldn't want even the hint of an extra bulge ruining her nearly perfect figure. 'Oh, screw it,' she finally said. She grabbed the FedEx envelope from her desk to deposit in the box on the square and headed for the elevator. She'd skip dinner.

When she came back from her coatless dash across the

square, coke in her pocket and hot sausage in hand, Hank still hadn't called. Lainie lifted her long, slender legs up onto the desk and bit into the succulent snack. She practically moaned with pleasure. This was better than sex. Much better. As she ate, the image of the singers in the square came back, and she felt a sudden longing for a child of her own to celebrate Christmas with. A little boy or girl to love and protect. Like her mother protected her? No. Better than that. Much better. No child of hers would ever go through the kind of hell she'd endured. She'd make sure of that. No child anywhere should ever have to suffer that. Or would if Lainie could help it. Anyway, it all seemed a stretch. Maybe someday, she supposed, but for now she had to be tougher than that. *Ambition should be made of sterner stuff*, Marc Antony told the Romans.

Yes, she thought, *ambition should be made of sterner stuff*. Did she have what it took to get where she wanted? Lainie Goff from Rockport via Rockland. The overachiever and star student. The valedictorian of her high school class and winner of a nearly free ride through four years at Colby and another through three years of law school at Cornell. Lainie Goff, who everyone, including Hank, saw as a brilliant, tough, self-confident winner. Lainie Goff, who was capable of anything, even fucking her way to the top. Did she have what it took? She wasn't sure. So far at least, she'd fooled them all. Only she knew the truth. Superstar Lainie didn't exist. The real Lainie was a woman unworthy of anyone's love, even her own. A woman who could only achieve the success she so desperately wanted lying on her back, knees up and knickers down. Wallace Stevens Albright would be so proud of his creation. He wanted her to call him Daddy. Once again, he'd gotten his way. She'd become his daughter through and through.

The phone rang. Lainie swallowed the last bite of sausage and picked it up.

Nearly nine o'clock. Lainie Goff's teeth were clenched in quiet rage as she walked toward her car in Palmer Milliken's private underground garage. The clickity-click of her heels against the concrete punctuated her fury in a rhythmic tattoo. He hadn't turned her down. No. He was much too slick for that. In fact, he hadn't said much of anything at first. Just teased her with the possibility until he'd gotten his rocks off. Then, while she was standing there, still half naked, he pulled the rug out from under her.

'Lainie, I'm afraid you'll have to be patient,' he said.

She said nothing. Just stood there seething. Staring at him with the same intensity of hatred she once reserved for Albright.

'Just a couple more months,' he said, zipping his fly, pulling up his suspenders. 'I'm working on it. It will happen. I promise. It will happen. There are a couple of other good candidates. Janet Pritchard. Bill Tobias.'

She wondered if he was fucking Pritchard, too. Wondered if Janet was as good as Lainie at her performance reviews.

'You know as well as I do,' he continued, 'the committee almost never approves partnerships for anyone who hasn't been here seven years, and you've got a way to go yet. The three of you will probably all be invited at once.'

Didn't he get it? She didn't want to wait until the others were invited, too. She wanted her recognition first. She wanted it now. But what the hell was she going to do? Yell? Scream? Hold her breath till she turned blue? She couldn't quit. She needed the job. She had car payments to make. And she sure as hell wasn't ready to give up on her dream of a Palmer Milliken partnership. But she finally figured it out. As long as Hank kept dangling the promise without actually delivering the goods, he had her where he wanted her. Literally and figuratively. Down on her knees with her mouth around his cock. The minute she got it, screw him. He could find himself another eager young associate to fuck.

Her car stood waiting in its assigned spot in the nearly empty garage. Just her Beemer and Hank's Merc remained. Everyone else had long since left for the holiday. She pressed the little button on her key ring. The car's lights flashed. Its doors unlocked. Still distracted, she didn't notice the absence of the accustomed click. She slid into the front seat. She sat there for a minute, still fuming, before she finally turned the key. The engine smoothly hummed to life. She glanced in the rearview mirror.

She froze.

'Hello, Lainie,' a familiar voice murmured. 'There're a couple of things we still need to discuss.'

Two

Portland, Maine
Friday, January 6

McCabe poured the Scotch, freehand, nearly to the top of the glass. Twelve-year-old Macallan single malt. No ice. No water. Smooth, expensive whisky, made more for sipping than for serious drinking. But right now he didn't much care. It was his first of the evening. Though, at eight ounces, the glass held nearly three times as much booze as the drinks they served at Tallulah's – and Tallulah had a generous hand. Even so, McCabe was thinking a few more might follow. Maybe more than a few. However many it took, he supposed, to figure out why he was feeling so shitty about what just went down with Kyra. Not exactly a fight. But not exactly not. Whatever you wanted to call it. It began with a safe enough routine. A pas de deux they'd gone through a number of times before. He asked. She declined. Familiar words. A familiar tune. But this time, wanting a different result, he pushed beyond the familiar and into uncharted territory. Terra incognita where monsters dwelled and ships fell off the ends of the earth.

He was wearing a pair of sweats with nothing underneath. The pants were maroon, frayed and torn at both knees. The words ST BARNABAS TRACK ran vertically down one leg, the last physical reminder of McCabe's days as a middle distance runner at his high school in the Bronx. Taking a good-sized slug of the Scotch, he padded in stockinged feet across the dark hardwood floor of his living room and settled himself in the big window seat that overlooked Portland's Eastern Prom. With his back propped against one wall, feet against the other, knees bent to accommodate his length, he gazed out the window. At five o'clock on a cold January afternoon, it was already dark. Weather reports were calling for snow, maybe a big one, but so far, at least, the sky was crystal clear. The moon, nearly full, rode low in the sky. A few cars passed below. He could make out the dark silhouetted limbs of the young trees that lined the other side of the street. Beyond the trees, a broad expanse of dirty snow, some plowed into giant mounds. Beyond that, the even broader expanse of Casco Bay. A long shaft of moonlight glittered, jewel-like, across the surface of the water. A few silvery chunks of ice floated free. In the middle of the bay, he could see the distinctive squat shape of Fort Gorges, a six-sided pile of stone and dirt built to defend Portland harbor from the Confederates during the Civil War. Lights from houses on Harts Island shone on the opposite shore.

McCabe felt the calming, comforting buzz of the alcohol kick in. He thought again about what had happened and wondered if he should give therapy another try. He'd gone through a few sessions last year. The therapist, a psychiatrist named Richard Wolfe, was smart and sympathetic and told McCabe he felt they were making progress. But McCabe had backed off. He was uncomfortable opening up to a stranger. He knew that was his fault and not the therapist's, so maybe he should try again. He'd never told anybody in the department about the sessions, hadn't even put in for them on his medical insurance. Dumb, he supposed, but he didn't want his detectives looking at him like he couldn't handle the stress. Or his boss, Lieutenant Bill Fortier. Or worse, Portland police chief Tom Shockley. Shockley was such a political animal that McCabe knew he wouldn't hesitate to somehow use the knowledge as a lever to bend McCabe to his will. McCabe finished the whisky, got up, poured a second, and returned to his perch. He watched a jogger, ignoring the cold, run by in the dark.

Today began as a nothing kind of day at the end of a nothing kind of week, and McCabe was bored. No rapes. No assaults. No murders. Not even a garden-variety case of domestic abuse he could sink his teeth into. It was as if everybody in Portland suddenly started taking nice pills. It was making him cranky.

Around ten thirty he went downstairs to the firing range on the ground floor of police headquarters and spent an hour putting tight clusters of holes in man-shaped targets. He thought about going to the gym, putting on the gloves, and continuing to work out the angst he was feeling by banging away at the heavy bag. Instead he went back to his desk and made a show of doing paperwork. Around one in the afternoon, Kyra called.

'Congratulate me,' she said.

'Okay, congratulations,' he replied. 'Now tell me what for.'

'Well, we finished hanging the show this morning and

guess what? Gloria's put three of my pieces right in the middle of the front wall.'

'That's good.'

'Wait. It gets even better. There's me right out front, and meanwhile, she's relegated Marta Einhorn and a couple of the other so-called *major Maine artists*' – Kyra's voice underlined the words with a dose of sarcasm – 'to the back room.'

'So they're pissed?'

'Not yet, but they sure as hell will be when they see it.'

'You said three pieces. What about the fourth?'

'In the window.'

'Well, alright! Congratulations again. How about I buy a *major Maine artist* a fancy lunch?'

'That your idea of a good time?'

'Yeah, maybe.'

'I've got a better one,' she said.

'Okay. Like what?'

'Like why don't you meet me at the apartment and find out.'

'What and skip a wholesome lunch?'

'Oh, you never know,' she said, her voice getting low and growly, 'I just might decide to nibble at a little something.' If this was Kyra's idea of phone sex, it was sure as hell working.

He glanced around the room to see if anyone was looking. Or listening. Nobody was. Less than a minute later, McCabe had his desk cleared, his coat on, and was heading for the door. He wondered what he'd say if Bill Fortier asked where he was going. *Following a lead on an ongoing investigation?* No way. Bill'd want to know what investigation.

Going down to the gym for a workout? Possible. That wouldn't elicit anything more than a grunt and a nod. Of course, it might be fun just telling the truth. *Well, actually, Bill, I'm going home to get laid.* That'd turn the old puritan fart a couple of shades redder. McCabe grinned at the idea. He glanced over at Maggie Savage, his number two in the Portland PD's Crimes Against People unit. She was on the phone, probably for a while. He hand-signaled that he was taking off. She nodded and mouthed 'Okay.' Today even Casey wouldn't be a problem. McCabe's fourteen-year-old daughter was leaving right from school with her friend Sarah Palfrey. Sarah's parents owned a condo at Sunday River and had invited Casey up for a weekend of snowboarding. He'd call from the car to make sure that she had everything she needed and that there'd be no unexpected drop-ins.

An hour later, McCabe and Kyra were lying side by side in the afterglow of lovemaking, Kyra on her back, eyes closed, McCabe on his side, idly tracing figure eights with two of his fingers around her damp and naked body. He thought about how different Kyra was from Sandy, his first wife. He leaned over and found her lips with his. 'Ummm,' she said, her eyes still closed, her arms reaching up to circle his neck. 'Wanna go again?'

'Only if you ask very nicely.'

She opened those liquid blue eyes he loved, looked right at him, and smiled. 'Please, sir, I want some more,' she said, her voice a passable imitation of young John Howard Davies as Oliver Twist in David Lean's 1948 film version. They'd watched it on TMC, together with Casey, just last night.

And so, in the fading half-light of a cold January after-noon, they made love again. And when they finished, he looked at her gravely and asked her again if she was ready to marry.

She didn't move, but he could feel her body stiffen. She lay there for a minute or two. 'No,' she said finally.

'When you say no, do you mean "No, not now" or "No, not ever"?'

'No, not now.'

'Why not?' he persisted. 'We've been together two years. That ought to be long enough.'

'Do we have to talk about this now?'

'You're thirty-one years old. I'm thirty-eight. I don't want to get too Irish on you, but it's time we got married.'

She turned onto her side and propped her head on her hand. His hand slipped from her chest. She studied him for a minute. 'Up until this instant this has been a per-fectly lovely day. Please, don't fuck it up.'

McCabe pressed on anyway. He wasn't sure why. 'You've said you'd like to have kids of your own. Our own. Hell, with Casey turning fifteen next spring, we'd even have a built-in babysitter. At least until she goes off to college.'

'I told you. I'm not ready.'

'Is it because I'm a cop?'

'That's part of it. But not all.'

'What's the rest of it? That maybe you've got a prob-lem with commitment?'

'I really don't want to talk about this anymore.'

He felt a surge of anger. 'Well, dammit, I do.' He swung out of the bed and found the sweats that were lying in a heap in the corner. He put them on. 'If it's about me being a cop, being a cop is what I do. What I am. You knew that when we started seeing each other.'

She studied him for a minute. 'Yes, I did,' she said. Then she rolled off her side of the bed and began walking around the room, picking up her clothes from where they'd fallen on the way in.

'So why'd you get involved with me?'

She looked back at him, and suddenly there was an edge to her voice. 'Because you were a good fuck.'

'Oh, really? So that's the headline? WASP princess from Yale School of Art gets her rocks off playing house with Irish stud from the Bronx? Is that what this is all about? Is that *all* this is?'

'McCabe, you can be such an asshole. You know damned well that's not what this is about, and, by the way, that was a really shitty thing to say.'

'Oh, really? And "You were a good fuck" wasn't?'

'Yes. It was. I'm sorry. I shouldn't have said it. Listen, can we stop this and maybe start over?'

'Okay. I'm sorry, too. Yes, let's start over. If being a cop is such a terrible thing, why *did* you get involved with me?'

She started getting dressed. 'A, being a cop is not a terrible thing. And B, as for why, I suppose it was for all the obvious reasons. Because you were fun. And smart. And good-looking. And yes, you were good in bed. Anyway, at the time, I didn't really plan on falling in love with you. I wasn't planning on falling in love with anybody.'

She sat down on the corner of the bed and continued pulling on her clothes.

'But you did? Fall in love with me, I mean?'

'Yes. I did.' Kyra was still naked from the waist up. McCabe found himself looking at her breasts and felt his desire for her growing again. It felt like a weakness. Sensing this, she turned her back on him and slipped on her bra. She took a deep breath. 'McCabe, I do love you. Though sometimes I'm not entirely sure why. So why don't we both shut up before we do or say something we'll both regret.'

She took the rest of her clothes, walked to the bathroom, and closed the door. He could hear sounds of running water. Kyra washing. The door opened. Kyra came out.

He knew he ought to drop the whole thing, but he didn't. 'Just talk to me. Okay?' His voice was calmer now. Less combative. 'You once told me you weren't sure you could marry someone who could take another human life. Is that it?'

'I did. But it's not. I've come to terms with that,' she said. 'I believe you killed those men because you had to. I also believe, as you do, that the world is better off without them.' She was looking around the room. 'Have you seen my sweater?'

'Over there on the rocker. Under my stuff.'

'Thank you.' She pulled it out and tugged it down over her head. Then she retrieved a brush from her bag and stood before the full-length mirror on the back of the bathroom door.

He stood behind her, watching her reflection, as she began brushing her short, curly blond hair. 'You know there's nothing wrong with what I do,' he said. 'It's an honorable profession. It's important. And it's what I care about doing.'

She turned and stroked his cheek. 'I know that. I respect it. I don't want to stop you being who you are any more than I'd want you to stop me being an artist.'

'So there's gotta be something more.'

'Alright.' She sighed deeply. 'Since you seem utterly incapable of letting it go, yes, there is something else. Something that frightens me, and, try as I might, it's something I can't seem to get out of my head.'

'And what is it that frightens you?'

Kyra didn't answer right away. She stood there looking at his reflection in the glass. Seconds passed. Then a minute. 'Please,' he said, 'just tell me what it is.'

'Alright, if you really must know, Carol Comisky frightens me. In fact, she scares the shit out of me. Do you remember Carol Comisky?'

Of course he remembered Carol Comisky. She was the widow of a cop who'd been killed the year before. He'd had his throat cut and bled to death trying to stop a killer from attacking a witness. The same guy came within a hair's breadth of killing McCabe as well.

'Yes. Kevin's wife. Kevin's widow. What about her?'

'Remember her standing there at the funeral?'

She knew McCabe remembered. He remembered everything. All the words he ever heard or read. All the images he'd ever seen. At least all the ones that were important enough for him to notice when he first saw them. He had an eidetic memory. The scene at the cemetery reassembled itself in his mind in extraordinary detail, right down to the last blade of grass. 'Mostly I see a woman in mourning. No crying. Just sort of a grim, determined look on her face. Black linen suit. Black shoes. Low heels. Dark hair cut short.

No hat. Three kids, all under six, standing next to her. Next to them are Kevin's parents. Standing right behind, Shockley and Fortier, in full dress uniform.'

'Look closer, McCabe,' she said. 'Look at her face. Her expression isn't grim. Or determined. It's angry. She's looking right at us. You and me. And she's pissed. Pissed at Kevin for becoming a cop. Pissed at herself for marrying him. Pissed at you because you're the one who sent him up to that room and, I suppose, because you're still alive and he isn't. She's pissed at me, maybe me most of all, because I'm not alone and she is. What I see in Carol Comisky is a woman, about my age, standing there with a bunch of little kids next to an empty hole in the ground and seeing any chance she ever had in life going right into that hole along with her dead husband.'

'Her dead husband the cop?'

'That's right. Her dead husband the cop. And you know what else she's thinking? She's thinking if only her husband had been an accountant or a salesman or a tugboat captain – almost anything but a cop – she wouldn't be burying him, and she wouldn't be raising those three kids on her own, and all the flowery speeches from Chief Shockley, all the twenty-one-gun salutes, all the bagpipe players marching up and down in their stupid kilts playing "Amazing Grace" won't make a shit's bit of difference.'

'She may get married again.'

'Yes, maybe, but the odds are against her. And even if she does, that's not really my point.'

'Then what is?'

'I understand if we get married the chances are you won't get killed. Most cops don't, and, as you point out

27

every chance you get, this is Portland, Maine, and not New York or Baltimore or Detroit. The problem is, McCabe, even assuming you live to a ripe old age, I'll still have to lie here night after night for the next fifteen or twenty years, while you're out chasing some nutcase, worrying that you may not come home, that I may never see you again. Maybe that's unfair. Maybe it's cowardly. I don't know. I do know that right now, I just don't want to put myself through that.'

'Kyra, you want us to break up because you're worrying about something that almost certainly won't happen?'

'No, I'm not saying that.' Kyra put her arms on his shoulders and looked into his eyes. 'I love you too much to even contemplate giving you up. All I'm saying is, every time I think about us getting married and maybe having children, the image of Carol Comisky pops into my head, along with your brother Tommy's wife and all the others who've been left behind.'

McCabe's narcotics cop brother Tommy, Tommy the Narc, had been shot dead by a drug dealer five years earlier. 'I know it's my problem, not yours,' Kyra said. 'Maybe someday I'll get over it and we can go on with our lives. But for now I'm just not ready. I'll let you know when I am.'

'Kyra,' he said, 'people die. Truck drivers get killed in accidents. Cowboys get thrown from their horses. And God knows how many sedate business executives die every day from heart attacks or cancer. When Casey gets her license, and that's less than two years away, I'm gonna lie awake at night like every other parent in the world dreading the idea that the phone might ring and some-body will tell me she's been killed or maimed in some horrible crash. But that doesn't mean I'm going to keep her from going out or getting a license. Or that I wish I never had her. We can't stop living our lives together because something bad might happen.'

'I know. You're right,' she said. 'Just don't push me for now. It's something I have to work out for myself, and one way or another I will. It won't be the reason I don't marry you. If that makes sense.'

'It doesn't. Not much.' He let it go, but he wasn't sure what he was feeling. Something between anger at being rejected and fear that he might actually lose her.

Kyra nodded, then went to the hall closet, retrieved a fleece vest, and slipped it on over her sweater. Her bright red L.L. Bean down parka went over that. She headed for the door. Before going out, she paused. 'Remember, tonight's First Friday, and I've got those four new pieces hanging at North Space.'

'Our cause for celebrating.'

'Yes. And I'm very happy we did. I'm very happy I have you. And I'm sorry if I'm making you unhappy. But this will pass.'

From his perch on the window seat, McCabe stared down across the bay and wondered if he could summon the emotional energy to make small talk with the art crowd. On First Fridays most of the forty or so galleries in Port-land stayed open late, many with opening receptions for new work. North Space was the most successful and best established of the lot. Kyra was proud Gloria Kelwin, North Space's owner, thought so highly of her work. She'd be dreadfully disappointed if he didn't show.

On the other hand, he could just sit here and say the hell with it all. With Casey gone till Sunday night, he could sit and drink all weekend if he wanted to. He didn't even have to go out for more booze. There were three fresh bottles of the Macallan just sitting in the pantry waiting for him. All the makings for his own *Lost Weekend*. His mind flashed on images of the alcoholic Ray Milland throwing his life away in the 1945 Billy Wilder classic. Another bit of detritus from McCabe's alternative life twenty years ago, as a young wannabe director at NYU film school. Would Kyra have wanted to marry him if he'd gone into the movie business instead of the police business? He supposed so. The artist and the auteur. A better fit than the artist and the cop. Except he never would have met her. Alternative lives.

He watched the lights of a giant tanker, laden with half a million barrels of North Sea crude, work its way into Portland harbor. A couple of tugs pushed and prodded its blue hulk toward the marine terminal in South Portland where the oil would be pumped into holding tanks to await transmission via pipeline to refineries in Quebec. As he watched he wondered about the men who worked big ships like these. Lonely men, he imagined. Hard men as well. Used to living without the comforts of women. Would they think him soft or self-indulgent? Whining about a woman who gave him everything up to a point. And then stopped. He supposed they would, but he didn't much care.

He got up, took a last sip of the whisky, walked to the kitchen, and poured the rest, more than half the glass, down the kitchen sink. Hell of a waste of fine single malt.

He was already feeling the effects, though, and he realized getting drunk wasn't what this was about. He washed out the Waterford glass, the last of a set of four his sister Fran, twenty years a nun, gave Sandy and him for a wedding present. He thought about the irony of that. Of Sister Fran, the daughter of a drunk and the bride of Christ, giving her younger brother whisky glasses to celebrate his marriage to a slut. A beautiful slut, but a slut nonetheless. When the marriage failed and Sandy walked out on him, she took two of the glasses with her to her new life as the wife of a rich investment banker. The third was broken in the move to Portland. This was the last, and it was precious to him. He dried it carefully and placed it back on its high shelf out of harm's way.

McCabe glanced at his watch. Nearly six o'clock. If he was going to make it to Kyra's opening at all, he'd better get moving. He called Casey's cell to make sure she'd arrived safely at Sunday River. She had. He took a quick shower. Before dressing, he clicked on the small TV in the corner to look at the Weather Channel. Fifteen degrees. Wind chill of minus five. Going down to single digits overnight with heavy snow predicted for after midnight. Jesus. When was this goddamned cold ever gonna let up? It'd been brutal all winter. Even forced him to renounce his inner New Yorker and buy some thermal underwear at the Bean's outlet on Congress. He found a clean pair still in their plastic wrapper and put them on. He hated wearing the things but had to admit they did make the cold more tolerable. His small closet was stuffed with his minimal selection of clothing plus boxes of stuff he hadn't unpacked from the move to Portland four years ago. He picked out a pair of brown corduroys and slipped them on over the long johns. Then a dark brown crewneck pullover. Then his sport jacket. Brown wool, butter soft.

A present from Kyra, purchased just before Christmas at a high-end men's boutique in Copley Place in Boston. 'Somebody's got to dress you decently, McCabe,' she said at the time. 'Since you're obviously incapable of doing it yourself.'

He remembered the weekend with pleasure. Casey was away that weekend, too, visiting her mother in New York. Sandy had only begun seeing Casey again last year after three years of total abandonment. This was the first time she'd be staying in her mother's apartment, meeting Peter Ingram, Sandy's new husband. Thinking about it had been making him edgy. Anxious. He needed a distraction. Turned out a friend of Kyra's from Yale was heading out of town and offered Kyra the keys to her apartment in Cambridge. So they snuck down, just the two of them, for a romantic interlude. The idea was to eat well and maybe take in a Celtics game – the Knicks were in town, and Kyra's friend, an art director at one of Boston's hot young ad agencies, had access to season tickets. On Sunday, they planned to see a Hockney show at the MFA. As it turned out, they did eat well. But skipped both the Celtics and the Hockney and wound up spending the weekend alternately in restaurants and in bed. It was probably what both of them had in mind in the first place.

He strapped on his service weapon, a heavy Smith & Wesson 4506. The PPD was changing over to Glock 17s. Lighter. More accurate. In McCabe's mind a better choice. Though he hadn't made the switch yet. He pulled the sweater down over the gun. He considered his choice of outerwear. Either a lined army field jacket. Warm, but it'd look ridiculous over the sport coat. Or the old black cashmere that'd come with him from New York. Not warm enough for this kind of winter, but it'd have to do. Next year, if it was cold again, maybe he'd trade it in on a fleece-lined parka. Maybe not. He still preferred dressing like a grown-up.

Frigid air smacked him full in the face as he stepped out of his condo. Even so, he decided to walk the mile and some to the North Space Gallery on Free Street. The snow wasn't supposed to start until after midnight, and the idea of being picked up for drunk driving wasn't appealing. He didn't feel like messing with a cab. Besides, a good dose of cold fresh air might be the best way to clear the buzz in his brain. He didn't want to look the clown for Kyra's opening. Even if he might be. If he walked fast enough, maybe he wouldn't succumb to frostbite.

A steady wind was blowing in off the bay. *Force five or six on the Beaufort scale.* McCabe's mind played with the words. He didn't have a clue what the Beaufort scale was, but he always liked the sound of it. It was the kind of thing David Niven might say before sending a squadron of Spitfires out to confront the filthy Hun. McCabe sometimes wondered if his own secret life might be a little too much like Walter Mitty's. Is that why he became a cop? To live out his fantasies? *Freeze, asshole!* Easy to do in this weather.

McCabe turned right and headed down the Prom, pulling the coat more tightly around himself. Dating back to his early days on the NYPD, it looked and felt its age. Worn elbows. Fraying cuffs. Maybe Kyra'd take him shopping to Boston again. He turned right on Vesper. The wind was at his back now, which felt better. He passed a couple of dog walkers, identities and gender hidden under heavy hooded parkas and boots. Great night for a mugging. *What did the mugger look like, ma'am? Well, Officer, he was wearing this heavy parka with a furry hood out front.* Nanooks of the North. More than ready to tackle the tundra. He remembered reading *Endurance.* The British explorer Shackleton spent a winter on an Antarctic ice floe with only a lined Burberry for warmth. Stiff upper lip? Absolutely. Not because Shackleton was British. The lip was just frozen in place. He turned left on Congress and headed west down Munjoy Hill. In spite of a decade of gentrification, the Hill still retained the look and feel of its working-class roots. Smallish wood-frame houses built sometime around 1900. Most divided into apartments. Tonight they were all closed up tight, curtains drawn. He continued down the hill, passing a few couples heading for one or another of the bars and restaurants that were sprouting like weeds. The Front Room, the Blue Spoon, Bar Lola – and, of course, his home away from home, Tallulah's. All crowded on a Friday night. Each with a few intrepid twenty-somethings hanging out front, desperate enough to brave the cold just to suck up their daily ration of nicotine.

His mind went back to Kyra. To the fight, if that's what it was. Why was he so hot to marry again? His marriage to Sandy had been a disaster. Except, of course, that it produced Casey, who was, without question, the best thing that ever happened to him. Amazing how such a great kid could ever have come out of that selfish bitch's body. All she said after nine hours of labor was 'Never again.' Didn't even want to hold her new daughter. Breastfeed? Not on your life.

So why go through the marriage thing again? Well, for one thing, Kyra wasn't Sandy. They were about as different as two gorgeous, sexy women could be. Okay, so why not just enjoy his relationship with the gorgeous, sexy Kyra and leave marriage out of the equation? That's what any therapist would want to know. He'd have to think about the answer.

By the time McCabe passed Washington Avenue, the cold was getting to him. His ears and toes were starting to go numb, and, drunk or not, he was beginning to regret the decision to walk. He figured he was sobering up, but not fast enough. He passed a new place called the Frost Line Café, coffee bar by day, open mike cabaret by night. He stopped and peered through the windows. They were all misted up from the body heat inside.

He went in and worked his way through the noisy crowd to the bar and ordered a small cup of coffee from a large, heavily pierced young woman wearing so much makeup that she looked to McCabe like a refugee from the set of Ernst Lubitsch's *Gypsy Blood*. Probably was. Just couldn't find her castanets. Incongruously, in spite of the getup, her accent was pure Downeast. She handed him an earthenware mug big enough to double as a soup tureen and pointed to a row of insulated pots on the far side. Told him to help himself. He did, adding a generous dollop of milk to the strong brew. He hadn't eaten in a while and figured he could use the nutrition.

On the far side of the room, a tinny-voiced girl singer

was belting out her version of the Dixie Chicks' 'Not Ready to Make Nice' to a crowd that seemed more interested in talking than listening. Natalie Maines had nothing to worry about. McCabe was scanning the room for a place to park himself and his mega cup when he felt his cell vibrate. By the time he fished it out from under three layers of wool, the line had gone dead. The call was from Maggie. McCabe was tempted not to call back. It couldn't be anything good, and he needed to be with Kyra right now. But even as he thought it, he knew it wasn't an option. If something was going on, he needed to know what it was. He headed for the men's room, where he figured he could hear Maggie, stay warm, and have some privacy all at the same time. He closed and locked the door. The sound of the Dixie Chick wannabe receded. He punched in Maggie's number.

'Where are you, McCabe?'

'At the moment? In a men's room on Congress Street.'

'Fine. Whatever it is you're doing there, when you finish, would you please get your ass down to the Fish Pier. The far end by the water. Seems we've got a little problem.'

This wasn't great timing. 'What kind of problem?' he asked.

'The murder kind,' Maggie replied.

Maggie – Detective Margaret Savage – was McCabe's number two in the PPD's Crimes Against People unit. They'd been working cases together ever since Chief Shockley bucked the unions and brought McCabe in from New York four years ago. In spite of a long Portland PD tradition of supervisors supervising and detectives working cases, McCabe liked getting into the weeds, especially when it came to homicide, and Maggie was always his partner of choice.

'Anything I oughta know?'

'I don't know much myself. A uniform discovered the body during a routine check. No positive ID yet. Young female Caucasian. Stuffed into the trunk of a car, possibly her own, parked illegally on the pier. She's dead, naked, and frozen solid.'

The frozen part was no big surprise if she'd been in the trunk a while. Unfortunately, a frozen body meant there'd be no decomposition. No decomposition meant there'd be no way to establish time of death. No time of death meant no way to check alibis. Somebody knocked on the restroom door. 'Be right out,' McCabe shouted to the knocker. He faced away from the door and turned on the taps to drown out the sound of his voice. 'Anything else?'

'Only that the car's a brand-new BMW convertible. Registered to an Elaine Elizabeth Goff of Portland. A marine insurance guy who works on the pier spotted it yesterday morning, parked where it shouldn't be. He didn't call it in until today. About an hour ago.'

'You call Fortier?'

'Yeah. Told him what I just told you. He said he'd brief Shockley.' Chief Shockley wanted to be kept up to the minute on any homicides. There weren't many murders in Portland, and when they happened he hated to look dumb in front of reporters. Especially the one he was sleeping with.

The knocker knocked again. 'Just a damned minute,' McCabe yelled at the door. Then he said into the phone,

'Okay, Mag, I'll be right there.' He hit end call and exited the men's room. The knocker gave McCabe what he figured was supposed to be a withering look. McCabe smiled back sweetly. 'All yours.' He threaded his way through the crowd and out the door. He called Kyra from the street.

'Don't tell me,' she said. 'I can guess. You're not coming.' She sounded more disappointed than angry.

'No, I'm not, but not for the reason you think. I was on my way to the gallery when Maggie called. They found a dead body dumped on one of the piers.'

'Murder?'

'Looks that way.'

'I'm sorry,' she said.

'Me, too. About everything. I want you to know that. And I want you to know I want to be there. How's the turnout?'

'Great, considering the weather.'

'Any reaction from the *other* major Maine artists?'

'Actually, Marta Einhorn's being very gracious. The others haven't said much. Oh, and Joe Kleinerman from the *Press Herald* –'

'The arts critic?'

'Yeah. He wants to do a piece about my work.'

McCabe spotted a PPD black-and-white unit heading east on Congress. He stepped into the middle of the street and flagged it down. 'That's great. Listen, I've got to go now. I love you. I wanted you to know that as well.'

'Yeah. Me, too.'

McCabe hung up. A young Asian patrol officer pulled up. McCabe leaned in and flashed his shield in case the guy didn't recognize him. It wasn't necessary. The Lucas

Kane case last year had made McCabe a minor celebrity, not just in the department but pretty much all over the city. He'd even gotten some press in New York. 'Hiya, Sergeant. What do you need?'

The cop's name tag identified him as T. Ly. Probably the shortest last name in the history of the department. Cambodian, McCabe guessed. There were quite a few Cambodians living in Portland. Most resettled as refugees back in the nineties.

'Ly?' McCabe asked, pronouncing it Lee. 'Right pronunciation?'

The man nodded. 'It'll do.'

'Can you get me to the Fish Pier? Like fast?'

Three

McCabe squeezed into the front seat, space made tight by the unit's onboard computer. Ly flipped on lights and siren, pulled a U-turn on Congress, and took off. It took less than two minutes to reach the Fish Pier. A sprawling waterfront complex off Commercial Street, the Portland Fish Pier was home to businesses serving the city's working waterfront, especially its struggling groundfish industry. A PPD unit blocked their way. Ly cut the siren and rolled down the window. The wind was howling even louder than before. A cop leaned in. 'Hiya, Sergeant. Go on down to the end of the pier.' He pointed. 'You'll see a bunch of units pulled in by the Vessel Services building. Can't miss 'em.'

Ly followed the road that looped around to the end of the pier. On their left, McCabe noted the boxy silhouette of the Portland Fish Exchange. A few years ago it would have been lit up and busy. Tonight it loomed dark and empty. A once thriving auction market where trawlers working out of Portland and a handful of other Maine ports sold their catches, the exchange had fallen on hard times. Federal regulations aimed at replenishing fish stocks cut trawlers' days at sea to a bare minimum. Catches and income were way down. Adding insult to injury, McCabe remembered reading, legislation backed by Maine's powerful lobstermen's lobby was keeping the fishermen from making a few extra bucks by selling the lobsters they snared in their nets. They had to throw them back. Or sneak them home to share with friends.

Without enough fish coming in, the Fish Exchange auctions, once held daily at noon, had become intermittent. Half the time they didn't happen at all. Some longtime Portland fishing families were being squeezed out of the business. Others moved down the coast to Gloucester, where selling stray lobsters was allowed. The captains who remained weren't happy.

Near the end of the pier, McCabe could see a pack of PPD units, light bars flashing. They were clustered next to the Vessel Services facility. Behind them yellow crime scene tape cordoned off the far end of the pier. Ly joined them. Half a dozen cold cops, clouds of breath streaming from their mouths, were stamping their feet, clapping their hands, or just moving around to keep warm. Two had positioned themselves by the tape to keep unauthorized visitors out of the active crime scene area. The others were keeping them company. A MedCU unit was just leaving. A dead body meant there was nothing for the paramedics to do.

'Hey.' Maggie Savage greeted McCabe as he emerged from the car. She was bundled in a dark blue Gore-Tex parka, hands in her pockets, a wool watch cap pulled down around her ears, her shield pinned to the outside.

'Hey, yourself. What's going on?' McCabe borrowed Ly's Maglite, and they headed toward a bronze BMW convertible parked facing in toward the city from the far end of the pier. Its driver's side door and trunk lid gaped open. Senior evidence tech Bill Jacobi and one of his guys were busy taking their pictures and measurements, drawing their diagrams, and writing their notes. The car was elegantly framed at a three-quarter angle between two concrete arms that poked out from the end of the pier into the Fore River, the tidal estuary that formed the far end of Portland harbor. Its rear wheels were two or three feet from the edge, leaving just enough room for the techs to walk behind the car without falling in. McCabe could see reflections of ambient light from nearby buildings as well as the more distant Casco Bay Bridge bouncing off the showroom-shiny fenders. Like an ad in a glossy magazine, the damned thing practically shouted, *Hey, look at me! Ain't I sexy?* To McCabe, it seemed too artfully placed for it to have been accidental. Someone wanted the car to be noticed.

As they stood there, Maggie handed him a plastic box of Tic-Tacs. 'Here. Before you breathe on anyone else, you might want to suck on a couple of these.'

'That bad, huh?'

'Not for anyone who appreciates the finer qualities of single malt. I just don't think it's something you want Jacobi noticing. Or the uniforms either, for that matter. Big night on the town?'

'I guess I had a few.' He left it at that and tossed two white pellets into his mouth. If truth be told, he felt a bit sick. He might have trouble walking the proverbial straight line. He handed the box back. 'Anything new?' he asked. He wondered if he was slurring his words.

'Just what I told you on the phone. Woman's body is stuffed in the trunk,' Maggie said. 'Frozen solid.'

42

McCabe shivered. 'I know how she feels.'

'She's packed in there so tight, I'm not sure how we're gonna get her out. At least not till she thaws.'

'Who called it in?'

'Guy named Doug Hester a little after six.'

About the time he was deciding to go to Kyra's show.

'Hester's office is over there,' Maggie continued. 'The one with lights on on the second floor. He runs a one-man marine insurance agency. Says he could see the car from his desk. It's been sitting there, illegally parked, since at least seven thirty yesterday morning when he came to work.'

Thirty-six hours. 'What took him so long to call it in?'

'It wasn't just him. There must have been fifty people who saw that car parked where it shouldn't be, and for two solid days none of them called it in. Either to us or to a towing service. I asked Hester why. He said people on the waterfront don't like to pry into other people's business.'

McCabe nodded. A familiar scenario. Citizens not wanting to get involved. Too polite. Too fearful. Too lazy. It was a problem for police departments across the country. It bugged the hell out of McCabe, but it was tough to figure out what to do about it.

'He said the car wasn't bothering him,' Maggie continued. 'Didn't seem to be bothering anyone else. So he, quote, didn't pay it no never mind, unquote. Also he says it's not that unusual for the wife of one of the captains to leave a car for her husband for when his boat gets in.'

'So what made him change his mind?'

'He started thinking how none of the fishing families

he knows is likely to have a brand-new BMW convertible. Not with the business in the dumper the way it is now. And, even if they did, they sure as hell wouldn't leave it sitting at the end of the pier for two days. So, at long last, he walks over and takes a closer look. Sees the keys in the ignition. Tries the door. It's not locked.'

'Getting his prints all over everything?'

'Probably. Though he says just the door. Anyway, he gets suspicious and finally decides to call.'

'Okay, so the car wasn't here when Hester left work Wednesday night, but it was here when he arrived Thursday morning. So sometime during that twelve-hour window somebody, presumably the killer, but possibly the victim, drives it in and parks it in the most prominent position on the pier.'

'Looks that way.'

'Why?'

'We don't know.'

'Hester pop the trunk?' asked McCabe.

'No. That was the responding officer. Uniform named Joe Vodnick. He popped the trunk and found the body. Little over an hour ago.'

'Was there probable cause for opening the trunk?'

'I think there may be some question about that.'

McCabe thought about it. Opening the trunk was no big deal if the car belonged to the victim. Elaine Goff or whoever it was wasn't going to complain about illegal search or seizure, dead as she was and stuffed inside. On the other hand, if the dead woman wasn't Goff, if Goff was the killer or somehow connected to the killer, the investigation could be compromised even before it began. 'Which one's Vodnick?'

'The big guy over there on the right.'

Vodnick was big alright. Six foot six. Built like a linebacker. Probably weighed 260, maybe more. He was busy bullshitting with a couple of the other cops. 'Did you ask him about probable cause?'

'He said the car roused his suspicions.'

'Roused his suspicions? That's nice. Anything a little more substantive?'

'Nope. He just said here was this expensive car, parked in a place it shouldn't have been for two days. Doors unlocked. Key in the ignition. He checked with Dispatch, and the car wasn't reported stolen. So he looked in the trunk. Listen, Mike, I don't know what a judge would say about probable cause, but I do know we probably wouldn't have found her otherwise. Hell, she could have been sitting in a tow yard until she thawed and somebody noticed the smell. I say he made a good call.'

'Assuming some slick-ass lawyer doesn't have the whole case thrown out on a technicality. I assume Vodnick's prints are on the car as well?'

'He says just the outside door handle and trunk release button, which is under the dash to the left of the wheel. Claims he was careful. Tried not to smear other possible prints.'

McCabe stood silently for a long minute, breathing in cold, damp air that smelled like seaweed and rotting fish, scanning the scene, burning its details into the hard drive he carried in his brain. A brand-new Beemer, unlocked, keys in the ignition, sitting there for two days. Amazing nobody tried to steal it. In New York it would've been gone in the blink of an eye. Maybe that was the bad guy's intention. Have some clueless kid take it for a joy-ride. Get his prints all over it. Get blamed for the murder when he was finally caught, nobody believing his denials. Not a bad plan. Might've worked. Except this was Maine, and nobody bothered stealing it.

He could see half a dozen trawlers tied up, two abreast, on either side of the pier. All good-sized commercial fishing boats. Some of the names were visible. *The Emma Anne. The Katie James. The Old Jolly.* They looked dark and empty, and none of them looked very jolly. McCabe wondered if any of them might have been here the night the car was driven onto the pier. If anyone might have seen anything. Probably not. Trawlers must be in and out of this place all the time. Taking on ice and fuel. Unloading fish for the auctions. Worth checking, though.

'Who takes care of the boats while they're here?' he asked Maggie.

'What do you mean, takes care of?'

'Services them. Fuel. Water. Ice. Stuff like that.'

'Actually, I do know. Company called Vessel Services. Right over there. I know someone who works for them.'

'Suppose they keep a record of which boats were here from Wednesday afternoon into Thursday morning?'

'Probably. But if you're thinking witnesses, why would someone spend a freezing cold night on board when he didn't have to?'

'It's possible.'

'An out-of-town boat, maybe. A Portland boat, I doubt it. These guys spend too much time at sea not to be home

46

with their wives, girlfriends, or whoever they can rustle up. Specially in this kind of weather.'

'Would you mind calling your friend at Vessel Services anyway? Maybe we'll get lucky.'

Maggie told him she'd call. McCabe's mind went back to the scene. The BMW was backed up close to the edge of the pier. Why? Was the killer getting ready to toss the body overboard? If so, why hadn't he? Maybe it was already frozen into the trunk and he couldn't get it out. Maybe he was interrupted by someone walking by or someone on one of the boats. Again, a possible witness.

'Have we learned anything about Goff?' he asked.

'Not much. Full name's Elaine Elizabeth Goff. She's a lawyer at Palmer Milliken. Twenty-nine years old. Single. Lives' – Maggie stopped herself – 'or possibly *lived* at 342 Brackett Street here in town. Car's brand-new. Initial registration dated the first of December.'

'We think that's Elaine in the trunk?'

'That's what we think. Officially, she's still Jane Doe.'

'You tried reaching her?'

'No listed number. Probably only uses a cell. I tried her extension at Palmer Milliken and got voice mail. I'm waiting on the Call Center to come up with a number for the cell. I asked Tom Tasco to track down her landlord.' Tasco was one of the unit's senior detectives.

McCabe took another deep breath of cold air. His head was clearing, but he still felt a little sick. 'Do we know what killed her?'

'Can't tell from looking.'

'No obvious wounds or trauma?'

'Some marks that look like bruises, that's all.' Maggie

47

paused. 'They don't look lethal. She's lying on one side with her knees tucked up tight, so you can't see that much of her.'

'Could be a wound on the other side.'

'Could be. Also her hair's covering her face, so you can't see that at all.'

'Terri on her way?' Terri was Terri Mirabito, a deputy ME with the chief medical examiner's office in Augusta, an hour and some away. Because she lived in Portland, Terri was always the first choice when a body turned up at night in the city. She was McCabe's first choice anyway. He couldn't stand her boss, Maine's chief medical examiner, Donald A. Fry, a.k.a. the Donald. A pompous know-it-all who never missed an opportunity to demonstrate to McCabe and his detectives how dumb they were and how smart he was. *Oh, for heaven's sake, Mac, it's obvious what happened here, isn't it?* No, Donald, it's not obvious. Also he had that habit of calling McCabe 'Mac.' It was a nickname McCabe loathed. Even when Fry was right, as far as McCabe was concerned, Fry was wrong.

Maggie nodded. 'Yeah. I called her cell. She was on her way out for a big evening with some new guy I think she has the hots for.' McCabe smiled. He enjoyed the image of the short, bubbly pathologist nursing a case of 'the hots.'

'Where was she headed?'

'A night at the opera.'

McCabe smiled again.

'No,' Maggie said with a sigh, 'not the Marx Brothers. The Kirov. They're singing at Merrill. I caught her just as she was parking her car. Tough ticket to get. She wasn't real happy hearing from me. Anyway, she said she'd let her friend know and then run home and get her kit.' Maggie glanced at her watch. 'Should be here any minute.'

'Okay. Let's take a look,' he said. In spite of Maggie's concern for his boozy breath, McCabe felt sober, his head clear at last. He slipped under the crime scene tape. 'You coming?'

'I'm coming.'

He headed toward the car, watching where he walked, shining Officer Ly's light on the concrete platform of the pier, flashing left and then right, trying to spot anything that shouldn't be there. There was nothing visible. Not even any tire tracks on the dirty patches of ice and snow. Too cold. Too hard. He reached the car. He peered in through the open driver's side door. Moved the light around the interior. Looked clean and new. He noted the key, still in the ignition. No other keys on the ring. No house keys. No office key. Just a plastic membership tag for Planet Fitness, a gym over on Marginal Way. He knew the place. Kyra went there. He wondered if they'd ever run into each other. McCabe squatted down and moved the light slowly across the floor and under the seats. He could just see the edge of a small plastic bag pushed under the driver's seat. He pulled it out. Pure white powder. Possibly coke. Jacobi could run a field test to be sure, but it looked like either Jane Doe or her killer was a user. Or maybe a dealer? He pointed it out to Maggie. She shook her head, indicating she hadn't seen it before. Either way, probable cause was established. They just had to let Vodnick know what he'd seen.

A couple of scenarios ran through McCabe's mind.

One, Goff drives here to meet someone. Maybe her dealer. He gives her the coke. She hides the bag under the seat. They have a disagreement. He gets pissed, kills her, and takes off. Possible. But if that was the case, why would the body be naked? Maybe the dealer demands sex for payment. She says no. He rapes her. Panics and kills her and takes off either in a second car or maybe a boat. Again possible, but it didn't feel right. Not the way the car was positioned in the most public place on the pier. Unless he backed it up to the edge after he killed her to dump the body overboard. So why didn't he? It wouldn't have been frozen yet. He could have tossed her into the harbor easily and driven off. Instead, he packs her into the trunk and leaves her. No. None of that felt right. More likely somebody brought the body here already stuffed in the trunk. Somebody who wanted the car to be noticed. Who wanted the body to be found.

Finally McCabe flicked off the light and stood up. He took a deep breath and walked toward the trunk, preparing himself for the first few seconds he'd spend alone with the victim. The cop and the corpse. A unique and strangely intimate relationship. Just the two of them. It didn't matter to McCabe who the victim was. A gangbanger or an innocent child. Either way, for him, it was this moment of shared intimacy that turned what for some cops was merely a job into an obligation. A sacred trust. To find and punish the killer, to right the wrong, to balance the scales. The Lord may someday get His turn – but for now, McCabe believed, vengeance is mine. I go first.

In the dim light of the open trunk, the woman's frozen body shone back at him bluish white, her flesh waxen. She was on her side. Head down. Knees and arms curled in. Like the tuck position divers squeeze into after they leap from their boards. Yet even in this position there was something familiar about her.

He flipped on the Maglite and suddenly found himself looking at a body he knew better than his own. Sandy. His faithless bitch of an ex-wife. The one who'd walked out not only on their failed marriage but also on their only child. How many times had he silently wished her dead? Now, somehow, she was. Dead. Frozen. Stuffed in a trunk. What in hell was she doing here? It made no sense.

He moved the beam to the thick waves of dark hair covering her face. It was longer than he remembered, but he hadn't seen her in a while. He knew he shouldn't touch any part of her body, not even the hair, until Terri got here. Too bad. Jacobi had his pictures, and there was no way he wasn't going to look. He felt around in his pockets for the plastic ballpoint he was sure was there. Grasping it by one end, he slid it under her hair, wondering briefly if, like her limbs, the hair would be frozen stiff. It wasn't. He lifted it off her face, squatted down, and shined the light in. Couldn't see much, but it was enough. The curve of her lip. The tilt of her nose. Worst of all, one lifeless blue eye staring out. Still mocking him even in death.

'McCabe, are you alright?'

Maggie's voice. He didn't answer. Just raised his left hand and waved her off. The rational side of his brain told him the body couldn't be Sandy. But if not Sandy, who or what was it? Some kind of delusion? Brought on by what? Too much booze? Too much emotion? Maybe he was going nuts. In his dreams he'd seen her dead often enough.

In some of those dreams he even killed her himself. But always with a gun. Never like this. Never without marks. Never left her to freeze in the trunk of a car. Not even a BMW. Though, to be sure, Sandy would rather be found in a Beemer than a Ford.

He wondered again about calling Richard Wolfe, the psychiatrist. Maybe it was time. He'd first seen Wolfe a little over a year ago, right after the end of the Lucas Kane affair, after Casey's first one-on-one encounter with her mother in more than three years. It was Kyra who urged him to go. He'd been getting the shakes and having trouble sleeping, and when he did sleep, his sleep was disturbed by violent nightmares that more often than not included Sandy. Kyra thought he might be having a nervous break-down. Wolfe told him no, it wasn't a breakdown. Just the aftermath of a high level of stress combined with anxiety about Casey and Sandy getting together again. He pre-scribed Xanax, which seemed to help, and though Wolfe recommended continuing therapy, either with him or someone else, McCabe decided that was that. He wouldn't take it any further.

'McCabe. You feeling okay?'

'Yeah. Fine.'

'You don't look fine.' Maggie was directly behind him. If he moved too fast he'd knock her right in the water. Once again, he felt her hand on his shoulder. 'Can you talk to me?' She was using her gentle voice. So effective in interrogations. All the bad guys fell for it. 'McCabe?'

He didn't answer. Instead, he examined the body one more time, finishing up by running the Maglite along her leg, searching for the small mole on the outside of her knee that should have been there. It wasn't. At least not where he could see it.

No, this wasn't Sandy. He was sure of it now. Just someone who looked like her. To prove it, even to the doubting little voice that inhabited his brain, he took out his cell and punched in her number in New York. It rang. Once. Twice. Four times. *Hello. You've reached the Ingrams. Sandy and Peter. Please leave a message, and we'll get back to you as soon as we can.*

'Sandy, it's me. McCabe. Call back as soon as you can. It's important.' Then, as an afterthought, 'Oh, it's not about Casey. She's fine.' He clicked off and tried the house in East Hampton and then her cell. Same result both times. He left messages.

No, he told himself again, this wasn't Sandy. She was in New York, safe and sound. On a Friday night she and her rich-as-Croesus husband were probably at the theater. *We request that everyone in the audience please turn off all cell phones for the duration of the performance. Thank you very much.* Or maybe they were home lying in front of the fire in their West End Avenue co-op, not answering the phone because they were otherwise engaged. He pictured Sandy having sex with Ingram. Without warning, the image changed and it wasn't Ingram on the floor by the fire, wrapped in the familiar scent and feel of Sandy's naked body. It was McCabe himself, thrusting into her over and over in a ferocious surge of desire. He was shocked by how much he still wanted her. Equally shocked by how much he hated her. It struck him that the need to exorcise the ghost of Sandy once and for all might be the real reason he kept pushing Kyra toward a marriage she wasn't ready for. That was something he'd have to deal with. Something he'd have to resolve. He loved Kyra too much to use her that way. Perhaps he should stop seeing her. At least until the exorcism was complete. He wondered what a therapist like Wolfe would say about all this. He wondered if he could even tell Wolfe. But maybe he would. He sure as hell couldn't tell anyone else.

As suddenly as it began it was over. Even the little voice in his brain accepted the fact that the woman in the trunk wasn't Sandy. She was a look-alike, most likely one named Elaine Elizabeth Goff. Yes, the resemblance *was* strong, but that's all it was, a resemblance. Maggie was still behind him, her hand still on his shoulder. 'I'm okay,' he said.

'I'm not even going to ask.'

McCabe focused the light once more on the body in the trunk, looking this time not for moles but for evidence. For something that might tell him who had killed this woman and how. He noticed reddish marks on the one wrist and one ankle he could see, suggesting she'd been physically restrained prior to death. He saw the bruising Maggie mentioned on the visible portions of her legs, buttocks, and arms. Maybe she'd been beaten as well. Or maybe the marks were nothing more than freezer burn. He hadn't seen any bruising around her face, and there was no sign of blood, either on her body or in the trunk.

Four

'Why is it you two always find your bodies on Friday nights? Haven't you ever heard of Tuesday?' Maggie and McCabe looked up at the sound of Terri Mirabito's voice. The deputy state medical examiner was standing at the front of the car holding a small black bag, like a Norman Rockwell doctor making a house call. Even bundled in a heavy sheepskin coat with a matching hat pulled down over her dark, curly hair, McCabe could tell Terri was dressed for a night on the town. He didn't think he'd ever seen her wear lipstick or mascara or even high heels before. She looked good. The two cops moved out of the way to give her room to look in the trunk.

'Hmmm. Frozen like a rock,' she said. 'That's what I heard. That'll make things interesting.'

'Any sneaky way to estimate time of death?'

'No. Freezing right after death keeps a body fresh. Like she died five minutes ago. Think Butterball turkey.'

'What if decomposition already started?'

'Freezing would have stopped it. We might be able to estimate the elapsed time between when she died and when she was frozen, but pinpointing actual time of death? No way.'

'So we could be talking weeks?'

'Sure. Assuming the body froze in position inside the trunk, which I think is the case.'

'That's too bad.'

'Well, yes and no,' said Terri, pulling on a pair of surgical gloves. 'Freezing also keeps any evidence we find on the body fresh. Poison, if that's what killed her. Drugs. Alcohol. Whatever she ate for her last meal. Semen, if the killer left any behind.' She ran a small high-intensity light over the body and began her examination.

'She is dead, isn't she?' asked Maggie. 'None of this "Frozen corpse comes back to life. Leaps off autopsy table"?'

Terri looked up, amused. 'Y'mean, like you see in the *Enquirer*?'

'Yeah. Like that.'

'Sorry, Mag. No leaping for this lady. She's dead.'

'Any idea what killed her?' asked McCabe.

'Yes.' Terri was now leaning deep into the trunk. She was holding Jane Doe's hair up with one gloved hand and shining the light on the back of her neck with the other. 'It looks like the killer knew what he was doing. Here. Take a look.'

McCabe squeezed in next to Terri. She pointed a gloved finger to a wound in the small indentation in the back of Jane Doe's neck. Right where the head and the neck connect. A small wound, no more than half an inch across. 'That's what killed her?' he asked.

'Yes. Looks like the killer pushed a thin-bladed knife or possibly an ice pick up into the base of her skull at the C1 vertebra. Probably went through the foramen magnum and into the brain stem.'

'The foramen what?'

'The foramen magnum. It's a small opening at the base of the skull. The spinal cord goes through it to attach to the brain stem. If the killer gets it right, he severs the spine from the brain; cardiac and respiratory systems stop working. The victim falls to the ground dead.'

'Just like that?'

'Just like that.'

'Doesn't look like there was much bleeding.'

'He didn't hit any major blood vessels.'

'Death was instantaneous?' asked Maggie.

'Yes. It's called pithing. It's one of the very few injuries that cause virtually instantaneous death. Victim goes down like a rag doll.'

'If he hits the wrong spot?'

'He ends up with a messy, possibly nonlethal wound.'

'So the creep knows his anatomy.'

'Yes. Unless he was just lucky, he knows his anatomy well enough to know the effect. Though, if the victim is immobilized, and it looks like she may have been, it's pretty easy to put the knife where you want it.'

'You're sure that's what killed her?'

'About as sure as I can be until I get her in for the autopsy, and we can't do that until she thaws out. It'll be three or four days at the very least. Probably more like a week.'

'A week? Jesus. Can't we do it faster?' asked Maggie. 'Maybe soak her in a tub under running water? That's how my mom handled the Butterballs.'

'Unfortunately, she's not a turkey. We thaw her too fast and we end up with tissue damage. The outside starts decomposing while the internal organs are still frozen. That'll interfere with some of the tests I need to run. Plus, soaking her in water could wash away any trace evidence on or in the body. We'll just have to wait.'

'A week?'

'For a total thaw, yes. We'll put her in the refrigeration unit at the lab, and at a constant thirty-eight degrees, it'll take about a week. Doing it that way minimizes decomp. Helps us learn more about what or who killed her. However, we should be able to get some information sooner.'

'Like what?'

'Well, I'll be able to check the body surface almost immediately, and clip her nails in case she scratched her attacker. If there's any hair or saliva or skin cells that aren't hers, we'll find them. Also I should be able to move her limbs enough in a day or so to do an internal swab and check for semen.' Even going over the gory details Terri sounded cheerful. She was one of those people who loved her job. *Unraveling the mysteries of the dead*, as they might have said on the Discovery Channel. McCabe found forensic pathology a strange way to get your jollies, but he guessed that's what made Terri so good at it.

She went back to her task of looking over the body. She was squatting down, shining her light at Jane Doe's face, when she called out, 'McCabe?'

'Yeah?'

'She's got something in her mouth.'

'Like what?' McCabe pushed in next to Terri again and looked where her light was pointing. Jane Doe's lips and teeth were slightly parted. Behind the teeth he could see a small flash of white he hadn't noticed before.

'Looks like paper,' said Terri.

'A gag?' asked Maggie.

'I don't think so,' said McCabe. 'It's not balled up like a

gag would be. Looks folded. Maybe some kind of note? Like maybe the murderer left us a message. Can you get it out?'

'I don't know. Her jaw's frozen in position. No more than an eighth of an inch clearance. I'll try to thread it through the opening with forceps.'

'Won't the paper be frozen, too?' asked Maggie.

'Mouth would have to be wet for the paper to freeze, but it might have been. Possibly with saliva. Or, if decomp already started, there might be some purge fluid.'

Terri rummaged in her bag and came out with an instrument that looked like a pair of delicate tweezers with small blunt teeth at the ends. She slipped it between Jane Doe's parted lips, grasped the paper, and gently tugged. It didn't move. 'It's frozen, alright,' she said. 'I'll see if I can wiggle it free.'

It took three or four minutes of carefully pulling and prodding, first one way, then the other. Finally the paper moved. 'I think maybe I've freed it. Now let's see if I can extract it without tearing it.'

Holding Jane Doe's frozen jaw in place with her left hand, Terri coaxed the paper through her parted teeth. Finally it was free.

'Can you unfold it?' asked McCabe. 'Let's see what's written. If anything.'

'Not till we warm it up a bit,' said Terri. She was holding what looked like a standard 8 1/2' by 11' sheet of copy paper between the teeth of her forceps. The paper was folded over and over into a one- by two-inch wad. It had been discolored, probably by fluid in the mouth.

'Here, Doc, put it in here.' Bill Jacobi was holding out a

small stainless steel pan. 'We'll warm it in the van. Then maybe we can take a look.'

Terri dropped the folded sheet of paper into the pan. They walked back toward Jacobi's crime scene van. It only took a minute for Bill to warm the paper enough to unfold it. He flattened it on a tray and took two shots of it, front and back, with a digital camera.

McCabe looked down. The paper was blank except for two words printed in the center in twelve-point type in an ordinary font.

Amos. 9:10.

'From the Bible?' asked Maggie.

'Yes,' said McCabe. 'Unfortunately. It may not be good news.'

Maggie looked at him sharply. 'Why? What's it say? Who's Amos?'

'One of the minor Old Testament prophets. Book of Amos. Chapter nine. Verse ten.' McCabe closed his eyes and let his brain take him back to sixth-grade Bible class at St Barnabas. There he was, eleven-year-old Michael, the oddity standing uncomfortably before the entire class. And there was Sister Mary Joseph, standing over him, smiling benignly down, celebrating God's gift of eidetic memory to her young student, making him recite yet another passage from an obscure book of the Bible. Her version of Trivial Pursuit. Could she stump him? No, she couldn't. Not even with the Book of Amos. Twenty-seven years later in the cold and dark of the Portland Fish Pier,

McCabe's mind brought the words back. 'It seems some-one was punishing our victim for her sins.'

'What's it say?' Maggie asked again.

'*All the sinners of my people shall die by the sword, which say, The evil shall not overtake nor prevent us.* That's what the Book of Amos was all about. God punishing the Israelites for their sins.'

'What kinds of sins?'

'The standard list. Greed, corruption, oppression of the poor.'

'It did say *all* the sinners – so there might be more?'

'Well, she might be the only sinner he planned on pun-ishing, but I'm not sure I'd count on it.'

Jacobi stared at McCabe. 'Book of Amos? Chapter nine? Verse ten? I heard you have a fancy memory, but how in hell would you know a thing like that?'

'Trust him, Bill. He knows,' said Maggie.

'You know the whole Bible by heart?'

'No. Just the parts we learned in class.' He passed Terri the note.

Terri glanced at the note and shrugged her shoulders. 'Wonder what sins he was punishing her for.'

'The sins of the flesh, I suppose. It's a pretty common syndrome among whackos all the way from Jack the Rip-per to that guy Picton they just put away in Vancouver.'

'Those guys were hunting prostitutes,' said Maggie. 'Elaine Goff was a lawyer, not a prostitute. And yes, McCabe,' she added, looking directly at him, 'there is a difference.'

He smiled and shrugged.

'Bill, I'd like to get the body up to Augusta as soon as we can,' Terri said to Jacobi. 'How long do you think it'll take to pry her out of the trunk?'

'When we're finished with the scene here, we'll flatbed the Beemer to 109. We'll probably end up cutting the car out from around her. Take a couple of hours to do it neatly.'

'You can get her up to Augusta tonight, though?'

'Yeah, I think so.'

'Okay, I'll call Jose Guerrera so he's there to receive.' Guerrera was Terri's lab assistant.

Joe Vodnick up close looked even bigger than he did from a distance.

'It's Joe, right?'

'Yes sir, Sergeant.'

McCabe looked him up and down. Mostly up. 'You ever play ball?' he asked.

Vodnick smiled. 'Yeah. A few years back. U. Maine Black Bears. All-conference defensive end. Twice, '01 and '02.'

'I think I saw you play once. Real nice moves.' McCabe was bullshitting. He'd been to one U. Maine game in his life, and that was a couple of years after Vodnick graduated. Still, the big man seemed pleased at the compliment, which was what McCabe intended in the first place.

'Yeah. I was pretty quick for my size.'

McCabe smiled at Vodnick, threw an arm around one massive shoulder, and steered him away from the cluster of cops to the other side of the pier. 'Joe, you and I need to talk,' he said, keeping his voice low, his tone friendly. 'Tell me what went down tonight.'

'It was just like I told Detective Savage. I was patrolling

the Old Port. Not much going on. At least not on the streets. Too damned cold. Anyway, I get a call. Dispatch tells me to check out an illegally parked car at the end of the Fish Pier.' Vodnick repeated the rest of the story pretty much the way Maggie had told it.

When he finished, McCabe nodded thoughtfully. 'Why'd you pop the trunk?'

'Why?'

'Yeah. Why. You know? Probable cause?'

Vodnick shrugged. 'Car wasn't locked. Keys sitting in the ignition. Didn't feel right. A 40K car left like that. First I thought maybe the car was stolen by some joyrider, then just dumped here, but I checked, and it wasn't.'

'But you *did* notice that little plastic bag full of white powder that was sticking out from under the driver's seat? Isn't that right?'

Vodnick hesitated. 'White powder?' He shook his head. No.

McCabe's eyes bored into the bigger man's. 'You remember, Joe. That small plastic bag of white powder that's now in the evidence van. That's what caused you to pop the trunk, isn't that right?'

Vodnick hesitated again. Then, as understanding dawned, 'Yeah, right,' he said, nodding slowly. 'That small plastic bag. Under the driver's seat? The one I thought might contain an illegal substance?'

McCabe nodded back at him. 'That's right. That's the one. So what did you do when you saw it?'

'Well, I figured I better open the trunk to see if there might be more illegal substances back there.'

'And did you find any?'

'No. All I found was the woman's body.'

'And you haven't discussed this with anyone else?'

'Just Detective Savage.'

'Not with any of your pals over there?'

'No. Nobody else.'

There was something so earnest and childlike about Vodnick's response, McCabe found himself resisting a temptation to reach up and pat the big man on the head. He settled instead for a more manly slap on the back. 'Okay. That's good. Where's Hester now?'

'Sitting in his office keeping his butt warm.' Vodnick pointed up to a couple of lit windows on the second floor of the building nearest the end of the pier. 'I told him to sit tight till you talked to him.'

'What does he know?'

'I didn't tell him about the body, but he'd have to be blind, deaf, and dumb not to have figured something was up.'

'Alright, I'll let him know we want to talk to him at 109. Then I want you to take him downtown, get a set of prints, then park him in an interview room on four. Got it?'

'Got it.'

McCabe slapped his shoulder again, turned, and headed for the building. Maggie fell into step alongside. 'All set with the big guy?' she asked.

'All set.'

'Good.'

A small sign identified the three-story aluminum box as the MARINE TRADE CENTER, 2 PORTLAND FISH PIER. They took the stairs up one flight and found a door with HESTER ASSOCIATES, MARINE AND GENERAL INSUR-

ANCE painted on frosted glass. It was basically a one-room office. Maybe three hundred square feet. Doug Hester was sitting at his desk, sipping a cup of coffee, looking out at the scene below. He didn't look happy. Probably hated being here this late on a Friday night. That was alright. McCabe hated it, too. Hester was a chubby little guy, maybe five foot six. McCabe put him somewhere in his mid-fifties. He combed his reddish brown hair over in a fruitless attempt to hide male pattern baldness.

'Mr Hester?' asked Maggie. Hester looked up. 'I'm Detective Margaret Savage. This is Detective Sergeant Michael McCabe. We're in charge of the investigation, and we'd like you to come down to police headquarters to review everything you reported related to the incident.'

'Is this really necessary? I already told the other officer, the big guy, everything I know. Which isn't a whole lot. It's my sister-in-law's birthday. We're having a dozen people over to celebrate. They're probably already there.'

'I'm sorry about that,' said McCabe, 'but I'm sure your sister-in-law will understand. A woman's body was found in the trunk of the car.'

'A dead body?'

'Yes.'

Hester blanched. 'Jesus. A dead body sitting there for two days. How'd she get in the trunk?'

'That's what we're trying to find out.'

'Jesus, why the hell would anyone leave a dead body in a car on the pier?'

'We don't know. But like Detective Savage said, we'd like you to come down to Middle Street and tell us what you know.'

Hester just shook his head in apparent disbelief. 'I'm not sure what I can add.'

'Going over it again may help you remember things you didn't realize were important when you talked to Officer Vodnick. Or maybe didn't realize you saw.' Maggie gave him her best smile. 'Anyway, since you apparently touched the car we'll also need to get a full set of your fingerprints. Unless you were wearing gloves at the time.'

'I wasn't. I just ran downstairs to look at the car. I wasn't even wearing a coat.'

'Okay. Officer Vodnick will drive you down. It shouldn't take long.'

'Can't I take my own car?'

'We'd rather you went with him.'

'Alright,' Hester said nervously, 'but one of you is gonna have to explain to my wife why I'm missing her sister's party. She's going to be mightily pissed.'

Five

Murder is major news in Portland, and major news travels fast. By the time McCabe and Maggie slipped out the back door of the Marine Trade Center, a cluster of reporters and photographers was already gathering at the front. The two detectives snuck along the side of the building, using a pair of parked vans bearing the logos of the local NBC and Fox affiliates as cover. The idea was to get to Maggie's car and drive away unnoticed. It didn't work. Luke McGuire, the crime beat guy for the *Press Herald*, spotted them first. 'Hey, McCabe,' he shouted. McCabe stopped. Game over. The reporters surged forward, shouting out questions and shoving microphones in his face. He turned to face them. Dealing with the press had never been McCabe's strong suit. In fact, Chief Shockley had warned him more than once that if he didn't stop snarling at journalists he'd be involuntarily enrolled in a course at USM called Effective Media Relations. Or, as Maggie put it, SmileyFace 101.

'Hey, McCabe,' McGuire repeated, 'who's the dead woman? What's her name?'

McCabe tried to put on his best friendly yet serious face. 'Sorry, Luke, I'm afraid we don't yet have positive identification. Until we do, she'll be listed as Jane Doe.'

Two or three others shouted out questions more or less

simultaneously. 'How was she killed? Are we calling it murder? What's the body doing on the Fish Pier?'

McCabe held up one hand for silence. 'Ladies and gentlemen, please. The ME's office hasn't made an official determination on cause of death. We'll let you know as soon as they do. To answer your second question, the circumstances of her death are under investigation.

'Is it true the body's frozen solid? Stuffed in the trunk of that car over there?' The question came from Josie Tenant, an on-camera reporter for NBC's News Center 6. Tenant was, without question, the most aggressive of the locals. Rumor had it she was also Tom Shockley's secret playmate du jour. Tenant's record as the conduit of leaks on major cases suggested it was more than rumor.

'Well, since the body's been outside in subfreezing temperatures for at least two days, I'll let you draw your own conclusion. I'm afraid that's all for now. Detective Savage and I have a lot of work to do. I'll ask you all please to stay back and respect the crime scene. Officers have been instructed to keep everyone out of the area until it's been totally cleared. Thank you.'

They managed to reach Maggie's car without answering any more questions. In the background McCabe could hear Tenant begin her live report. 'Tonight there's breaking news from the Portland Fish Pier. Earlier this evening the body of an unidentified woman was found stuffed into the trunk of a car illegally parked at the end of the pier. According to anonymous sources close to the investigation, the victim, who appeared to be in her twenties or early thirties, may have been Portland attorney Elaine E. Goff. However, identity has not yet been confirmed.

68

Detectives on the scene told News Center 6 the victim's body had been stored in the trunk long enough for it to freeze solid in the record low temperatures . . .'

'Goddammit!' McCabe slammed his fist hard against the dashboard of Maggie's car. 'Sonofabitch just couldn't resist rewarding his little bedmate.'

McCabe pulled out his cell phone and speed-dialed Shockley's direct line at police headquarters. As Maggie eased the car forward, Shockley picked up. 'Hey, Mike. How you guys doing down at the pier?' He sounded echoey, as if he were talking on speakerphone. 'By the way, Bill Fortier's been briefing me on the case.' Well, that, at least, answered one question.

'With all due respect, Chief, we'd be doing a whole lot better if you could hold off talking to your special friends in the press.' These last words were delivered with more than a spoonful of sarcasm. 'At least until we know for sure who the victim is – and maybe inform her next of kin?'

'McCabe, that's an outrageous accusation. I don't know what you're talking about.' McCabe heard Shockley asking Fortier to leave and to shut the door. Then the chief switched off the speakerphone and spoke in a low, threatening voice. 'McCabe, if you want to stay in this department, if you even want to stay in Portland, you'd better learn to keep a tighter handle on your righteous indignation.' Then, almost as an afterthought, 'You also better learn to get your facts straight.'

'If I was mistaken, Chief, I apologize. But maybe you want to turn on News Center 6.'

There was a brief silence as Shockley turned on the set

in his office. In the background, McCabe could hear what sounded like Josie Tenant's live report. Shockley came back on. 'That's unfortunate,' he said. 'Josie ought to know better than that.' His voice sounded tight and angry. A second later he hung up. If he hadn't managed to get himself fired, McCabe figured he might at least have damaged Tenant's inside line to the department.

Maggie exited the Fish Pier and turned right on Commercial, heading east into the heart of the Old Port. McCabe leaned back against the headrest and closed his eyes. With the windows closed and the heater starting to blast warm air, the strong, greasy smell of Chicken McNuggets filled the car. McCabe's foot found the empty container. He picked it up and peered in. There were a couple of cold McNuggets left on the bottom. 'Mind if we get rid of this? It's making me feel sick.'

'Sorry. My dinner,' said Maggie, an unrepentant junk food junkie. Somehow it never seemed to affect her. There wasn't much fat on her long, lanky frame. She pulled over by a curbside trash bin, and McCabe tossed the box in. He left the window open to release the smell.

'You okay?' she asked. 'Not going to puke or anything?'

McCabe was leaning back, looking out the open window, breathing in cold air. 'No,' he said, 'I'm fine.'

She turned left onto Market. Cold or not, it was still Friday night in the Old Port, and the bars and clubs were hopping. Kids armed with ID, fake or real, darted from one noisy doorway to another.

'Y'know, it's weird,' she said. 'I've seen you look at, what, a dozen murder victims over the years? Some cut up, some shot up, some missing arms, legs, and other body parts. Some bloated and turning green. Almost all of them bloodier than Our Lady of the Icicles. Yet never once have I seen you turn the color you did back there. Remember the song "A Whiter Shade of Pale"? That was you.'

'A Whiter Shade of Pale,' 1967. Procol Harum. Number one on the British charts for six consecutive weeks. Only made number five in the U.S. Sometimes McCabe wished he had a delete button for all the crap sloshing around in his brain. 'Okay. What about it?'

'Just that I've never seen you react like that before. I was wondering why this time.'

'You said you wouldn't ask.'

'I changed my mind.'

'Too much booze on an empty stomach. Nothing to worry about.'

'Come on, McCabe, I know you better than that.'

'It was the booze,' he said flatly.

'Bullshit. It wasn't the booze. It was the body. You did a triple take. Like you knew her or something. And those phone calls to Sandy? What was that all about?'

He looked at Maggie looking at him. He supposed he ought to tell her something. She was the closest thing to a friend he had in Portland, not counting Kyra or Casey. Finally he shrugged. 'No, I didn't know her. I just thought I did. She looked like my ex-wife.'

'Sandy?'

'The one and same. Casey's mother. The wonderful woman who walked out on both of us and never looked back. I took one look at the body in the trunk, and, boom, I wasn't looking at Jane Doe or Elaine Goff or anyone else. I was looking at Sandy. Dead. Naked. And frozen like a rock. It was like it really was her.'

'Weird.'

'Yeah. Weird.' He didn't tell Maggie the rest of it because he didn't know how, and he wasn't sure it was her business anyway. His cell rang. He checked caller ID. Sandy. He put the phone back in his pocket and let his voice mail pick up. He didn't want to talk to her now. He realized he was sweating. He turned the heater down.

Six

Less than a minute later, Maggie threaded the big Ford down the narrow alleyway that led to the police garage. She pulled into a free space near the back door between two black-and-white units. Wordlessly they entered the building and took the elevator to four. The bureau was empty except for Tom Tasco, who was on the phone, and Brian Cleary, who had his feet up on his desk and was chewing away on a slice of pizza. Cleary, recently promoted to plainclothes, was the new kid on the block. Tasco was a seasoned detective with more than eighteen years in the PPD. McCabe figured Tasco was the right guy to show Cleary the ropes. McCabe had assigned Tasco's former partner, Eddie Fraser, to work with the sometimes difficult Carl Sturgis.

Cleary looked up as McCabe and Maggie approached. 'A couple more pies down the conference room if you guys want some,' he said.

McCabe realized he was famished. He hadn't eaten all day except for a bagel at breakfast. 'Okay, let's talk down there,' he said. He signaled Tasco to follow when he finished his call. A couple of open boxes of pizza and some warm Cokes sat on the big table. A detective named John Hughes from Crimes Against Property was helping himself to a slice. 'Who do I owe?'

'Shockley's treat,' said Cleary.

'That's a first,' said Hughes. 'He must like you guys.' Hughes took his food and left. Tasco came in.

'Shockley still here?' asked McCabe.

'No. He just left. So did Fortier,' said Cleary.

'Anything else going on?'

'You mean other than your frozen corpse?'

'Yeah. Other than her.'

'A couple of assholes decided to ring in the new year by beating the shit out of a homeless guy over on Preble Street.'

'Just for the fun of it?'

'Looks that way. Though it may have been racial. The vic was black and he didn't have anything worth stealing. Bill 'n' Will are checking it out now.' Detectives Bill Bacon and Will Messing had been universally known by their rhyming first names since McCabe teamed them up three years earlier.

'We know who did it?'

'Not yet, but the vic's in the ICU at Cumberland. Might not make it.'

Detective Carl Sturgis stuck his head in the door. 'This a private party, or can anyone play?'

'C'mon in, Carl,' said McCabe. 'Where's Eddie?'

'At a school play. *Peter Pan*. His daughter's playin' the head fairy.'

'Tinker Bell?' Maggie smiled.

'Yeah. Tinker Bell. Probably over by now,' said Sturgis, checking his watch. He helped himself to a slice of the pizza and a Coke and sat down.

McCabe signaled Maggie, who nodded and flipped open her cell. 'Hey, Eddie, it's Maggie.' Pause. 'Sorry to call you at home, but if the play's over we need you to come in tonight.' Pause. 'Yeah. A murder. Plan on a long night.' Pause. 'No. Wait till the star's tucked in. We can manage till then. Hope she brought the house down.'

'By the way, some oversized uniform named Vodnick just deposited a witness in the small interview room,' said Sturgis. 'Guy named Hester?'

'Hester can sit for a minute,' said McCabe.

Tasco came in and handed everyone a set of color photos. Three shots of the same woman. 'Elaine Goff?' asked Maggie.

'Yup,' said Tasco. 'Elaine Elizabeth Goff, attorney at law and, as you all know, the owner of a brand-new BMW 325i convertible. I assume this is your corpse?'

McCabe spread his set of pictures on the table one after the other. The resemblance to Sandy was even more startling in the photographs than it had been with the dead and frozen woman in the trunk. 'Yeah,' he said finally, 'that's her. Where'd you get the pics?'

'Google Images. Amazing the stuff you can find there.'

McCabe studied each picture in turn. The first was a business headshot in black and white. A formal Fabian Bachrach kind of thing. The second must have come from someone's vacation blog. It showed Goff by a pool, wearing a skimpy bikini. Palm trees in the background. She was looking straight into the camera and sipping what looked like a piña colada. In this shot she looked more like Sandy than in either of the others. Sure as hell more than she did lying dead in the back of a Beemer. It wasn't just the setting or the bikini that made the resemblance startling. It was the attitude. The same half smile, half smirk he'd seen a thousand times.

The one that said, *Eat your heart out, asshole, I'm way too hot for the likes of you.* It gave him the feeling he knew everything there was to know about Elaine Elizabeth Goff. Even though they weren't the same woman. Even though there had to be differences. It was a feeling he had to be careful of.

In the last of the pictures Goff was wearing a strapless black evening dress at some kind of function. Looked like the kind of shot a press photographer might take at a fancy charity event. The *Press Herald* ran that stuff all the time. She was standing in a small group with another young woman, an attractive freckle-faced blonde, and three guys in black tie. Two of them were gray-haired and probably in their fifties. The third, the one to Lainie's right, was maybe ten years younger. He was looking straight into the camera with intense dark blue eyes. He had a thin face, a crooked nose, and longish dark hair. McCabe wouldn't have called him handsome, but there was something in those eyes that drew attention. Star quality. Charisma. Call it what you will, but even in competition with a beauty like Lainie Goff, one's eyes might well go to him first – and stay with him the longest.

'Who's the guy with the violet eyes?' asked McCabe.

'Name's John Kelly,' said Tasco. 'He's executive director of a small nonprofit called Sanctuary House. Shelter for runaway kids located off Longfellow Square. Doesn't seem like a black-tie kind of guy, so I figure the party must have been a fund-raiser for them.'

'Who's the woman and the other two guys standing with Goff?'

'Don't know yet,' said Tasco. 'That's something we have to track down.'

McCabe slipped his set of pictures into the breast pocket of his jacket.

Tasco passed another printout around the table. 'Elaine Goff's bio page from the Palmer Milliken Web site.'

Elaine E. Goff
Associate
Direct Dial: 207·555·1041
egoff@palmermilliken.com

Elaine Goff joined Palmer Milliken as an associate in the firm's Mergers & Acquisitions Practice Group in 2000. Prior to joining the firm, Lainie served as law clerk to United States District Court Judge Edward Mellman.

Education
Lainie earned a B.A. from Colby College (1997) and a J.D., magna cum laude, at the Cornell University School of Law (2000). At Cornell, she was a member of the Cornell Law Review and served as articles editor her final year.

Bar Admissions
Lainie is admitted to practice in Maine.

'Hell of a waste of a fine-looking woman, is all I can say.' It was Brian Cleary. He was still gazing at Goff in her bikini. 'Looks like that actress. You know. What's her name? The one who played the math guy's wife in *A Beautiful Mind*?'

'Jennifer Connelly,' said McCabe.

'Yeah. Jennifer Connelly. Like her.' Cleary shook his head in admiration. 'Man, I don't know why a hottie like this ever bothered going to law school. She coulda been a model, an actress, anything.'

'A hottie? Gee, Brian, that's not what I heard. I heard this babe's ice cold.' Sturgis guffawed at his own wit.

'Oh, for chrissakes,' said Maggie. 'Brian, why don't you do us all a favor and stop drooling over that picture like a horny twelve-year-old. The woman's dead. And Carl, can the jokes, alright? They're not funny.'

'Oh. Yeah. Gee. Okay . . . Sorry, Mag,' said Cleary, his normally red face turning even redder.

Sturgis just glared. He didn't like being rebuked by a woman. Especially a younger woman who outranked him in spite of serving fewer years in the department. There was a short, embarrassed silence around the table.

McCabe broke it. 'Okay, enough,' he said. 'Let's get back to work. Maggie, would you go talk to Hester? He's been cooling his heels long enough. Any longer, he'll take a walk.' If Hester was hiding anything, Maggie was the one to find it. She was as good as anybody McCabe had ever seen at ferreting information from reluctant witnesses. He'd seen her go from sympathetic to tough to friendly to threatening in the blink of an eye, all without pissing witnesses off or closing them down. Most never knew what hit them. 'Meantime, I'll brief these guys on what we saw on the pier.'

Maggie nodded, collected her copies of the printouts, and left. McCabe spent the next fifteen minutes going over what they'd found, including the frozen note pried from Goff's mouth and Terri's opinion on the cause of death.

'She was pithed, huh? Somebody stuck a knife in my

neck, I guess I'd be pretty pithed, too,' said Sturgis, again chortling at his own wit.

McCabe threw him a warning look. 'All right, Carl, like Maggie said, it's time for you to stop with the humor. A woman's been murdered, and if you or any of you other guys think that's funny, trust me, I can have you out of this unit and back in a uniform before you even stop laughing.'

Sturgis murmured an apology. McCabe turned back to Tasco. 'Tommy, did you manage to track down Goff's landlord?'

'Yeah. Guy named Andrew Barker. Lives downstairs in the same building she lived in. It's a six-unit over on Brackett. Number 342. Barker told me Goff's apartment sits right above his on the second floor. Also says he hasn't seen her in a while. Thought she was on vacation. I asked him if her mail was piling up. He said no.'

'You check with the post office?'

'Yes. That's who I was talking to when you and Maggie got back. Goff submitted a hold-mail request to start Saturday, December twenty-fourth. Deliveries scheduled to resume this Monday.'

'Anything else?'

'Yeah. I told Barker we were investigating a possible homicide and that we'd be sending the techs over to take a look at her apartment. Guy seemed kind of excited about that. Anyway, he said he'd be there to let them in and that he hoped nothing bad happened to Lainie. That's what he called her, Lainie. I said we didn't know yet.'

'He'll figure it out soon enough,' said McCabe. 'At least he will if he watches TV. Any luck with her cell phone?'

'Yeah,' said Brian Cleary. 'I worked on that. She uses Verizon.' He glanced at his notebook and read out the number. 'Number's 555-4390. I got a subpoena and asked the company for a record of all her calls, incoming and outgoing, for the past three months. Also for access to voice mail messages for the last thirty days. I told them it was urgent. Supervisor there said they'd get it together, have it for me in the morning. Asked me to fax over a copy of the subpoena. I did.'

'Good.'

'Got something else, too.' Cleary was hunched forward in his chair, his foot tapping nervously on the floor. McCabe had high hopes for the young detective. He saw Cleary as a throwback to the Irish cops of thirty and forty years ago. McCabe's father's generation. Smart and aggressive with a wise-guy cockiness that reminded McCabe of the young Jimmy Cagney. *Made it, Ma! Top of the world!* He looked a little like Cagney, too. Short, maybe five-eight or five-nine, with reddish blond hair and a face full of freckles. Cleary had been a bit of a brawler as a kid. Until his old man put a stop to it. Told young Brian if he enjoyed beating people up so much, he'd be better off doing it inside a boxing ring instead of in schoolyards. Turned out to be a pretty good welterweight. Won a bunch of bouts at the Portland Boxing Club. Even thought about turning pro, then thought better of it. He joined the department instead.

'I found the head of HR on the Palmer Milliken Web site. Woman named Beth Kotterman. Called her at home. Asked her if anyone at PM would know about Goff's vacation plans. She said yeah, she would. Seems all staff at

Palmer Milliken have to let the office know where they'll be on vacation in case there's an emergency.'

'A legal emergency?' asked McCabe.

Cleary shrugged. 'I guess. She asked me why we wanted to know. I told her Goff's car was found on the pier and we thought something bad might have happened to her. She dropped everything and went to the office to check her files. I guess she lives nearby, 'cause she called back a few minutes later. Said Goff was away for two weeks, returning next Monday. Her last day in the office was Friday, December twenty-third.'

'Two weeks ago.'

'Yeah. That's why nobody reported her missing. She had reservations starting the twenty-fourth at a place called the Bacuba Spa and Resort on Aruba. Bacuba on Aruba.'

'Traveling alone?'

'I think so. At least she wasn't sharing a room. I called the resort, and they had her down as a single.'

'Place sounds expensive.'

'It is. Twelve hundred bucks a night. When she didn't show, they charged her credit card two nights as a penalty. I checked with Visa, and other than the penalty charge the card hasn't been used since the twenty-second, when there was a charge for sixteen dollars and fifty-two cents from the Jan Mee Restaurant on St John Street.'

'Is Kotterman still at the office?'

'She said she was going home, but we should feel free to call her if there was anything else we needed.'

'You still have her number?' asked McCabe.

Cleary wrote it down on a piece of paper. McCabe

glanced at it and then crumpled it up. 'Okay,' he said. 'The timing's a gift. It gives us back our chance to check alibis. Whoever killed her had to have grabbed her between the time she left her office on the twenty-third and before she was supposed to get on her flight to Aruba. Did you find out anything about her travel plans?'

Cleary shook his head no.

McCabe turned to Sturgis. 'Carl, I want you to find out what airport she was leaving from, what flight she was supposed to be on, and if she ever checked in.'

'Think he might have grabbed her at the airport?' asked Tasco.

McCabe shrugged. 'Let's find out.'

Sturgis didn't move. McCabe figured it was because, as a senior detective, he resented being asked to do what he considered routine clerical work. Tough shit. A lot of being a detective, senior or not, consisted of nothing more than routine clerical work.

'Like now, Carl,' said McCabe.

Sturgis finally nodded, got up, and left. He passed Maggie on his way out the door without saying a word.

'What got into him?' she asked.

'Don't ask.'

'Okay.' Maggie rejoined the others at the table and sat down. 'Hester doesn't know anything.'

'You're sure.'

'I'm sure. I poked, I prodded, I pleaded. All he knows is what he told Vodnick down at the pier.'

McCabe filled Maggie in on what she'd missed. After that he sat for a long minute piecing the investigation together in his mind.

Tasco broke the silence. 'Okay. Where do we go from here?'

'You're going to Brackett Street,' said McCabe. 'I want you and Brian to round up as many warm bodies as you can. That includes Fraser when he gets here and Bill 'n' Will when they finish checking out the assault. Split into teams. Make sure everyone has a copy of her Palmer Milliken bio picture and start banging on doors. You know the drill. Start with the other tenants in Goff's building, then fan out to include surrounding buildings on Brackett and then the neighborhood. Wake people up if you have to. Include any small businesses she may have patronized. Dry cleaners. Convenience stores. Whatever. It's not that late. Some may still be open.'

Maggie looked at the pictures again. 'Let's not ignore the obvious. Goff would've attracted men like flies,' she said. 'If she had a regular boyfriend, we need to bring him in and grill him. Maybe this whole thing was nothing more than a lovers' spat that got out of hand.'

'Doesn't fit the MO,' said McCabe. 'Abusive boyfriends are usually a little more direct in their approach than neat little holes in the back of the neck, and they don't leave quotations from the Bible. Still, you're right, we ought to check it out. Tom, see if any of the neighbors can give you names or descriptions of current or former sexual partners.'

'Could be somebody she dumped recently,' said Cleary. 'Somebody who maybe wasn't too happy about it and decided to take it out on her. We'll also check to see if anyone other than Goff was seen driving the Beemer. That's a car people would notice. And remember.'

Tasco's droopy bloodhound face was looking even more worried than usual. 'Y'know, we're not going to be able to cover all this stuff tonight.'

Maybe I should start calling him Deputy Dawg, thought McCabe. 'I understand,' he said. 'Just get started and keep at it until something turns up. Also send some of the uniforms to start knocking on doors down at the Fish Pier.'

'Okay, I'll have a team take a whack at it,' said Tasco, 'but you gotta remember we're talking about a commercial area here. Empty at this hour. Probably empty when the guy drove in with the body. Could be empty all weekend.'

'We're not waiting till Monday,' said McCabe. 'This happened in the middle of the city. Someone might've been around. Might've been watching. Maybe someone with a security camera. Maybe someone who works nights. Aren't there people working at the Fish Exchange at all hours?'

'Once upon a time,' said Cleary. 'Fishing ain't what it used to be.'

'Well, unless and until you have a better idea, let's see what we can find. I'll ask Fortier to get you enough people to help knock on doors.'

'You want me to work the canvass?' asked Maggie.

'No. I'd like you to go downstairs and see how Jacobi's doing cutting Goff out of the Beemer. After she's on her way to Augusta, I want you to go with the techs to check out her apartment.'

'Where are you off to?'

'I'm going to talk to Beth Kotterman. See if I can find out who Goff's next of kin is. Maybe find out who she palled around with at the office.' McCabe stood and collected the small pile of printouts. 'Anybody have anything else?' He looked at each of his detectives. Nobody responded. 'Okay. That's it, then. Call my cell if you find anything meaningful. Otherwise, let's meet back here tomorrow morning, ten o'clock. And don't forget what the note said. *All the sinners of my people shall die by the sword.* "All the sinners" sounds like more than one to me. If that's the case, he could already be looking for a new playmate. Let's find him before he finds her.'

Seven

McCabe's footsteps echoed off the marble walls and floor of Ten Monument Square as he walked across the semi-darkened lobby toward a circular security desk. A young black man wearing horn-rimmed glasses and a blue blazer watched him approach. The words METCO Security were stitched in gold letters above the blazer's breast pocket. A gray-haired woman stood at the side of the desk, hands thrust into the pockets of her open wool coat. Under the coat she wore faded blue jeans and a blue U. Maine sweatshirt, clothes thrown on for an unexpected trip to the office. McCabe placed her in her early fifties. She looked anxious.

'Ms. Kotterman?' he asked.

'Yes, I'm Beth Kotterman. You must be Sergeant McCabe?'

'That's right. I'm sorry to keep interrupting your Friday night.'

'It doesn't matter. Not in a situation like this. Do you know anything more about' – she paused, searching for the right word – 'about what happened?'

'I'd rather talk in your office, if you don't mind.'

'Of course. Come with me.'

'Uh, excuse me, sir,' said the guard, 'would you mind signing in first?'

'He's with me, Randall. He's a police officer.'

'Sorry, Ms Kotterman. Police or no police,' said the guard, 'he's still gotta sign in. Rules say everybody signs in. Don't say "except police."' The guard smiled. He probably didn't have a lot of opportunities to hassle cops, and he was enjoying the moment.

'Not a problem,' said McCabe, returning the smile. 'Wanna see my ID?'

The guard shrugged. 'Sure.'

McCabe flipped open his badge wallet, laid it on the desk, picked up the pen and clipboard, and scrawled his name in the first open space, adding the time 10:32 P.M. in the second. There was a long list of names above his own. He didn't recognize any except Beth Kotterman's.

The guard glanced at McCabe's ID and handed it back. 'Thank you.'

'My pleasure. Does everyone who comes into the building also have to sign out?'

'If they don't work here, yeah. If they sign in, they sign out.'

'What about people who do work here?'

'They only have to sign in or out after 6:00 P.M.'

'Does everyone show you ID?'

'Nope. Rules don't require identification.'

Stupid rules, thought McCabe. Anybody could sign in using any name they wanted. 'Ms. Kotterman, could you give me a minute just to ask Randall here a couple more questions?'

Kotterman nodded. She obviously wanted to be finished with this, but she said, 'That's fine. I'll be in my office. When you're ready, ask him to call my extension. I'll come down and get you.'

The guard eyed McCabe. 'What do you want to talk to me about?'

'Just want to ask you a few questions.'

'I don't have to answer any questions.'

'No, I guess you don't, but I'm pretty sure my friends over at METCO Security would be a whole lot happier with you if you did. Now, what'd you say your last name was?'

'Jackson. Randall Jackson.'

'Okay, Randall,' said McCabe, 'let me make sure I understand the rules. You said all visitors to the building have to sign in and sign out, but anyone who works here only has to sign in or out after 6:00 P.M. Is that right?'

'Yeah. That's right.'

'So how do you know who's who?'

'Whaddaya mean?'

'You know everybody who works in the building?'

'Most of 'em. By face anyway. The ones I don't know either sign in or show me ID.'

'Nobody ever slips through without signing?'

The guard studied McCabe for a minute. 'Not on my watch.'

'How about anybody else's watch?'

'Can't speak to that.'

'Is there someone on this desk around the clock?'

'Yep. Twenty-four seven.'

'You work alone, or do you have a partner?'

'During the day there are two of us. At night I'm alone.'

'Where do you go to take a leak?'

'There's a break room in the basement. With a toilet.'

'So somebody might be able to slip through while you're taking a leak?'

'No. That door you used to come into the building? I lock it if I have to go downstairs.'

'And there are no other ways in?'

'Not at night. Back door only opens from the inside, and the garage is gated. You need a card key to raise the gate. Only the lawyers have card keys.'

Fairly typical building security. Not bad, but not good enough to keep a determined or clever bad guy from sneaking in. 'Do you always work this building, or does METCO shift you around?'

'Usually here. Occasionally I work other buildings. METCO's got contracts with most of the big buildings in town.'

'Were you here the night of December twenty-third?'

'What do you want to know that for?'

'A minute ago I asked you if anybody ever slips by you without signing in, and you said, "Not on my watch." I wondered if your watch happened to include the night of the twenty-third.'

'The twenty-third?'

'Yes. The twenty-third.'

The guard stared at McCabe. After a long minute he said, 'That would've been the Friday before Christmas?'

'That's right.'

'Yeah, I was here. I worked a double that day. Traded with another guard so I could take Christmas off. Started at 4:00 p.m. Stayed on till eight the next morning.'

'Long hours.'

'Yeah, I wanted to be home with my kids on Christmas.'

Okay, he was a dad. Did that make him any more trustworthy? Maybe not. 'Did you notice anything unusual that day, anything that sticks out in your mind? Think about it.'

Randall thought about it. He didn't say anything for a minute. Then he nodded as if reconstructing the day in his mind. 'The only thing unusual was all the people who left early 'cause of the holiday. A lot of 'em didn't come back from lunch. Place was pretty much empty by five o'clock except for the big bosses, who all left together around six, six thirty. Most of 'em seemed pretty happy, gave me something for the holiday. Best as I can remember there were only a couple of late sign-outs. Usually a lot of folks work late.'

'Who were the late ones that night?'

'First one was one of the younger lawyers, Miss Goff. Real pretty woman. Fact is, I saw her a couple of times.'

'When?'

'First time was around eight o'clock or so. I remember 'cause she wasn't wearing a coat and it was colder'n –' Jackson stopped himself.

'Colder'n shit?' asked McCabe.

'Yeah. Colder'n shit. Anyway, she didn't sign out. She had a Federal Express envelope in her hand and said she'd be right back.'

'Was she?'

'Yeah. Two minutes later. Carrying a hot dog from the cart in the square. Must've been hungry.'

'And the second time?'

'She left for the night about an hour later. Around nine.

Stormed out of here like hell wouldn't have it. Must have been real pissed off about something. Didn't sign out that time either. I called after her to come back. She just flipped me a bird.' Randall smiled at the memory. 'That was one angry lady.'

'What'd you do?'

'Nothing. I knew her. It was no big deal. She went out through the door that goes down to the lawyers' private garage.'

'That door there?' He pointed to an unmarked gray steel door next to the main entrance.

'Yeah. That one.'

'Have you seen her since?'

Randall shook his head. 'No. I don't think so.'

'You said there was another late sign-out?'

'Yeah. Ten minutes or so after she left, Mr Ogden came down. Henry Ogden. He's one of the senior partners at Palmer Milliken.'

'Was he angry, too?'

Randall shook his head and shrugged. 'No. He seemed okay. He looked like he always looks. Like a rich white guy. Handed me an envelope. Christmas card with a hundred bucks inside. Last year it was just fifty. Told me to get something nice for my kids.'

'Anybody else leave the building after Henry Ogden?'

'No.'

'Working a double like that, Randall, any chance you might have dozed off and missed somebody else coming in and out?'

Jackson stiffened. 'No. No chance at all.'

'You're sure?'

91

'I'm sure. Only people to leave after Ogden were the regular cleaning crew. They get here around six and are usually outta here about one in the morning.'

'How many people?'

'Half a dozen, give or take.'

'They have to sign in or out?'

Randall shook his head. No.

'Same folks all the time?'

'Not really. Company mixes 'em up. Specially around the holidays.'

'They work for METCO?'

'No, METCO just handles security. Some other company does the cleaning. You wanna know who, you'll have to ask building management.'

'You still have the sign-in sheets from that day?'

'Not here. METCO might. I don't know how long they hold on to them.'

'Would anybody be there now?'

'Nope. Office won't be open till eight o'clock Monday morning. We've got a number we're supposed to call in case of emergency. You want that?'

'Yes.'

Jackson opened a drawer and pulled out a business card. He handed it to McCabe. The name on the card was Scott Ginsberg. He knew Ginsberg. He'd retired from the PPD's Community Affairs Division two years earlier. Maybe there was life after leaving the force. His cell number was 555-1799.

McCabe pointed to a bank of small screens behind the desk. 'How about your video. Are you recording, or is it just live?'

'Recorded.'

'Tape?'

'No. Digital.'

Made sense. Digital meant there was no good reason not to record. The images could be fed right into a computer at METCO's offices. Storage wasn't a problem. Neither was the cost of videotape. There was no reason not to hold on to the images more or less forever. McCabe called Eddie Fraser and, after congratulating him on Tinker Bell's rave reviews, gave him Scott Ginsberg's number and asked him to start reviewing the video. ASAP. So far all they had was the body and the note. They needed more. Starting with a next of kin.

McCabe gave Jackson his card. Told him to get in touch if he thought of anything else. Then he asked him to call Beth Kotterman.

They exited the elevator at five. 'My office is at the end of the hall to the right,' said Kotterman. She led. McCabe followed. The corridor was dimly lit and empty. The air was cold.

Kotterman read his thoughts. 'Heat's programmed to go down to fifty at seven o'clock unless somebody calls to have it left on.'

'Nobody working late tonight?'

'I'm sure some of the lawyers are.'

'No lawyers on this floor?'

'No. Five's mostly administrative. HR. Accounting. Office management. That sort of thing. We tend to be more nine-to-five types.' She unlocked her office door and flipped on the lights.

As head of HR, Beth Kotterman rated a corner office. It was furnished in generic midlevel modern. Not what the partners would get, but a hell of a lot more comfortable than anything at 109. Kotterman had added a lot of touches that kept the place from being generically boring. A small jungle of indoor plants that included a ceiling-sized ficus dominated one corner. One wall was covered with family photos and a large crayon drawing titled *Gramma Bethby*. Bethby was wearing a bright green dress and had oversized feet and big glasses. The portrait was framed and carefully hung in a place of honor. It was signed BECKY.

Kotterman didn't bother taking off her coat. She sat and pointed McCabe to a straight-back chair in front of her desk. The interview chair, McCabe guessed. 'How old's Becky?' he asked.

Kotterman relaxed a little. 'Seven now. She was four when I sat for the portrait. How sure are you that the body you found is Lainie Goff? The other officer, Detective Cleary, said you didn't know yet.'

'We've tentatively confirmed her identity from photographs,' said McCabe. 'We're ninety-nine percent certain the dead woman is Elaine Goff.'

'Not one hundred? It could still be someone else?'

'I wouldn't hold out much hope. We'll do a dental records check to be absolutely certain, but I think you can assume it's Goff.'

'I'm going to have to let people in the firm know.'

'That's fine. Most of them probably already know. News Center 6 jumped the gun on that.'

'That's unfortunate.'

94

'I agree. We always like to inform next of kin before they hear it from the media.'

'Of course. And you think Lainie, assuming it is Lainie, was murdered?'

'Yes.'

'Odd.' Kotterman looked away. 'One doesn't expect that sort of thing to happen in Portland, but I guess there are no safe places anymore. Maybe there never were. Any idea who did it?'

'No. We're just beginning the investigation.'

'How can I help?'

'Like I said, the first thing I need is next of kin. I was hoping you'd have the name on file.'

'We should.' Kotterman woke up her sleeping computer and started tapping keys. 'All employees give us an emergency contact number on their first day of work,' she said. 'It's usually a relative.' Her brow furrowed. 'This may not help you.'

'Why not?'

'Well, most people list a family member. Lainie didn't.'

'Who'd she put?'

'A woman named Janie Archer. New York City address.'

'Maybe a sister?'

'Lainie lists her as a friend.'

'Lainie and Janie, huh? Can you give me the contact info for Ms Archer?'

She wrote an address and telephone number on a Post-it note and handed it to McCabe. Upper East Side Manhattan address, 212 area code. He committed both to memory and tossed the note.

'That contact info is six years old,' said Beth Kotterman.

'Everyone's supposed to update their information annually, but a lot of people never bother. Lainie's friend may not live there anymore.'

It wasn't a big problem. He should be able to track Archer down using either of the public databases Portland PD subscribed to, Accurint or AutoTrackXP. 'Do you have anything else to indicate next of kin?'

'Yes. There's one more place I can check.' Kotterman started tapping keys again. 'All employees get a term life policy as part of their comp package. I'm looking to see who Lainie put down as beneficiary.'

'How much is the policy worth?' asked McCabe.

'One and a half times annual salary. For Lainie that'd be in the neighborhood of one hundred and eighty thousand dollars.'

Not a bad neighborhood, McCabe thought. Certainly enough to offer a reasonable motive for murder. But if money was the motive, why go through all the show-off stuff down at the pier? Why not make the death look like an accident? The only reason McCabe could think of was to throw investigators off track, and that didn't seem likely. 'Does the policy pay out if the employee is murdered?'

'I'll have to double-check with our agents, but I would think so, yes. Hmmm.' Kotterman was peering over her glasses at the screen. 'Now isn't that interesting?'

'Isn't what interesting?'

'There's no family member listed as beneficiary either. Lainie's primary isn't even a person. It's an organization. Something called Sanctuary House. Portland address. I have no idea what that is.'

'I've heard of it,' said McCabe. 'Don't know much

about it. Just that it's a small charity, some kind of shelter for kids.' It was beginning to look like there was no next of kin. Like Lainie Goff was an orphan. He wondered what her connection to Sanctuary House might be.

'Well, they're about to get a healthy chunk of money.'

'From what I hear, they can use it.'

Kotterman closed down her computer and leaned back. She looked tired. 'I'm afraid that's all I've got. Is there anything else I can do for you, Detective?'

'Did you know Lainie well?'

'No, hardly at all. Palmer Milliken has over three hundred employees. I've only talked to her occasionally. Usually about HR procedures.'

'When was the last time you saw her?'

'At our Christmas party.'

'When was that?'

'Friday, December sixteenth. At the Pemaquid Club. Most of the partners are members, and the firm took over the whole place.' The Pemaquid Club was a membership-only gathering place for Portland's rich and well connected. It was housed in a century-old redbrick mansion on the city's West End.

'Did you speak to her at the party?'

'Just in passing. Merry Christmas. Have a great holiday. That sort of thing. Lainie wasn't a woman who'd waste much time chatting up someone like me. She had bigger fish to fry.'

'Such as?'

'Such as the partners. Especially the senior partners. Most especially the male senior partners. She was, from what I hear, an extremely ambitious woman.'

'Really?' said McCabe. 'Now, who did you hear that from?'

Kotterman rolled the question around in her mind before answering. 'The grapevine. People talk.'

'While they were talking, did any of them say anything about Lainie Goff being involved?' he asked. 'Maybe with one of the partners? Maybe with more than one?'

'You know, Detective, it's late and I'm tired. I've probably said too much already.'

'I appreciate that, Ms Kotterman, but I'd also appreciate it if you could tell me who you saw Lainie talking to at the party. Who she spent time chatting up, as you put it. Anyone in particular?'

'I didn't notice.'

McCabe knew Kotterman wouldn't give him much more, but he had nothing to lose by trying. 'A minute ago you said she had bigger fish to fry? I'm wondering who that might have been.'

'I'm sorry, Detective. I probably misspoke. I didn't know Lainie all that well. As you can imagine, I'm very upset by the news of her death. I'm sure everyone in the firm will be. Why don't we just leave it at that?'

'Just a few more questions.'

'I don't think so.'

McCabe wondered if the head of HR was going to refuse to tell him anything more. It was her right to do so. 'It's important,' he said.

Kotterman sighed. 'Alright. As long as your questions aren't of a personal nature.'

McCabe nodded assent. 'Okay. How long has Lainie Goff been with the firm, and what exactly did she do here?'

'She's an attorney. A senior associate. She started here shortly after she graduated from Cornell Law in 2000. She worked in the Mergers and Acquisitions Group.'

'Was she on track for a partnership?'

'I have no idea. The partners don't generally share their intentions with me. My role is more administrative.'

'But she would have wanted one, right?'

'Of course. All associates want partnerships. The ones who don't get offers usually leave the firm.'

'Do you know who her friends were at the office? Who she hung out with?'

'I already told you I didn't know Lainie very well. Why don't I make you a list of the people who worked in the same practice area? That might be the simplest thing.'

'Okay. Let's start there.' McCabe watched as Kotterman turned back to her computer. It was clear the older woman didn't like Goff. That wasn't surprising. The Beth Kottermans of the world didn't like Sandy much either. So how much of what she implied was based on truth and how much on simple resentment of the beautiful diva? He needed to find out. 'Who was Lainie's boss?'

'The senior partner in charge of M&A. Henry Ogden. She reported to him.'

Ogden. Okay. He was the guy who signed out of the building ten minutes after Lainie. Had Henry Ogden seen Lainie that night? Was he the last person to see her alive? McCabe had no answers. Just possibilities. He had a lot of work to do. 'Does Ogden know about Lainie's death?' he asked.

'Not from me. I was waiting until I knew for sure it was

Lainie. Until after I'd spoken to you. I'm going to call him at home after you leave.'

'I need to speak to Mr Ogden as soon as possible. Can you give me his home number and, if you have it, his cell?'

She wrote both numbers on another Post-it note and handed it to McCabe.

'Is there anything else you need from me, Detective, before I go home?'

'Yes. I'd like to take a look at Lainie Goff's office.'

'I can show you where her office is, but I'm afraid you can't go in. She almost certainly kept her files in there, and we'd have big client confidentiality issues.'

'That could present problems.'

'You can check with Henry Ogden, but I'm sure his answer will be the same. That Lainie's office, her files, and her computer are off-limits unless and until you get a subpoena. Even with a subpoena I'm not sure we can give you access to our client files.'

'Fine. We'll request a warrant first thing in the morning. In the meantime I'm going to post a uniformed officer and have a padlock put on the place. We'll also put a DO NOT ENTER sign on the door. I'd appreciate it if you could let everyone at Palmer Milliken know that the office is off-limits.'

Eight

Harts Island, Maine
Friday, January 6
11:30 P.M.

Abby Quinn didn't know how long she'd been in the closet at the Castellanos' empty summer cottage, but it seemed like a long time. The thin strip of daylight that earlier seeped under the closed door had faded hours ago. This was her fourth hiding place since Tuesday, the fourth in four days, but now she'd made the decision to leave the island it would also be the last. Her plan was simple. The Castellanos' house was no more than a hundred yards from the ferry landing. The last boat Friday nights left the island at eleven fifty-five. Bobby Howser was the mate on the late boat. She went to high school with Bobby. He used to be a friend. As soon as she saw him getting ready to haul in the gangway, she'd sprint the hundred yards and, if she timed it right, leap on just as the boat was pulling away from the dock, leaving the monster stranded on the island. The monster she thought of as Death.

Abby pushed the button that lit the face of her old, cheap digital watch. Twenty-five minutes to go. She pressed back against the wall of the closet and wrapped her arms around her knees. She squeezed as hard as she could, as if by squeezing, she could push the fear from her body, the urge to run screaming into the night.

Last Tuesday replayed itself in Abby's mind for the thousandth time. The day had started out normally enough. Another day so cold Abby couldn't think of a good reason to get out of bed. She slept late, and when she finally woke up she spent most of the afternoon lying under her heavy quilt reading the latest Stephanie Plum and listening to her mother clank around downstairs.

Things were going pretty good for a change. She was staying on her meds, and they seemed to be working. The Voices were quiet. She was living like a real person and not some freak. She was working the dinner shift at the Crow's Nest and doing okay. Taking orders and getting them right. Reciting the specials from memory. Writing out the checks. Asking customers how they were. Telling them she was doing fine. She was making money and saving it and thinking she might somehow have a life.

Yes, the drugs were making her fat like they always did, but this time she was fighting back. No beer. No snacks. No desserts. Plus, most nights after she finished at the Nest, she jogged the four-mile circuit around the island even though it was late, even though it was cold. Abby was too self-conscious about her jiggling flesh to even consider jogging in the daylight. Someone would see her and laugh at the crazy lady trying to get her floppy body into shape. The Voices might even wake up and start mocking her. No. That wasn't acceptable. Night offered cover, and cover was good. If she could keep up the diet and exercise, maybe in the spring she'd enroll in a couple of courses at USM. Get a few more credits toward her accounting degree. Yes, she decided. That's what she'd do if she could stay on her regimen and lose the weight and could keep the frigging Voices quiet.

Her psychiatrist told her over and over the Voices weren't real.

'No,' she insisted, 'they are real. I can hear them.'

'Hearing voices is a symptom of your illness, Abby. A symptom we can control with medication.'

She didn't answer. Her shrink was full of shit. The Voices were real.

'When you hear them,' he asked, 'are they loud? Or are they quiet?'

'Sometimes quiet. Sometimes loud. Sometimes so loud I can't hear anything else.'

'When they're loud, do other people hear them? Or just you?'

'Other people hear them. They just pretend they can't.'

He thought about that. 'Do you ever hear them in this office?'

'Sometimes. Yes.'

'Do you hear them now?'

She listened. 'Yes.'

'What are they saying?'

She smiled slyly. 'They're saying that you're full of shit.'

He returned her smile. 'Sometimes I am full of shit,' he said, 'but not about this. I can't hear them, Abby. Really, I can't. I'm not pretending.'

She didn't buy it. The Voices were real. They hated her. They wanted to kill her. She didn't tell him any of that. She just thought it.

But he always seemed to know what she was thinking. Maybe he had a way of listening in.

'In one way the voices are real, Abby,' he said. 'They're real to you. But they're real only in your brain. Not outside. And while we can't get them out of your brain, we can control them. We can keep them quiet. Keep them from interfering with your life. Isn't that what you want?'

She nodded silently. Yes, that's what she wanted. If only he knew how desperately she wanted it. She nodded again, this time more vigorously.

'Okay. If that's what you want, you have to take your medication every day. No slipping or skipping or pretending you don't need it.'

'The pills make me fat.'

'We can't totally prevent that, Abby, but you can minimize it. Watch what you eat. Exercise. You were an athlete in high school, weren't you?'

Yes, she was. Emphasis on the past tense. *Was.* Seven years ago. Varsity field hockey and lacrosse for the Portland High School Lady Bulldogs. The Barkin' Bitches, the boys called them.

'Weren't you?' he asked again.

She nodded.

'Tell me in words, Abby. Don't just nod.'

'Yes, I was.'

'Then train your body like you're still trying to make the team.'

She listened, and together they wrote out a diet and exercise plan. And she was sticking to it, It seemed to be working. She felt normal. She was still fat, but not as fat as before. She was getting stronger. Even though, when she

104

looked at her naked body in the bathroom mirror, it still looked more bloblike than she could bear.

Tuesday was a quiet night at the Nest. Only two couples came in for dinner all night, and they were early birds. Paid up and gone by seven o'clock. After that, just a couple of the regulars hung out at the bar. Hard-core drinkers who wanted a break from the bar at the Legion. Lori was annoyed about staying open with just a couple of drunks for customers. But what the hell else did she expect on a freezing Tuesday in January with nobody but year-rounders still on the island? The big spenders, the summer people, had long since drained their pipes, boarded up their windows, and fled back to their real lives in Boston or New York, Dallas or Atlanta.

Abby spent the hours till closing sweeping the floor, putting stuff away, and bullshitting with Travis Garmin, who was tending bar and, as usual, hitting on her. Sometimes she was tempted to take Travis up on it. He wasn't the brightest bulb in the box. In fact, Lori said Travis was so dumb if a customer gave him a penny for his thoughts, he'd have to give 'em change. Still, he looked good and didn't seem to mind that she was fat. Didn't even notice when she started getting weird. Just smiled at her with that goofy grin of his.

By eight thirty, Lori said the hell with it and announced they were closing early. They finished putting stuff away and locked up around nine. Travis asked if she wanted to go park on the backshore, look at the waves and maybe smoke some weed. She said no, she wanted to go for her run. He didn't push it. Just said okay and dropped her off at her mother's house behind Tomkins Cove. She climbed out of his truck and stood on her front steps for a couple of minutes. She watched his taillights disappear up the hill. Probably going off to smoke by himself. Or maybe find some other island girl to fool around with. Abby breathed in the cold fresh air and gazed at the full moon and the million stars that were spread across the dark sky in a wide swath. She sometimes thought that's where the Voices came from. They were visitors from *a galaxy far, far away*, and they were taking over the bodies of earthlings one by one by one. Sooner or later they'd control everybody. One time she told her shrink about this theory. He got this worried look on his face that made her wonder if he might not actually be one of the aliens. Maybe he planned to kill her to keep her from telling the authorities. So she backed off real quick. Told him she was just kidding. He didn't laugh. Just asked her if she'd gone off her meds. Afterward Abby tried telling the police about the aliens and about how humans were controlled by them. She was pretty sure they didn't believe her either.

She went inside. No key needed. Her mother's front door hadn't been locked in twenty years. She shut it fast to keep the heat from escaping. What heat there was. Inside, she could hear some jerk screeching away on *American Idol*. What crap. Even the Voices sounded better than that. She clicked the TV off and glanced at her mother, Gracie, to see if the sudden silence would wake her up. It didn't. She was lying nearly prone on the recliner. Her head was back, her mouth open. A wet rasping sound, half snore, half gurgle, was coming out. Abby picked up the half-dozen empty Bud Light cans scattered on the floor around the chair and tossed them into the recycling bin. She'd try to remember to return them to the store before work tomorrow. Thirty cents was thirty cents. She tossed a log into the woodstove and checked the monitor. It was throwing about as much heat as it was capable of. Before heading upstairs, she studied the worn face of the woman who'd given her life. Not fifty yet but fat and pasty looking. Like the Pillsbury Doughboy's grubby older sister. Gracie was stuffed into a dirty Old Navy sweatshirt that was two sizes too small for her and baggy jeans that were two sizes too big. Her teeth were brown and stained, the ones she had left, anyway. Even counting the broken ones Gracie's mouth was a whole bunch short of a full set. Please God, Abby thought, don't ever let me end up like her.

She went up to her room and pulled off the black pants and white button-down shirt she wore at the Nest. She stepped on the bathroom scale. Not bad. Down another half pound. She still looked blobby in the mirror, though. Still had a ways to go. Her running clothes were piled on the chair in her bedroom. She put them on, layering them for warmth. Long polypropylene underwear over her bra and pants. A long-sleeve cotton turtleneck. A Thinsulate-lined shirt. A pair of black Gore-Tex storm pants. A fleece vest. Some thermal socks and her Nikes. Last, she ripped open a plastic bag and pulled out a brand-new Blue Lightning Neoprene Face Mask. She slipped it on and checked her image in the mirror. She smiled broadly. Spider-Man was looking back at her. Only this Spider-Man was blue, not red. Either way she'd scare the shit out of anybody she passed on her run tonight. The idea pleased her. She growled at herself in the mirror.

Downstairs, Gracie looked like she was out for the count. 'Go to bed,' Abby yelled in her ear. No reaction. 'Say good night, Gracie.' Her father's old joke. Still no reaction. The hell with it. Abby sat on a kitchen chair and pulled on her ice cleats over the Nikes. The last thing she needed was to slip on the ice and break something. Finally she put on her black Gore-Tex jacket and her fanny pack with a mini flashlight and her meds already inside. She clipped a key ring to her belt. It held thirteen keys. One for the back door of the Crow's Nest. One for each of the twelve summer cottages Abby kept an eye on while their owners were away. Her jogging route took her past all twelve. Easy work. Easy money. More important to Abby, it proved that a whole bunch of people could trust her with their expensive homes.

The thermometer nailed to the tree in the yard read twelve degrees. There was no wind. Abby figured that'd change when she hit the backshore and the open ocean. No worries. She was prepared for the cold. She took off and broke into an easy jog. Hard-packed snow crunched under her feet. A full moon lit her way. A moon made for creatures of the night. Weirdos and werewolves and crazies like her. She followed the dirt track that led for about a half mile from her house to the backshore. The ice cleats slowed her down some, but that was okay. They made her feel sure-footed climbing the icy rises.

She passed the Healys' log cabin. One of her houses. Only deer tracks marred the crunchy layer that covered the snow, and she ran on. Watching the cottages involved little more than keeping an eye out for storm damage or signs of a break-in. Nothing much ever happened. One time she did notice a broken window at the Morrisseys'. A B&E, the cops called it. Breaking and entering. Turned out vandals had spray-painted dirty pictures all over the walls. Men with big dicks and dangling balls banging away at bent-over women with huge boobs. Some stuff was stolen, too. A flat-screen TV, some stereo equipment, and, according to Dan Morrissey, three bottles of Kahlúa. The cops thought stealing Kahlúa was weird, but Abby knew lots of island kids who loved the stuff. Shit, why wouldn't they? It not only got them drunk, it tasted like dessert. The cops never caught anyone. Just wrote up an incident report so the Morrisseys could file an insurance claim. That was the cops for you. Do-nothing assholes.

One other time Abby saw a light flickering from one of the bedrooms at the Callahans' place. She went in and found Marie Lopat and Annie Carle, stark naked and going at it hot and heavy on the Callahans' bed. She told them to get dressed and go home before she called their parents. Abby never figured Annie and Marie for lesbos, but hey, whatever turns you on.

She emerged from the woods and turned left onto Seashore Avenue. A cold wind from the northeast smacked her right in the face, but thanks to her Blue Lightning mask she barely felt it. Big breakers slammed into the rocks below the road, creating plumes of spray twenty feet high. The full moon glittered on the water. There were now even more stars than before. Abby felt good. She was running. She was laying off the beer. She was on the meds. The Voices were mostly quiet. She was even starting to feel good about herself as a woman again, the way she did seven years ago at Portland High and for two years after that at USM. That was before the Voices invaded her head. Before she tried to shut them up by jumping off the rocks at Christmas Cove. Not once but twice. That was before the two years locked up at Winter Haven, and a chunk of another year living with a bunch of runaways and druggies at John Kelly's halfway house in town. Now she was home, but not home free. Abby knew from experience she had to be vigilant. The Voices lived. Meds or no meds, it could all come crashing down.

She picked up her pace on the paved, nearly level surface. Most of the houses were newer and bigger on this side of the island, none of them owned by island families. About half belonged to rich retirees from away. They mostly left for four months in Florida right after New Year's. The other half belonged to even richer summer people who spent most of the year in places like New York or Dallas or L.A. One couple even came over from London and built a McMansion right on the water near Seal Point. Probably cost two million bucks. More money than most islanders made their whole lives. And they used the place all of four weeks a year. The other forty-eight weeks it was locked up and empty. There had always been summer people on Harts Island, but never people rich enough to live like that. The island was changing, and Abby was sorry about that. She liked it better the way it was when she was little. She wished the Londoners would just go home to London and take their big fat house with them. Or let it float out to sea. Yes, they paid her to watch the place, and yes, she liked getting the money. Still, she wished they weren't here.

A hundred years ago, most islanders would never have

dreamed of building anything more than a fishing shack out here on the open ocean. Even twenty years ago when Abby was a little girl there were only a few houses on the backshore, and most of those were pretty modest. It was too damned cold and the nor'easters too punishing. People today had no problem coming to the island, changing the place, pushing real estate prices and taxes ever higher and challenging nature in ways that seemed to Abby arrogant and wrong.

If Abby had been running a step or two faster, if she'd rounded the bend at Seal Point a second or two sooner, or if she'd just been looking out to sea when the match flared in the second-floor window, she never would have seen it. In this, however, as in so much else in her life, luck didn't fall Abby's way. The match flared. She saw it. Then it was gone. It happened so fast, she wasn't sure it happened at all. She stopped running, then stood and looked at the window where it had been. Todd and Isabella Markham's house was a large, gray-shingled, neo-Victorian designed in what Isabella liked to call 'the island vernacular.' It was built high up on about ten truckloads of fill to give it an even more commanding view of the ocean. It had a triangular front roofline with a rounded turret on the right. A dozen steps led up to a large, open wrap-around porch. Abby stood in the shadows, gazing at the window and wondering if she'd just imagined the whole thing. Then, just as she decided that maybe she had and was about to resume her run, another match flared. Whoever lit it must have used it to light a lantern or a candle, because this time the light stayed on, flickering dimly.

Abby wondered if the Markhams might be on the island. They lived in Boston, and they sometimes came up in winter, but Isabella always called a day or two ahead and asked Abby to open the house, turn up the heat, and leave a few lights on. They wanted everything warm and cozy when they arrived. Besides, if it was the Markhams, why didn't they just turn on the electric lights? Why bother with candles?

The idea of candles suggested romance. Were Marie and Annie playing house again? Or some other island teenagers? Abby tried to remember if she'd ever seen Kahlúa in the Markhams' liquor cabinet. She hoped she wouldn't find dirty pictures painted on the walls. Either way, the Markhams paid her to watch the place, so she'd have to check. They didn't pay her much, but she took the money, and they trusted her to do the job.

If she'd brought her cell phone, she could have called the police. Or maybe Travis. But cell phone service was hit or miss out here at Seal Point, and the police would just give her a hard time. As for Travis, if he wasn't home sleeping, he was probably busy trying to get into some other girl's pants. He'd see Abby's name on caller ID and not pick up.

She tried to remember the layout of the Markhams' place. The only time she'd been upstairs was when Isabella showed her around and gave her the key. She was pretty sure the candlelight was coming from the master bedroom. It was a big room on this side of the house with a wall of windows that looked out over the open ocean. She remembered thinking how glorious it would be to wake up warm and cozy in the Markhams' king-sized bed and watch the sun come up over the horizon. How wonderful to have someone to make love to in a setting like that.

Abby moved toward the house, trying to stay in the shadows like a TV detective. She had a feeling that who-ever or whatever was inside, it wasn't Annie or Marie or any of the other island kids – and if not them, who? Her anxiety rose. She reached the house and climbed the twelve steps up to the porch. Then she pressed herself against the front of the house and crept sideways to the front door. She pushed her ear against the door and real-ized instantly how dumb that was. Between the blowing of the wind and the crashing of the waves against the rocks, there was no way in hell she'd hear anyone inside even if they were screaming at the top of their lungs.

But then she did. Someone talking quietly. Then some-one else. Then a chorus whispering. The Voices were waking from their slumber. *Go on, stupid bitch, go inside. Go, you fat slug. Go inside and get yourself killed. That's what you really want, isn't it?* Ignore them, she told herself. Don't respond. Answering back just encourages them. She pushed herself forward. She had to do this. If she couldn't ignore the Voices and do her job, she might just as well leap off the rocks. That's what the Voices wanted her to do. This time they'd make sure there were no lobstermen around to fish her out.

Abby felt wetness under the mask and realized she was crying. The Voices were getting louder. She had to shut them up. She pulled off her gloves, reached into her fanny pack, and found her Zyprexa. Pulled off the mask and dry-swallowed a 20 mg tablet, her second of the day. Twice what she was supposed to have. She didn't know how long it would take to work or even if it would work, but she hoped it would. It was her only weapon.

She put her mask and gloves back on and crept around to the back of the house. She peered in the window of the garage. There was more than enough moonlight to tell the car inside wasn't the Markhams' Escalade. It was something smaller, sleeker.

Abby riffled through her keys until she found the one marked I.M. She opened the back door and stepped inside, closed it, and listened again. She stood stock-still. Moonlight poured through the big front windows, lighting the whole ground floor, which consisted of one big room, a kitchen area that led seamlessly into open dining and living spaces. Outside, foamy explosions of moonlit waves crashed into the rocks. The house was so solidly built, she could barely hear them. She didn't think the extra pill could have worked that fast, but the Voices seemed quieter. Reduced to a grousing and grumbling like restless sleepers turning in their beds. Otherwise there was silence.

The room felt warm. Abby knelt down and placed a bare hand flat on the hardwood floor. The underfloor heating was on. She looked around for coats or boots or other signs of winter intruders. Nothing. To Abby's right a staircase led up to the second floor and whoever or whatever awaited her there. She stood by the bottom step and listened. From upstairs, she heard a long, low mournful cry. Her heart beat faster. Was it the Voices? She didn't think so, but she told them to shut up anyway. She stood for a minute, closed her eyes, and took a deep breath. If she could do this one thing and do it right, maybe she could silence the Voices forever. Besides, it was her job. She had to try. She looked around the kitchen for a possible weapon. She spotted a nine-inch chef's knife. Lethal – but the thought of actually stabbing anyone, even in self-defense, frightened her too much. She settled instead for a small cast-iron skillet. The notion of fracturing a skull was somehow more appealing.

She took her mittens off and clipped them to her belt. She took another deep breath, waited a few seconds, then began to climb the stairs, one by one, as silently as possible. She was clutching the skillet so tightly her right hand began to hurt. She stepped onto the landing floor. A thick carpet muffled her steps. The wordless cry came again, soft and utterly without hope. It seemed to Abby the saddest sound she'd ever heard. Was it real or was it the Voices? She had no way of knowing. The door at the end of the dark hall was ajar. Dim, flickering light shone through an opening of an inch or maybe less. Abby pushed herself against the jamb and, with one eye, peered in. For a moment she stood transfixed, unable to move, unable to speak, unable to comprehend the scene before her.

The room was lit only by a few candles scattered around. A naked woman knelt on the bed. Her wrists and ankles were bound to the bedposts with what looked like silk scarves. Another scarf was tied around her mouth. Her head was down. Dark hair hid her face. At the side of the bed a man stood, facing the woman, his back to Abby. He, too, was naked with a slender, muscular body. He held a thin-bladed knife in his right hand. As Abby watched, he lifted the woman's hair with his left hand, raised the knife with his right. He brought the knife downward in an arc. Stopped. Positioned it carefully in the center of the woman's neck. Then pushed. The blade penetrated flesh. The woman slumped. Abby's brain exploded in a cacophony of Voices. She screamed. The man turned; he had no face, just a fiery mane with icy eyes peering at Abby through the flames. Shocked by Abby's scream, the man with the face of fire pulled the knife from the woman's neck, tore open the door, and slashed at Abby's throat. She leapt back. The blade missed. He raised his arm to strike again. Abby swung the skillet. Missed. The Voices screamed. Abby ran. The man, still naked, ran after her. Abby's head filled with horrible sounds. A chorus screaming for her death. She took the stairs two at a time and raced for the front door. It was locked. The man closed in. Abby swung the skillet and missed again. Flames flew from his bestial eyes. The Voices laughed hysterically. Abby flipped the bolt. Death touched her arm, his hand burning like the devil's own. She turned, crouched, and swung the skillet in a low arc like the field hockey player she once was going for a goal. This time it connected. He went down, choking, gasping for air, clutching his injured testicles. Abby spun and ran through the open door and down the steps, tossing the skillet into the shrubs at the side of the house. She raced across the frozen yard. Glancing back, she saw his naked form charging down the porch stairs and out into the frozen night. She leapt the icy slope down onto the road. Her cleats somehow held on the slick surface. Looking back again, she saw him slip, feet flying out from under him in a kind of circus pantomime. A naked clown with a head of fire slipping on a frozen banana peel. His momentum took him up into the air, then down again, hard on his back. He lay still. Abby ran off into the night. She ran blindly, certain he would follow, determined to outrun not just her own death but also the Voices shrieking inside her head.

She ran for nearly a mile, expecting at each step to feel Death's hand touch her shoulder, expecting his blade to plunge into her neck as it had the woman's. Finally, winded, she paused. Behind her there was nothing. Just moonlit ice shining off the empty road. He was gone. Abby stared into the darkness, catching her breath. Still nothing. Had she imagined it all? Would her doctor tell her it was nothing but her illness creating visions that didn't exist except in her mind? She didn't know. Maybe that's all it was.

Five minutes passed before Abby saw reflections of the headlights coming in her direction from Seal Point. She cursed herself for stupidity. Of course. The car in the Markhams' garage. It was only a half mile, maybe less, behind her and was closing fast. She looked left. She looked right. Not thinking, just reacting. The Voices screamed, *Turn left! Turn left! The rocks, the ocean. Dive in the ocean. The water will save you from the knife.* No, she screamed back, I'm not ready to die. She turned right, away from the rocks and onto a narrow trail that wound its way through a salt marsh toward the island's interior. Frozen tracks carved into the ice by cross-country skiers slowed her down. They made the way treacherous, too easy to twist an ankle, even with the cleats.

Had he seen her turn off the road? She didn't know. If he did, he'd follow on foot. The trail was way too narrow for the car. Head down, arms pumping, Abby charged ahead. Behind her she heard the engine stop, the car's door open, then slam shut.

She ran as hard and as fast as she ever had, praying her foot wouldn't catch in one of the ski tracks. Praying she wouldn't fall and break an ankle. Every third or fourth step a foot broke through the icy surface to crusty snow below, slowing her further. How long before he caught up? However fast she was going, she knew it wasn't fast enough. If she couldn't outrun him, maybe she could lose him. She'd played on this maze of trails all her life. She knew how they looped around through dense piney woods, randomly crossing back on each other. Easy to get lost. Hard to follow someone, especially in the dark. Even on a moonlit night. Or so she hoped. That was her only advantage. Ahead of her the trail forked. The wider fork, the one to the left, led to the back end of the island dump and from there to a paved road that led down front. The fork to the right was narrower and trickier to negotiate. It would take her through a random series of trails and icy ledges where her cleats and knowledge of the terrain would give her more of an advantage. She veered right.

It was nearly 1:00 A.M. before Abby emerged from the edge of the woods. She worked her way through the dark streets down front to the small police station where two Portland PD cops were, no doubt, snoozing. She tried the door. Locked. Of course. She rang the bell. Nobody came. She looked around. Island Avenue in each direction lay dark and empty. Finally exhausted, Abby leaned against the bell and held it down. She wouldn't let go until one of them let her in or until Death pushed his thin-bladed knife into the back of her neck. Whichever came first. She tried to organize the frantic succession of images in her mind.

She had to be coherent or the cops would never believe her. Still no one came. She lowered her head. A low, keening whimper escaped her lips. Almost like the cry of the woman on the bed. The Voices taunted her. She pretended not to hear. Dark visions closed in from every side. Finally the big cop with the black mustache peered around the drawn shade. He looked annoyed to have been woken up. He opened the door and let her in.

That was Tuesday. This was Friday. It was 11:52 P.M. Time to run for the ferry.

Nine

By the time McCabe signed out at Randall Jackson's security desk, he was pretty much running on empty. All he really wanted was to go home, take another hot shower, and climb into bed. With Kyra if possible, alone if necessary. Unfortunately, at the moment, neither was an option. Instead, he parked himself in a corner of the lobby and tapped in Janie Archer's number in New York. He needed to find out for sure whether or not Lainie Goff had a next of kin. If she did, he'd have to arrange for a police officer to visit their home and break the news if they hadn't heard it already. There were a few other things he wanted to question Archer about as well. Like Goff's relationship with Henry Ogden. Maybe she'd know if it extended beyond the purely professional. Jackson told him Lainie left the office looking pissed. Ogden left ten minutes later. Had they been together? If so, McCabe wanted to know why. He also wanted to know why an ambitious young woman like Lainie Goff would leave nearly two hundred thousand dollars to a tiny, practically unknown charity dedicated to helping runaway teens. It didn't seem to fit with her persona, and he didn't like things that didn't fit.

After four rings a young woman's cheery voice came

on. 'Hi, this is Janie. Leave a message and I'll call ya back.' At least Archer was still in New York and still had the same number. 'Ms. Archer. This is Detective Sergeant Michael McCabe of the Portland, Maine, Police Department. It's important that you call me back as soon as you get this message. It concerns your friend Elaine Goff.' He left both his office number and his cell. Then he called the PPD Call Center and asked whoever was on duty to please track down a cell number for Janie Archer in New York City and, sorry, no, he didn't know who the service provider was.

Before he could try Henry Ogden's number, Maggie called. 'Yeah, Mag, what's up? You still at Goff's apartment?'

'No. I just left. I'm on my way to the ferry terminal. Can you meet me there? Like right away? The fireboat's waiting for us. We're taking a little trip over to Harts Island.'

'Harts? What's on Harts?'

'A possible witness.'

He began to ask questions. She cut him off. 'I'll tell you more about it when I see you.'

'Don't hang up,' said McCabe. He exited the building and walked over to the unmarked Crown Vic. 'Tell me what you know about Sanctuary House.' He got in and started the engine.

'Well, I've certainly heard of it. I'm a cop's kid from Machias, and Sanctuary House is kind of controversial, even famous, up there. Or at least it was when it first opened, which was, I don't know, maybe seven or eight years ago. John Kelly, the guy who started it, was standing next to Goff in that party picture Tom gave us. You find some connection?'

McCabe's windshield was coated with a solid layer of ice. He could scrape and talk to Maggie later or let the defroster do the work and talk now. He opted for now. 'I'm not sure yet exactly what the connection is, but it looks like Sanctuary House is about to get a healthy chunk of change.' He flipped the defroster blower to high. 'Lainie Goff had company-paid life insurance, a hundred and eighty thousand dollars' worth, and Sanctuary House is the sole beneficiary.'

'Hmm,' Maggie snorted. 'Now isn't that interesting? Here's what I know. Sanctuary House is a shelter for runaway kids. A lot of them are from my folks' neck of the woods.'

'How old are the kids?'

'Mostly teenagers. Both girls and boys. Most are victims of sexual abuse. That was the original mission. But they also take in drug addicts, kids convicted of petty crimes, some with mental or emotional problems, basically any young person in need of a safe haven and adult support. Father Jack – that's what all the kids call Kelly – he's an ex-priest, and he makes them all go for counseling. Therapy if they need it. Tries to help them clean up their acts, help them find jobs.'

'You said it was controversial. What's the controversy?'

'The place was set up a year or so after word was beginning to spread about the priest abuse scandals. Father Jack was a young Franciscan at the time, and when he told the diocese he wanted to work with sexually abused teens, the bishop went ape-shit, figured Kelly was going to stir up a hornets' nest when the Church was hoping the whole thing would just simmer down and go away. The bishop put a lot of pressure on Kelly to back off. He said no. The bishop said yes. Kelly said fuck you and turned in his collar.'

'Left the priesthood?'

'Yeah, and it was too bad, because he's just the kind of young idealistic guy they desperately need. Instead he went out on his own, raised enough money to get started, and bought a big old house on one of the side streets off Longfellow Square. I've never met Kelly personally, but from what I hear he's a hell of a charismatic guy. A real charmer.'

Charismatic fit with the face they'd seen in the picture. Charismatic and intense. The windshield was clear now, and he slipped the car into gear. What Maggie told him was interesting, but it still didn't explain Goff's interest in Sanctuary House. 'Anything else I should know?'

'Just a rumor that John Kelly was abused by a priest himself when he was a teenager.'

'Unsubstantiated?'

'I don't know, but the story goes that's what made him so determined to help other kids, church or no church.'

The Casco Bay Lines ferry terminal sat on the edge of the Old Port between Commercial Street and the water, less than a five-minute drive from Ten Monument Square. By the time McCabe clicked off the phone he was already there. The Bay Lines' half-dozen ferries provided frequent and regular service to the handful of out-islands that fell within the city limits of Portland. Harts, with a year-round population of just under a thousand, was the biggest. McCabe left the unmarked Crown Vic in a five-minute parking space at the side of the terminal building, its PPD plates protecting it from the packs of contract towers that circled the place. He got out and headed toward the dock where the PFD fireboat, the *Francis R. Mangini*, was tied up. At midnight on a Friday, McCabe could hear loud Irish music spilling across the water from the bar that occupied the adjacent pier.

As he approached, he speed-dialed Kyra's number to let her know she wouldn't be seeing him for a while. She didn't answer. He left a message and put the phone away. He spotted Maggie and a couple of firefighters waiting for him in the stern of the *Mangini*. A pair of twin diesels was already churning up the water behind the sixty-five-foot steel-hulled vessel. McCabe eased himself down an icy aluminum gangway and climbed aboard. As soon as he was safely on, one of the firefighters unhitched the lines, and the boat pulled out. He led McCabe and Maggie to a small galley behind and below the wheelhouse where they could stay warm and have some privacy. Then he went up and joined his buddy and the officer piloting the boat. Inside the galley, McCabe noticed a pot of hot coffee. He held it up. Maggie shook her head no. He poured a mug for himself, dropped a buck in the can, and sat across from her at the dining table.

'Okay, what's going on?' he asked.

'Like I said, we may have a witness.'

'On Harts?'

'Yeah. While I was at Goff's apartment I got a call from one of the uniforms assigned to the island. Guy named

Scotty Bowman? You may not know him. He used to work in town, but he's been out on the island for a while now. Always been kind of a pain in the ass. Perpetually pissed off because his career never took off like he thought it ought to. Sees himself as one of the best and the brightest.'

'And he's not?'

'Scotty's smart enough, but he tends to be a whiner and a malcontent. Also a chauvinist. He likes patting fannies.'

'Ever pat yours?'

'Only once. I cured him of that affliction in a hurry.'

McCabe smiled. Knowing Maggie, he imagined the cure must have been painful.

'Anyway,' she continued, 'I get this call from Bowman, and he tells me he's not sure how significant it is, but a woman named Abby Quinn came charging into the station on the island Tuesday night claiming to have witnessed a murder.'

'Four nights ago?'

'Four nights ago.'

'Did you ask what took him so long to report it?'

'I asked. The short answer is he didn't believe her.'

McCabe frowned. 'What's the long answer?'

'It seems Abby Quinn has a history of mental illness. She's been in and out of Winter Haven at least a couple of times. Diagnosed with paranoid schizophrenia. She's given to delusions and hallucinations. Sees things that aren't there and hears voices nobody else can hear. She's tried to kill herself more than once.'

Not exactly an ideal witness. If the cops on the island didn't believe what Abby Quinn was telling them, why would any jury? Beyond that, if Goff really was killed on Harts, why and how had the killer transported her body across the bay to the Fish Pier? It didn't make a whole lot of sense. He guessed they'd cross those bridges when they got to them.

'Quinn lives with her mother in a cottage on the island,' Maggie went on. 'Bowman says she's okay as long as she stays on her meds. He also says this wasn't the first time she's come barging into the station spouting some craziness or other. Last time it was aliens from outer space taking over our bodies.'

Scenes from the fifties sci-fi classic *Invasion of the Body Snatchers* flashed through McCabe's mind. Walter Wanger and Don Siegel's black-and-white original. Not the remakes from '78 or '93. He wondered if Abby Quinn had seen any or all of them.

'So he didn't bother checking her story out?'

'No. Not at the time. Just figured she'd gone off her meds again.' Maggie helped herself to a sip of McCabe's coffee. 'Figured she was having a psychotic episode.'

'Did he do anything at all?'

'Not really. He says he thought about bringing her in to the emergency room, but when he told her that's what he was thinking, she quieted right down. Apparently the idea of going to the hospital scared her more than any murderer. First she pleaded with Bowman not to take her, then told him he was right, it was a hallucination, but it was over now and she was okay. She must've convinced him, because, quote, against his better judgment, unquote, he took her home. Back to her mother's house. After that he took a quick run by the alleged crime scene.'

'Which is?'

'An empty summer house on the backshore.'

'Where he doesn't find a body?'

'Where he doesn't find anything. Inside or out. Just some tracks in the snow between the road and the porch, which he figured were Abby's. No body, no weapon, no murder. The only thing remotely questionable was a frying pan he spotted lying in the snow under some shrubbery.'

'A frying pan?'

'Yeah. He figures it's random junk, picks it up, and takes it back to the station and forgets about it until tonight. If you want my personal opinion, McCabe, Bowman was just too lazy to seriously investigate a story coming from a known crazy. Too lazy to even send her to the hospital and spend time writing up a report. He just took the easy way out and dropped the whole thing.'

McCabe gave her a half-smile. 'You really like this guy.'

'Gee, how could you tell?'

McCabe sat at the galley table, sipping his coffee, staring out the window, thinking about what Maggie had told him. His eyes followed a yellow and white island ferry chugging through the icy waters back to the Portland terminal. He checked his watch. After midnight. He didn't realize the boats ran so late. 'Okay,' he finally said with a frustrated sigh, 'so Bowman drops it. Then four days later he changes his mind and calls it in. Why? What suddenly makes him think maybe Abby Quinn wasn't hallucinating?'

'He heard about our murder,' said Maggie, helping herself to another sip of his coffee.

'Y'know, they have a whole pot of this stuff right over there. I'll be happy to get you some of your own.'

'No, thanks.' She smiled. 'I'll just sip at yours.' She took one more swallow and returned the mug to the table. Sometimes, he thought, she behaves more like a wife than Sandy ever did. Or Kyra for that matter.

'Anyway,' Maggie continued, 'Bowman was off duty tonight, sitting at the bar at the Cross-Eyed Bear.' The Cross-Eyed Bear, in spite of its cutesy name, was a serious drinkers' joint on Silver Street, just down the block from 109. A lot of the cops coming off shift hung out there. So did guys who worked the waterfront. Not too many tourists or kids, though, and the few who did wander in rarely ventured beyond the front door. 'He's having a quiet drink by himself when a couple of his buddies come in and join him. They all start bullshitting, and they tell him how they were just working a crime scene down at the Fish Pier and how the reporters and TV crews showed up and how they're all gonna get their faces on the eleven o'clock news. Naturally, they also tell him about our frozen stiff.'

'And he decides to call you?'

'Not right away. He says he still thought Abby Quinn might have been hallucinating and maybe the body turning up at the pier was just a coincidence. Says he wanted to make sure he had something worthwhile before wasting our time. So he catches the next ferry out to Harts. His idea was that he'd find Quinn and have her go over her story one more time. Maybe visit the crime scene again and have her walk him through it. If it made any more sense the second time around, then he was gonna call us. Probably thought he could score a few brownie points by insinuating himself into a big murder case.'

McCabe nodded. 'Either that or look less like an asshole

128

for not following up on what Quinn told him in the first place.'

'Anyway, he gets to Harts and guess what? He can't find her. She's not home, and she's not at her job. Nobody's seen hide nor hair of her since Tuesday night.'

Great, thought McCabe, not only is the witness a nutcase, now she's a missing nutcase. It didn't sound promising. 'So he finally calls you?'

'He finally calls. Tells me what I just told you. Naturally, I question him about the details of what Abby Quinn said.'

'Anything I need to know?'

'Yeah. Two things. Number one, when she came into the station she was too agitated to describe what the killer actually looked like. She just went on and on about some monster with icy eyes and a head exploding in fire. Even if we do find her, there's no guarantee she'll describe him any better.'

Maybe Bowman had been right. Maybe it wasn't worth following up on. 'What's number two?' he asked.

'Number two is why we're on the fireboat. Apparently, in the middle of all her ranting, Quinn did manage to communicate that what she saw was this so-called monster, and again I quote, plunge a thin-bladed knife into the back of a woman's neck.' Maggie paused. 'A naked woman with long dark hair.'

They both knew the cops drinking at the Cross-Eyed Bear wouldn't have had access to those details. They could only have come from Quinn. McCabe found himself hoping what they'd find on Harts Island was a live witness and not just another frozen corpse.

Ten

The fireboat slowed noticeably, and the officer at the wheel began maneuvering it alongside a wooden dock. When he had it in position, one of the firefighters leapt onto the dock and secured the boat fore and aft to a pair of steel cleats. McCabe could see a black-and-white PPD Ford Explorer waiting by the landing. The department's slogan, painted in gold on the SUV's rear fender, had been changed from PROTECTING A GREAT CITY TO PROTECTING A GREAT ISLAND. Two cops were keeping themselves warm inside. One was in plainclothes. McCabe guessed Bowman hadn't bothered changing back into uniform before returning to the island.

Maggie and McCabe walked up from the dock to the car, and Bowman climbed out to greet them. He was a big man, maybe six-two, with an athlete's stance and body. No hint of a paunch in spite of his age, which McCabe figured for just south of fifty. He had a hard face with blotchy red skin, maybe from the cold, maybe from booze, or maybe it was just blotchy. He sported a short, neatly clipped mustache. He was dressed in faded blue jeans and a lined windbreaker with a fake fur collar. He had his badge pinned to the windbreaker. There was no weapon strapped around his waist, and McCabe guessed he was wearing a shoulder holster under the jacket. Probably liked playing detective.

Maggie made the introductions. 'Scotty Bowman, Sergeant Mike McCabe.' The two men shook hands. The officer in the SUV lowered the driver's side window and waved. 'Mel Daniels,' he called out. Daniels looked too young to be a cop. He had a soft, almost feminine face and an open, eager expression. McCabe calculated backward. Since today was Friday, Daniels wouldn't have been on duty Tuesday night. Cops assigned to the island worked fire department hours. Twenty-four hours on, twenty-four off, another twenty-four on, then five days off. McCabe and Maggie climbed into the back of the Explorer. The car felt warm enough to suggest it'd been running awhile. Maybe looking for Quinn. Daniels turned the vehicle around and started up the hill away from the landing. 'You guys found our witness yet?' asked McCabe.

There was a short, tense silence before Bowman sighed. 'No. Not yet. We don't know where she is.'

'You don't know where she is?' McCabe repeated. He hadn't realized how pissed off he was about that. 'That's great, Bowman. That's just fucking great.'

The island cop turned in his seat and held up his hands, palms out. 'Hey. We've been trying to find her since nine thirty when I got back to the island. But like I told Maggie on the phone –'

For the second time in ten seconds Bowman had rubbed McCabe the wrong way. 'Just for the record, you didn't tell "Maggie" anything on the phone. You told Detective Savage. You got that straight?'

The red-faced cop eyed McCabe cautiously. He didn't like being corrected, especially not in front of a junior officer, but they both knew there wasn't a whole lot he could do about it. 'Fine,' he said, his voice flat and unfriendly. 'I told *Detective Savage* we checked Quinn's house. She wasn't there. Her mother, a woman named Grace Quinn, said she hasn't seen her daughter since Tuesday. However, since Gracie's usually blind drunk, she probably hasn't seen much of anything since Tuesday. We also talked to Lori Sparks, the owner of a restaurant called the Crow's Nest where Abby waits tables.'

McCabe knew the place. He and Kyra and Casey had all made a mess eating lobsters out on the deck one evening last summer. Gorgeous views of the bay and the sun setting down behind the Portland skyline. 'Quinn hasn't been there since Tuesday either. Lori was pissed 'cause it left her shorthanded. Friday's her busiest night.'

'Have you tried calling her cell phone?'

'Yeah. Half a dozen times. Message keeps kicking in right away. Like it's turned off. Or out of power.'

McCabe took out his own phone and punched in some numbers. 'This is McCabe,' he said. 'Hold on a sec.' Then, addressing Bowman, he asked, 'What's Quinn's number?' Bowman gave it to him, and McCabe repeated it to the woman who picked up at the PPD Comm Center. He asked her to try to pinpoint the phone's current location, and no, he didn't know who the service provider was.

Daniels pulled the Explorer into a parking space in front of the small brick building that housed the Harts Island police and fire stations, a branch of the Portland

Public Library, a community room, and the only public restrooms on the island.

'Have you looked anywhere else?' asked Maggie. 'Maybe she's hiding out with friends.'

The young cop turned to face them. 'There aren't a lot of people who hang out with Abby. Not the way she is now. It's too tricky. I checked with a couple of her classmates, *our* classmates, from high school. The ones who are still on the island. Like me, they remember Abby the way she used to be. A totally different person.'

'You and Quinn were in the same class?' asked Maggie.

'Yeah. Portland High. Class of '99.'

'The classmates haven't seen her either?'

'No. Not since Tuesday. Neither has the guy who tends bar at the Nest. Young guy, twenty-one or twenty-two, named Travis Garmin.'

'Anybody out searching the island?'

'Just getting started,' said Bowman. 'The other cop on duty tonight, a guy named Sonny Cates, is out organizing a search party. Mostly people who work city services plus some of the volunteer firefighters. Planning to round up eight or ten in all.' The island was only a little over two square miles. McCabe figured ten locals could cover it quickly and effectively without bringing in outside resources.

'We'll find her,' Bowman said flatly.

McCabe stared in the dark at the back of Bowman's head. It was as if Bowman could sense frustration pouring across from the backseat. 'Listen, McCabe,' he said, turning around, 'we handled this right. I handled it right.'

'You don't think you did anything wrong?'

'No. I don't.'

McCabe nodded and climbed out of the vehicle. The others followed. He threw an arm around Daniels's shoulder. 'Why don't you go on inside,' he said softly. 'Detective Savage and I need to have a private chat with Officer Bowman.'

Daniels looked from face to face, probably feeling like the kid being sent out of the room so the grown-ups could talk. Still, he didn't object. He just walked to the station, unlocked the door, flicked on the lights, and went inside. McCabe waited until the door swung shut, then turned to Bowman. 'You had a witness to a murder sitting right in your lap.'

The cop's eyes narrowed. 'No. I didn't,' he hissed. 'What I had was a psychotic nutcase jumping around my station, screaming her fuckin' head off.'

McCabe kept his own rising anger under tight control. 'Abby Quinn may be a psychotic nutcase,' he said. 'I don't know about that. What I do know is that, even agitated and probably terrified, she was cogent enough to provide an accurate description of, one, the murder weapon, two, the MO, and, three, the victim. Details nobody else knows anything about. And what do you do? Nothing. You assume she's gone off her meds and let her slip through your hands. You're an experienced cop, Bowman, with what, twenty years in the department? And you didn't even bother getting her the medical attention you told Detective Savage you thought she needed. If you'd done that, at least we'd have her in a safe place. Instead, you just drove her home. The very first place the bad guy would go looking. Let's just hope we find her before he does, if he hasn't already. Shit, Bowman, I'll bet you didn't even record what she said, did you?'

Bowman said nothing, so McCabe continued. 'That's what I figured. So now, four days later, not only do we not have any idea where our witness is, we don't even have an accurate record of what she said. In fact, thanks to you, we don't have bupkis. In case you haven't been to New York lately, that's Yiddish for goat-shit.'

Bowman stood facing McCabe on the cold, empty village street, his eyes slits, his hands clenched into fists, the distant glow of a streetlamp accenting his features in an irregular pattern of light and shadow. Two alpha males, facing off, with nothing between them but the whoosh of an icy wind sweeping in off the bay.

Bowman blinked first. 'We'll find her,' he said again. 'If she's still on the island, we'll find her.'

McCabe remembered the ferry they passed on the way in. 'Let's hope she is,' he said, 'and let's hope we do. Because if she's not, she could be anywhere. Like stuffed into the trunk of a fancy car. Stabbed, stripped naked, and frozen solid.' McCabe felt Maggie's hand on his shoulder, squeezing gently, bringing him down, urging him toward the building.

'Let's go inside,' she said, 'or we'll all be frozen solid.'

Eleven

McCabe had never seen the Harts Island cop shop before. There wasn't much to it. Up front was a small office space outfitted with a desk, a couple of chairs, a police radio, an all-in-one printer/scanner/fax machine, and a pair of computers. One was an aging desktop model, the other the sort of silver laptop usually found mounted in PPD units. Daniels was sucking on a Coke, his butt planted on one end of the desk. Behind him, through an open doorway, McCabe could see a second room. He walked over and glanced in at a small, sparsely furnished break room, dominated by a grubby-looking brown couch with worn, nearly threadbare arms, a pair of puke green vinyl chairs, and a circular coffee table, littered with out-of-date magazines and a few paperbacks. A wooden staircase rose against the wall to the left. McCabe knew the island cops kept cots upstairs so they could catch some sleep during their long twenty-four-hour shifts. There was an office-sized fridge topped with a coffee setup under the stairs. To his right, a fuzzy-looking Red Sox game flickered away on a TV in the corner. Had to be a replay. The Sox didn't play in January.

As McCabe turned back from the doorway, he spotted a small stack of color photos lying on the desk. 'Quinn?' he asked, picking them up.

'That's her,' said Daniels. 'We found them at her mother's house.'

McCabe studied the pictures, three in all. In the first, Abby was standing on the rocks by the shore, smiling at the camera, a big, healthy-looking girl with a generous figure and a face full of freckles. Probably still a teenager when the shot was taken. Waves crashed behind her, and the wind was sweeping her long reddish brown hair down over one eye in an unruly mass. McCabe never would have called Abby pretty, but she was still appealing in that open, outdoorsy way so common in Maine. She wore a sweatshirt with a picture of a strong-looking woman flexing a muscular right arm. Under the picture were the words GRRRRL POWER! McCabe smiled. A Harts Island feminist.

The second photo showed Abby standing in the stern of a lobster boat. She was clowning for the photographer, who must have taken the shot from the end of a pier or maybe from a second boat a little ways away. She wore a plaid flannel shirt and a pair of the orange waterproof overalls that seemed mandatory for anyone lobstering in Maine. She was holding a big lobster, maybe a five-pounder, by the tail and pretending to be frightened by the creature writhing at the end of her arm.

'How old is she?' McCabe asked.

'My age,' said Daniels. 'Twenty-four or twenty-five. Like I said, we graduated Portland High the same year.'

'Were you friends?' asked Maggie.

'Not particularly. The island kids mostly hung together. My folks lived in Portland, so I wasn't part of their crowd.

But I do know that Abby in high school was a totally different person from who she is today.'

In the third picture, she did indeed look like a different person. So different the photo might have been used as the 'after' shot in a before-and-after demonstration of the toll mental illness takes on the human spirit. She looked thirty, maybe forty pounds heavier and at least ten years older. Her hair hung lank and lifeless. Her eyes were clouded by a joyless empty expression, and there were dark circles under them. Her skin looked pasty and almost gray. One hand was up, trying to shield her face, as if to say, *Please don't take a picture of me. Not like this.*

'Is this recent?' McCabe asked, holding it up, before handing the stack to Maggie.

Daniels shook his head. 'No. Probably taken after her last stay at Winter Haven. About a year ago. That's her mother's cottage in the background. I've got a feeling Gracie didn't have enough sense or sensitivity not to take a picture of Abby looking like that.'

'Is it how she looks now?' he asked.

'Well, she's not as fat now – twenty, thirty pounds less – and she's washing her hair. Looks more normal. Chubby but normal. The last time I saw Abby was about a week ago going in to work at the Nest. She looked almost happy.'

McCabe slipped the photos into his breast pocket. 'You don't mind if I borrow these?' he asked. Nobody did. He glanced over at Bowman, who was sitting in a swivel chair, his eyes locked on McCabe's, one leg mounted on the desk. A few chunks of ice had fallen from his boot and were melting into small pools on the fake wood surface.

'You know out there?' he said. 'If you were worrying that your killer's gonna hunt Quinn down to eliminate a witness, you can relax. I don't think that's likely.'

'Really?' McCabe studied him. 'Any reason for that? Or just your natural optimism bubbling to the surface?'

Bowman ignored the sarcasm. 'A couple of reasons. Starting with your assumption Quinn actually saw the murder take place –'

'Not a bad assumption, Scotty,' Maggie interjected. She was leaning against the door, arms folded across her chest, the photos of Quinn still in one hand. 'A knife to the back of the neck is a pretty specific detail.'

'It is, *Detective Savage*.' Bowman laced the last two words with a heavy dose of his own sarcasm. 'But isn't it at least possible Quinn only saw the body after the fact? A naked woman. Dead. With a small wound in her neck. Don't you think seeing that might've freaked her out enough to push her into making up the rest? Hallucinating it. Or imagining it. Or whatever the hell else you call what schizophrenics do when they're stressed.' Bowman looked pleased with his hypothesis.

McCabe shrugged. 'Slightly tortured logic, but I suppose it's possible.'

'Oh yeah? Tortured in what way?'

'Well, if that's how it happened, where, exactly, is the killer while your schizophrenic is discovering the body? Hiding in a closet? Wandering around outside in the cold, waiting for her to finish freaking out so he can go back up and collect the remains? Or maybe he's just over at the Crow's Nest having a beer? Like I said, possible. Just not very likely.'

Bowman sighed in reluctant agreement. 'Okay. But even if we assume Abby did catch the killer in the act, even then he probably didn't see her face.'

'What do you mean?' asked Maggie. 'She saw his face. Why wouldn't he see hers?'

'Because,' Bowman announced, 'she was wearing a mask.' He smiled with grim satisfaction, like an athlete savoring a meaningless point scored in the last seconds of a losing effort.

Maggie gave him a questioning look. 'What kind of mask?'

'A cold weather ski mask. Y'know, the kind that covers your face with holes cut out for the eyes, nose, and mouth. It was blue. Sort of an imitation Spider-Man design. She was still wearing it when she came to the station.'

What if Quinn *was* wearing a mask? McCabe thought about the implications of that as Maggie and Bowman continued their back-and-forth.

'She was wearing this mask because . . .?' asked Maggie.

'She was out jogging that night. The winds on the backshore can be brutal on bare skin, and I guess it was part of her gear. Anyway, when she passed the Markhams' cottage –'

'That's the crime scene?'

'Yeah. As she passed she saw candlelight in one of the windows. Since it's one of her houses –'

'What do you mean, her houses?'

'Abby makes a few bucks keeping an eye on some of the summer cottages for the owners. She has keys to all of them. This was one of them. According to Lori Sparks at the Nest, she takes the responsibility seriously. I guess that's why she went in to investigate.'

McCabe's eyes, narrowed almost to slits, bored in on Bowman. 'Wouldn't she have taken the mask off when she went inside?'

'I don't think so. She had it on when she got here, and she kept it on. I couldn't tell who she was, and I had to ask her twice to take it off. She finally did, but only reluctantly, and even then she wouldn't let go of it. I think she saw it as some kind of whatchamacallit, a talisman or something.'

McCabe's mind played with the possibilities. If Abby was wearing a mask when she saw the murder, if the killer couldn't see her face, as Bowman suggested, it changed the dynamic of what they were doing. 'You're sure Sonny Cates didn't tell the searchers why they were looking for Quinn?' he asked. 'He didn't say anything about her witnessing a murder?'

'No,' said Bowman. 'He couldn't have. Like I told you, he didn't know that himself. All I told Cates was that Quinn was missing and we needed to find her. In fact, that's all Daniels knew till we went to pick you up off the boat.'

Okay, that was good. 'How about her mother and the people at the Crow's Nest?'

'Same thing. I just asked them if they knew where Abby was, they said no. Travis Garmin told me to try her cell number. He knew it by heart. We did. Got no answer.'

McCabe walked to the window and peered out at the dark street. Snow was beginning to fall. Small hard flakes, not the fat fluffy ones he preferred. He let the idea of the mask perk around in his brain for a minute or two. Clearly they had to find Quinn ASAP, either here or on the mainland. At the same time, they didn't want to put Quinn's life in danger by letting the killer know who it was who had barged in on the murder. He thought about classifying Abby as a confidential police informant, a CI. That way they could legally keep her identity secret pretty much indefinitely, or at least until the discovery phase of a trial, if this thing ever got that far.

McCabe's only problem was that this particular CI was missing, and it was going to be a hell of a lot harder to find her if they couldn't tell anyone who they were looking for. No. Formal CI status wouldn't work. They had to play it both ways. Tell people who they were looking for when they had to, but under no circumstances tell anyone why. At least Bowman hadn't screwed that up yet.

McCabe took out his cell and tapped in Starbucks's number. The PPD's resident computer brain, Starbucks's real name was Aden Yusuf Hassan. A Somali kid, he'd arrived in Portland back in 2000, in the city's first wave of Sudanese and Somali refugees fleeing genocide in their own lands. When he started working for the department a couple of years later, the cops dubbed him Starbucks because of his addiction to strong coffee. The name stuck. Starbucks had never touched a computer in his native country, but he learned fast. He was a natural. One of the best McCabe had ever seen.

His mother picked up on the third ring. 'I'm afraid Aden is not at home, Sergeant,' she said in heavily accented English. 'He's out for the evening with a friend.'

McCabe thanked her, said he hoped he hadn't woken her up, and tried Starbucks's cell. 'Yes, Sergeant.' Starbucks was shouting over loud music. 'What can I do for you?'

'Sorry to break up your night on the town,' McCabe shouted, 'but I need you to get over to 109 now.'

'Oh.' Disappointment in his voice. 'Okay.' Pause. 'That's fine.' The voice brightened up. 'I'll have to apologize to my friend and take her home first.'

'Apologize for me, too.'

'I will, but not to worry, Sergeant, the job comes first. What can I do for you?'

'I'm having three photos of a woman e-mailed to you. When you get to the office, take the one where she looks old and fat. Photoshop about thirty pounds off of her. Then take the other two and add maybe five years. Could you hear all of that?'

'Yes, Sergeant,' Starbucks shouted back. 'I hear you very well.'

'Good. When you're done, send the photos to Cleary's computer.'

'Is he at 109?'

'He will be soon.'

Maggie started to ask a question. McCabe held up a finger, signaling her to wait. He called Cleary.

'Hey, boss, you solve the murder yet?' Nearly one in the morning and Cleary was still full of beans and ready to take on the world. That was good. McCabe needed somebody aggressive on this.

'Not yet,' McCabe told him. 'The canvass turn up any results?'

'Not yet either. We're still working it.'

'Tell Tommy I'm pulling you off.'

'Yeah?' Cleary sounded surprised. 'Why? Whaddaya need?'

McCabe filled him in on everything they had learned so far, including the fact that Quinn couldn't identify the killer and that the killer might not be able to identify Quinn.

'Does the bad guy *know* she couldn't ID him?'

'No. Which is why we need to find her before he does. As quick as we can. Without letting people know why we're looking, and without using her name any more than we have to. Otherwise we could have another corpse on our hands.'

'Jesus,' said Cleary, 'this is all kinda weird.'

'Yeah, kinda. Anyway, Starbucks is working on some pictures. By the time he's done with them they ought to be pretty good likenesses. I want you to send out a confidential ATL to all of our units plus every other department in Maine, plus the staties both here and in New Hampshire. Get someone to check with all the taxi companies in town. And cover the train and bus terminals. She might head there. Trailways has a 3:15 A.M. departure to Boston.'

'Who goes to Boston at three in the morning?'

'I don't know. Just make sure Quinn's not one of them. Also check for early departures out of the Jetport.'

'Nothing's gonna be flying out of there for a while. Not with this snow coming in.'

'Probably not, but tell our guys to keep an eye open anyway. If I were Quinn I'd be running as far and fast as I could.'

'Yeah, but you're not crazy. She have a car?'

'I don't know. Check that, too. See if there's one registered in her name. Or maybe her mother's. Grace Quinn. Same Harts Island address.'

'Anything else?'

'Yeah. Call my cell when you're done.'

McCabe hung up.

'You know, McCabe,' Bowman snorted, 'you're tryin' to keep this so damn hush-hush – but what about Quinn herself?'

'What about her?'

'Your witness has no control over her own mouth. She's probably out there right now blabbing her head off.'

McCabe shrugged. 'Yeah. She might be. Nothing we can do about that. But hey, maybe nobody'll believe her. You know. The rantings of a psychotic nutcase and all? Now I'd like you to stop worrying about that and take me through the rest of what happened Tuesday night.'

'You pretty much know it all. She came here. She ranted. She raved. Then I took her home. End of story.'

'You visited the crime scene afterward? Isn't that right?' he asked.

'Yeah, I did. It's a fancy backshore cottage right across the road from the water. Belongs to some banker type from Boston. Guy named Todd Markham.'

'Everything look normal to you?'

'Yep. I went through every room, including the master bedroom, which is where she says it happened. I saw nothing out of place. No weapon. No body. No blood. Not where she said it was and not anywhere else.'

'On the other hand, you weren't expecting to see anything out of place, were you?'

'What do you mean?'

'Just that if there was something not quite right there, if you weren't expecting it, it wouldn't be surprising if you didn't see it.' McCabe knew all too well how expectations create their own reality. How they cut off even a smart cop's ability to consider other possibilities – and Bowman wasn't all that smart. 'Let's just hope you didn't destroy any evidence.'

'I didn't.'

'How'd you get in?'

'The door was open.'

'Front door? Back door?'

'I went in the front.'

'How about Abby?'

'I don't know.'

'Was the back door locked?'

'I don't know.'

'No signs of B&E?'

'No. I told you. Abby had a key. She let herself in.'

'Yeah, I know. You told me. Abby had a key. How'd the killer get in?'

Bowman's brow knitted. 'I don't know.' Pause. 'I hadn't thought about that.'

He hadn't thought about it because he was so damned sure Quinn made the whole thing up.

'You guys have Markham's number in Boston?' asked McCabe.

'We can get it.' Daniels woke the desktop computer from its sleep and began tapping keys. He wrote some numbers on a Post-it note. McCabe nodded at Maggie, who nodded back, took the Post-it, and disappeared into the back room to check on Todd Markham's whereabouts Tuesday night.

'Abby couldn't describe what the bad guy looked like?'

'No. Just a lot of craziness that didn't make any sense.'

'Like what exactly?'

'You really want to know?'

'Yeah.'

'She said he looked like a man from the back, but when he turned to look at her he was a monster. Let me see if I can remember her exact phrases. "A fiery fiend. An evil animal face. Icicles for eyes."' There was a nasty mocking tone to Bowman's voice.

McCabe let it pass. 'Maybe he was wearing a mask as well.'

'I don't think so,' said Bowman. 'Abby's a whacko. She hallucinates. That's all her description of a monster was. A hallucination brought on by the stress of the moment.'

'What did she do after she saw the murder?'

'Not clear, but I think she turned and ran. There were footprints broken into the ice and snow leading to and from the front door. All messed up like they were made by someone running fast. Looked to me like they were all Abby's. In one spot it looked like she took a fall.'

McCabe glanced out the window. It was snowing even harder than before.

'Todd Markham says there is a key to the back door. It's hidden inside a lantern on the exterior wall next to the door,' said Maggie, coming back into the office. 'I asked him who knew it was there. He said half the island. Plumbers. Electricians. Anybody who ever worked on the house when the Markhams weren't there. By the way, Markham was in Chicago Tuesday night. Says he had dinner with a couple of clients. Stayed at the Hyatt. Didn't get back to Boston till –'

McCabe nodded. 'Okay. Tell me about Markham's alibi later. Right now I need you and Daniels to get over to his house. Photograph and preserve any readable footprints before the snow out there covers them up. You guys have any plastic sheeting here?'

'No sheeting,' said Daniels, heading toward the rear of the station, 'but we've got a bunch of tarps out back.'

They piled the tarps into the back of the Explorer, along with metal tent pegs to secure them, a digital camera, and a couple of lights. It wasn't perfect, but it'd have to do.

The front door opened just as they left. 'Jeez,' said Sonny Cates, stamping snow off his boots, 'it's colder'n a witch's tit out there.' He was a round, jolly-looking guy with white hair. Santa Claus without the beard. He pulled off his glove. 'Mike McCabe, right?'

McCabe waited at the window until the Explorer pulled out before nodding and taking Cates's extended hand. 'Any luck?'

'Nah. Not yet.'

'Take me through what you're doing.'

They walked over to a large laminated aerial map of the island pinned to one wall. An erasable marker was hanging next to it. 'Basically, I divided the island into six more or less equal sectors.' He drew a red line horizontally

148

across the center of the island, then two vertical ones. 'Assigned a team to each.'

'Communications?'

'All the teams have cell phones.'

'How's the reception?'

'Sketchy. Some places okay. Some places nonexistent. Two of our teams have trucks with radios. I put them in the areas where cell reception's worst. We're checking outdoor areas first. In this weather, if she's stuck outside, she's gonna be in trouble pretty quick. We're also checking the old bunkers here, here, and up over here.' Cates pointed to three places on the map. 'You know about the bunkers?'

McCabe did. During World War II, North Atlantic convoys sailed in and out of Portland harbor, and the army made Harts a key element of Portland's shore defenses. Concrete bunkers and observation posts were still dotted all over the island. Some had been converted into garages, storage sheds, and summer houses. Others were simply abandoned. One, Battery Victor, was big, dark, and empty, with multiple rooms and plenty of hidey-holes.

'How about the empty summer houses? The ones she had keys to?'

'So far, visual inspection only. Snow makes it easy to see if anyone's been marching up to them.'

'Anything suspicious?'

'Other than deer tracks, not so far. Just around the Markham place, which is here.' Cates pointed to a spot on the map. 'This new snow's gonna cover everything up pretty quick, though. Then we'll have to start calling the owners and looking inside.'

'Anybody ask why we're looking for her?'

'Just told them she's missing and we've got to find her. They all know she's got mental problems and tried suicide twice, so nobody's asking too many questions.'

They saw headlights pulling up outside. Maggie and Daniels were back.

Twelve

It was a little after one thirty in the morning when Maggie pulled the Explorer up in front of an oversized gray house on Seal Point. McCabe studied the place from the passenger seat. There were just the two of them. Bowman and Daniels had been left behind, and Cates had rejoined his search teams. The fewer people who tramp around a crime scene the better, even one that might already be compromised. Forensics 101.

Different cops work in different ways, and McCabe liked to look at a crime scene with the eye of the filmmaker he once dreamed of becoming. He broke events down into discrete scenes, choreographed the movement of the principal players through each scene, considered the lighting, and shot the action with the camera in his mind from as many angles as he could. Later he'd edit the mental footage until it told a complete and, hopefully, coherent story. For McCabe it was the closest he could come to actually having been there.

He sat next to Maggie in the dark, not talking, just looking out the window and listening to the slap of the wipers. Heavy gray tarps, stretched end to end across the middle of the front yard, were already nearly invisible under new snow. Finally he asked, 'Any useful prints under those things?'

Maggie nodded. 'A few.'

'Bowman's?'

'No. His are all clustered away from the others. Looks like he was being careful not to destroy evidence.'

Good. At least the asshole had done something right.

'Someone, I think Abby, entered the property, wearing ice cleats. You can see some cleat prints on top of the ice. She broke through in a couple of places. She took a circuitous route, staying close to the shrubbery over there on the right. Then she stayed close against the house till she reached the porch steps.'

McCabe remembered the full moon Tuesday night. Assuming Abby got to the place around ten or eleven o'clock, it would have lit the front yard almost like daylight. She was trying to stay in the shadows. Not be seen by whoever was in the house. The layer of crusty snow extended up the steps and onto the porch. Blown in by the wind off the sea. 'She go in the front door?'

'No, but she must've thought about it. There's a couple of her cleat prints right in front of the door. Everything's kind of messed up in that area, 'cause that's how they came out, but there is a nice clear trail of cleats going around the side of the porch to the back. Best I can tell, she checked out the garage, then went into the house through the back door.'

'And came out the front?'

'Yeah. With somebody chasing her. Coming out, she went straight down the middle, and the bad guy came after her.'

'What do you have from him?'

'Everything's pretty messed up. Looks like somebody, the bad guy I think, slipped and took a fall. Still, we got a couple of decent imprints. Looks like he was barefoot.'

Must have been desperate. Running barefoot on snow and ice in ten-degree weather. McCabe wondered if he was totally naked. Might have been if he raped Goff just before killing her.

'A couple of partials of his feet are pretty clear. One heel and two toes. Good indication of size. Should be able to make casts of them.'

'See anything that looks like it might have been Goff's?'

'No. He might have carried her in. Remember, she didn't come out again. Goff only had a one-way ticket.'

A one-way ticket to the Hotel California. The old Eagles song started up in McCabe's head. *You can check out any time you like, but you can never leave.* Goff didn't. Quinn barely did.

'When's Jacobi coming?'

'Tonight. Weather report's calling for a heavy snow drop, so he wants to get out here and get as much of the scene tied down as possible before the snow wipes out any more of it. They're already finished at Goff's. He's arranging barge transport for the van.'

McCabe sighed. 'Long night.'

'Bill's okay with that. Says Bernice will love spending the overtime.' Maggie looked over and gave him one of those lopsided grins of hers, with one side of her mouth going up more than the other. A brunette version of Ellen Barkin. 'So will I,' she added. 'If I ever get to go shopping.'

'Anything else?'

'Yeah. A couple of sets of tire tracks leading into and out of the garage. Looks like two different vehicles to me.' Then, as if sensing his thoughts, she said, 'Todd Markham told me he hasn't been on the island in months. He wasn't sure about Isabella. When he's traveling on business, which apparently he does a lot, he says she likes coming up here instead of staying in Boston.'

'A little lonely, I would've thought.'

Maggie just shrugged. 'Who knows? Maybe she's anti-social. Or maybe she's got a friend.'

'Has she been up here in the last month or so?'

'We'll have to ask.'

'Did you ask him what kind of car she drives?'

'Yup. A Caddy Escalade.'

McCabe nodded. 'Any of the tracks readable?'

'I think so. There's a couple of nice fat frozen tire prints just inside the door. Different tread patterns. I figure one could be the Escalade, the other the Beemer.'

Would the freak have taken Goff's car over on the ferry? With Goff inside? Or maybe tied up in the trunk? Then back again with her body? Pretty careless if he did. There were no surveillance cameras on board, but there were plenty of witnesses who might remember a new BMW convertible going across in January. Who might have noticed the driver. Who might be able to describe him. Or her. McCabe checked his phone. There was a signal, but it was weak. With the bulk of the island between Seal Point and the nearest cell tower, that was no surprise. He called Cleary again and managed to connect.

'ATL in place?'

Cleary told him it was.

'Okay. Next thing I need you to do is find the home number for the director of the Casco Bay Lines. Wake him up if you have to, but get the crew rosters for every ferry between Portland and Harts Island from the night of the twenty-third until the last boat tonight. Both coming and going. Get the crews' home numbers, cell numbers, whatever. Just find them. We need to know ASAP if anyone remembers seeing the BMW and if they can remember the driver. Or if anyone actually remembers seeing Goff. Also see if anyone remembers a Caddy Escalade. Massachusetts plates.'

'Got it.'

'Also find out if anybody saw Abby on any boat leaving Harts between Wednesday morning and tonight. If you need help, call Fortier. He gives you any shit, tell him to call me.'

'No problem.'

McCabe smiled. He knew why he loved Cleary.

They found flashlights, stuffed evidence gloves and paper booties in their pockets, and exited the Explorer. The two of them walked south along Seashore, to the bend in the road where the Markhams' house disappeared from view. Then they turned and looked back. Abby had first seen the candlelight somewhere between here and the path leading up to the porch. They walked back, trying to see things the way Abby saw them as she jogged toward the house four nights ago. It had been an icy night, clear and bright with a full moon and no snow. Native Americans used to call the January full moon the wolf moon to honor the ravenous hunters who once roamed these regions in winter. Driven by cold and hunger and the absence of prey, lone wolves howled their discontent at the heavens. To survive, they needed something warm to kill.

McCabe tracked Quinn's progress as she rounded the curve into a straight patch. The large wall of windows in the center of the second floor came into view. Had Abby seen candlelight right away? Jogging on an icy road, even with cleats, she might have been looking down, keeping an eye on the icy patches and only glancing up occasionally. McCabe walked gingerly himself; Maggie did the same. He imagined himself in a head-over-heels pratfall, a Keystone Kop slipping on a banana. He'd just as soon avoid a side trip to the hospital with a broken bone.

He reached the stone steps leading up from the road to the front path. By now Abby must have seen the light flickering in the window. He imagined her standing there debating what to do. Did she have a phone? If she did, why didn't she call the cops? Maybe she figured they wouldn't believe anything reported by someone they thought was crazy. She would have been right.

What was Abby feeling as she stood there? Curiosity? Fear? Something less rational? Was she already in the middle of a full-blown psychotic episode by the time she looked up, saw the light, and decided to enter the house? For what it was worth, he didn't think so. How many 'psychotic nutcases,' as Bowman called her, ran four miles a night? Bowman had also said, *Abby makes a few bucks keeping an eye on some of the summer cottages for the owners. She has keys to all of them. This was one of them. That's why she went in to investigate.* Cause and effect. A deliberate decision. A rational, even courageous, decision. It didn't seem like the behavior pattern of a schizophrenic who was 'off her meds.' He made a note to find and interview Abby Quinn's doctor as soon as he could. Check Bowman's assumptions. Check his own.

Of course, even if Abby *was* totally rational when she

156

entered the house, no jury would ever take her testimony seriously. No prosecutor would even put her on the stand. He imagined a defense lawyer interrogating her on cross, Abby sitting there helpless. *You do have a history of seeing things, don't you, Ms Quinn?* Yes. *Hallucinations?* Yes. *Things that aren't there?* Yes. *Things that never happened?* Yes. *Hearing them as well, according to your medical records.* Yes, once again. The killer, if they ever caught him, had little to fear from Abby Quinn in a court of law. McCabe, if he ever found Abby, would have to use her in a different way. Perhaps to lead him to the murderer, but not to count on her testimony to convict. It would take something other than Abby's testimony to right the wrong of Lainie Goff's murder. He shoved the thought away. He didn't need to be thinking about that now.

Instead of adding their own footprints to the chaos that was already there, Maggie and McCabe went around to the driveway at the side of the house and headed toward the garage. McCabe slipped on the latex gloves and raised the door a couple of feet. He and Maggie squatted. She pointed at one set of tire treads and then the other. Both were clearly visible, frozen into icy permanence, and would stay that way at least until the temps went above thirty-two and stayed there for more than a day or two. Jacobi would be able to read and photograph them without any problem.

McCabe slid the garage door shut and followed Maggie up the four steps that led to the back of the porch. He shined his light at the area around the door. Like Bowman said, no sign of a B&E. He tried the door. Still open. They waited while Maggie found the key inside the lantern where Markham said it would be and slipped it into a paper evidence bag. If the bad guy used that key to gain access, his prints might still be on it.

McCabe wondered if Lainie walked to her death. Wondered if she was still conscious at that point. Blood tox results would show any drugs used to knock her out, but they wouldn't have those until well after she thawed. They bent down and donned their paper booties. McCabe pushed the door open, and they went in. He flipped half a dozen dimmer switches and adjusted a ceiling-full of bright floods downward. They worked their way around the room, checking for bits of evidence Bowman might have missed that would tie the scene to Lainie or, even better, to the man who took her life. Except for the fact that the heat was on, nothing seemed out of place. They went upstairs.

The room in which Lainie Goff died was nearly as big as McCabe's entire apartment, at least if you counted the luxurious bathroom and the two walk-in closets, each spacious enough to serve as individual guest rooms. Through the wall of windows, he could see the rocks and the open sea beyond. Everything in the room was neat, tidy, and in its place. He wondered why the bad guy bothered to light candles. The full moon shining through the wall of windows would have provided more than enough light to dispatch the victim without alerting the curious jogger passing by below. Had he intended some kind of ritual murder, a ceremony of death? *All the sinners of my people shall die by the sword.* Or did he simply find rape and murder by candle-light romantic? Perhaps the true reasons could only be understood by the killer himself.

Thirteen

'I'm not in real good shape to talk right now,' Janie Archer told McCabe, 'but you said it was urgent, so, hey, here I am.' He was standing on the deck of the *Francis R. Mangini*, waiting for one of the crew to finish tying the fireboat up to her regular slot on the Portland side.

Archer was slurring her words. McCabe could hear a male voice shouting something unintelligible in the background. He was tempted to tell her to get some sleep and he'd catch her in the morning, but it already was morning, and from the sound of her she might be out of commission for most of the rest of the day. He decided to get what he could now.

He followed Maggie up the slippery ramp to the pier. 'Ms Archer. My name's McCabe –'

'Yeah, I know. You're a cop. You said that on the message.' He heard a giggle. Then Archer must've pressed her hand over the receiver, because he could just make out her next muffled words. 'Stop it, Brett. I'm talking.' Then a loud whisper, 'To a cop.'

Maggie mouthed the words 'Good night' and signaled she was headed home to bed. McCabe threw her a distracted wave and watched her disappear into the night. It was snowing even harder on this side. Three or four inches already, and the wind was swirling it into drifts. They predicted a big one, and it looked like, for once, they'd be right.

'Are you sure you can talk now, Ms Archer? Sounds like you're busy.'

'No. I'm okay. It's alright. You said it was about Lainie. What is it? What'd she do?'

Had Janie Archer been next of kin, McCabe would have been required to arrange for someone from the NYPD or another agency to visit her apartment and inform her of Lainie's death in person. But she wasn't. She was only a friend. 'Ms. Archer. I'm sorry to have to tell you, your friend Elaine Goff is dead.'

He heard an intake of breath. 'Oh shit.'

My sentiments exactly, thought McCabe.

'Lainie's dead?'

'Yes.'

'Lainie's really dead?'

'Yes. I'm afraid she is.'

'I thought she was in Aruba.'

'She never made it to Aruba.'

'What happened? Was she driving that fucking Beemer too fast again?'

'No. It wasn't an accident,' he said.

'Not an accident? Then what? She didn't OD or anything like that?'

No attempt to hide Goff's drug habit. Maybe with Goff dead Archer figured it didn't matter. 'Was she a heavy user?' he asked.

'Occasional. Social. It wasn't a big deal with her.'

McCabe reached the five-minute parking zone to find his car covered in a layer of snow. He wasn't going anywhere until he had a chance to scrape it off. 'Do you know the name of her dealer?' he asked, unlocking the door.

There was hesitation on the other end of the line. 'Uh . . . gee . . . no. No, I don't.'

He climbed in and started the engine. 'Ms. Archer, Elaine Goff's body was found earlier this evening. If you can give us the name of her dealer, it would be a big help.' He waited. There was no response. He decided to press harder. 'Your friend didn't just die. She was murdered. Drugs were found in her car. There may be a connection.'

Now there was shock. 'Murdered? Lainie was murdered?' He could hear the depth of it in her voice. People like Janie Archer, nice people, middle-class people, people with real homes and good jobs, never believed the people *they* knew, their friends or family, could ever be the victims of anything as ugly as murder. That sort of thing didn't happen to them. Not in a city like Portland, Maine. Not anywhere. In their minds it only happened to poor people, black people, people in the projects.

'Do you know the name of her dealer?'

'She never told me his name. She called him the hot-dog man. "Gotta go see the hot-dog man," she'd say.'

It didn't mean anything to him. He wasn't sure if 'the hot-dog man' was a dealer's tag or if selling hot-dogs was what the guy ostensibly did for a living. Easy enough to find out unless he was a total amateur. The narco guys were aware of most of the pros in town. Even the part-timers. There were a few seconds of silence.

'You're really a cop? This isn't some kind of stupid joke?' The slurring of words was gone.

'I'm really a cop. Detective Sergeant Michael McCabe, Portland, Maine, Police Department, and no, it's not a joke.'

'Funny. I was pissed off 'cause she hadn't sent me a card from Aruba. Stupid me. You better give me some ID. A badge number or something I can check later.'

McCabe repeated the number slowly so she could copy it down.

'That's McCabe? M-C? Not M-A-C?'

He told her M-C was correct. After that he could hear her talking to her boyfriend again, this time more calmly. 'Alright, Brett. It's time for you to go home.' Pause. 'No, I'm sorry, but tonight's over.' Brett said something McCabe couldn't make out. Then he heard Archer again. 'Yes, something's happened, and no, I don't need your help. Just go.' Pause. 'Thank you.' Then another pause and a muttered 'Asshole.' Finally he heard a deep breath, and Archer was addressing him again.

'Where did you get my name?' she asked.

He pushed the defroster to high, but the car hadn't yet warmed up enough for it to accomplish much of anything. He realized he was shivering. 'Elaine Goff listed you as her emergency contact at Palmer Milliken. I got your number from the head of HR.' Behind him he could hear the loud scraping of a snowplow. He hoped the guy didn't block him in behind a wall of snow, forcing him to dig his way out of the parking space.

'Jesus, Lainie was murdered,' Archer said. This time it wasn't a question. It was a statement, delivered in a flat voice. Quietly, without affect, as if Janie Archer were merely trying the idea on for size. As if by saying it aloud, she'd be able to tell if such a thing was even possible.

McCabe waited for her to say more, but there was only silence on the other end of the line. 'Ms. Archer, do you know if Lainie had any family? Anyone who should be notified of her death?'

'What? I'm sorry. What did you say?'

He repeated the question.

'No. I'm probably the closest thing to family Lainie had.' Archer's voice morphed from disbelief to sadness as if she'd just accepted the reality of her friend's death and was beginning to mourn. 'Janie and Lainie they called us. We were so close it was almost like we were two sides of the same person.'

'What happened to Lainie's parents?'

'Her mother died while we were in college. At the end of sophomore year. After that and right through law school, she spent Thanksgivings and Christmases and a couple of summers with my family in New Jersey. Lainie was the sister I never had.'

'How about her father?'

'She never knew her real father. He was killed in a car accident when Lainie was a baby.'

'His name was Goff?'

'I'm not sure. I think so. It may have been her mother's maiden name.'

'There were no siblings?'

'No. She was an only child.'

'You just said, "She never knew her *real* father." Was there ever a stepfather who might still be around?'

'She had a stepfather, but he hasn't been part of her life since she was a kid.' Archer hesitated again. 'I don't think she'd want him notified of anything.'

'But he's alive?'

'Not as far as Lainie was concerned.'

'Can you give me his name?'

'Albright. Wallace Albright. He lives in Maine. Camden, I think.'

'What was Lainie's problem with Mr Albright?'

Archer didn't answer right away. When she did, all she said was 'I think you better ask him that.'

McCabe thought about pressing the issue but decided instead to wait until he talked to Albright. He changed the subject. 'How'd she pay for school?'

'She had a scholarship. And loans. And summer jobs. After her mother died, she also had the equity on her mother's house and the proceeds of a life insurance policy. Couple of hundred thou altogether. She used that to live on all the way through Cornell and for a little time after. Until she started at Palmer Milliken. It was barely enough. Lainie had expensive tastes. Always did. Officer ... I'm sorry, what's your name again?'

'McCabe. Detective Sergeant Michael McCabe.'

'Officer McCabe, you said Lainie was murdered – but you didn't tell me when or how. Do you know who did it?'

'There isn't very much we can tell you yet. We only found her body a few hours ago, and the investigation is just getting under way.'

'Are you sure it was Lainie you found?'

'As sure as we can be. Because death was the result of a homicide, there'll have to be an autopsy. Probably at the end of the week. After that it looks like it'll be up to you to make funeral arrangements once the body is released.'

'I guess so,' Archer said. 'Somebody has to be there for Lainie, and I guess I'm it. I'm the only one she has. What kind of . . . I don't know how to put this delicately. What kind of shape is her body in? Did the killer . . .'

'She's not mutilated or grotesque in any way, if that's what you're getting at. She's simply dead.' There was a brief silence; then McCabe asked, 'Is there anyone you can think of who might have wanted to harm her?'

'No.'

'Or any reason anyone would want to see her dead?'

'Not that I know of.'

'Did she ever mention a Palmer Milliken life insurance policy to you?'

'No.'

He asked her a few more pro forma questions; then, just as they were about to hang up, she said, 'Ogden.'

'What?'

'Ogden.'

'What about Ogden?' *Lainie left the office looking pissed. Ogden left ten minutes later.* Was he pissed as well? *He looked like he always looks. Like a rich white guy.*

'You ought to talk to him about Lainie. Talk to Henry Ogden.'

'Were they having an affair?'

There was only a slight pause and a sigh before Archer answered. 'Talk to Ogden.'

Before he could ask her anything more, the phone went dead. He didn't call back.

*

McCabe pulled out of the ferry terminal and turned right onto Commercial Street. At a little after three o'clock on a snowy January morning, the streets were empty in a way New York's never would have been, not even in the middle of a blizzard. There was no traffic, and there were no people. Bars and hotels were shut up tight, and the last of the Old Port revelers had long since gone home. With an overnight parking ban in effect, there weren't even any parked cars. Nothing moved but the snowplows, scraping their way up and down the streets, orange lights flashing, giant insects on the prowl.

The Crown Vic's heater was finally generating some warmth, and he turned the blowers on high. He took a left by the Japanese restaurant on India and a right at the treatment plant on Fore Street, steering the big Ford gingerly through the snow, hoping that the Eastern Prom had been plowed and that the car's rear wheel drive would get him up the hill.

The road turned out to be passable, and it took only a minute or two longer than usual to reach the big white Victorian at the top. He looked up. Kyra had left a living-room light on to welcome him home. *Home is the sailor, home from the sea, And the hunter home from the hill.*

But instead of turning left into the building's parking area, he pushed on through the deepening snow, straight up the Prom all the way to Congress, where he took a left. He drove three blocks, made another left, and then another, completing the circle. He pulled to a stop across the street from the building.

He sat in the dark, engine running, and imagined Kyra waiting upstairs. This afternoon's lovemaking seemed weeks and not mere hours ago. *Here he lies where he longed to be.* It was true. Still, something else tugged at him.

Did you love her then? Do you still love her now? Richard Wolfe had asked him during their sessions.

Not in the way you mean.

In what way, then?

In the only way I ever loved Sandy.

He needed time and space to understand why he reacted the way he did down at the Fish Pier. Why he was pushing Kyra so hard to marry. That would be impossible to do with her lying next to him. He knew that no matter how silently he crept into their room, she'd wake and smile. No matter how carefully he pulled off his clothes and slid between the sheets next to the warmth of her, she'd open her arms and wrap them around him in greeting. She'd ask about what happened at the Fish Pier and later on Harts Island. He'd tell her to go back to sleep, promise to tell her about it in the morning. She might do that. Might give him space to think. But she might not. And if she didn't, if, instead, she raised her head and propped it up on one hand and looked at him with those glorious, inquisitive eyes and said no, no, it was alright, he could tell her now, well, that just might be a problem. Because he wasn't ready yet to talk to her about the feelings Goff's resemblance to Sandy had triggered in him. He needed to understand all that himself first.

He glanced over at the snow-covered mound that was his own car. The classic '57 T-Bird convertible he and Sandy splurged on the first year they were married. The Bird was the only project that ever held both their hearts for more than a minute. And that included the daughter she never really wanted, the pregnancy she threatened to abort. He remembered how the two of them spent weekend after weekend working on the car together, restoring it to a gleaming newness that drew stares and admiring whistles from everyone who laid eyes on it. A thing of beauty and a joy forever. Sort of like Sandy herself. At least the beauty part. The car and Casey were all that remained from the ten years he invested in a failed marriage. Except, of course, for the rage and desire he sometimes felt in his dreams. Tonight on the Fish Pier those things made him feel, on some level, like he was being unfaithful to Kyra. He wasn't happy with that. It was something he needed to deal with.

McCabe slipped the car into drive and plowed his way back into the road. Once again he turned left toward Congress Street. This time he didn't drive in a circle.

Fourteen

Three forty-two Brackett was a three-story brick Victorian with a slate mansard roof set in a neighborhood where the elegance of Portland's West End began its slow transition into the small apartment houses, strip malls, and gas stations that lay farther north and east toward Longfellow Square. McCabe pulled in across the street and sat for a minute, engine running, and studied the building. Nice enough to serve as appropriate digs for a young lawyer on the upswing of her career, but not, he was sure, what Lainie ultimately aspired to.

There were no other cars on the street, the overnight parking ban having chased them all to designated downtown garages or school parking lots. He couldn't even see any evidence of Tasco's canvassers. They'd probably already covered the area and by now were blocks away.

On the porch McCabe could make out six small black mailboxes hung in two rows to the left of the glass-fronted doors. Six mailboxes. Six apartments. Headlights from a police cruiser approached in his rearview mirror. The unit passed by without slowing. When its taillights disappeared in the distance, McCabe pulled out and took a right around the corner. Fifty yards up, the familiar stone spire of St Luke's Episcopal loomed out of the snow-filled sky. The parking lot behind the church had already been plowed, probably a couple of times. He found a protected spot in the lee of the building and pulled in. He stuffed a flashlight and a pair of evidence gloves in the side pocket of his overcoat. He scrounged around the glove box but couldn't find any lock picks. Shockley sneered at such stuff as 'TV copudrama bullshit.' Maybe so, but useful bullshit as far as McCabe was concerned. Well, he'd have to do without.

He wrapped his coat tightly around himself, walked back to Brackett, crossed the street, and climbed five steps up to the porch. The tenants' names were printed on strips of white card stock and inserted into slots at the bottom of each numbered mailbox. E. Goff had lived in 2F. *F* had to stand for 'front,' because the only other letter designation was *R*. Apartment 2R was occupied by someone named K. Wilson. Like Tasco told him, Andrew Barker, the landlord, lived directly below Goff in 1F. A. Rosefsky and P. Donelley shared 1R. S. Hanley resided in 3F. And a pair of Chus, N. and T., were in 3R. None of the names meant anything to McCabe, and Tasco's team would have already knocked on all their doors and spoken to those who answered. Still, he might want to talk to them later. Apartment dwellers in Portland tended to notice the comings and goings of strange faces. He wondered which of them had known Lainie personally, which had been willing to share information about their dead neighbor.

Twin ovals of beveled glass, covered on the inside by white lace and framed in polished oak, graced the double front doors. He thought about ringing the bell for 1F and waking Barker but decided if he could handle the locks he'd rather go in unnoticed. He glanced back at the street.

No one in sight. He slipped on the evidence gloves and pushed down on the brass handle. To his surprise the door was unlocked. No copudrama bullshit required.

He found himself in a handsome if slightly faded hallway. Etched glass sconces bathed beige walls in soft light. The dark oak floor and stairs were covered with an Oriental runner that, despite a few worn spots, would muffle the sound of his steps. The place looked like Barker was trying. As he passed, McCabe glanced at his own image reflected in a large gilt-framed mirror hanging at the bottom of the stairs. He looked like shit.

He climbed up to the second floor and turned back toward 2F. There was no padlock on the door, no yellow crime scene tape crisscrossing the opening. Jacobi's team must've finished going over the place. He tried the lock, hoping it, too, had been left open. It hadn't, but it didn't much matter. The lock was an old-fashioned lever tumbler. *Easy pickin's, my man McCabe, easy pickin's*, he could hear his ex-NYPD partner Dave Hennings whispering in his comforting baritone. He fished in his wallet for two paper clips he kept stuffed at the bottom. He hadn't practiced the trick in a while and never had the deft hands Hennings had. Still, he was pretty sure the lock wouldn't present much of a challenge. He opened the first clip and bent one end to a ninety-degree angle. Then he opened the second and folded one of its ends over on itself, forming a loop. He squeezed the sides of the loop as closely together as he could and pushed it into the lock, applying steady tension to the left. At the same time, he inserted the angled end of clip number one into the lock just above the loop. He poked around until he found the first pin and pushed it down. Then he froze. He'd heard a sound. Had it come from inside the apartment? A radiator turning on? The creak of a floorboard from someone sneaking around inside? He stood silent and listened. Nothing. He waited a few seconds. Still nothing. He went back to his work. One by one he found the other pins and pushed. The lock slid open. It might have been easier with a set of professional picks, but not a whole lot faster or quieter.

McCabe pocketed the flashlight, drew his weapon, reached across, and slipped the latch. He pushed the door, waited a count of three, and swung into the room. He swept the .45 across the open space in a wide arc. Goff's living room lay empty and silent before him. From the opposite wall, ambient light from streetlamps reflected off the flakes of snow falling from the sky and spilled through the uncovered panes of a pair of large double-hung windows. He closed the door and flipped the lock. He stood motionless. Job number one was making sure he was alone.

In front of him were a white couch, two matching oversized easy chairs, and a glass-topped coffee table on its stainless steel base. All nearly identical to things Sandy bought for the apartment they shared on West Seventy-first Street and hauled off seven years later to Peter Ingram's house in East Hampton. It seemed beyond coincidence. Was God laughing at him, making him the butt of some sort of cosmic practical joke? The thought provoked an involuntary shiver. Then he pushed it away. Oversized white couches and glass coffee tables were as common as dirt, and the rest of the furnishings were different from anything he and Sandy had. Besides, Goff's stuff was new. Right out of the carton. By the time Sandy moved out, theirs was anything but.

He looked down at the high-concept Angela Adams rug in brownish reds that covered the floor under the coffee table. Kind of an autumn leaves motif. Nothing like anything on West Seventy-first Street, though he had seen the same one in the Adams window on Congress Street a few months back. Sandy might have liked it, but they'd never owned anything remotely similar. Goff had a lot of new stuff. New Beemer. New furniture. New rug. Plus an even newer two-week vacation at a high-end resort. Seemed to be upgrading her life to first class. Her six-figure salary was more than ample for a single woman living alone – sure as hell more than he was making – but why buy all these things at once? Had she just landed the partnership Kotterman said all young associates lusted after? He'd ask Ogden.

A small French writing desk stood against one wall. Rosewood with a leather top. It was either a real and very expensive antique or a very good repro. A pretty thing, beautiful wood and elegant curves – but, like the beautiful woman who owned it, the desk had recently been violated. Its three drawers hung open, a clutter of papers carelessly pulled from each. Most lay scattered on the floor below. A few stragglers floated indecisively, halfway in and halfway out. The bookcase on the opposite wall had suffered similar indignities. Volumes pulled from its shelves lay on the floor in haphazard piles. Many were still open, spines facing up, as if they'd been shaken to unearth papers hidden inside, then carelessly discarded.

Jacobi's crew never would have done this. They were

too methodical, too professional. Maggie certainly would have told him if they'd found it this way. No. Someone had searched the place since Jacobi left. A searcher who might still be here, hiding somewhere in the inner recesses of the apartment, his search interrupted by McCabe's unexpected appearance. What else could the sound he'd heard on the landing have been?

There was a single wood panel door to the right of the bookcases. McCabe stood to one side and yanked it open. He ran the beam of his flashlight across the interior. Coats and clothes on hangers. Boots and boxes on the floor, boxes neatly taped. The searcher hadn't looked in them. At least not yet. And no one was hiding behind them. The kitchen also showed signs of a hurried search. The cupboard drawers had been left open. One, Goff's junk drawer, had been upended, the drawer and its contents left in a pile on the floor. McCabe knelt and poked through the mess with a gloved hand. Nothing of interest that he could see.

He moved to the bathroom and entered gun first. A shade covered the locked window, and instead of raising it he used his light to see. It was an older bathroom, nicely outfitted. A shower curtain, decorated with staggered rows of little green palm trees, covered the claw-footed tub. He swept it aside in a single motion. No knife-wielding killer was hiding inside. Nothing to notice except some mascara and lipstick lying on the marble vanity next to the sink. A toothbrush and a tube of Crest were in a glass. Stuff she would have taken to Aruba. If she'd gone. Unless she had a duplicate set.

That left the bedroom. The searcher's last hidey-hole if

he was still in the apartment. McCabe checked his watch. Less than two minutes since he'd picked the lock. Not much time, but if the freak was in the bedroom, it was enough. His anxiety would be well cooked by now, pretty much reaching fever pitch. That made him more dangerous, more likely to do something stupid. Like attack a cop. McCabe had to assume he'd be armed. He killed Goff with a knife, but a gun was more lethal, and who said bad guys had to be consistent? *A foolish consistency is the hobgoblin of little minds.* Ralph Waldo Emerson, American philosopher, poet, and essayist. Born May 25, 1803, died April 27, 1882. More detritus from the brain-files of Michael McCabe. If the bad guy had a gun and killed McCabe, think of all the useless shit that would die with him.

Right now he wouldn't have minded backup, and he kind of wished Maggie were here. Too bad. The visit hadn't been planned, so he was on his own. But hey, they didn't call him the Lone Ranger for nothing. Right? Right. Hi-yo, Silver. He pressed his body against the side of the wall, hunkered down as low as he could get, and aimed his .45 slightly up and dead center. At that angle, if the bad guy was standing on the other side of the door, McCabe's shot ought to blow his balls off.

He rapped on the door with the barrel of the gun. No sound came in response. No bullets exploded through the thin oak panel. He rapped again. Still silence. He rose from his squat to a runner's crouch, slid his arm across the door frame, grasped the knob, and turned it as silently as possible. He willed the little hammer in his heart to stop pounding. He counted. One. Two. A pause. A sigh. His mouth formed the word 'three.' The door flew open.

McCabe moved in fast and low, sweeping the room, light in one hand, .45 in the other ready and eager to start blasting away.

The room lay empty and silent before him. He pointed the light this way and that. Nothing. He peered under the bedskirt. Still nothing. Just a book, a single slipper, and an impressive collection of dustballs. He crossed to the closet and pressed himself to one side of the door. He flung it open. Something black and silky fluttered in the whoosh of air. Everything else was still. McCabe peered in. Poked his light through the hanging clothes. More boxes. All stacked, sealed, and presumably checked only by Jacobi's ETs. He turned from the closet and looked at the windows. Draperies across all three. In *Hamlet*, Polonius met his maker behind the arras. Would the same hold true for the searcher? McCabe yanked the curtains aside. Nothing. Nobody. Just the windows, closed and locked.

He breathed easier. Maybe the searcher had found what he was looking for and left, or maybe he slipped out when he heard McCabe enter downstairs. Either way McCabe was alone. He holstered the .45 and took a deep breath. He was getting too old for this shit.

He looked around at a good-sized room, not crowded with furniture. The king-sized bed had been left unmade. Next to it was a nightstand with a lamp and an open paperback. Sue Grafton's *S is for Silence*. The lone drawer had been opened and searched. Ditto the drawers in the bureau on the opposite wall. A pile of neatly folded clothes sat next to a tub chair in one corner; a red canvas suitcase lay open and half filled on the floor. No ambient light entered this room. None would escape. McCabe turned on the lamp on the nightstand.

The wall above the bureau was covered with good art photography. He moved closer. Black-and-whites. Chemical prints, not digital. All matted and identically framed in black. A dozen pieces in all. Half were abstracted visions of a derelict urban landscape. Abandoned mills and factories. Broken bridges. Rotting piers. Hard black shapes crisscrossing in starkly graphic depictions of ruin and decay. The photographer had talent. Whoever he was. None of the shots was signed. All but one of the rest were female nudes. Erotic images of a single model, white body caught in angular, athletic poses silhouetted against an even whiter seamless background. In each, delicate patterns of light and shadow played against the model's pale flesh. All were beautiful, all anonymous. In three of the shots, dark hair covered the model's face. In two, head and face were cut off from view.

One image in particular held McCabe's gaze. Here a naked torso arched backward across a large black exercise ball. White legs were parted and thrust forward, knees bent, feet on the floor. Pubis, stomach, and ribs formed a smooth runway rising away from the camera to a far horizon of breasts and nipples, behind where both head and arms disappeared from view. Gazing at the picture, he felt a familiar stirring. Odysseus drawn by a siren's song. Was he lusting for a dead woman he'd never met? Or was it the wife he hated, yet still longed to possess? Awareness of desire brought revulsion. He turned his eyes away.

The one photo that didn't show Lainie's body showed her face, a silhouetted oval, luminous features emerging, seemingly disembodied, from the inky blackness of the background. Her eyes, light blue in life and gray in the black-and-white of the photograph, seemed to follow him as he moved from left to right in front of the picture. He closed his own eyes, not wanting to let what he was feeling overtake him. Like an addict resisting an alluring display of the opiate that once held him captive. Like a dry drunk hanging out in a bar. No. He couldn't go back. He wouldn't. Yes, Goff was dead. So, in her way, was Sandy. He knew he had to keep it that way.

Four o'clock. Hours until dawn. Feeling nothing inside but an aching weariness, McCabe went back to the kitchen. Except for the evidence of the search, the room was both empty and ordinary. Cupboards, cabinets, and appliances lined the wall to the right. An oak table with two chairs sat against a single window to the left. A pile of dirty dishes was stacked on a counter above an open and half-filled Bosch dishwasher. A dirty bowl and spoon sat on the table, contents dry and crusted – the remains of breakfast cereal eaten two weeks earlier. It was unlikely Goff would have left it this way before leaving for Aruba. Further evidence she never made it home that Friday night. McCabe squinted at the fridge door. A Concord Trailways timetable, held in place by a magnetized version of Slugger, the Portland Sea Dogs mascot. The 8:30 A.M. departure to Logan Airport was circled in red. He opened the fridge a crack, squeezed his arm inside and unscrewed the lightbulb, then opened the door wider and shined his own light in. Looked like Lainie was a fan of Stonewall Kitchen, a local purveyor of high-end jams, jellies, and sauces. There was also a plastic box of eggs laid by free-range hens fed, according to the label, a strictly vegetarian diet, a half-empty bottle of Vouvray, a bottle of skim milk with a use-by date of January 2, and two cardboard cartons of Chinese takeout. McCabe opened one. The chicken and pea pods inside had developed a serious case of fur. Had Goff ordered this stuff after leaving the office on the night of the twenty-third? No. Cleary said she used her Visa card at a Chinese restaurant on the twenty-second. If she'd made it home Friday, she would either have eaten or tossed any leftovers, knowing she'd be away for the next two weeks.

He closed the fridge and rooted around until he found what he was probably really looking for in the first place. A mostly full bottle of Chivas Regal. He looked at the amber liquid inside. He found a glass, poured out a couple of inches, closed the top. Then he reopened it and poured the whisky back, washed and dried the glass, and returned both bottle and glass to the pantry, exactly in the position he found them. He wasn't so far gone that he had to start drinking a murder victim's Scotch.

He went back to Goff's bedroom, moved the pile of clothes from the tub chair to the floor, and sat. Empty stomach or not, the whisky would've felt good going down. Just what he needed. Just what he didn't need. He closed his eyes and let his mind wander. Why had Lainie posed for the nude photographs? Why had she hung them here? If she was an exhibitionist, she was a careful one, exposing herself only in the most private of places. Whose eyes were the pictures intended for? Lovers and potential lovers? If so, why? To arouse them to a higher level of excitement? That idea seemed both ridiculous and redundant. Lainie in the flesh would arouse far more powerfully than any framed image, no matter how erotic. No, he decided. The pictures weren't for her lovers. They were for her.

He looked across at the bed and saw Lainie, or Sandy, he wasn't sure which, lying under him, dark hair fanned across white pillows, pleasure skittering across her face, shallow and transitory like cat's-paw ripples on the surface of the sea. From a vantage point of years, McCabe the auteur observed McCabe the lover's urgent thrusts, trying always to reach something deeper in the woman he married. Trying but failing. He knew their lovemaking was an act. It had always been an act, but it was an act that for years he couldn't resist. He looked into her eyes, preposterously blue, filled with love, but not for the extraneous, if sometimes useful, appendage she had married. Instead she focused on the images on the opposite wall. Narcissus at the pool, utterly enchanted with the perfection of her reflected self.

McCabe was jarred from his reverie by the sound of the apartment door opening and closing. Had the searcher returned to finish the job? McCabe slid the .45 from the holster to his hand, switched off the light, and felt his way through the dark to the other side of the room. He pressed himself into a corner between the bedroom door and the wall of photographs. He heard a soft thump, a whispered shout of 'Shit.' A dim light came on, leaking under the closed bedroom door. Not a steady light but moving like the beam of a flashlight in someone's hand. He heard steps coming closer. He held his breath.

The bedroom door opened. The searcher stood there,

moving a circle of light across the wall above the bed. He paused on the chair where McCabe had been sitting, then moved on. Seconds passed. A small man advanced into the room, his back to McCabe. He was no more than five-three or -four and slender. No, not slender. Skinny. One thirty, one forty tops. Thinning hair. Maybe the oddest thing about him was that, with ten-degree temperatures outside, the searcher wasn't wearing a coat. Just a checked shirt and an open cardigan. Mr Rogers visits a murder. He supposed the guy could have left his coat in the hall or taken it off in the other room, but why would he? Maybe he lived in the building.

The intruder had no sense he wasn't alone. No sense someone was standing less than four feet away pointing a .45 at the center of his back. Most people can tell. This guy couldn't. McCabe watched as he continued moving the beam of light around the room. He stopped when he got to the nude photographs. He moved closer and gazed at them, transfixed. Then he looked down into the open dresser drawer. Instead of continuing to rifle through the contents as McCabe expected, he pulled out a pair of Lainie Goff's lacy black thong panties and pressed them against his cheek. Finally McCabe raised the .45 so the guy would see it. 'First I'd like you to put the flashlight on the bureau,' he said, 'nice and slow, beam up. Then drop the panties.'

The guy turned toward McCabe, his expression more puzzled than surprised. He looked down at his own right hand, the one holding the light, but made no move to do as he was told.

'Be a good boy.' McCabe wiggled the barrel of his gun. 'No discussion. No arguments. Just put it down.'

The guy did. 'Are you the one who killed her?' he asked. His voice was quavery, as if he thought he might be next on the hit parade.

Maybe it was an honest question. Or maybe just a way to divert suspicion. McCabe moved to the bureau, picked up the flashlight, and pointed the beam against the opposite wall. 'Please step over there, lean against the wall with both hands, and spread your legs.'

'You mean assume the position?'

'Very good. Assume the position.'

'Who are you?' the guy asked in a high-pitched voice.

'I'm the man with the gun. That means I get to ask the questions and you get to do as you're told.'

The guy went to the wall and leaned against it. His left hand was still clutching Lainie's panties.

McCabe switched on a standing lamp next to the bureau. The sudden brightness revealed that the intruder was a soft, nerdy-looking man in his early forties, more milquetoast than murderer. He was wearing a brown leather tool belt around his waist. Pliers, screwdrivers, a hammer, some other stuff.

'Undo the tool belt and let it drop to the floor.'

The guy did.

'Very good. Now, my first question is, who are you?'

'Me?' the guy squeaked.

'I don't see anyone else in the room. Do you?'

'No. No, I don't. Name's Andy Barker,' the guy said. 'I own this building.' Then, as if it just occurred to him, 'Actually, you're trespassing on my property.'

McCabe ignored the last remark. 'Got any ID, Mr Barker? Don't reach for it. Just tell me where it is.'

'In my wallet. Back pocket. Left.'

McCabe walked over and kicked the tool belt out of reach. He patted the guy down, then fished out the wallet. He found a Maine driver's license. Andrew Barker. Age forty-two. Address 342 Brackett Street. He shoved the wallet back in Barker's pocket. 'Thank you, Mr Barker. For the record, I'm Detective Sergeant Michael McCabe, Portland police.'

Barker let out a long breath he'd been holding in for a while. Probably thought a cop was less likely to shoot him than some random guy with a gun. 'Police, huh. Yeah.' He nodded. 'Yeah. That's what I figured.'

'I have another question.' McCabe holstered the .45. 'What are you doing here?'

Barker shrugged. 'Like I told you, I own this building. I'm Lainie Goff's landlord.'

'Do you normally visit your tenants' apartments unannounced –'

'Unannounced? Who am I supposed to announce it to? Goff's dead.'

'Unannounced at four fifteen in the morning?'

'I'm an early riser.' Now he was playing the wiseguy.

'Keep talking.'

'Well, I figured I was gonna have to find a new tenant. I wanted to see what kind of shape the place was in. How much stuff'd have to be moved out.' They both knew that was bullshit. Barker was just trying it on for size.

'You were carrying the tools for what reason exactly?'

Barker shrugged again. 'I don't know. I usually wear a

tool belt. In case anything needed fixing?' His voice rose at the end of the last sentence, making it more question than assertion.

McCabe decided it was time to cut the crap. 'I think you can do better than that, Mr Barker. Now, what were you doing entering a murdered woman's apartment carrying a flashlight and a set of tools in the middle of the night? And what exactly are you doing with her underwear?'

Barker started looking around like he wanted to be anywhere but leaning against a wall in front of McCabe. 'Mind if I sit down?' he asked.

'Over there,' said McCabe, pointing to the tub chair. Barker lowered his hands and sat.

'Now answer the question, Mr Barker. Why are you here?'

'I was curious. Like I told the other detective, the woman, Ms Savage, I'm kind of a fan of police stuff. Wanted to have a look around. Scene of the crime and all that.'

More bullshit. 'You were up here before, weren't you, Mr Barker?'

'Yeah. Sure. I've been up here a couple of times. When Ms Goff needed something fixed or had a problem with something.'

McCabe went to where Barker was sitting, put his hands on the chair's two arms, and leaned in close. 'I want some straight answers, Andy,' he said. 'You don't mind if I call you Andy, do you?'

Barker looked up and shook his head no.

'That's good, Andy. Now no more bullshit. You came up here earlier tonight, didn't you?'

Barker shook his head again. 'No. Well, yes, but only to let the other detectives in.'

'Then you came back. After they left. And you started going through Lainie Goff's belongings like you were looking for something, didn't you, Andy? And it wasn't just underwear, was it?'

Barker shook his head, confused.

'What were you looking for?'

'I wasn't looking for anything. I wasn't even up here.'

'Was it something incriminating? Something that might tie you to the murder? Is that what you were looking for?'

'I told you, I wasn't here. I wasn't looking for anything.' Barker tried to get up out of the chair, but McCabe was blocking the way. He sat back down. 'I want to go home now.' He sounded like a child who wasn't having fun with his playmates anymore.

'I'd rather you stayed where you are, Andy. I'd rather you told me what you were looking for when you came up and ransacked Lainie Goff's personal things earlier tonight.'

'You're trying to make like I had something to do with her murder, aren't you? 'Cause if that's what you're trying to do, that's just total bullshit.'

Barker seemed near tears. He was looking everywhere except at McCabe. Mostly he was glancing over at the wall of pictures above the bureau. The nudes of Lainie Goff.

'She was a good-looking woman, wasn't she, Andy?'

'Who?'

'Your tenant. Ms Goff.'

'Yes. She's beautiful. She *was* beautiful.'

'Woman like that could make a man do all kinds of things he might not do otherwise, don't you think, Andy?'

'What are you talking about? I don't know what you're talking about.'

'Are you a married man, Andy? Is there a nice little Mrs Andy downstairs in 1F waiting for you? One who'll vouch for where you were Tuesday night around, oh, I don't know, eleven o'clock or so?'

'No. I'm not married. Besides, I don't see what business it is of yours where I was Tuesday or any other night.' Barker's voice was swinging wildly between panicked and petulant.

'You've got a key to this apartment, isn't that right, Andy?' asked McCabe.

'Of course. I've got keys to all the tenants' apartments.'

'And you just used that key to gain access to this apartment?'

'Yes.'

'Did you find what you were looking for?'

'I told you I wasn't looking for anything.'

'Not even a pair of Lainie Goff's black lace thong panties?'

Barker looked down and realized he was still clutching the panties in his left hand. He dropped them like they were on fire.

'Maybe you also used your key to gain access to this apartment earlier tonight? After the crime scene people left and before I showed up.'

'No.'

'Maybe you came in and went through Lainie Goff's drawers and personal effects?'

'No.'

'What were you looking for, Mr Barker?'

'I'm not talking to you anymore.'

'Something personal? Maybe something even sexier than those panties? Something that might turn you on?'

'I know my rights, and I don't have to talk to you. I have the right to remain silent.'

'I know. I'll bet you were looking for more pictures of Goff naked. I mean, if she's got those over there right out in the open, she's probably got even better ones in her drawer, don't you think? Is that what you were looking for?' McCabe pointed over to the open drawers in the bureau. 'Or maybe you're just into underwear? Frilly, lacy black underwear? She probably has lots more of it in there. You the kind of guy that gets turned on by a good-looking woman's underwear? Is that what you were looking for?'

'I have the right to remain silent,' Barker said again. 'Anything I say can and will be used against me in a court of law. I have the right to have an attorney present during questioning –'

'Yes you do, Mr Barker, but you're not under arrest or anything like that. We're just having a friendly little chat. Guy talk, that's all.'

'I have the right to remain silent,' Barker repeated.

'I'm just trying to figure out what you were doing wandering around up here with a flashlight and a bunch of tools at four o'clock in the morning.'

'I'd like you to leave my house now,' Barker said.

'What were you looking for, Barker?'

'I want you to leave my house. Or get yourself a warrant and come back later.'

This was a murder victim's apartment, and McCabe didn't need a warrant to be here. On the other hand, it was pretty clear he wasn't going to get anything else out of Andy Barker. He needed to find out what, if anything, the evidence techs had found here and what they'd found in the house on the island. More than either of those things, he needed some sleep.

In the end McCabe told Barker to go back down to his apartment but not to leave town and to make himself available if he was needed for further questioning. Then he called 109 and told Dispatch to send over an evidence tech to see if the searcher had left behind any fingerprints or other evidence and then padlock the place and make sure nobody else snuck in. When the tech got there, McCabe left.

The snow was still coming down at 5:00 A.M. when McCabe got back to his own place on the Eastern Prom. The light in the living room was still on; Kyra was in the bedroom still asleep. He stripped down and slid into bed next to her. He had that ten o'clock meeting but still had time for a few hours' sleep. With Casey at Sunday River, he wouldn't have to wake up until about nine thirty to make it downtown by ten. Trying not to disturb Kyra, but feeling a need for her warmth, he pressed his body, spoon fashion, against the bend of her back. He rested one arm along the curve of her hip.

'I'm glad you're back,' she said. 'I was beginning to worry.'

'I'm sorry. I didn't mean to wake you.'

'You didn't. I've been awake pretty much all night. Anyway, welcome home.'

He pushed himself even more tightly against her. 'It's good to be home,' he said. He meant it. He was glad he did.

Fifteen

Abby moved, mask on, head down, Spider-Man trudging through a fog of silence. The snow, whipped by gusting winds, was blinding. Forced by drifts to walk on the road, she could barely see the houses behind the mounds of snow, let alone make out their shapes or colors. Not even the ones on the near side of the street. The ones on the far side were totally invisible. She'd been walking for hours, or was it days? She was sure she was going around in circles. She couldn't concentrate on where she was or where she was headed. She was just too tired. All she knew was that there were no people and there were no cars. There was only the snow and the wind and the endless empty streets. She'd never felt so alone in her life.

At least the Voices were quiet. The meds were doing what they were supposed to do, keeping the crazies locked in their box where they couldn't jump out and torment her. Even so, all it would take was a little bit of bad shit and, boom, there they'd be, popping up like jack-in-the-box clowns, loud and vindictive. On top of that, the extra pills were making her dopey. Forcing her to fight for every clear thought through a fuzziness that seeped in and around and through her brain. Screw it. She didn't have to think right now. She just had to keep walking. Street to street. Block to block. Don't think. Just walk.

As she walked she repeated a low rhythmic chant. *Gotta find Leanna's house. Gotta find Leanna's house. Gotta find Leanna's house.* Leanna Barnes, her friend from Winter Haven. Leanna would take her in. Abby knew she would. Bury her in the big extravagant folds of her flesh. Keep her safe. Leanna wouldn't tell anyone she was there, either. Except Abby couldn't find the right house or even the right street. She'd only been to the house a couple of times before, and then always in the summer when everything was green and gold and you could see where you were going. Not this blinding white, this emptiness where even the street signs were impossible to read. She was too tired and too cold to walk much farther. She was starting to go numb.

All she really wanted to do was lie down on top of the snowbank at the side of the road and drift off to sleep. She'd be covered up in no time. The plows'd dump more snow on top of her and that'd be that. The trash collectors wouldn't find her body till spring. Trash. That's all she'd be in the end. Frozen trash. She remembered seeing on the Discovery Channel how people who freeze to death feel warm before they die. They just slowly go to sleep and never wake up. It seemed a pleasant idea. Burning to death would be a lot more painful. One time, when she was off her meds, the Voices tried to get her to pour gasoline over her head and set herself on fire. *Gonna turn you into a crispy critter,* they told her. She went and found the gas can in the shed next to the house and a box of matches

191

and almost did what they said. She remembered their mocking voices. *Crispy critter. Fried golden brown. Crispy critter.* She thought the fire would purify her, exorcise the evil, rid her of the Voices. At least she hoped it would. She unscrewed the top of the gas can and held it over her head. In the end, though, she chickened out. The idea of burning up scared her too much, and she put the can away. She wasn't *that* crazy. But the Voices kept spewing their filth and ugliness. How they hated her. She must deserve it.

Abby looked up and saw a low dark thing moving toward her. A black form, now visible through the whipping snow, now obliterated by it. With each step it grew clearer and bigger. At twenty feet it began to take shape. Animal. Not human. A large dog, gray fur glistening under crystals of snow, cruel icy eyes shining through the night, more wolf than dog. She stopped, but the animal kept coming. She could hear its rumbling growl. Low. Menacing. Commanding. Her heart beat against the walls of her chest so hard she was certain it would break through. She knew what the creature wanted. She knelt on her hands and knees. It bared a fang long enough and sharp enough to penetrate the soft flesh at the back of her neck. She lowered her head and waited for release . . . but release didn't come. Finally, after a minute or two, she looked up, and it was gone. She could see nothing in front of her but the snow-covered street and the windswept flakes still hurtling down through the night sky. She stayed where she was, kneeling in the snow. She could hear a child crying. She listened. After a bit she realized the sound was coming from her. She got up and started walking again.

She wrapped her arms around her body and rubbed to warm herself. She was still wearing the running clothes from four nights ago. After the cop dropped her off, she hadn't taken the time to change or brush her teeth or even to wash. She didn't know when Death was going to come walking in through the door. So she just stuffed the seventeen dollars and sixty-three cents she had in the desk drawer into one pocket, her wallet with her license and nearly maxed-out Visa card into the other, and took off. She had her cell in her fanny pack, along with the bottle of Zyprexa, but the phone was dead and the charger was in her bedroom back on the island. Dumb. She couldn't worry about that now. All she knew was that she had to get to Leanna's house. If only she could find it. She thought about a hot shower. God, that would be heaven. She'd take a hot shower at Leanna's.

Ahead of her, up the hill, she saw the lights of a twenty-four-hour Mini Mart on Congress. She was sure she'd passed the place twice before. This time she'd go in, warm up, try to figure out where it was Leanna lived and how to get there. A comforting wave of heated air hit her as she opened the door. The woman behind the counter was munching peanut M&M's out of one of those big yellow family-sized bags and watching a small black-and-white TV. She stiffened as Abby approached. Didn't move. Just sat there staring, eyes widening in fear. Abby whipped around, expecting Death to be right behind her, but he wasn't. Nothing was there.

'What do you want?' the woman asked in a quavery voice. 'We ain't got much cash here.'

Abby puzzled over that until she finally figured it out. She was still wearing the Spider-Man mask. She pulled it off along with her ski hat and stuffed both into her pocket. She ran a hand through her matted hair and forced herself to smile. 'Sure is cold out there.'

'Jesus Christ, girl. You scared me half to death. What the hell you doin' walkin' around with that thing on?' The woman seemed to relax a little. 'I almost hit the damned alarm.' She took a deep breath, relaxed some more. 'It's cold, alright,' she said. 'Down near zero.' Then, after a few more seconds, she added, 'They say we're gonna get more'n a foot.'

Act normal, Abby reminded herself. No crazy stuff. Not here. She nodded to the woman's comment, as if considering its wisdom and, upon due consideration, concurring. 'Probably got pretty near that much already.' Abby smiled again, figuring you couldn't smile too much. Then she walked over to the coffee station, took off her gloves, clipped them to the bottom of her jacket, and pulled out the smallest of the three sizes of cardboard cups. She pushed down the spigot on the hot chocolate machine and watched steamy brown liquid trickle into her cup.

'Pretty near that much,' the woman agreed, peering out the window. 'It don't look like it's stopping anytime soon, either.'

Abby pushed one of the plastic lids onto her cup until it clicked into place. She walked back toward the counter. The cup felt hot under her hands. She shifted it from one hand to the other, thawing her fingers, enjoying the warmth.

The woman swept her arm toward a car shape outside

the window, completely covered with snow. 'That there's mine. Hope I don't have any trouble getting home.'

'Hope not,' Abby said, putting the cup on the counter.

'That do it for you?'

Abby nodded.

'Be a dollar fifty-eight.'

Abby counted out exact change from the seventeen dollars and sixty-three cents she had in her pocket, smiled again, and headed back toward the bathroom. She set the hot chocolate on the edge of the sink, locked the door, peed, and washed her hands, surprised how much the warm water stung her frozen skin. She stared for a minute at her face in the mirror. The last four days had taken their toll. She had dark circles under her eyes. Her hair looked dirty. She was surprised the woman wasn't more scared of her with the mask off than with it on.

She only half noticed the big blond guy when she exited the restroom, and then only because all her systems were on high alert. He was standing in the grocery aisle pretending to study the plastic microwave cups of beef stew and Chef Boyardee pasta. His eyes followed her when she walked past him to the newspaper and maga-zine rack. She picked up one of the freebie newspapers, the *West End News*, and pretended to read. The guy was still looking at her. He wasn't big. He was huge, six foot five, maybe more. Big neck and shoulders. He was wear-ing jeans and a lumber jacket. She turned back to the paper and sipped her hot chocolate slowly, trying to figure out what to do next. She couldn't go back out in the cold. Not yet. She needed to stretch her drink out for as long as it took her to really get warm again. But he was making her nervous. She glanced over again. He smiled. At least it was a friendly smile. Not a leer. She quickly looked away. Shit, he was coming toward her. Act normal, she thought. Tough it out. Her heart was pounding. She could hear the Voices starting to rouse themselves from their slumber. *Here comes Death*, one of them said. Even though he didn't look like Death. At least not like Death had looked in the bedroom at the Markhams' place.

'You okay?' he asked, walking up close to her, cradling an armful of plastic Chef Boyardee containers. 'You look kind of upset.'

Tell him to go fuck himself, the Voices said. *Tell him to go stick his big fat dick in his big fat ass.*

'Yes. No. Yes,' Abby said to the guy. The words came out in too much of a jumble. 'I'm fine.' She realized she was craning her neck to look up at him. He was so tall it was like looking up at the top of the Observatory. Or the Empire State Building. 'I'm fine,' she said again. 'Nothing the matter with me.' She was still talking too fast. Too loud. She had to slow it down. She took a deep breath. 'I'm just walking to my friend's house,' she said. There. That was better.

'Walking? In this? Are you crazy?'

The Voices cackled. They thought that was a good joke. She closed her eyes, determined to ignore them. 'It's not far,' she said. 'Just over on . . .' She thought as hard as she could, and suddenly there it was. The name of the street. 'Just over on Summer Street.' Yes. Summer Street. Where she'd gone in the summer. Maybe that was the problem. Maybe you couldn't get there in winter.

'Y'know, Summer Street's a good hike away. Why don't I give you a ride?'

'No. No.' She concentrated on sounding normal. 'That's not necessary.'

'Well, it might not be necessary,' he said, scratching his head with his free hand, 'but it'd sure as heck be warmer than you walking all that way. Probably safer, too, on a night like tonight. I wouldn't forgive myself if somebody froze to death walking, when I could just take 'em over to where they were going in a couple of minutes. What do you say? My truck's right outside. I left it running.' He gave her a big toothy grin. 'To keep it warm,' he added.

She wasn't sure why, but she felt herself giving in. This man just didn't feel dangerous, and the idea of driving to Leanna's in a warm truck was practically irresistible. She pointed at the half-dozen plastic containers resting in his arm. 'You eat that stuff?' she asked.

He blushed. 'Yeah.'

Yes, it was okay. Death wouldn't blush. She didn't think a rapist would either.

'Actually, I kind of like it.'

Death probably wouldn't eat Beefaroni either, even though enough of that stuff could probably kill you. Abby let herself relax. The Voices slid back into their box. She followed the tall man to the front of the store.

'Hey, Esther,' he said to the woman behind the counter. He dumped the microwave containers in front of her.

'How you doing, Joe?' she said, waving a handheld bar code scanner over each. 'You guys caught that killer yet?'

'Not yet.' He looked back at Abby. 'What's your name?' he asked.

'Abby.'

He waited a few seconds before asking, 'Don't you want to know what my name is?'

She shrugged.

'I'm Joe.' He held out a hand. She shook it.

It was only when he reached for his wallet to pay for the Beefaroni that she noticed the gun poking out from under his jacket. Her heart started doing its pounding thing again. The woman behind the counter gave him his change and put the containers into a plastic bag.

'Let's go,' he said, smiling again.

She followed numbly. The storm was, if anything, worse than before. As they headed for his truck, she thought that maybe she ought to make a run for it. But, in the end, she decided she'd rather die inside a warm truck than freeze to death out there on Congress Street. That wasn't being crazy, she told herself. Just smart. He clicked the doors open, and they climbed in. He stowed the bagful of Chef Boyardee behind the seat on top of a pair of snowshoes and what looked like a rolled-up sleeping bag and some other stuff as well. Under it there was an ice ax. He saw her looking at it.

'I'm on my way up to Katahdin,' he said. 'I've got a couple of days off, and I'm gonna do a little snowshoeing and some winter camping. Some ice climbing as well. That's what that ax is for.'

She put the hot chocolate in the cup holder and rested her hands on her lap. If he was going camping in this weather, he was even crazier than she was.

He must have sensed what she was thinking, because he said, 'No, really. It's fun, Abby. Least it is if you have the right equipment.'

She didn't say anything. Just tried to get another peek at the gun. He was putting on his seat belt and she couldn't see it. Then he waited while she did up her belt. She watched him release the parking brake and turn in his seat so he could see to back up. When he did, there was the gun again, poking out.

'Are you going to shoot me?' She hadn't planned on asking him that. The words just spilled out all by themselves. He stepped on the brake and stopped the truck halfway in and halfway out of the parking space.

'What? What in hell are you talking about? I think maybe you *are* crazy.'

'You have a gun. I saw it.'

'Yes, I have a gun. I'm supposed to have a gun,' he said.

'Nobody's *supposed* to have a gun.' Maybe he was Death after all.

'I am. I'm a cop. Really, Abby, it's okay.'

He smiled again. That friendly reassuring smile that made the Voices yawn and go back to sleep. He took out a wallet from a jacket pocket and flipped it open. A badge and an ID card with his picture on it. Portland Police Department. Joseph L. Vodnick. He handed her a card and said, 'Listen, Abby, if you're ever afraid of something or worried or anything, you just call the number on this card and I'll come right over. Okay?'

Abby looked at the card and nodded, but she didn't say anything back. After that she just stared straight ahead as they drove, watching the wipers wipe the snow away.

Sixteen

Portland, Maine
Saturday, January 7
9:00 A.M.

McCabe inched toward consciousness, eyes closed, sunshine warming his face. Someone must have opened the blinds and let the sun in. The brightness hurt even behind his closed lids. Not a nice thing to do to someone who'd only had a couple of hours of sleep. He slid his hand over to the other side of the bed, felt around, and came up empty. Explored further. Nothing but sheet.

'Looking for something?'

Kyra's voice came from behind him. She sounded amused, and he thought she had a hell of a nerve sounding amused at this ungodly hour of the morning. He thought back and remembered all he'd drunk and all he hadn't eaten the night before. Amazingly he didn't have a headache. Just a hell of a thirst. Nothing that would qualify as a hangover. He figured that most of what he was feeling was from lack of sleep. He flopped over onto his left side and squinted at her. 'What time is it?'

She was sitting in the bentwood rocker sipping coffee. 'Nine fifteen.'

He absorbed this information. Nodded. Okay. Nine fifteen. Four hours' sleep. Plenty enough for anyone. He opened his eyes farther. She was wearing an oversized New York Giants jersey with Tiki Barber's number twenty-one on it and a pair of plaid pajama bottoms. Both were his.

'Can I get you some coffee?'

He grunted something vaguely affirmative. She pulled herself out of the rocker and headed for the kitchen. By the time she got back he was sitting up. She put a mug of coffee on the bedside table and handed him a large glass of orange juice.

'Here. You looked like you could use this as well.'

'Thank you.' He chugged it down in a couple of gulps, then traded the glass for the coffee. 'How was your show last night?'

'Excellent. Over a hundred people. Two red dots and a lot of positive ego massaging from all and sundry.'

'Including Kleinerman?'

'Umm. Yes. He interviewed me. Said there'd be a piece in tomorrow's paper.'

'Tomorrow tomorrow or tomorrow today?'

'Tomorrow tomorrow. Sunday. How was your murder?'

He took a deep breath. 'Pretty ugly,' he said, sipping at the coffee. 'A young woman. Lawyer here in town. Somebody stuck a knife in her neck and stuffed her body into the trunk of her own car. She was frozen solid. The weird thing, at least for me, was that she was the spitting image of Sandy. I mean identical.'

She looked at him curiously. 'Did that bother you?'

He didn't respond for a minute. Finally he said, 'Yeah. It did. At first. For a minute I had this crazy idea that it was Sandy and that I'd done it, like in my dreams. But once I got used to the idea that the victim wasn't either my ex-wife or my kid's mother and that I wasn't the murderer, I calmed down.' Not quite the whole truth, but close enough to holler at. Even better, it hadn't bothered him telling her about the murder or Goff's resemblance to Sandy, which he figured had to be a good sign.

'Do you know who did it?'

'You know the old cliché, everyone's a suspect, which, roughly translated, means we haven't got a clue.'

'Which, roughly translated, means this case is going to take all your time and attention.'

'For a while, yeah, I think it will.'

Kyra sipped her coffee, thinking about what he'd said. Finally she nodded. More to herself than to him. 'Okay. I'm going to move back to my own place.'

'For good?'

'No. For the time being. Until this is resolved. Until we can really be together again.'

'That isn't necessary.'

'I think it is. It's what I was talking about yesterday. I don't want to spend all my time wondering what you're doing or what time you're going to be coming home. If I'm at my place I won't be thinking about it so much. Just let me know when it's over, and I'll come on back, happy as a clam, wagging my tail.'

He ignored the mixed metaphor. Or simile. Or whatever it was. 'So we're not going to see each other at all?' He noticed his bare foot tapping on the floor. 'What about having dinner together?'

'We can do that. If you're ever free for dinner, which, based on past experience, I don't think is likely. The way

I figure it is when you're up to your ears in a murder we don't see each other anyway.'

'You won't mind if I call you?'

'I'd mind if you didn't.'

'Okay. I guess.' McCabe brightened. 'How about conjugal visits? Like they allow in prison?'

'Really? They allow that? In prison?'

'In New York they do. And I think California.'

'How about Maine?'

'I don't think so.'

'Well, there you go, then.'

While Kyra went off to take a shower and collect her stuff, McCabe threw on a robe and went into the living room to call Henry Ogden's home number, the one Beth Kotterman had given him. The lawyer picked up on the third ring. McCabe told him who he was and why he was calling, but before he could ask for a meeting Ogden slipped smoothly into corporate bullshit mode, letting McCabe know that Beth Kotterman had called him late last night and informed him of Lainie's death and what a shock it would be to everybody at the firm, especially to those who worked closely with her, as he did, in Palmer Milliken's M&A practice area. Yes, it was a terrible thing, and the firm would have to do something special in the way of a memorial service. McCabe closed his eyes and let Ogden rattle on for a while, only half listening, trying to attach a face to the voice. Randall Jackson's description of that last Friday before Christmas ran through his mind. Ogden sounded like Jackson said he looked. A rich white guy.

Finally McCabe cut in on the oration. 'Excuse me,

Mr Ogden. I understand how upset everybody must be, but I was hoping you and I could have a little chat in person.'

'About Lainie?'

What the hell did he think McCabe wanted to talk to him about? 'Yes. About Lainie, and about her murder.'

'I'm not sure what I can add . . .'

'As an attorney, I'm sure you understand how important it is that we talk to everyone who knew her, everyone who worked with her. We want to get as complete a picture as possible of Lainie's life and why someone might have wanted to end it.'

Ogden tried to interrupt, but this time it was McCabe who kept talking. 'I'd like to meet with you as soon as possible. Later this morning or early this afternoon if that works for you.'

'I'm afraid it's not terribly convenient. Barbara and I are having guests from out of town over for lunch. She's been planning it for some time, and you know how women are when husbands mess up their plans.' He chuckled in a man-to-man way.

McCabe wondered if Ogden was trying to avoid a meeting – and if so, why? He wouldn't let him off the hook that easily. 'It's important, Mr Ogden, and it shouldn't take very long.'

'Couldn't we do this tomorrow?'

'Today would be better.'

'Oh, alright,' Ogden said, not trying to hide his impatience. 'If you can be here at ten thirty I'll see if I can spare you half an hour or so.'

'Where do you live?'

'Cape Elizabeth.'

McCabe checked his watch. It was nine thirty. No part of Cape Elizabeth was more than twenty minutes away. If he moved fast he could grab a shower and still be there easily. He'd rather meet with Ogden at 109, but then again, going to his house would give him a chance to see how the man lived. The only other problem was the ten o'clock meeting with his detectives. He'd have to ask Maggie to run it and fill him in later. He was sure she'd be okay with that. 'Fine,' he said. 'I'll see you at ten thirty sharp.'

'Good. Our cottage is at 367 Ledge Road. Do you know where that is?'

'No, but I can find it.'

McCabe was showered, shaved, and out the door by ten. The parking area downstairs was plowed, and it took him less than five minutes to clear the snow and ice from the Crown Vic and pull out onto the Eastern Prom. He headed down Fore Street and then veered left by the statue of John Ford onto York Street heading toward the bridge. He'd be on Ledge Road with time to spare unless the bridge was stuck in the open position for the passage of a freighter or high-masted sailboat. It wasn't. He followed Route 77 through South Portland and into Cape Elizabeth. The town was one of Portland's most affluent suburbs and consisted mostly of broad, curving streets with large, comfortable colonials and Victorians set on oversized wooded lots. It housed a significant percentage of Portland's doctors, lawyers, and stockbrokers and, he guessed, the largest percentage of stay-at-home moms in the entire state.

It was a bright, clear day. Crisp and cold but still beautiful. Virginal snow lined either side of the roads. Following the directions he found on Google Maps, he turned left at Old Ocean House Road, left again at Trundy Point, then a slight left onto Ledge Road, which ran no more than a hundred yards inland from the open ocean and had to be one of the best addresses in town. Number 367 was on the left, marked by a large black rural mailbox. Just numbers. No name. The house itself, as well as the ocean behind it, was hidden from view by a dense stand of birch and maple, bare limbs covered in a delicate filigree of snow. He turned down a private drive that, at ten thirty on a Saturday morning, after a more than twelve-inch snowfall, was already neatly plowed and sanded. The drive curved through the woods for nearly a hundred yards before opening onto a white gravel parking area, also immaculately plowed. He pulled the Crown Vic into a parking area to the right of the house between a black Mercedes-Benz 500 S-Class – appropriate wheels for one of the top lawyers in town – and a ten-year-old Ford Taurus with a dented rear fender. No snow on the Merc. Ogden had already been out and about this morning.

McCabe got out and looked around. The hundred-year-old shingle-style cottage, as Ogden called it, was a cottage the same way Mt Washington was a hill. McCabe gauged the house at a minimum of six or seven thousand square feet set on at least three acres of spectacular oceanfront property. He was five minutes early but had no intention of standing around in the cold until the appointed hour. He headed up the path to the front door and rang the bell. Chimes echoed inside. The door opened, and a middle-aged woman, wearing jeans and a sweatshirt and holding a plastic bucket, stood looking at him.

'Mrs Ogden?' he asked, pretty sure it wasn't her.

'No. I'm Chloe. I'll go get her for you.'

'Actually, I'm looking for Mr Ogden. I'm Detective Michael McCabe.'

'I know who you are. Come on in. You're letting all the heat out.'

McCabe moved into the front hall.

'I recognize you. I saw you on TV last year. After that murder of the teenaged girl. Katie Dubois. That was you, right?'

They called Portland a city, but it was amazing what a small town it really was. Everybody knew everybody. In New York no one would have remembered. 'Yup. That was me.'

'I'll get him. Take your shoes off before you walk any-where. I just finished the floors.' He did as he was told. 'You can give me your coat.'

She went off, bucket and coat in hand, and disappeared down the hall to the back of the house.

McCabe looked around. Oversized cottage or not, the place was spectacular. High ceilings, fabulous moldings, and stained glass windows. From where he stood he could see at least two fireplaces. Both had wood fires burning away in them.

'Lieutenant McCabe?' A good-looking man, tall and slender, with expensively cut gray hair and a confident manner, walked toward him. Even dressed down in faded blue jeans and a Helly Hansen fleece jacket, and even with a day's growth of gray bristle covering his pink cheeks,

Ogden looked like a Hollywood casting director's dream choice for an A-list lawyer. 'Hank Ogden,' he said, extending a hand. McCabe shook it. He recognized Ogden as one of the guys standing next to Goff, wearing black tie, in the photo Tasco had shown them.

'Thanks for the promotion, Mr Ogden, but it's Sergeant. Detective Sergeant, actually.' McCabe held up his badge wallet. Ogden ignored it, so McCabe put it away. 'Beautiful place you have here.'

'Yes, it is. An early John Calvin Stevens. Built in 1897 and, except for the kitchen and bathrooms, still mostly original. It's been in my wife's family for some time.'

McCabe had heard of Stevens. The best-known Portland architect of the last century, he'd been the go-to guy for fancy houses in and around the city from about 1890 until the 1930s. Anybody who lived in a John Calvin Stevens house bragged about it. Even taciturn Yankees. They just bragged more discreetly.

Ogden led him into a small book-lined study. A fire was gently crackling in yet another fireplace, this one an Adam. He pointed McCabe to one of two red leather wing chairs. He sat in the other. He studied McCabe for a moment, then took a sip of coffee from a bone china cup with pink flowers printed on the outside. McCabe wouldn't have minded coffee himself, but Ogden didn't offer any, and McCabe wasn't about to ask.

'As I told you on the phone, Sergeant, my time's limited, so let's get right to it. What would you like to know?'

'Tell me about Elaine Goff.'

'What is there to tell? Lainie was a brilliant, beautiful woman and a fine lawyer. Well on her way to becoming a partner at the firm. She would have been one of the youngest we've ever had.' He put on his sad face. 'Her death is a tragedy beyond words.'

'Do you know why anyone would want to kill her?'

'I can't imagine. I have to believe it was a random attack. Robbery or maybe rape as the motive. You know more about these things than I do.'

'You and Elaine Goff were the last two attorneys to sign out from Palmer Milliken her last day at the office. That was Friday, December twenty-third.' McCabe paused, wondering if Ogden would care to comment. He didn't. 'You signed out ten minutes after she did, at ten after nine. Did you happen to see her in the office before you left?'

'Yes, as a matter of fact, I did. We had a late meeting. From about eight thirty to nine that evening. There were a couple of things Lainie wanted to wrap up before she left for vacation.'

'Such as?'

'I don't see how that's pertinent to your investigation.'

If you were fucking her on your desk, asshole, it might be very pertinent was what McCabe wanted to say. He settled for the weaker and less incendiary 'Whatever was on Goff's mind, whatever she talked about, may have affected her actions later. It might help us find her killer.'

Ogden didn't say anything, and his blank face revealed nothing. Probably a hell of a poker player. Finally he spoke. 'Well, I don't see what this could possibly have to do with her death, but the meeting was about Lainie's partnership. She was eager to get it before the end of the year. It would have been a very early offer. She's only been with Palmer Milliken for six years. However, I thought the quality of her work warranted consideration. For that reason I sponsored her for admission to the firm at a partners' meeting held earlier that evening.'

'Was an offer extended?'

'No. My colleagues thought it was too early and that Lainie should wait another year. That's when most PM partnerships are awarded. I argued in her favor, but to no avail.'

'You told her that when you met?'

'Yes.'

'How did she take it?'

'Naturally, she was disappointed.'

'Was she angry?'

Ogden looked at McCabe as if trying to gauge how much the detective knew. A moment passed before he said, 'Not that I could see.'

'Did she tell you where she was going after she left the office?'

'No, and I didn't ask. But I would have thought she'd go home to pack. She was leaving on her vacation the next morning.'

'I'd like to have my people go through her office and computer files to see if we can find any notes or e-mails that will help in our investigation.'

'If she was killed by a random mugger . . .'

'I have reason to believe she knew her attacker.' That wasn't quite true, but it might throw Ogden off stride. 'There may be some evidence of that relationship in her office.'

'Well, it sounds like a fishing expedition to me.' Ogden pursed his lips, then shook his head. 'No. I won't allow it.'

'I can get a court order.'

'I don't think so. Her files are protected by attorney-client privilege.'

'We only want to look at her personal files. You, or someone from your firm, can be present while we look. Make sure we don't compromise confidential client information.'

'Not good enough. I'm not sure her personal files can be separated from her business files. Certainly e-mails can't. Naturally, I'd like to help in any way I can, but I can't compromise my clients' confidential business. If you request a court order, I'm afraid we'll have to file a motion to quash. I think we'll be successful.'

Ogden might be right about that. McCabe might have to establish some sort of likelihood that Goff's files contained relevant information. He'd have to talk to Burt Lund in the AG's office about how to proceed. Lund might be able to work out a deal with Ogden, otherwise they'd go for the warrant. For the moment he decided to try another tack.

'Where did you go after you left the office that Friday night?'

'I had a drink to celebrate the season with a friend, and then I came home, to this house, to spend the rest of the evening with my wife.'

'Who was the friend?'

'Another attorney at my office. We had the drink at the bar at the Portland Harbor Hotel, and yes, I can prove it. I have the American Express receipt at the office.'

'Who was the other attorney?'

'I'm not sure that's any of your business.'

'Humor me.'

Apparently not one to suffer fools lightly, Ogden sighed. 'Another of the associates in the M&A practice. A woman named Janet Pritchard.'

Interesting. A woman. Probably a young woman since she was still an associate. Was Ogden fucking her, too? McCabe filed the name away for future reference. 'One more question.'

Ogden glanced at his watch.

'Where were you between 10:00 P.M. and 3:00 A.M. last Tuesday night?'

'Sergeant McCabe, I'm afraid I'm out of time. And, aside from that, this conversation is getting a little tiresome. I'll have Chloe bring you your coat.' With that he got up and walked out of the room, leaving his nearly empty cup on the table and McCabe still sitting in the red leather chair. McCabe stared at the cup, wondering if he could slip it into his pocket without being seen. The dregs of the coffee might wet his pocket, but traces of Ogden's saliva, and thus his DNA, would remain on the rim. He doubted the Ogdens would notice the loss of a single cup. However, he knew that if he took it without either a search warrant or permission, any evidence obtained would be inadmissible in court.

'Here's your coat, Detective.'

'Thank you, Chloe.'

As McCabe put it on, he deliberately swung the tail of the long overcoat behind him. Ogden's cup crashed onto the hardwood floor.

'Oh, damn, look what I've done.' He knew there was some reason he still wore a full-length coat.

Chloe ran off to find a dustpan and brush. 'I'm terribly sorry,' he called after her. Then he knelt down and carefully slipped as many pieces of the rim into his pocket as he could. He put on his shoes, waved good-bye to Chloe, and closed the front door on the way out. Didn't want too much heat escaping.

Henry C. 'Hank' Ogden stood at a window on the second-floor landing and watched, with a kind of loathing, as McCabe walked across the icy gravel toward the big black Ford. He felt a tightness in his gut, and he didn't like the feeling. No. He'd have to keep this nosy prick of a detective, with all his questions about Lainie and who was where and when, from probing too deeply into his affairs. It wouldn't do for him to know too much. No. It wouldn't do at all.

Deep into his thoughts, he didn't notice Barbara coming up behind him. He started at the touch of her hand on his shoulder.

'You'd better shower and change, Henry. Jock and Sonia and the boys will be here in less than an hour.'

He nodded absently, still keeping his gaze on the car as it pulled from its parking space and disappeared down the driveway. His eldest son and daughter-in-law and their two sons were coming up from Boston for the weekend. It would be hard playing the devoted father and grand-pops when he had so many other things to think about.

'Who was that in the black car?' she asked.

'A policeman. Something bad happened to someone in the firm. He came to ask some questions.'

'Really? What happened?'

'One of the associates died. No. That's not strictly true. Actually, she was murdered.'

'Oh my God, Henry, that's horrible. I'm so sorry,' she said. 'Who was it?'

'A young woman who worked for me in M&A. No one you know. Elaine Goff.'

'Murdered. My God. Do they have any idea who did it?'

'No. Not yet.'

'Elaine Goff? I don't think I know that name. Was she anyone important to the firm?'

'No,' he said. 'Not anyone important.' He smiled and kissed her softly on the cheek. 'Not important at all.'

Seventeen

Instead of going back to 109, McCabe pulled up in front of the Coffee by Design on Congress Street. Leaving the car running, he ran in and ordered a large cup of the daily dark roast, Black Thunder, which at least sounded like it ought to keep him going for a while. As an afterthought he added a cranberry walnut scone. He sat in the car for a while, sipping and munching and looking at the picture of Goff in her black evening gown. Ogden to her left. Jack Kelly to her right. The guy who was about to pick up nearly two hundred grand as a result of Lainie's death. McCabe turned the Crown Vic around, made a right on Avon, then a quick left and another right. He turned into the driveway of a large, ramshackle Victorian. Two smaller buildings to the rear also seemed to be part of the property. He pulled in between a red Jeep Cherokee, one of the old boxy ones, and a battered school bus with light blue paint covering the original yellow-orange. Black hand lettering on top of the blue read SANCTUARY HOUSE. Below that, in smaller letters, was written, WHERE HOPE IS REBORN. McCabe could see the outline of other letters, painted over but still visible under the blue. They read WEST PARIS SCHOOL DISTRICT.

Up on the porch, a boy and a girl, both a little older than Casey, lounged against the railing, sucking hard at the butt ends of cigarettes, doing their best to ignore him.

The boy looked away when McCabe approached. The girl stared back disdainfully through a heavy coating of makeup. Her addiction to black lipstick and even blacker eyeliner appeared to be at least as strong as the one to nicotine. Beneath her painted face she wore a short, fluffy white fake fur jacket over a thigh-high miniskirt, which in turn covered dark gray long johns stuffed into fluffy boots that kind of matched the fluffy jacket. Except for the long johns, an accommodation to the weather, the package screamed hooker. He didn't know what he was expecting to find at Sanctuary House, but somehow this wasn't it.

McCabe put on his best smiley face. 'Either of you know where I can find John Kelly?'

Neither answered, so he repeated the question.

Finally the girl nodded slowly. 'Yeah. We know.'

'Well, good. That's a start. Now maybe you can tell me where that would be?'

She took a last deep drag and tossed her butt into a number ten can apparently set out there for the purpose. 'I'll go get him for you,' she said and headed into the house. The boy continued smoking and looking out toward the street, his acne-scarred face almost lost under the array of hardware pierced into the flesh.

'Pretty nice day today, huh?' said McCabe.

No answer.

'Still pretty cold, though. You might need a jacket.'

Still no answer.

'You have a name?'

'No.' The kid flicked his spent butt into the can and headed for the door. McCabe shrugged and followed. Once inside, he found the girl walking back toward him.

'He says to wait in his office. That's it there.' She pointed toward a closed door with a hand-lettered sign Scotch-taped to it that read KNOCK!

'Says he'll be right with you.' She disappeared up the stairs. McCabe went in without knocking and closed the door behind him. There wasn't much to Kelly's office, and what there was looked shopworn. Third- or fourth-generation hand-me-down furniture. An old oak desk. A couple of folding metal chairs for visitors. A tall metal filing cabinet in the corner. Pretty much every surface was covered with paper – files, manuals, piles of newspaper clippings – most of which appeared to be about Sanctuary House or Kelly himself. All highly laudatory. The one on top had a picture of Kelly with his hands resting on the shoulders of a couple of teenagers, both of whom looked more cleaned up than the pair on the porch. A HERO OF THE STREETS, the headline declared.

Two facing walls were covered with books stacked on shelving constructed out of cinder blocks and unpainted boards like in a college dorm. Hundreds of them. Most of the titles seemed appropriate for someone in Kelly's line of work. *Broken Lives: The Tragedy of Child Abuse*; *The Psychotherapy of Abandoned Children*; *Fund-raising for Nonprofits: Building Community-Based Partnerships*. He pulled out a volume called *The Healing Power of Play: Working with Abused Children* by a woman named Eliana Gil, skimmed a few pages, and then put it back. He squatted down and checked out the bottom shelves. Mostly books about religion and theology. Two titles stuck in the right-hand corner behind Kelly's desk caught his eye. The first was *The Theology of the Prophetic Tradition*. He pulled out the second, *An Introduction to the Old Testament Prophets and Their Message*. He flipped through it. A lot of the pages were marked by yellow highlighter. He flipped to the table of contents and was hit by a surge of excitement, followed by a surge of doubt. He stared at the words in front of him. Chapter 17. Page 463. *The Prophecies of Amos: Historical Relevance to the Modern Age*.

He was interrupted by a deep voice. 'Checking out my library?'

McCabe looked up. A pair of dark blue eyes behind heavy black-rimmed glasses looked down at him. He closed the book and rose from his squat.

'John Kelly?'

Kelly nodded.

'Detective Sergeant Michael McCabe. Portland PD.'

They shook hands.

'How can I help you?'

'All the sinners of my people shall die by the sword,' McCabe said, watching Kelly's face. No reaction other than a mild curiosity.

'I beg your pardon?'

'All the sinners of my people shall die by the sword. Sound familiar?'

'I'm afraid I don't know what you're talking about.'

He held up the book. 'It's a quote from the Book of Amos. Chapter nine. Verse ten. I wondered if you remember hearing it before.'

'I don't recall, but I've probably come across it.'

'This is your book?'

'Of course it's my book. They all are, though that one dates back quite a few years. I wrote a paper on the Roman

Catholic view of Old Testament prophets in graduate school.'

'With references to the Book of Amos?'

'Yes. Though that wasn't the focus.'

'But you don't remember that line?'

'Not specifically, but Amos was all about smiting sinners, so it sounds appropriate.'

'Interesting.'

'If you say so.'

'Are you still interested in biblical scholarship?'

'I suppose so. It's what I got my doctorate in. What I taught at the college level before deciding to put my money where my mouth is and start this place. I still do some reading – and writing. When I have time. Which is not often.'

'Who knows about your paper on the prophetic tradition?'

Kelly heaved a sigh. 'Y'know, this is getting old. I have no idea. I suppose my thesis adviser might remember it. Maybe my roommate at the time. Why on earth are you questioning me about quotes from Amos?'

'Is it available on Google?'

'My paper?' Kelly looked oddly at McCabe 'Good heavens, no. It was never published. It wasn't that good.'

'Do you still have it?'

Kelly thought about that. 'It's probably buried in a box along with the rest of my stuff from grad school.'

'Where do you keep the box?'

'I have a summer cottage. No. Cottage is too grand a word. A shack, really. I store a lot of stuff there.'

'Unheated?'

'There's a woodstove. I don't use the place in winter, though. It's not insulated. I haven't been there in months.'

'Where is it?'

'On one of the islands.'

'Which one?'

'Harts.'

McCabe tried not to let excitement show on his face. 'Do you have any objections if we take a look at your cottage? Assuming, of course, you have nothing to hide. If you'd rather, we can always get a warrant.'

Kelly looked more puzzled than annoyed. 'Be my guest. The doors are never locked. Walk right in.' Kelly told him where the cottage was located. 'Now why don't you tell me what all this has to do with Lainie's death. That is why you're here, isn't it? Lainie's death? Are you suggesting somebody read Amos, took it to heart, and smote her as a sinner?'

'Smote? Is that the past tense of smite? Not smited?'

'Smote is correct. Now please answer my question.'

'Sorry. I can't. I just needed to check something out. Why don't we start over?' He extended a hand. 'Like I said, I'm McCabe. Detective Sergeant Michael McCabe.'

'I recognize you. When the kids told me a cop was here, I figured it had to be you.'

McCabe smiled and waved a hand, indicating his civilian clothes. 'How'd they know?'

'These kids can sniff out a cop a mile away.'

Just like the kids in New York, McCabe thought. They always knew. Uniform or no uniform. Even when there was no color difference. 'What makes your kids so good at it? Sniffing out cops, I mean.'

'Experience. Most of them are runaways, throwaways, and other assorted leftovers from the societal scrap heap. They've been bullied, hassled, and chased down by guys in blue suits most of their lives.'

'I haven't worn a blue suit in a long time.'

'It's not the suit, McCabe. Trust me. They know. Anyway, I've been expecting you ever since I heard the news about Lainie.'

Kelly pointed McCabe to one of the folding chairs. 'Just dump those files on the pile over there.' He slipped behind the desk and sat down and looked at McCabe. His eyes, even behind the glasses, were hard to ignore. They were even bluer and more intense than they'd seemed in the photo. They radiated energy. *From what I hear he's a hell of a charismatic guy*, Maggie'd told him, *a real charmer*. His crooked nose looked like it'd been broken more than once. McCabe guessed a scrapper. Sort of like Cleary.

'Ever do any boxing?'

'Amateur. As a teenager back in Pittsburgh.'

'Any good?'

'Not really. As you can see from the nose, guys tended to hit me more than I hit them.'

'So what made you do it?'

'I like defending myself. When I was young, people picked on me. One in particular. I wanted him to leave me alone.'

'So you hit him?'

'Just once. That's all it took. He stopped.'

'Picking on you?'

'Yeah. Picking on me.'

'Do I call you Father Jack?'

'No. Just John. Or Jack, if you prefer. I'm not a priest anymore. Haven't been for a long time.'

'But you're still a believer?'

'Yes, but it's different now. God sets the course by which I guide my life. The pope no longer does.'

'Do most of your kids dress like the girl on the porch? The one who went to find you?'

'What were you expecting? The Brady Bunch?'

'She's what? Fifteen years old?'

'Tara's sixteen.'

'Sixteen, then. Any reason you let her hang out on the porch sucking on butts and looking like a Times Square hooker?' Not the best way to start off with Kelly, but screw it. The girl was just a couple of years older than Casey. McCabe needed to get it off his chest.

'Look, McCabe, if that's where this conversation is going, why don't you pick yourself up and go on back to Middle Street. My kids aren't angels, and as a former street cop you ought to know that. A lot of them are vengeful, dirty, unrepentant sinners. All of them are wounded. I can't change that in a day or a week or even a month. They tend to wear whatever they arrived in plus whatever appeals to them in the donation bags we get from the churches around town. Which, frankly, isn't much.'

McCabe knew he had pressed the wrong button. He also knew it was dumb. If he was going to get any more out of Kelly, he'd have to back off. Let the anger subside. At the moment Kelly was on a roll, and McCabe figured he was better off letting him finish.

'If Tara looks like a hooker,' said Kelly, 'hey, guess what? You're right. That's how she survived for the last

222

year or so, and I'll bet if you asked, she'd tell you fucking strangers for money was better any day than fucking her father for nothing. Which is what he forced her to do most of her life. At least when he wasn't beating her silly and telling her she was a worthless piece of shit. The good news is she's stopped hooking. She's starting to put her life together. She just hasn't changed her clothes yet.'

'I'm sorry.'

'You're sorry?'

'Yeah, I'm sorry. I shot my mouth off, and it wasn't called for. So I'm sorry.'

'Okay.' Deep breath. Pause. 'Apology accepted.' Another deep breath. Another pause. 'McCabe, you've got to understand our first job here is to get Tara and others like her off the streets and convince them their lives are worth saving, worth caring about. Fashion makeovers and smoking cessation, as important as they may be to you, are well down the line as far as I'm concerned.'

'You're pretty passionate about all this.'

'You noticed.'

'Any truth to the rumor you were abused yourself as a kid?'

'It's not a rumor, and yeah, there's truth to it. It's not something I try to hide. I was fourteen, and I was raped by my parish priest. The first time it happened I told my old man, and all he did was beat the crap out of me for blaspheming the Holy Mother Church. So I figured I'd have to defend myself. Remember I told you how somebody picked on me? Well, the second time it happened I beat the crap out of the priest. He was bigger and older than me, but I gave him two black eyes and a bloody nose.'

McCabe suppressed a smile. 'What happened to you for that?'

'Nothing. He couldn't tell anyone what he'd done to deserve it. So he just told everyone, including the cops, that he'd been mugged on the street. Told them a couple of big black guys did it.'

'Naturally. Doesn't everyone?'

'I suppose – but y'know what angered me then and still makes me angry now? Knocking the good father silly didn't really change anything. He just kept on doing the same thing to other kids.'

'Whatever possessed you to become a priest yourself?'

'You mean aside from the fact that I felt I had a calling?'

'Yeah. Aside from that.'

'Like a lot of others, I had this cockamamie idea I could reform the institution from the inside. Didn't take long to realize that idea was delusional. In those days, the institution wasn't interested in reform. It was only interested in avoiding scandal, which it did for decades. It wasn't until the *Boston Globe* turned the whole thing into national news that the Church really did anything to change. And by that time Sanctuary House was already up and running, and I was gone from the priesthood.'

McCabe remembered the *Globe* series well. In January 2002, a team of investigative reporters from the paper broke the story of pedophile priests wide open, detailing the sins of hundreds of priests, the victimization of thousands of children. The country was shocked. McCabe wasn't. He'd learned about priestly abuse decades earlier because he knew a kid who was one of its victims. He hadn't thought about Edward Mullaney in a long time.

Fourteen years old. Shy and serious. An altar boy. A pious believer, utterly powerless to resist the God-like figure in a turned-around collar who liked taking him on 'outings.' McCabe had often wondered what had become of Edward. He'd found out last year. That's when he learned Mullaney had been convicted of raping an eight-year-old girl.

'How many kids do you have living here?'

'Depends. Anywhere from thirty, which is our legal capacity, up to sixty, which is about all we can stuff in. Kids who sleep on the street in the summer sleep here in January. Right now we've got them three and four to a room.'

'They come and go?'

'It's not a prison. Kids are always welcome here. Any kid. If they leave, we don't usually try to hunt them down. Although I have done that with a few I thought were a danger to themselves or to others. Even called you guys for help a few times.'

'How long's the average stay?'

'Some come for one night and then disappear. Others are here for weeks or months, which gives us a chance to work with them. We don't turn anyone away, and we don't kick anybody out unless they break our rules.'

'Which are?' asked McCabe.

'We only have three, and, like I said, they don't include a smoking ban. Number one's no violence. Against yourself or anyone else. Number two's no booze or drugs. Here or anywhere else. Number three, everyone has to show everyone else respect. Break a rule once and I'll usually give you a second chance. Break it twice and you're out. In return the kids get a place to sleep, food to eat, and an obligation to do some work to help keep this place running. Cooking. Cleaning. Shoveling snow. Plus an obligation to work with one of our counselors to develop a program to turn their lives around. We try to help them get jobs in town. Find permanent housing. Send them to school or tutor them for the GEDs. Thanks to our volunteers we can offer therapy to those who need it. Counseling for the others.'

'Permanent staff?'

'Me and three counselors. One's a young friar who's been with me a couple of years. The other two are USM grad students studying social work. They'll rotate out at the end of the semester and be replaced by others. We also have a number of volunteers.'

'Lainie Goff one of them?'

'Yes, Lainie was a volunteer. She was also on our board of trustees.'

'Active?'

'Very. This organization meant a lot to her.'

'What was her role?'

'She did some fund-raising. She was very good at that. She was also our attorney. Pro bono, of course.'

'Yours or the kids'?'

'Both. We get hassled by the powers that be all the time – the city, the child welfare agencies. She fended them off. Sometimes abusive parents want their children back. She fended them off as well. Lainie was a tough, smart, take-no-prisoners kind of lawyer. This is the kind of work she should have been doing full-time instead of slaving away in that corporate sinkhole.'

'Palmer Milliken?'

'Yes. She was better than that. A better lawyer. A better person, though she probably didn't know it. The fourteen-hour days she spent there would have counted for a lot more if she'd spent them here.'

'Why do you think she did it? Work there, I mean? Was it just for the money?'

'Money was important to her. Too important in my view. See, the thing you've got to understand about Lainie is she was insecure. She always needed to prove she was the best. The smartest, the toughest, the sexiest, the most beautiful. Whatever. That's what drove her. Still, no matter how well Lainie did, and she always did very well, somehow it was never good enough. Insecurity does terrible things to a person. It's a sad thing to say, but I think the only time I ever saw her genuinely happy was when she was here working with the kids.'

'Really?'

'Strange, isn't it? The tough-as-nails lawyer as surrogate mother. She always seemed to gravitate toward girls like Tara who'd come from sexual abuse situations. They trusted her. She seemed to have an intuitive understanding of what they'd been through.'

She had a stepfather, but I don't think she'd want him notified of anything. What Janie Archer said to him now made more sense. 'Do you suppose Lainie went through an abusive childhood herself?'

'I don't know, but that's what I've always thought. Work with these kids long enough and you learn they give off a certain vibe. You can feel it. I felt it in Lainie. I even asked her about it once or twice, but she never wanted to talk about it. She's a very private person. *Was* a private person.'

McCabe made a mental note to find out more about Wallace Albright. Find out if he was still alive, still in Maine, and maybe still abusing young girls.

'Lainie only worked with the girls?' he asked.

'Yes.'

'Interesting.'

'If she was abused as a child, I think it fits. She saw males as the enemy. People to be used and manipulated but not to be trusted.'

'She trusted you, didn't she?'

'I think so.'

'What was your relationship with her?'

'We were close. As close as she ever let anyone get to her.'

'Except for the kids?'

'Yeah. Except for them.'

'Were you intimate?'

'You mean sexually?'

'You tell me.'

'No. We weren't intimate. Not sexually. Not in any other way either, except that we both cared about the kids. She was a private person and didn't share much about her personal life.'

'She was also a beautiful, sexy woman, and you're not a priest anymore. Weren't you ever tempted? Physically, I mean?'

Kelly stared at him. 'I'm otherwise involved.'

'Who with?'

'None of your business.'

'Ever been to her apartment?'

'No.'

'Where were you last Tuesday night from about 9:00 p.m. till midnight?'

Kelly smiled at the inference. 'It would seem I'm a suspect.'

'Everyone's a suspect.'

'Last Tuesday night I was where I am every Tuesday. Sitting right here writing grant proposals till about two in the morning.'

'Then what?'

'I went to sleep.'

'Where?'

'There's a staff bedroom upstairs. One member of the staff is always on premises. We rotate. Tuesdays and Thursdays are my nights.'

'Anybody see you?'

'Nobody any jury would ever believe.'

'Who?'

'Just a couple of street kids who banged on the door about midnight. They wanted beds. We didn't have any, but it was too cold to let them sleep outside. So I gave them something to eat and let them sleep in the kitchen.'

'They have names?'

'Sure. One calls himself Bennie. Male prostitute. Gives blow jobs for drug money. He's about seventeen. He lived here for a while last year, but we had to bounce him out.'

'Bennie have a last name?'

'He says it's Bennie Belmont, which may or may not be his real name. He's a liar and a troublemaker. He broke the rules twice and then some. You might be able to find him if you prowl around the right bars. The other one said his name was Gerald R. McGill, which I know was phony.'

'How do you know?'

'Had to be. Unless he owns the funeral parlor across the street. Anyway, Bennie and Mr McGill left the next morning, and I haven't seen either of them since.'

'How about Friday, December twenty-third? Two days before Christmas. Where were you, say, around 9:00 P.M.?'

Kelly thought for a minute. 'At home. In my apartment. On Howard Street.'

Howard Street was just a few blocks from McCabe's place on the Eastern Prom. 'Anybody with you?'

'Yes.'

'Who?'

'My partner. We share the apartment.'

'You're gay?'

'I'm gay.'

'What's your partner's name?'

'Edward Childs. People call him Teddy.'

'Mr Childs will confirm you were together that night?'

'I'm sure he will.'

'There were just the two of you, home alone two days before Christmas? No parties to go to? No celebrations?'

'We like it that way. We had dinner. Wrote some last-minute cards. Read. Went to bed.'

'How long have you and Teddy been together?'

'Eight years.'

'Do you have any idea why someone would want to kill Lainie?'

'No, I don't.'

'You have any kids here who are mentally unstable?'

'If you're talking about emotional problems, anxiety, depression, stuff like that, it's pretty near one hundred percent. If you're talking about being bipolar or schizo-phrenic, we've had a few, but not many. Mostly we're not equipped to deal with it.'

'Can you give me a list of the kids Lainie had closest contact with? We'll need to interview them.'

'You saying one of the kids might have done this?'

'It's possible, but I doubt it.' McCabe knew a street kid leaving obscure messages from the Bible was more than unlikely, and the same kid driving a new BMW would be as conspicuous as an elephant dancing a waltz. 'We just want to talk to them. Somebody may know something.'

Kelly nodded. 'How far back do you want to go?'

'Since Goff started working with you.'

'That's over three years. Probably a dozen kids. Maybe more. You may have trouble finding some of them.'

'We have resources. We'll also want to interview the rest of the staff.'

'Okay. I'll e-mail you both lists as soon as we can put them together. What's your e-mail?'

McCabe handed Kelly his card, then asked, 'You ever hear the name Abby Quinn?'

'Of course. Abby lived here for about six months last year. She's older than our usual profile, but her psychiatrist is also on the board, and he thought the experience would be good for her. We treated her as kind of an unpaid intern. She did a little of everything.'

'What's her psychiatrist's name?'

'Wolfe. Dr Richard Wolfe.'

It amazed McCabe once again what a small town Portland was. You kept running into the same people every-where. 'How can Abby afford a fancy doctor like Wolfe?'

'Medicare. Abby's on disability. At least she was when she lived here.'

'Was Dr Wolfe right? About Sanctuary House being good for her?'

'I think so. Abby's a diagnosed schizophrenic, but she stayed on her meds, did her chores, and tried hard to fit in. She did well.'

'Why did she leave?'

There was a slight hesitation before Kelly answered. 'She was ready. It was time for her to go home.'

'No other reason?'

'No.'

'Did she ever meet Lainie?'

'I don't know. They may have bumped into each other once or twice. Lainie never worked with her. Only Dr Wolfe did that.'

'Do you know where she is now?'

'Harts Island, I imagine. That's where she lives.'

'She's not here, is she?'

Kelly squinted at him, then shook his head. 'No. What would she be doing here?'

'Just wondering. Did Abby make any particular friends while she was here? Kids she might still be in contact with?'

'None that I can think of. Why?'

'We need to talk to her.'

'In connection with the murder?'

'Yes. Can you think of anyone here she palled around with?'

'Check with Wolfe. He'd be the first one I'd ask. Or go out to Harts Island and ask her. Is this going to take much longer?'

McCabe ignored the question. 'How's Sanctuary House doing for money?'

'Finances are not so great. They never are for organizations like ours. We depend mostly on small foundation grants and donations from well-meaning citizens. We don't accept any state or city money. That gives us more freedom to operate.'

'You said Lainie was a good fund-raiser.'

'Yes. She was. In fact, she helped bring in a gift of ten thousand bucks just a month ago.'

'You get a lot of gifts that size?'

'A few, but it's never enough. Just look around you. Do we look rich? We've got building violations coming out of our ears, which the city, thank God, has so far ignored. They don't want my kids back on the street any more than I do. Or your department does, for that matter. Without Lainie running interference, it'll be tough.'

'Any danger you'll have to close your doors?'

Kelly shrugged. 'It's always a danger. Always a struggle. Maybe you'd like to make a contribution?'

McCabe smiled. 'Maybe I would. How does one hundred and eighty thousand dollars sound to you?'

Kelly looked at McCabe curiously. 'You're kidding, of course – but that kind of money would be a game changer for this place.'

'No, I'm not kidding. Lainie had life insurance. Sanctuary House is the beneficiary.'

'You're serious?' Kelly looked stunned. 'One hundred and eighty thousand dollars?'

'You didn't know about it?'

'No. She never said a word.'

'I guess she didn't plan on dying,' said McCabe. 'Where exactly were you last Tuesday between eleven at night and three in the morning?'

'I already told you.'

'Tell me again.'

'Right here.'

'You're sure?'

'Are you suggesting that I may have killed Lainie for the money?'

'I'm not suggesting anything. Now that you bring it up, did you?'

'No.'

'You're sure?'

'I'm sure.'

'So I guess that means you wouldn't mind coming down to police headquarters this afternoon so we can get a set of your prints and a DNA sample.'

'Because everyone's a suspect?'

'Yes. Everyone.'

Kelly agreed to go to Middle Street, and McCabe left.

Eighteen

It was nearly one thirty before McCabe got back to 109. He slipped the shards of Henry Ogden's china cup into an evidence bag and locked it in the bottom drawer of his desk. Then he called Joe Pines, the DNA guru at the state crime lab in Augusta. Saturday or not, McCabe was pretty sure Pines would be in his lab. He'd never known Joe to be anywhere else.

'Hey, Joe, I've got a question.'

'Relevant to a case or just a question?'

'Just a question. Let's say someone drinks from a coffee cup and the cup is allowed to dry out for, I don't know, days or maybe even weeks. Will you still be able to pick up DNA from the guy's saliva?'

'Might not be as intact as we ideally like – so there could be some issues with long sequencing reads, but yes, we should be able to get you something. Who's the guy?'

'Like I said, just a question.'

'Okay. Let me know when you're going to send me the cup.'

He'd have to check what day trash got picked up on Ledge Road in Cape Elizabeth so he'd know what day it was he found the bits of china in the bin by the side of the road.

Next call was to Tony Krawchek, head of the PPD's three-man Narcotics unit.

'Hiya, Mike. That frozen stiff you guys found last night still frozen stiff?' Krawchek guffawed. Another comedian.

'Yeah, still frozen. That's what I'm calling you about. You ever hear of a small-time dealer who calls himself the hot-dog man?'

'Probably a guy named Kyle Lanahan. Runs a sausage stand in Monument Square. Basically an amateur, but he peddles a little blow from time to time. We just haven't been able to catch him at it yet.'

'You have any problem if we bring him in?'

'What's your interest?'

'Goff had a bag in her car. I'm pretty sure it came from him.'

'Sure. Why not? While you're at it, see if you can get him to tell you who his distributor is. That's what we really want to know.'

McCabe agreed, called Tom Tasco, and asked him to invite Mr Lanahan in for an interview.

After he hung up, he googled the name Wallace Albright. He got more than four hundred hits. It only took a couple of minutes to narrow them down to the right one, Wallace Stevens Albright, a prominent attorney practicing in Camden. Albright had been married three times. His second wife was named Martha Tynes Goff. McCabe googled that name and found a number of articles mostly concerning the fact that Martha Tynes Goff, Lainie's mother, had committed suicide in May 1995. The end of Lainie's sophomore year at Colby. Finally he went to Google Images and found and printed a couple of images of Mr Albright. Good-looking guy. Thin face. Angular features. Gray hair.

I don't think she'd want him notified of anything, Archer had said.

But he's alive?

Not as far as Lainie was concerned.

Later he'd asked Kelly, *Do you suppose Lainie went through an abusive childhood herself?*

I don't know, but that's what I've always thought.

As soon as he could, he'd head up to Camden and have a little chat with Mr Albright. But there were a few other things he had to do first.

Maggie wandered over.

'Pick up the other line,' he said. 'I'm calling Burt Lund.'

She pulled over a chair while McCabe made the call. In Maine all homicides are handled out of the attorney general's office, and Assistant AG Burt Lund was McCabe's favorite prosecutor. He just hoped the prosecutor wouldn't be halfway down a slope at Sunday River and unable to talk. He wasn't.

'You know, McCabe, I didn't give you my cell number so you could pester me at home on weekends.'

'C'mon, Burt, you know how hurt you'd be if I didn't slip you the skinny first on murder cases.'

'Are we talking Goff?'

'Who else? By the way, Maggie's on the other line.'

'Hiya, Mag.'

'Hi, Burt.'

'What do you need?' asked Lund.

'A warrant to search Elaine Goff's office at Palmer Milliken. Henry Ogden won't let us in. Claims it'll compromise client confidentiality.'

'It probably would.'

'Says he might try to quash.'

'Hmmm. That seems excessive. There are ways Palmer Milliken could segregate sensitive client material. Ogden ought to know that.'

'I think he's hiding something.'

'Do you think he's the killer?'

'I think it's possible. I'm pretty sure he and Goff were sleeping together, and yes, Burt, I do know screwing around at the office doesn't necessarily translate to killing.'

'No, it doesn't. Rumor is Hank's been dipping his highly privileged wick into one good-looking associate or another for years. As far as I know, most of them are still alive. A few have even become partners.'

'There may be a difference here,' McCabe told Lund.

'Really? Keep going.'

'The night Goff disappeared, Lainie and Ogden had a late meeting in his office. I think Henry promised her an early partnership. That night he told her she wasn't getting it. According to the building's security guard, Lainie left looking majorly pissed. I'm wondering if she threw a hissy fit when Ogden turned her down. Maybe threatened to tell the wife about the affair. Or the other partners. Or maybe really go public and accuse the firm of sexual harassment. What do you think?'

'Would he kill her over that?' asked Maggie. She sounded doubtful.

'Given Ogden's domestic situation, it's possible,' said Lund. 'How much do you two know about the lovely and talented Mrs Ogden?'

'Nothing,' said McCabe.

'Among her friends, Barbara Milliken Ogden is known as Attila the Hen.'

'Cute,' said Maggie. 'What do her enemies call her?'

'Beats me, but nothing good. She's not only unattractive, she's nasty and vindictive. Handsome Henry married her for her money.'

'Her maiden name is Milliken?'

'Yes. My guess is Barbara tolerates Henry's little sexcapades as long as they remain discreet, but if any of Henry's playmates ever humiliated her in public, she'd cut his preppy little balls off.'

'What are we talking about here?' asked Maggie. 'An expensive divorce? Big alimony payments?'

'Alimony's not an issue. Henry makes a good living, huge compared to the likes of us, but the really serious money in the family is all Barbara's. Some comes from the Milliken side, but a lot more comes from her mother's family. Ever hear of the Dexters?'

'As in Dexter Oil?' asked McCabe. Dexter's red diamond-shaped logo stared McCabe in the face practically every morning, painted, as it was, on the sides of all those big storage tanks on the South Portland side of the harbor.

'Yeah, as in. We're talking big bucks here. Probably hundreds of millions. If Babs ever kicks Henry out of the honeymoon cottage, he won't see another dime of it. Ever. He might even lose his job. Dexter Oil was Palmer Milliken's first big corporate client. Established the firm as a major player back in the fifties. And it's still number one by a wide margin.'

'You think Barbara could get him dumped?' asked McCabe.

'I know she could. Dexter's still privately held, and Barbara's the majority shareholder. If she told Henry's partners they'd lose Dexter as a client if they didn't make Henry walk the plank, he's done. Finished. Toast. He'd be lucky to get a job as dog catcher in this town, let alone as an attorney.'

'Pretty dumb to put all that at risk just to get into Lainie's pants,' said Maggie.

'Also pretty common. If you recall, we had a president not so long ago who couldn't keep his fly zipped either. Not to mention a gaggle of governors and senators. I'm just wondering what's in Lainie's office that's making Henry so determined to keep you out.'

'Who knows?' said Maggie. 'Phone records. Pictures. E-mails. If proof of the affair exists, Ogden'll want to find it before we do.'

'That would suggest Henry's not the killer,' said McCabe. 'If he was, he would have started looking two weeks ago. Right after he nabbed her.'

'On the other hand, if he only heard about the murder last night,' said Maggie, 'he'd want to keep us out until he had a chance to look.'

Maggie was right. Which meant it was probably Ogden who tossed Goff's apartment last night. Right after he found out she was dead. Maybe he checked out the office, too. Or maybe he didn't have a master key and couldn't get in until Monday morning. *There are ways Palmer Milliken could segregate sensitive client material.* All kinds of sensitive material, McCabe decided.

'Okay,' Lund said, 'let's see if we can discover what it is Henry might be looking for. Write up the affidavit, and we'll find a judge to issue the order. Of course, if Ogden tries to quash, we could be wrangling about it for a few days anyway.'

They hung up.

'Get your coat and let's get some lunch,' McCabe said to Maggie. 'We'll talk while we eat.'

Tallulah's, halfway up Munjoy Hill, was jammed with the late weekend brunch crowd. As usual Tallulah was guarding the door. She greeted McCabe with her customary hug, squeezing her ample bosom into his chest. 'How you doing, Mike? Heard there was a murder in town last night. Some lawyer lady.'

'I'm good, Lou – and yeah, you heard right. In fact, we need a quiet table in the corner where we can talk business.' He looked around the crowded room. 'That is, if you can find one.'

She scanned her clipboard and made a few notations. 'No problem, Sergeant. I've got your reservation right here.' She looked up with a smile. 'You're right on time.'

Tallulah led them past a noisy gaggle of thirty-somethings, hanging at the bar, drinking beer and Bloody Marys and waiting for tables. Like they say in the American Express ads, membership has its privileges. She seated them in back, about as far from the action as possible. 'Can I start you two off with a couple of Bloodys?'

McCabe pondered the question and was about to nod yes, but Maggie beat him to the punch. 'Not today, Lou. We're working.'

'Yeah.' McCabe sighed. 'Mag's right. Just make it a Virgin. And a burger and a chopped salad for me.'

Maggie handed back her menu. 'Make it two. Medium rare. And an order of onion rings.'

'I'll go tell Mandy.' Tallulah passed on their order to the pretty blonde who was serving drinks two tables away. Mandy was a part-time waitress and a full-time artist and friend of Kyra's. Like most artists, she couldn't make a living selling her work, so she waited tables.

'How come you never get fat?' asked McCabe. 'You eat like a twelve-year-old. You don't exercise. And you still look great.'

Maggie smiled brightly. 'Just a metabolic powerhouse, I guess.' She waited till Tallulah was out of earshot before continuing. 'You know, I didn't say anything to Burt, but I have some other problems with Ogden as the freak.'

'Other than his not checking out her office in the two weeks since she was nabbed?'

She nodded. 'Yeah, other than that. Ogden just doesn't strike me as the kind of guy who'd leave obscure quotes from the Bible in his victim's mouth. The Book of Amos? I mean, they don't teach that kind of stuff at Harvard Law, do they? Plus hauling her body back and forth to Harts Island? Why would he do that? If Ogden was going to kill someone, he'd keep it simple. You know the headline by heart. "Woman assaulted and slain in deserted garage. Assailant flees." Or maybe assailant doesn't flee. Maybe he dumps her body in Casco Bay or maybe in the middle of nowhere. Maine's a big state. Over thirty-five thousand square miles, most of it wilderness. Could've been months, years, maybe never before anyone found her.'

McCabe nodded. 'I agree. I don't think Ogden's our

guy either. I didn't tell you, but I paid a visit to Goff's apartment after we got back from Harts last night.'

Maggie looked at him quizzically. 'Really? Why? I appreciate your devotion to duty, but couldn't your visit have waited till morning?'

'I wanted to see how Goff lived. Anyway, somebody tossed the place between the time you and Jacobi left, which was what?'

'A little before eleven.'

'Okay. I got there at roughly 3:30 A.M. In other words, after Goff's murder was announced. I'm willing to bet the searcher was Ogden.'

Mandy brought their drinks. 'Burgers'll be here in a sec,' she said. When she was gone, McCabe asked Maggie for a rundown of what transpired at the 10:00 A.M. detectives' meeting. 'Anybody make any progress?'

'Not much. The canvass went oh-for-four. Nobody saw anything. Nobody heard anything. Nobody knew anything. The only person who showed any interest was Goff's landlord.'

'Andrew Barker?'

'Yeah, and he showed too much. Kept asking questions about the murder like he was getting off on it. Creepy little guy. Wondered if he might not be our pither.'

'I don't think so.'

'Really? Why?'

'He snuck into the apartment while I was there, and we had a little chat. Why don't you tell me the rest of what you have first.'

'Just a bunch of odds and ends. First thing this morning

I ran a ViCAP check to see if I could find any other cases where a female victim had been raped and pithed. Found a couple.'

'Possible connection?'

'Only as a copycat. One of the bad guys is dead. The other, who killed at least six women that way, is currently doing life without parole at a supermax in Youngstown, Ohio. I also e-mailed other departments in Maine and New Hampshire plus the RCMP. So far nobody's reporting anything similar.'

'Cleary hear back from Verizon?'

'Yeah. They sent him a rundown on calls to and from Goff's mobile for the past three months. He's going over the list now, culling out people we might want to talk to.'

'Any calls on the twenty-third?'

'Nothing. If she called anybody that day, she must have used her office phone. Last outgoing was to the Chinese restaurant Brian mentioned on St John Street. That was at 8:37 P.M., Thursday the twenty-second.'

'Let me guess. She ordered chicken with pea pods.'

Maggie nodded. 'Three incoming messages after that. Two from the Bacuba Resort wanting to know what the story was on her not showing up. And one from a friend named Janie in New York, who said, quote, "What we talked about is cool. If you get this message on Aruba, give me a call. If not, no big deal. I'll see you when you get home." That was it.'

'What we talked about is cool?'

'Yes.'

McCabe tried Archer's cell. There was no answer. Just her voice asking him to leave a message. 'Ms. Archer. This is Detective McCabe again. Would you please give me a call as soon as possible? Thank you.' He clicked his phone off. 'Goff have a landline?'

'Didn't see one in her apartment.'

He hadn't either. 'E-mails?'

Maggie shrugged. 'There was no computer in the apartment, but someone like Lainie must have had a laptop. Could have been with her when she got nabbed. Or it could be sitting in her office downtown.'

'Or Ogden could have found it and tossed it into Casco Bay. Anything else?'

'Yeah. I checked with my pal at Vessel Services.' Maggie opened her notebook and leafed through the pages till she found the right one. 'Only one boat came in for service Wednesday night. The *Good and Plenty*. It stayed overnight and pulled out at four on Thursday morning. I was able to chat with the captain by satphone. He said he noticed the car sitting there but didn't see it come in or who was driving it. Nobody on the crew saw anything either.'

McCabe put the celery stick he'd been gnawing on back in his drink. 'Cleary still working on the ferry crew rosters?'

'He's down at the terminal talking to deckhands now. Said he'd have everyone covered by –' She looked at her watch. 'Pretty soon now. Also I stopped by at Winter Haven Hospital this morning, and, after forty-five minutes of bullshit over privacy issues, I finally got them to give me the name and contact number for Abby Quinn's shrink.'

'Dr Richard Wolfe?'

'Yeah, how'd you know?'

'Kelly told me.'

In spite of his deadpan, McCabe's expression must have given something away. 'What is it?' she said. 'Do you know him or something?'

'Yes. I know him,' said McCabe. 'Wolfe's a good guy.'

Maggie eyed him suspiciously. Her radar was just too good. 'Okay, he's a good guy. Is there something else you're not telling me?'

'Like what?' he asked.

'I don't know. Maybe like are you seeing a shrink or something? Maybe like Dr Richard Wolfe, for example?'

Mandy arrived with their burgers. McCabe handed her his empty Virgin Mary glass. Asked for a cold Shipyard Export.

'No. I'm not seeing a shrink,' he said after the waitress was gone. He picked up his burger and took a bite.

'*Were* you seeing a psychiatrist?'

He didn't respond.

'Please don't give me that Clint Eastwood squint, McCabe. I'm your friend. Remember?'

He still didn't answer.

'Oh, never mind.' She sighed. 'The only other thing going on is Scott Ginsberg at METCO sent over the sur-veillance videos from Ten Monument Square for both the twenty-second and twenty-third. Also sent his regards. Eddie spent a chunk of this morning going over the videos with Starbucks.

'They're still looking, but so far they haven't seen any-thing suspicious,' she said. 'Videos are from two cameras. One covers the security desk and elevators. The other's focused on the main entrance. Nobody came into the building after 6:00 P.M. either day except for the cleaning crew, who arrived all together in a crowd at 6:05 on Thursday and again at 6:08 on Friday. On Friday, Goff left, wearing no coat, at 8:04 and comes back five minutes later holding something in her right hand. Goff leaves again at 9:03, again doesn't sign out, walks right past the security guard – and he's right, she did look pissed. She gives him the finger and exits frame. A gray-haired male leaves at 9:12 –'

'Henry Ogden.'

'He doesn't look so happy either, but he shakes the security guard's hand and hands him a white envelope.'

'A hundred bucks. It was his Christmas present.'

'He also doesn't bother signing out. That's it for both nights except for the cleaning crew, which left, again together' – Maggie looked down at her notes – 'Thursday, or more accurately Friday morning, at exactly 1:00 A.M. and Saturday morning at 1:04.' She looked up. 'They're going over the videos one more time.'

McCabe had finished what he wanted of both his burger and salad, which was about half of each. He sipped at his Shipyard. 'How about the GO?' The GO was the unit's nickname for Chief Shockley, a.k.a. the Great One.

'Quiet as a mouse. I haven't heard boo from him.'

McCabe looked doubtful. 'That's out of character.'

'Yeah. It won't last. Aside from anything else, his bimbo will need something new for her viewers. That pretty much covers it except for our eight-hundred-pound schizophrenic.'

'What did you tell the boys about her?'

'Pretty much everything.'

'You gave them Quinn's name?'

'Yeah. I told them not to give it out unless they had to, and not to tell anyone why we're looking for her.'

'Okay,' said McCabe. 'My turn, I guess.' He signaled Mandy and ordered coffee for both of them. He spent the next twenty minutes filling Maggie in on his conversations with Janie Archer last night and Henry Ogden and John Kelly this morning.

'You think Kelly's the guy?'

'I don't know. Possibly. There are a lot of reasons to think so. His familiarity with Old Testament prophets. His house on Harts. A volatile personality. Plus, he's got weak alibis for both key nights. One from a pair of unreliable and possibly unfindable street punks. The other from a committed longtime partner. Motive is what bothers me. Tough to see why Kelly would want to kill her.'

'Sex?'

'Kelly told me he was gay. In a committed relationship.'

'He could swing both ways,' said Maggie.

'Maybe, but I don't think so.'

'There's money. A hundred and eighty K isn't exactly chicken feed.'

'I'm not sure he knew about that. Plus, I think he really cared for Lainie, and he couldn't have cared less about us searching his house on Harts.'

'Sure. Because he killed her at Markham's house. Which means we won't find a thing at his. Anyway, I'll call Jacobi and get it organized.'

'Ask Tommy to cover it with him. Tell them to look carefully. If there is something out there, let's find it.'

Maggie shrugged, nodded, and made the calls. 'Okay, all set. So you went to Goff's apartment last night?'

248

'Yeah.'

'How'd you like the pictures?'

McCabe smiled. 'What can I say? Such a sweet young thing, modest to a fault.'

'She still remind you of Sandy?'

'In some ways, yes,' said McCabe. 'Others, no.'

Maggie started to ask something about that but then, instead, just shook her head. 'Never mind. It's none of my business. Anyway, you said you found the place tossed?'

'Yeah. My theory is that Ogden, assuming it was Ogden, was in the apartment when I arrived. He either heard me on the porch or saw me approaching through the living-room window. He knew he couldn't go downstairs without bumping into me. So he went up instead and hid on the stairwell between the second and third floors. I get into the apartment and close the door. He takes off. I heard a sound while I was working the lock. I thought it came from inside. I was wrong. It came from the stairs. I should've had him. Basically I screwed up.'

'Okay, so you're not perfect. It happens. What was the damage?'

'Drawers were searched and some of them dumped. Books were pulled out of the bookcase, which means he may have been looking for something that would fit between the pages of a book.'

'Paper.'

'Yeah. I doubt Hank's the love letter type. More likely he was looking for photos or printouts of e-mails.'

'You're sure it wasn't Barker? You said he came waltzing in later. It could have been his second trip.'

'A bunch of things make me think not. First off, I came

down on Barker pretty hard about whether he'd been there before to search the place. It just kind of confused him. He wouldn't admit to a thing.'

'Doesn't mean it's not him.' Maggie was busy building little towers of sugar cubes on the table. 'When you arrived, the door was locked. So were the windows. That means whoever was in there locked up the place. Barker has a key.'

'If Ogden was her lover, he might have had one, too. And remember, there were no house or office keys attached to the key ring in the Beemer. If the killer took them, I assume it was for a reason.'

Maggie nodded. 'Okay. You said there were a bunch of reasons you didn't think Barker was the searcher. What's the other?'

'Lainie's underwear.'

'Lainie's underwear?' She stopped building sugar towers and frowned. 'What about Lainie's underwear?'

'When Barker still thought he was alone, he spotted a pair of Goff's panties, a black lace thong, lying on top in her open dresser drawer. He seemed surprised by it. Thrilled, in fact. Like a kid at Christmas with a brand-new toy. If he'd already searched the place he'd have seen the thong before, probably stuffed it in his pocket and taken it home.'

'What'd he do with it?'

McCabe just shrugged.

Maggie made a face as if there were a bad smell in the room. 'An underwear sniffer?'

McCabe shrugged again and nodded.

'And you don't think he's our freak?'

'I don't think so.'

'I don't know, McCabe. Means, opportunity, motive. It all fits. Means? Barker has a key that gets him into her apartment anytime he wants. Opportunity? She's going away on vacation. Won't be missed for over two weeks. Motive? That's easy. The guy's a creep. A sexual deviant. An underwear sniffer. Yuck.'

Mandy arrived just in time to hear Maggie say 'underwear sniffer.' 'Anybody want more coffee?' She smiled uncertainly.

'No thanks, Mandy, just the check,' said McCabe.

When she was out of earshot, Maggie picked up where she'd left off. 'Think about it, McCabe. Goff's a gorgeous woman. Barker lusts after her. Dreams about her. You told me yourself you saw him staring at the pictures. He probably jerks off to visions of Goff leaping around naked in his dirty little brain every night. Of course, what this guy really wants, Lainie won't give him, and he knows she never will. So he decides to get it and get her. The only way he can.'

Maggie was on a roll, and maybe she was right. Barker was a tempting suspect. Definitely a creep. Still, being a creep didn't mean being a murderer. Or even being the guy who searched Lainie's apartment.

'Let's say he sneaks into 2F on that Friday night,' said Maggie. 'Waits till she gets home from work, overpowers her –'

'Overpowers her?' McCabe laughed. 'C'mon, Mag. Give me a break. The guy's not just small, he's the proverbial ninety-pound weakling. Goff could have kicked the shit out of him. Hell, my daughter could have kicked the shit out of him.'

That stopped her, but only for a second. 'Yeah. Okay. Maybe. But what if he had a gun or a knife? *The* knife. Or if he slipped her a roofie?'

'You mean when they were sitting down to share a cocktail?'

Maggie glared at him. 'Don't be a wiseass.'

'Alright, sorry, but then what? After she's unconscious he drags her out of the apartment, puts her in her own car, and takes the ferry to Harts Island? Why? So he can kill her where there's a nice view of the ocean? Then, to top things off, he steals her apartment keys when he already has a set? Admit it, Detective Margaret. That dog don't hunt.'

'Alright, alright.' She held up her hands reluctantly. 'You're right. I still think the guy's a creep –'

'He's definitely a creep.'

'A creep who knows something he's not telling us. Like what he was doing sneaking into Goff's apartment with a flashlight and a tool belt around his middle at four in the morning. I think we need answers.'

McCabe nodded. They did need to find out what Barker was doing in the apartment, and what it had to do with Goff's murder. 'Okay. Bring him in, but I'm not sure how much you'll get from him. The minute I got too tough last night he started reciting me his own Miranda rights.'

'C'mon, McCabe.' She smiled. 'You're not Brian Cleary. You know tough's not the answer to everything.'

'Alright, Mag, work your wiles. Find out what he was doing there. But I still don't see Barker as the searcher.'

'Your money's still on Ogden?'

'As the searcher, yes. Like Burt said, Ogden has a lot to lose if the whole world finds out he was cheating.'

Maggie went back to building her sugar towers. 'Okay, so we're saying Ogden's not the killer and Barker's not the killer. Who's left? Kelly?'

'The evidence points that way. What we need to do is establish a motive.'

They split the bill fifty-fifty and headed back to 109.

Nineteen

Cleary was waiting on the other side of the elevator door when McCabe and Maggie stepped out onto the fourth floor at PPD headquarters. 'You guys got a minute? Wanna bring you up to date, and there's something you ought to see.' He led the way into the small conference room and closed the door.

'What did you find out?'

'Bunch of stuff,' said Cleary. 'First off, Quinn doesn't have a car and didn't rent one. At least not from any of the agencies in Portland. Didn't take a taxi anywhere either. Her mother's car is a '97 Subaru Outback, but Quinn didn't use it. It's still parked under a pile of snow at a lot off India Street. Possible friends' cars we don't know about.'

'How about the terminals?'

'Airport's closed till later this morning. Quinn hasn't been spotted there or at the train or bus stations.'

McCabe pursed his lips. 'Anything from the ferry crews?'

'That's the good news. Nobody's seen the BMW, but we do have a sighting on Quinn.'

'Go ahead.'

'According to one of the deckhands, she returned to the mainland on the last ferry last night.' Cleary sat down next to the TV monitor and pulled chairs into position for the others. There was a freeze-frame image of a nervous-looking man in his twenties on the screen. 'Left Harts Island at eleven fifty-five. Arrived in Portland twelve fifteen.'

Eleven fifty-five. The ferry McCabe watched from the galley of the *Francis R. Mangini* as the two boats passed midway across the bay.

'I was going through the crew roster, interviewing the deckhands one by one.' He tilted his head toward the monitor. 'This one told me he saw Quinn.'

'What's his name?' asked Maggie.

'Bobby Howser,' said Cleary. 'Howser and Quinn know each other. They were classmates at Portland High. At first Howser denied seeing her, but something in the way he said it, well, it was pretty easy to tell he was lying. So I bring him in, stick him in an interview room, and go at him for a while.' Cleary smiled. 'Y'know? Good cop. Bad cop.'

Maggie smiled. 'Oh yeah? Which one were you?'

'Both.' Cleary smiled back. He was rhythmically banging his right fist into his left palm.

'You didn't rough him up, did you, Brian?' McCabe asked. His tone was teasing, but the question was serious. Cleary had potential, but he was a born brawler. McCabe knew he might have to keep a tight rein on him.

'Nah. I wouldn't do anything like that.'

'I'm glad to hear it. I wouldn't want to have to cut short a promising career. What did Howser tell you?'

'Kid was pretty scared once he realized this wasn't a game. He hung tough for about five minutes and then blurted out the whole story.' Cleary hit PLAY, and the frozen image came to life. Howser was sitting at the table in the small interview room at the end of the hall, eyes darting around, looking everywhere but at where Cleary would have been. A hand entered the frame and slid a photograph across the table. Cleary's voice came out of the speaker. 'Alright, Bobby, I'm going to ask you again like I did down at the Bay Lines. Have you ever seen this woman on the boat?'

Howser glanced at the image, then looked away again. 'No. Well, yes, but not recently.'

'When was the last time you saw her?'

Howser looked around nervously. 'I don't remember.'

'Do you know her?'

'Yeah.'

'What's her name?'

Howser didn't answer right away. Suddenly Cleary's hand came down hard on the table. Howser flinched, the sound of the slap reverberating like a rifle shot. 'Bobby. I asked you a question,' Cleary said, his tone measured yet, for all its softness, full of menace, 'and I expect an answer.'

'Quinn. Her name's Abby Quinn.'

'Abby Quinn. Good. That's better. When was the last time you saw Abby Quinn?'

Howser closed his eyes, took a deep breath. He opened them again. For the first time he looked at Cleary. 'Last night,' he said. 'She jumped on the eleven fifty-five about thirty seconds before we pulled out. There were only a couple of other passengers. Hardly anyone takes that boat this time of year.'

'How long have you known Quinn?'

'All my life. We're both from the island. Grew up there. She's still living there. I've got my own place in town now.'

'Did you talk to her last night?'

'Like I said, she jumps on at the last minute and comes running up to me.' Howser paused. 'You know Abby's crazy, don't you?'

'No,' said Cleary. 'I didn't know. What do you mean by crazy?'

Howser shrugged. 'She gets weird sometimes. Does weird stuff. Says weird stuff. She's been in and out of that mental hospital in Gorham a couple of times.'

'Winter Haven?'

'Yeah. Winter Haven.'

'Was she doing weird stuff Friday?'

Howser nodded. 'Kind of. She came running on wearing this stupid ski mask. I could tell it was Abby, though.'

'How? You said she was wearing a mask.'

'I dunno. Her shape. Her voice. The way she was moving and talking. Like I said, I've known her all my life.'

No surprise there. It's not that hard to recognize someone under a mask. Not if you know them well enough. Which left the obvious question hanging. Did the killer know Abby? And if so, how well? McCabe didn't give voice to the thought. He didn't have to. He knew Maggie was thinking the same thing. On the screen Howser was still talking.

'Anyway, she pulls the mask off and tells me somebody's chasing her. She looks upset, so I ask her who's chasing her. She says Death. That's what she said. Death. I mean, that's weird right there, isn't it? Then she puts her face about an inch away from mine and makes me promise not to tell anybody that I'd seen her. Says I have to swear I won't tell. On a stack of Bibles. Cross my heart and hope to die. Like we were still in third grade or something. "Swear you won't tell," she said. "C'mon, swear it." She wouldn't stop till I actually used the words, "I swear I won't tell."'

'Did you? Use the words?'

'Yeah.'

'What, exactly, did she make you swear?'

'I just told you.'

'Tell me again.'

'That I wouldn't tell anyone that I'd seen her. Not even the cops, she said. Not even you guys. Death would get her if I did. Like Death was some dude she knew.'

McCabe wondered, *was* he some dude she knew? Cleary didn't ask the question. Instead he asked, 'How'd you feel about that?'

Bobby Howser looked down. Spoke in a low voice. 'I gotta tell you. When Abby gets crazy like that she scares the hell out of me. She's tried to kill herself a couple of times, y'know. She wasn't like that as a kid. We were pretty good friends back in middle school. Right through high school. She was normal. Like everyone else.'

'How is she now?'

Howser gave Cleary a frustrated look, as if he were tired of repeating himself. 'I already told you. Crazy. You never know where the stuff that comes out of her mouth comes from.'

'Okay, so you swore to her you wouldn't tell. Is that why you lied to me about seeing her?'

Bobby looked down, embarrassed. 'Yes.'

Cleary's voice softened. 'It's alright. You did the right thing. She needs help, and we're trying to help her.'

Bobby looked up, a flicker of hope on his face.

'Then what happened?' asked Cleary.

Howser shrugged. 'She locks herself in the head. Stays in there the whole way across. When we got to Portland, I had to knock on the door to let her know we arrived. She comes out, puts that stupid mask back on, and runs off into the night.'

'What else was she wearing?'

'Running clothes. A black Nike jacket. Nike shoes. Air Pegasus. I noticed 'cause I have the same kind. She was carrying a small backpack. And a fanny pack.'

Cleary hit stop. Howser's image froze again. 'That's pretty much it,' he said. 'I told the kid that what he told me was confidential. If he told anybody anything he'd be in deep shit. He said he wouldn't. I made him swear.'

'Cross his heart and hope to die?' asked McCabe. Cleary grinned.

'And he didn't know where she went?' asked Maggie.

'Nope. Like he said, she just ran off into the night. Gone. Poof. Just like that.'

McCabe supposed it was progress of a kind. Knowing for sure Abby was on the mainland. Knowing she was still alive, at least as of midnight last night. Knowing what she was wearing. Of course, the downside was it gave her a whole lot more geography to get lost in. Or get killed in. Or freeze to death in. Finding Abby had to be job one. For the cops and the killer. McCabe had the advantage of greater resources. An advantage that would be neutralized if the killer knew her well. Knew who her friends were.

Knew where she was likely to go. It was going to be a delicate balancing act. Eddie Fraser leaned into the room. 'There's something on the Monument Square videos you guys ought to see.'

Cleary switched off the monitor and said he'd get the information on what Abby was wearing out to all units. They followed Eddie over to Starbucks's cube. The area wasn't much bigger than a walk-in closet, but they all managed to squeeze in. It was lined with an array of the latest electronics. The young Somali's face broke into a huge grin as they entered. 'Sergeant McCabe,' he called out. 'We've found something good here, I think.' After only seven years in America, Starbucks spoke English almost without an accent. Only the occasional odd construction and a formality gave him away. 'I've been helping Detective Fraser review the surveillance videos from the lobby of Ten Monument Square. Both Thursday the twenty-second and Friday the twenty-third.'

'Cleaning crews came into the building both nights and left again later when they finished their work,' said Fraser.

'Here's the lobby just before the cleaners arrived Thursday,' said Starbucks. There were two video monitors mounted side by side on a shelf just above Starbucks's head. He directed their eyes to the one on the left. 'As you can see, the camera has a wide-angle lens and is shooting down from a height of ten-point-five feet.' The time code read *12/22/06. 6:05:40 PM*. The lobby's revolving door and two sets of regular doors on either side were all clearly visible. So was the steel door Randall Jackson said led down to the lawyers' private garage. Starbucks hit play, and McCabe watched a cluster of people enter the door on the left. Because of the angle, he was looking more at the tops of heads than at faces. They walked about eight feet into the lobby and then turned in a group like a school of guppies and exited through the garage door. 'Where are they going?' asked McCabe.

'There's a supply room downstairs where the cleaning stuff is stored. There's also a small locker room where they stow their coats and bags while they work, and a unisex toilet.'

'The entrance to the lawyers' garage is there, too, right?'

'Yeah. I went down and looked around,' said Fraser. 'You go down one flight of stairs to a short corridor, turn left for the supply room and locker room. Go straight ahead for the restroom. Turn right for the garage. There's also a freight elevator at the end of the corridor that takes the cleaning and maintenance crews to any floor in the building. Also an emergency exit to the street. Locked from the outside. Sets off an alarm if you open it from inside.'

'So theoretically our killer could have walked through that lobby door down to the basement and ended up anywhere in the building?'

'Yeah,' said Fraser. 'The question is how he got out again. I checked the alarm on the emergency exit. It was on and working. The only other ways out are up through the lobby or out through the lawyers' garage. You need a key card to open the gate in the garage.' Ogden, of course, had a key card. So did Lainie. So did every other lawyer at Palmer Milliken, all 192 of them. If they descended to the garage level via the freight elevator, they wouldn't have shown up on the videos. He asked Maggie if Jacobi had found Goff's key card in her car. He hadn't. 'Watch the rest of the video,' said Fraser. 'Starbucks picked up on something I didn't notice first time through.'

'Here are the cleaners arriving twenty-four hours later, on Friday night,' said Starbucks. On the right-hand monitor McCabe and Maggie watched a virtual replay of Thursday night's action. The cluster of people arrived at 6:08 instead of 6:05. Everything else was the same. They came in through the same entrance. Turned right at the same point and left the lobby through the same steel door.

'See the difference?' asked Fraser.

'No.' If there was something different, McCabe wasn't sure what it was. Not the first time through, anyway. 'Play Thursday again,' he requested. Starbucks did. 'Okay, freeze it right . . . there.' Starbucks stopped the video just as the cleaning crew cluster stretched out to pass through the steel door. 'Okay, now roll Friday and freeze at the same point.'

This time he caught it. The extra man. At least he thought it was a man, based on size and the way the figure moved. Bundled up in a long dark coat with a hood, you couldn't tell for sure. On Thursday six cleaners went through the door. What appeared to be three men and three women. On Friday there were seven. The seventh was pretty well hidden while the group was bunched up, shielded from the camera, practically invisible. Even as number seven filed through the door he kept his head down and turned away from the camera. He had one hand raised and blocking his face from the camera like a starlet avoiding the paparazzi. No question. He knew it was there. 'Gotcha, you bastard,' McCabe muttered. 'You check with the cleaning company?' he asked Fraser.

'Yup. Joe Maguire of Capitol Maintenance Corp. told me six cleaners were assigned to the building both nights. The same six. Maguire's son, Joe junior, dropped them off at Ten Monument Square in a company van, which is why they all arrived together. He also picked them up at the end of the shift. He said there were only six going each way each night. That's all the van holds, not counting the driver.'

'So the bad guy waits outside until the cleaners arrive and sneaks in with them?'

'Looks that way,' said Fraser. 'Maguire gave us names and contact info for all six cleaners. Sturgis is out tracking them down now. See if they remember the extra guy coming in with them.'

'How about the security guard? Name's Randall Jackson. He might have seen the guy's face.'

'Spoke to him already. He never noticed anyone extra at all. Just the cleaners.'

McCabe sighed. He wasn't sure how much they were going to get out of this. 'Can you show me the video of the cleaners leaving Friday?'

Starbucks fast-forwarded to the early morning hours. The steel door opens, the six cleaners file into the lobby and leave the building. No number seven. Lainie Goff's probable killer checked in, but he didn't check out. The time code read *12/24/05. 2:04:32 AM*.

'Nobody else left after that?'

'Nope.'

'So he kidnaps her, and they both leave in her car.'

'Looks that way.'

'Let's find our best shot of the guy.'

Starbucks rolled back to where the cleaners entered the building. Then he advanced the video frame by frame, until he settled on the best view they had of cleaner number seven. It wasn't great. His head was down. His hand was hiding the side of his face. The hood hiding the hair. A small patch of white chin was all that could be seen. Starbucks tightened the frame to a close-up of the head. That made it too blurry to see much of anything. All you could tell was that the person was Caucasian and taller than the other cleaners. The heavy hooded coat hid everything else. Normal enough in this weather. McCabe stared at the frozen image. Assuming this was the killer – and that was still an assumption – it was further evidence that Hank Ogden wasn't their guy. No need for Ogden to be sneaking into his own building when he was already upstairs in the Palmer Milliken offices both earlier in the day and later that night. He supposed it could all be a deliberate trail of disinformation designed to lead the cops away from Ogden as the killer. Maybe that was what all that other stuff was, too. The Bible notes. The trip to Harts. The body left on the pier. Maybe it was all a setup to divert suspicion. But McCabe didn't think so. If at 6:08 on that Friday night Ogden was still sitting in the partners' meeting and not sneaking into his own building, well, that'd pretty well settle the issue. Assuming, of course, that cleaner number seven was, in fact, the killer.

Twenty

Dr Richard Wolfe returned McCabe's call a little after seven. 'You said it was urgent. What's up? Is it the dreams again? Are they coming back?'

'No, it's not the dreams,' McCabe said. 'In fact, it's not about me at all. I'm calling as a cop. I need to talk to you about one of your patients.'

'Really?' Wolfe paused to consider that. 'Well, that could be a problem. You do understand professional ethics forbid me to reveal private information about any of my patients. To you or anyone else.'

'Yes, I understand that. But there are circumstances under which you would be able to talk, aren't there?'

'Yes. If I have knowledge that the patient has committed a crime. Or is about to commit one. Or if you can document that the patient or someone else will be put in danger by my failing to speak.'

'Then I don't think you'll have any ethical issues here. One of your patients has been involved in a crime and may be in serious danger. We need your help.'

There was a long pause on Wolfe's end of the line before he spoke. 'Alright. Can you tell me which patient?'

'I'll tell you when I see you. Where are you?'

'In my office. Trying to finish a paper I'm writing for one of the journals.'

'Why don't we meet there in, say, twenty minutes?'

'Alright. That's fine. I need to break for some dinner anyway. If you haven't eaten yet, why don't you join me? I'll order some takeout, and we can eat while we talk.'

'Deal.'

'Good. What do you feel like? Chinese? Thai? Pizza?'

'Your choice.'

'Ring the buzzer to the right of the front door. The building's locked on weekends. Office 301.'

'I remember.'

'Yes. Of course you do. If I don't come down and get you right away, it means I'm on the phone. So just wait and don't buzz again. Okay?'

McCabe decided to walk. It was ten minutes from 109 Middle Street to 23 Union Wharf, and the air was warmer than it had been in a month. Upper twenties, according to Weather.com, and still rising. Leaving the building, he overheard a couple of uniforms talking about a January thaw. Sunday temps, they said, might hit fifty or more. He imagined frostbitten Portlanders leaping out of their long johns into shorts and T-shirts, hoping for a winter tan. He might even join them. McCabe headed east on Middle, turned left, and walked down Exchange. The Old Port shopping district was crowded with people, some even pausing to check out shop windows instead of just darting from car to doorway and back again.

He called Kyra. Wherever she was, he could hear voices in the background. 'I'm having people over for drinks,' she explained. 'Reestablishing connections. Letting my friends know I'm still alive.'

'Anyone I know?'

'Mandy's here. Said she served you and Maggie lunch today. And Joe Turco. You know him.' Turco ran a letterpress printing operation in the old bakery building where Kyra's studio was. Limited edition portfolios. Art books. Other high-end print jobs. McCabe had met Turco a couple of times. 'We're heading over to Joe's studio in a while to look at the proofs for a new edition he's printing . . .'

Kyra talked some more about the portfolio edition. McCabe only half listened. He was missing her already, and she'd only moved out this morning.

'How's your murder going?' she finally asked.

'I guess we're making progress. Hard to tell sometimes. Actually, I have a question for you.'

'About the murder?'

'Yes. You know most of the good art photographers in town, don't you?'

'Most of them,' she said. 'The ones I don't know personally, I know by reputation.'

He described the shots on Lainie Goff's bedroom wall. 'I'd like to know who shot them.'

'Industrial detritus and naked lawyers? Interesting range. Does Goff still look like Sandy? With her clothes off, I mean.'

'Yes.'

'That's it?' Kyra teased. 'Just yes? No elaboration?'

He didn't answer, so Kyra changed the tone. 'The prints weren't signed?'

'No.'

'Interesting. If they're as good as you say, they're worth less without a signature. Besides, most serious photographers want people to know their work.'

'Maybe Goff asked the photographer not to sign them. Maybe she didn't want people to know who was photographing her in the nude.'

'Possibly. Or maybe the photographer isn't a pro. Just a talented amateur. Or,' she said, a tinge of conspiracy creeping into her voice, 'maybe Goff and the photographer were lovers and she wanted to keep the affair a secret?' McCabe smiled. Kyra was getting into this. 'I'll nose around for you,' she said. 'See if any of my friends have any idea who'd shoot that kind of stuff.'

'Thanks. Just be discreet. Don't tell them why you want to know,' said McCabe. She said she wouldn't. He continued, 'Any chance of me seeing you tonight?'

'None. I've got to make my willpower last more than one day, don't you think? Anyway, I love you.'

He sighed, told her he loved her, too, and put the phone back in his pocket. He turned right onto Fore Street and jaywalked to the other side. Overly polite Maine drivers stopped in the middle of the block to let him pass. Had he tried the same thing in New York, they would have been swearing and laying on their horns. Or maybe just running him over. He glanced at the sex toys in the windows of Condom Sense. Pasta boobs and marzipan penises. He wondered who bought that stuff. A few doors down was Edward Malinoff, Purveyor of Rare Wines. Malinoff also carried a great selection of single malts and the odd box of contraband Cuban cigars, the latter available only to Malinoff's friends at astronomical prices McCabe couldn't afford. Not a problem. McCabe hadn't smoked a cigar in years.

He turned left at Union Street by the Portland Harbor Hotel, went down the hill past Three Dollar Dewey's, crossed Commercial Street, and walked out onto Union Wharf, one of the many piers that form most of Portland's working waterfront. Wolfe's office was in an old three-story wooden building toward the end. He could see lights shining from a wall of windows on the third floor. A shiny black Lexus IS 350 was parked directly in front. He figured it had to be Wolfe's. The rest of the building looked dark and empty. McCabe climbed three steps, pressed the buzzer for 301, and peered through the glass into the dark lobby. Once a warehouse or maybe a fish processing plant, the building's interior space had been updated in a style McCabe liked to think of as SoHo Modern. Shiny black walls, exposed pipes crisscrossing the ceiling, big windows looking out on the harbor.

Dr Wolfe apparently wasn't on the phone, because he pushed the door open less than a minute later. McCabe's former shrink was in his mid-forties, six-one or maybe a bit more, with close-cropped gray hair that was considerably shorter than McCabe remembered it. He wore round rimless glasses that seemed to intensify the blue of his eyes. Dressed in a black pullover, black pants, and black canvas walking shoes, he looked more like the film director McCabe once dreamed of becoming than a successful Portland psychiatrist. More LA cool than L.L. Bean.

'Good to see you,' said Wolfe. He ignored the elevator and pointed McCabe toward the black steel stairs. They started up. 'Been about a year, hasn't it?'

'A little over.'

'How have you been doing?' Wolfe asked, the question clearly medical, not social.

'Fine,' said McCabe. 'How about yourself?'

'No more nightmares?'

'Nothing I can't handle.' Not quite the truth, but what the hell.

'Still taking the Xanax?'

'No.'

'Good. Glad you don't need it. Still drinking?'

'Some.'

'Too much?'

'I don't think so.'

Wolfe shared the top floor with another psychiatrist named Leah Peterson. 'Let's talk in my office,' he said.

The contrast between the office and Wolfe's treatment room next door, where the Abby Quinns and Michael McCabes of the world came to tell their tales, was startling. Two different worlds both inhabited by the same man. The treatment room was small and cozy with a big comfy couch facing the doctor's chair and walls lined with books and bric-a-brac. Designed to put patients at ease. The office was nothing like that. Instead it mirrored the cool, hard-edged modernity of the lobby. All shiny glass and chrome with floor-to-ceiling windows facing the harbor. McCabe looked out. A pair of tugs were pushing a large container barge toward the International Marine Terminal. The lights of cars moved in a steady parade across the Casco Bay Bridge.

There was a separate seating area with four chrome and leather chairs surrounding a free-form glass table.

'I ordered Thai,' said Wolfe, pointing McCabe toward one of the chairs. 'From the Siam Grill.' McCabe knew the place. High-end Thai and creative martinis on Fore Street. Some of the best Asian food in town.

'Coconut shrimp. Fresh spring rolls. Hot basil duck. Should be here in twenty minutes or so. Work for you?'

'Perfect.'

'Scotch?' asked Wolfe, producing a bottle of Dewar's from his desk drawer.

'Is that allowed?'

'Why not? You're not here as a patient.' Wolfe poured himself a drink from the bottle.

McCabe resisted temptation. He was working even if Wolfe wasn't. 'Not at the moment. You have any water?'

Wolfe went to a small fridge behind his desk, added some ice cubes to his drink, and found a bottle of Poland Spring for McCabe.

'Thanks. Helluva view.'

'Yes. Leah Peterson and I are both sailors and kayakers. When we can't be on the water we like being as close as possible.'

'You own the building?'

'The two of us do. How'd you know?'

McCabe smiled. 'You and the design seem to fit each other so well.'

Wolfe returned the smile with obvious pleasure. 'Thank you.'

They sat. The smiles faded. 'Now, who's my patient?' Wolfe asked. 'The one you say is involved in some crime?'

'Woman named Abby Quinn.'

'Abby?' Wolfe looked surprised. 'What on earth has Abby been doing?'

McCabe decided to lay it out. 'Witnessing a murder.'

Wolfe took a minute to absorb the information. 'The Elaine Goff murder?'

'Yes.'

'Abby saw it happen?'

'Yes. You knew Goff, didn't you?'

'Yes, but not well. We served on a board together. Sanctuary House. We saw each other once a month at board meetings.'

'When was the last time you saw her?'

'Goff or Abby?'

'Goff.'

'At the last meeting. They take place the second Tuesday of each month. That would have been . . .' Wolfe flipped through the pages of a Day Planner. 'Tuesday, December thirteenth. From seven till nine.'

'And Goff was there?'

'Yes. As I recall she came in late. The meeting had already started.'

'Who else attended?'

Wolfe rattled off a list of names. None of them rang any bells for McCabe except John Kelly.

'How long have you been treating Abby?'

'Since her first stay at Winter Haven. Right after her first suicide attempt. A little over three years now.'

'So you know her well?'

'Yes. Probably as well as anyone.'

'Who were her friends?'

'Abby doesn't really have any. Not close ones, anyway. I wish she did.'

'Who would she turn to if she needed someone to take her in? Perhaps to hide her?'

'Abby's hiding somewhere?' Wolfe asked. 'Is she in danger?'

'She may be. Where do you think she'd go?'

'I don't know. I would've hoped she'd come to me.'

'But she hasn't?'

'No.'

'Is there anyone else?'

Wolfe considered the question. 'Maybe John Kelly. He might take her in. Give her sanctuary, as it were. There's also Lori Sparks, the woman she works for on Harts Island.'

'Kelly said he hasn't seen her. So did Sparks.'

'I don't know, then. Are you sure Abby actually saw the murder take place?'

'Yes.'

Wolfe sipped at his Scotch. 'I'm really sorry to hear that. Abby's been doing so well lately. This could be a major setback.'

'Did you think she was cured?'

'No. Abby's schizophrenic. There's no cure for what she has. It's more about treatment and control. The last thing she needed was a major trauma.'

Wolfe peered at McCabe through the rimless glasses. He looked puzzled. 'One thing I don't understand, though. Since you apparently don't know where Abby is, how is it you know she saw the murder?'

'The night Goff was killed, Abby ran to the police station on Harts Island and told the officer on duty that she saw it happen.'

'And?'

'And he didn't believe her.'

'Because of her illness?'

'Yes. He thought she was hallucinating.'

'I see.' Wolfe nodded. 'And what, exactly, has convinced the Portland Police Department to change its collective mind?'

'Abby told the cop details of the murder she couldn't have known unless she was there. Unless she actually saw what she said she saw. By the time he reported it to us, she was already gone.'

'Was she able to identify the killer? Was it someone she knew?'

'No. That's where this gets messy and where I may need your help as her doctor. All she could tell us was that he was a naked male. When the officer asked her for a description, she couldn't provide one. Just said his face exploded in fire and he had icicles for eyes.'

'That's it? No further details?'

'The conversation wasn't recorded, but as far as we know, that's it. She said it a couple of times.'

Wolfe sighed. 'She is hallucinating. Which either means she's off her meds or the trauma's making them less effective.'

'Does that happen?'

'It can under extreme stress. I was worried something was wrong when she didn't show up for her session Wednesday.'

'When did you last speak to her?'

'Two weeks ago. Just before Christmas. Abby's sessions are Wednesdays at eleven. That would have been, let's see . . .' He flipped again through his Day Planner. 'December the twenty-first.'

'What about the following Wednesday? The twenty-eighth?'

'The office was closed between Christmas and New Year's. No sessions.'

'What about this week? Last Wednesday? You said she was a no-show?'

'Yes. I wondered why.'

'Did you check?'

'My receptionist called. She didn't get an answer.'

'Has Abby ever missed an appointment before?'

'Yes. Twice. Both times when she convinced herself she could cut down on her medication.'

'Why would she want to do that?'

'Because she thought she was okay. She felt normal. Let me give you a little background. Abby's on a drug called Zyprexa. It's a strong antipsychotic. She's on the highest dose I generally prescribe. It works well. Prevents most of the symptoms. However, it has a number of side effects. The primary one is weight gain. Abby doesn't like that. Not surprising, of course. Being physically attractive is important to a young woman in her twenties. So when she begins to feel normal, when she isn't experiencing psychotic symptoms, she'll say to herself, "Hey, I don't need this stuff anymore," and she either cuts down on the drug or, as she did on one occasion, cuts it out completely. She hasn't been experiencing psychotic episodes lately. Entirely possible she's gone off again.'

'What happens when she does?'

'Depends how long she's been off, but it seems she's already hallucinating. The emotional trauma of witness-ing a murder could also trigger that. Or exacerbate it.

Abby's tried to kill herself twice already. It could happen again. I think we need to find her quickly.'

'You're right. For two reasons.'

'What's the other?'

'We may not be the only ones looking.'

Twenty-One

Andy Barker smiled as he watched the thermometer stuck to the outside of the window rise. After weeks of wretched cold, things were finally moving in the right direction. Thank God. He just hoped it'd last. From early October to late May he kept all the windows closed and locked, all the cracks sealed with weather stripping, all the curtains drawn day and night. The same lined brown velvet curtains his mother had hung there more than forty years ago when Andy was a little boy. Even so, the cold had a way of seeping in.

Maybe if he had more fat on his body Maine winters, even bad ones like this, wouldn't be so miserable. Whale blubber keeps whales warm. Shouldn't people blubber do the same? All those bulbous blimps he saw waddling around the mall probably didn't even feel the cold. At least not the way he did.

Andy had had no personal experience with fat. When he was a kid Mimsy constantly urged him to eat. 'For your own good,' she'd say. 'Help you grow up big and strong.' No matter how hard Andy tried to force down the food, though, it never seemed to help. He was small and skinny and funny looking, and that was that. An ugly duckling who was never going to turn into a swan.

Aunt Denise, Mimsy's youngest sister, used to call him delicate. She was only ten years older than Andy, but she always treated him like a little kid. 'Don't worry about him so much,' she'd tell Mimsy when she came to take care of him when Mimsy was going away overnight. 'Andy's okay,' Denise would say. 'He's just a little delicate.'

God, how he hated that word. Delicate. Made him sound like some damned fairy. Well, he wasn't a fairy, and if anyone knew that it ought to be Denise. Hell, he knew she knew it. The way she walked around the apartment flashing her goodies in that see-through nightie when she came to take care of him when Mimsy was away. The way she'd tease him mercilessly when she caught him sneaking peeks. Bitch.

Sometimes Andy'd peek through the keyhole when Denise was in the bathroom taking a bath or shower. He always liked doing that, at least until that last time. There he was, fourteen years old, down on his knees, his eye pressed against the door, and, boom, she whips it open and catches him in the act. Bitch.

'Was there something you wanted to see, Andy?' she asked, standing over him without a stitch on with a smirky little smile on her face. Her voice oh so sweet, butter wouldn't melt.

'No, no. I was just . . . just here.'

'Haven't you ever seen a naked girl before?'

He didn't answer.

'You haven't, have you?'

He couldn't bring himself to say anything. Just got to his feet and stood there blushing. He was sure she could see the bulge in his pajamas where his erection was pushing out. Sure he was going to explode and start squirting all over himself.

'Well, go ahead and have a good look, Andy,' she said,

with a mean little smile. 'Just don't touch. That wouldn't be right, now would it?' Bitch.

He remembered her closing the door, leaving him on the other side. He was sure she'd tell Mimsy what he'd done. She never did, but the threat was always there. After that, when she came to stay over, the bathroom keyhole was always covered. He never saw her naked again.

No, Andy shook his head sadly, he liked girls alright. As much as anyone. It was just that they didn't like him back. None of them did. Thinking about it, he felt the old sense of despair breaking out. He tried to push it away. He didn't want to go there. Not now. He closed his eyes and took a deep breath to calm himself.

His mother was gone now, taken by cancer nearly five years ago. He missed her. He really did. Even though, if he was going to be super honest about it, her being dead wasn't all bad. Apartment 1F was all his. It didn't stink of dead cigarette butts anymore, and he didn't have to hide his stash of magazines or videos or worry about her finding them. It also meant he wasn't always being hassled to go out and *find a nice girl*.

Somehow Mimsy never got it. Girls didn't like him, not even ugly girls. Occasionally he worked up the courage to convince some girl he found on Match.com or eHarmony or Craigslist to go out with him. One who was ugly enough or desperate enough to give him a try. But it never worked. There never was a second date, and Andy was tired of being dumped on, stood up, and turned away. Besides, he didn't really want an ugly girl. He wanted a girl like Lainie. Now even she'd been taken from him. It wasn't fair. God had really fucked him over.

The hell with it. He didn't want to think about it anymore. In one sense he still had Lainie and he always would. He double-locked the door to 1F, latched the chain, and brought out his box of DVDs from their hiding place behind the false panel in the closet under the stairs. He set the box down next to his favorite chair, a brown corduroy La-Z-Boy recliner.

It was Lainie moving into 2F three years ago that first gave him the idea to install the spycams. Someone really worth looking at taking the apartment. Someone a whole lot sexier than Denise. He remembered showing Lainie the apartment, remembered following her through each of the empty rooms, showing her how big the closets were and how much light the windows let in, pointing out the new appliances in the kitchen, hoping against hope that she might want the place, absolutely certain that she was the most beautiful woman he'd ever seen in his life. Those incredible eyes. That gorgeous face. That amazing body. Maybe the best part of it all, maybe the best moment in his entire life, was when Lainie turned to him at the end of the tour, smiled, and said, 'It's perfect. I'll take it.'

Christ, it had been all he could do to keep himself from pumping his arms in the air and shouting 'Yes!' like some halfback who just scored the winning touchdown in the Super Bowl. Somehow he managed to hold himself in. Managed to just smile back calmly and say, 'Great. I'll run downstairs and print up a lease.'

Yes, Goff taking the apartment was what finally gave him the courage to turn his long-imagined fantasies into action. He knew exactly what he had to do, exactly what equipment he needed for the job, exactly how to make it work. Of course, why wouldn't he? What with him being a former video professional and all.

Andy's mind went to that cop who caught him in 2F last night. Guy treated him like he was some kind of pervert. Sure he was turned on by Lainie's underwear, but so what? Who wouldn't be? Lacy black thongs pressing into her you know what. Andy should have known the bastard was still there, but he was sitting in that chair just out of range of the bedroom spycam, and it'd been so quiet up there so long, he figured the guy was gone. Bastard sure fooled him.

Twenty-Two

'Look, you're her shrink,' said McCabe. 'You know how her mind works. If anyone knows where Abby would go to hide from a killer it ought to be you, right?'

Wolfe shook his head helplessly. 'I've already told you what I think.'

'Kelly?'

'Yes.'

'He says he doesn't know where she is.'

'Have you searched the place?'

'Are you suggesting Kelly may be lying?'

'All I'm suggesting is that Kelly's unpredictable. The minute anyone starts thinking they know who or what John Kelly is, it's time to think again.'

'Aren't you the one who placed Abby at Kelly's?'

'Yes.'

'Why? I thought Sanctuary House was supposed to be for sexually abused runaways. Mostly teenagers. I hadn't heard Abby was abused, and she's not a teenager.'

'She wasn't, and she's not. At the time, I wanted her out of Winter Haven. She was doing well. Staying on her meds. The voices were quiet –'

'The voices?'

'Yes. Abby hears voices. Auditory hallucinations. Common among schizophrenics. At that point, they were under control. But none of the halfway houses I usually work with had space, so I called Kelly and talked him into letting Abby work at Sanctuary House as a staff assistant, a kind of an unpaid intern/big sister. Convinced him her illness wouldn't get in the way. I thought taking on that kind of responsibility would be good for Abby. Build confidence. Self-esteem.'

'Did it work?'

'Yes. For several months it worked very well. Abby was proud of the trust people were placing in her. Especially Kelly. She worked hard. Did a good job.'

'Then what happened?'

'She fell in love with Kelly.'

'I thought Kelly was gay.'

'He is. She fell in love with him anyway.'

'What happened?'

'It kind of blew up in her face. In our sessions I told her pursuing Kelly wasn't a good idea. She said she couldn't help how she felt. So I suggested it was time for her to leave Sanctuary House.'

'What happened next?'

'She went to Jack. Told him how she felt. Made explicit sexual advances.'

'She told you that?'

'Eventually, but Kelly did first. He was worried about her. Said he told her he thought that she was a terrific young woman but that her feelings were inappropriate. That it was an impossible situation and that it would be best all around if she left Sanctuary House.'

'Sounds like an appropriate response.'

'I think it was.'

'How did she react?'

'She felt abandoned. Humiliated. He was the first man

she'd reached out to since her illness began, and he turned her away.'

'Did he tell her he was gay?'

'Yes. I think on some level she already knew it. Subconsciously, she was creating a situation she knew would lead to rejection.'

'Why?'

'I don't know. Maybe to demonstrate her own worthlessness.'

McCabe remembered the picture of the healthy young woman standing on the rocks by the sea. Only a couple of years older then than Casey was now. GRRRL POWER! her sweatshirt proclaimed. He felt a profound sadness at the curveballs life had a way of throwing at people. He knew there wasn't much he could do about it.

He pulled out the photo of Lainie Goff and the others at the party and handed it to Wolfe. 'Any idea what the occasion was?'

'Yes. A Sanctuary House fund-raiser. A week or so before Christmas. I was there along with about a hundred other people.'

'I recognize Ogden and Kelly, and Goff, of course. Do you know who the other two are?'

'The blonde is a Palmer Milliken attorney. Janet something or other. I only met her that night.'

'Janet Pritchard?'

'Sounds right.'

'How about the tall bald guy?'

'A money man from Boston,' said Wolfe. 'Goff hooked him for a decent chunk of change, and Kelly closed the deal.'

'How big was the donation?'

'Ten K.'

'Do you know the money man's name?' McCabe asked.

'Uhh . . . yes.' Wolfe paused, trying to remember. 'Give me a minute. I don't have your talent for total recall.' He squinted at the horizon. 'Tom? Ted? No, Todd. That's it. Todd Martin? No, that's a tennis player.'

'Todd Markham?'

'Markham, yes, that's it.' Wolfe nodded. 'Todd Markham.'

A buzzer rang. Wolfe looked at his watch. 'Food's here,' he said. 'Sit tight. I'll run down and get it.'

Jesus, McCabe thought, this was getting incestuous. He looked again at the photo. Every one of these people was in some way connected to Goff, and any one of them might have had reason to kill her. Kelly for the money. Ogden as her lover. Pritchard as a competitor for a Palmer Milliken partnership and maybe for Ogden's affections. Markham? All he knew was that Lainie was killed in Markham's house, in Markham's bed. Maybe they were lovers as well.

Markham was in Chicago Tuesday night, Maggie had told him. *Had dinner with a couple of clients. Stayed at the Hyatt. Didn't get back to Boston till* . . . Till when? He'd interrupted her before she finished the sentence. He'd have to check.

Wolfe returned carrying a brown paper bag filled with food. He set it on the coffee table. 'I don't know if I should even bring this up,' he said, pulling containers out of the bag, 'but there is one possibility we haven't discussed.'

'Which is?'

'Which is that maybe Abby didn't just witness Goff's murder. Maybe she committed it.' Wolfe opened a drawer in his desk and started pulling out paper plates, napkins, and chopsticks. 'Shall I split everything up? Half and half?'

'Sure. That's fine.'

As Wolfe began doling out equal portions of the food, McCabe walked over to the window and looked down at the water. The barge hadn't made a whole lot of progress in the time he'd been there. He guessed barges moved slow. He thought about what Wolfe just said. Could Abby have been the killer? He'd never considered that possibility. None of them had. Not Maggie. Not Bowman. Not any of his team. Probably dumb. It was a scenario too obvious to ignore. He knew she was present when the murder took place – she knew details she couldn't have known otherwise – and she had run away. Disappeared into the night. They'd all assumed she was hiding from the killer. Wasn't it equally possible she was hiding from them? From the police? Or maybe hiding from what she had done.

Wolfe held up the bottle of Dewar's. 'Sure you won't join me?'

McCabe glanced back. 'No thanks.'

'Another water, then?'

'Sure.'

Wolfe refilled his own glass and put another bottle of Poland Spring by McCabe's plate.

If Abby *was* the killer, McCabe wondered, why would she have gone to the police in the first place? Why wake up Bowman in the middle of the night? What about motive? But even as he was asking himself these questions, he knew they were irrelevant. Abby was crazy. Schizophrenic.

She suffered from hallucinations and delusions. For someone like Abby, normal concepts of reason and motive didn't apply. If she killed Lainie Goff, it would have been in the middle of a psychotic episode, probably without even realizing what she had done.

McCabe returned to his chair and took his plate of food. He picked up a spring roll, dipped it in sauce, and took a bite. 'You say you know Abby better than anyone else. Do you think she's capable of murder?'

'Capable of it? Of course she's capable of it,' Wolfe said, chewing on a mouthful of spicy duck. 'Abby's schizophrenic. She inhabits an alternative reality. If she's been off her meds for a while – or if they're starting to lose their effectiveness – she's capable of damned near anything.'

'So you're saying she invented the story of the monster with his face on fire?'

'No. Probably not,' Wolfe said. 'A monster with his face on fire may in fact be exactly what she saw, whether she killed Goff herself or just witnessed the murder. Either way.'

'You better help me with that, Doctor. I'm a little slow today.'

'Let me give you some background. Schizophrenia is a brain disorder that's characterized, more than anything else, by a profound disconnect between perception and reality. Like most schizophrenics Abby suffers from delusions, things that are false but that she believes to be true. She also suffers from hallucinations. False sensory perceptions. She sees and hears things that aren't there. She really does see them, though, and hear them. They're as real to her as that coconut shrimp is to you.'

'So if Abby did kill Goff . . .'

'She may really, truly have seen a monster do it. Maybe somewhere in her mind she feels it's something only a monster could do. What she doesn't recognize, if that's the case, is that the monster is her.'

McCabe leaned back and stared at the ceiling. He supposed what Wolfe was suggesting was possible, but the more he thought about it, the more certain he became that it just didn't happen that way. There were too many details that didn't fit. Details Wolfe wasn't aware of. Like the dumping of the body on the Fish Pier. Like the note in the mouth. Like the precise and careful way she'd been killed. No, McCabe was sure Abby hadn't done it. 'What if she's not the killer?' he asked. 'What if she did in fact see it happen?'

Wolfe shrugged. 'Then she's probably seeing the killer as a monster because what she actually saw was too frightening or too painful for her mind to accept. But really, I'm just guessing now.'

McCabe wiped his mouth with a paper napkin, got up, and tossed his empty plate in the trash. 'Is there any way to bring the real memory back?'

'Maybe. When nonschizophrenics repress painful memories, hypnotherapy sometimes works.'

'Hypnosis?'

'Yes. It isn't typically used with schizophrenics, but it's not necessarily contraindicated either. I've never tried it with one, but I've read about some experimentation. In fact, I'd be interested to see how it works with someone like Abby.'

'Do you know anybody who's an expert in, what did you call it? Hypnotherapy?'

'Yes. Me.'

'You'd be willing to hypnotize Abby?'

'Yes. Of course – but we'll have to find her first.'

McCabe nodded thoughtfully. 'Thanks, Doc. I'll let you know when we do.' He got his coat and put it on. 'And thanks for dinner.'

Twenty-Three

'It's Andy, right? Do you mind if I call you Andy?' Maggie leaned into the open back window of the black-and-white patrol car, looking down at the small figure hunched on the backseat. He glanced up at the question but didn't answer. Maggie smiled. Andy Barker blinked back. 'You don't mind if I call you Andy, do you?' She repeated the question. 'I've got a younger brother named Andy. He's my favorite brother, actually.' Her brothers' names were really Trevor and Harlan. 'Andy's always been one of my favorite names.'

Her eyes registered the green and black plaid wool pants the guy was wearing, the green suede ankle boots, the fake snakeskin jacket. Little perv even dresses creepy, she thought.

'Yeah. That's fine,' he said, still blinking. 'I guess that's fine. Can I call you Margaret?'

Could he call her Margaret? The name printed on the card she'd given him last night. 'Sure,' she said. 'You call me Margaret.'

She extended her hand. He looked at it but made no effort to shake it. 'Nice to meet you, Andy,' she said. 'And thanks for agreeing to come in and talk to us.' She pushed the hand toward him just a bit more.

Finally he took off a glove and shook. His hand felt cold and dry. Like a dead man's, she thought, letting go. She could see he was shivering. 'Hey, Castleman,' she called to the uniform behind the wheel, 'pump up that heat a little, would you? Man's cold back here.'

Castleman didn't do anything right away. Maggie knew the last thing he wanted was to make the guy in the backseat more comfortable. Tough shit. 'Hey, Castleman, you hear what I said?' Castleman's right hand poked at the temp gauge and flipped the fan on to high.

'Thanks, Castleman,' Barker said, a little gloat in his voice. Then he looked up. 'Why do I have to go with him anyway?' he asked. 'I'd rather drive with you. In your car.'

'Yeah. I know, I'd prefer that, too, Andy. Then we could talk privately on the way in. But we've gotta follow department protocol. You know what I mean?' She stood and tapped her left hand twice on the unit's front door, letting Castleman know it was time to leave. The rear window rolled up. The car pulled out onto Brackett. Maggie could see Barker turn and look back, watching her through the misted glass. She smiled, raised a hand, and gave a small wave. Like a mother sending her kid off to school.

She waited until the unit turned left on Pine Street and disappeared, then stepped over a pile of dirty snow that was starting to melt in the warmer air. She opened the door of her unmarked Crown Vic, pulled off her coat, tossed it on the passenger seat, and headed for 109.

Barker knew something he wasn't telling them. Maggie was as sure of that as she was of anything. Something that explained why he snuck into Goff's apartment at four in the morning wearing a tool belt. The trick would be getting it out of him. In spite of what she'd told McCabe, she had to play this one carefully. It wouldn't be all that easy.

*

Maggie parked herself in Fortier's office and watched Barker fidget on the TV set in the corner. He was nervous, looking this way and that. He'd been there ten minutes and was starting to get antsy. Time to get the show on the road. She nodded to Brian Cleary, who was standing next to her. Ten seconds later she watched the door to the interview room open. Cleary walked in.

'Hey, Mr Barker, how are you? Detective Cleary here.' Cleary disappeared from view as he sat down in the interviewer's chair. The camera stayed focused on Barker's face.

'Where's Margaret?'

'Who?'

'Margaret.'

'Oh. Detective Savage, you mean.'

'She asked me to call her Margaret.'

'Yeah. Well. She's my boss, so I gotta call her Detective Savage. Anyway, she's stuck in a meeting for a few minutes. Said to tell you she'll be with you as soon as she can. Shouldn't be very long. Asked me to cover a few of the preliminaries so we don't take any more of your time than we have to. Hey. Would you like me to get you a cup of coffee? Or water or anything?'

'I'll have a glass of water.'

'Okay. Sure thing.' Cleary's shoulder came into frame as he got up. A minute later Maggie could see his hand place a full glass of water in front of Barker. If he drank any he'd leave a DNA sample on the rim.

She could see Cleary's hands on the table opening a manila file folder. 'Okay,' he asked. 'Now, your full name is what?'

'Andrew Barker.'

'Any middle name or anything?'

'John.'

'Good. And you live in Apartment 1F at 342 Brackett Street here in Portland, right?'

'I own the building.'

'Oh yeah? Good for you. How long have you lived there?'

'All my life. I was born there.'

'Really? Right there in the apartment?'

'No,' Barker said, irritation beginning to creep into his voice. 'I was born at Cumberland Medical Center. My parents lived in the apartment at the time.'

'Your folks still live there?'

'Is Margaret coming soon?'

'Yeah. Just a few minutes. She said she's anxious to talk to you, so I'm sure she'll be here as soon as she can. Your folks still live there? In the apartment, I mean?'

'No. My parents divorced when I was little. Mimsy died about five years ago.'

'Mimsy?'

'My mother.'

'Mimsy was her name?'

'No. Her name was Gloria. Mimsy's what I called her.'

'Oh yeah? Sort of like Mom or Mommy or something like that?'

Barker squinted at Cleary. 'It wasn't like that. Mimsy's what everybody called her.' He started looking around the room. Everywhere but at Cleary. 'Where's Margaret? I thought she wanted to talk to me. I can't wait here all night, y'know.' The tone was petulant. Maggie figured it was time to make an entrance. Wait any longer and Barker's irritation would turn into anger and they'd probably lose him altogether.

'Mr Barker,' she said, walking into the interview room, 'I'm sorry we had to keep you waiting.' Then, to Cleary, 'Brian, I can take over from here.' When Cleary didn't move she added, 'Would you mind?'

'Hey, I'll be happy to stay, Marg . . . uh, Detective Savage,' said Cleary.

'Not necessary,' Maggie said. Walking behind Barker's chair, she stood behind him, facing Cleary. 'I'd rather speak to Mr Barker privately.'

Cleary held up his two hands, palms out, a signal of surrender. 'Okay, you're the boss,' he said. 'Call me if you need me.'

Maggie continued around the table in time to see a nearly imperceptible smile flicker across Barker's face as he watched Cleary collect his notes and walk out of the room. The carefully orchestrated dance was over.

'Asshole,' Barker muttered.

'Oh, don't mind him,' said Maggie. 'He's just trying to do his job. We all are.'

'You're different.'

'Thank you, Andy. I appreciate that.' She sat in the chair Cleary had just vacated.

He looked at her.

'I'd like to start by asking you some questions about your building and about Elaine Goff. And also about your other tenants. Would that be alright?'

'Okay. Yes. Sure. That would be fine.'

Maggie opened a small notebook and for about ten minutes took him through a series of general questions about the building, about his job as landlord. After that they went back and forth for a few more minutes about the other tenants in the building. Who they were. Where they worked. How long they'd lived at 342.

As they spoke Maggie could see Barker's eyes darting back and forth, going from her face when she was looking at him to her breasts when he thought she wasn't. Every time she looked down to write something in her notebook, boom, down they'd go. It was almost funny. The little creep would probably start salivating in a minute. Or jerking off. She considered buttoning her jacket and cutting off his view. Then she changed her mind and, instead, hoisted her long legs up on the table and leaned back in the chair and let the jacket fall open. Barker's lascivious looks weren't anything she couldn't handle, and the longer he thought he could sneak a peek, the longer he'd want to stay and answer questions. Maybe more important, the more excited he got, the more likely it was that he'd slip up and tell her something he didn't mean to. *I didn't mean to confess to the crime, Your Honor. I was distracted by the detective's boobs.*

'How long has Goff lived in the apartment?' Maggie asked.

'A little over three years. She signed a lease for a fourth year back in November. She was a good tenant. Quiet. Clean. The place was always picked up. She always paid her rent on the first of the month.'

The place was always picked up? Interesting. How

would Barker know that? 'Was she friendly with any of the other tenants?'

'Not really. Not that I know of. I saw her talking with the Chus occasionally.'

'The Chus?'

'Nancy and Tom Chu. The people on the third floor rear. She was pretty friendly with them, especially Nancy.'

'Interests in common?'

'I don't know,' said Barker. Maggie's pen went back to her pad; Barker's eyes went back to her breasts. 'Nancy's into photography. They talked about that a lot.' Maggie looked up. So did Barker. He gave her his best smile.

'Would you excuse me, Andy?'

He looked up questioningly.

'Just be a second,' she said. 'I have to go to the little girls' room,' she added in a conspiratorial whisper.

She left the room and found Cleary and Tasco. 'Did you guys talk to the Chus last night? Apartment 3R?'

'No. They didn't answer the door.'

'Okay. Find Nancy Chu. Bring her in. Tell her it's important.'

She went back to the interview room. 'There, that's better.' She smiled. 'So, tell me about Goff,' she said. 'What kind of woman was Lainie?'

'What do you mean?'

'What did you think of her?'

'I liked her.'

'Yeah, but what'd you think of her? I mean, did you ever talk to her?'

'Yeah, sometimes I talked to her.'

'What about?'

Barker shrugged. 'Stuff.'

'Stuff in her apartment?'

'I didn't go into her apartment.'

'Well, you must have gone in there occasionally to fix things. Y'know? That kind of stuff?'

'Yes. Occasionally.'

'Did you go in there a lot?'

'I said occasionally.'

'Was Goff there when you went in?'

'If something needed fixing, she usually told me to take care of it while she was at work. She always knew about it, though.'

'But you did go in there?'

'Yes. I already told you that.'

'Alone?'

'Yes.'

'What'd you think of the pictures? The photographs. On the bedroom wall.'

'They were . . .' Barker paused as if he were searching for the right word to use. 'They were . . . beautiful.'

'Yeah, they were, weren't they? Really beautiful. I thought so, too.' Maggie smiled warmly at him.

Barker seemed to relax.

'Did you ever talk to Lainie about the pictures?'

'No.' Now he looked puzzled.

'Never discussed them with her at all?'

'No. That would have been . . .' Again Barker searched for the right word. 'Rude. That's what it would have been. Rude. Them being pictures of her and all.'

'Really? Those were pictures of Goff? You're sure? I mean, you can't see her face or anything.'

Barker smiled. 'I'm sure.'

'Did Goff tell you she posed for the pictures?'

'Let's just say I'm sure.'

'That is so cool.' Maggie paused as if she were debating something. 'You know, Andy, I'll let you in on a little secret.'

'What?'

She leaned forward and spoke in a near whisper. 'I sometimes think . . . now, you've got to promise not to tell anyone.'

'What?'

'Nah, I probably shouldn't be telling you personal stuff like this.'

'No, c'mon, what?'

'Well.' Maggie looked left and right as if she were checking that there was no one else in the room. 'I sometimes think I'd like to get some pictures shot of me like that. Don't you think that'd be cool?'

Barker stared at her.

'Too bad you never asked Lainie who the photographer was.'

'I . . . I . . . know who it was.'

'Really? Who?' she asked.

'Nancy Chu.'

'Nancy Chu from 3R?'

'Yup.'

'Gee, she's good. Do you think she'd do me?'

'Oh, yeah,' Barker said, leaning in even closer. 'In fact, I could probably arrange it.' The little creep was positively radiating sexual tension.

'Gee, that'd be great.' Maggie leaned back again, letting

the jacket fall open. 'Just a few more things to cover, Andy, and then we can let you go home. Did you ever see anybody who didn't live in the building going into or out of Lainie's apartment?'

'You mean like boyfriends?'

'Yeah. Or other women.'

'She sometimes had a friend of hers from New York staying with her. Janie something or other.'

'How about guys?'

'There were some. Sure. I keep a pretty good eye on the place, and I noticed them.'

'Do you know any of their names?'

Barker thought about that. 'No, I really don't. Again, it didn't seem like any of my business.'

'Okay. Well, thank you, Andy.' Maggie stood up and held out her hand. Barker shook it. 'That's really all we need. You've been a big help.'

'You're welcome.' Pause. 'Maggie.'

'Do you need a ride home? I can have an officer give you a ride.'

'That's okay. I'll just catch a cab.'

Maggie watched him go. She waited until the elevator doors closed in front of him before turning and going into interview room number two, where an Asian woman was sitting at the table waiting for her.

Twenty-Four

At ten thirty on a Saturday night, the fourth floor at 109 was quiet, overhead lights dimmed to semidarkness, a feeling of loneliness about the place. McCabe came back to the office after leaving Wolfe's because he needed somewhere to go that wasn't his empty apartment. Here, at least, there was work to be done. A small lamp on Maggie's desk was lit. That and the glow from her computer screen threw twin circles of cold light across her face. She was hunched over, fingers dancing across the keyboard. He pulled up a chair and watched.

'Hi,' he said after a minute.

'Hold on a sec,' she said, not looking up. 'Just want to finish this. Okay. There.' She looked up. 'Hi.'

'Where is everybody?'

'Tasco's still out on Harts with Jacobi and the ETs. I told everyone else to go home to their wives, girlfriends, and kiddies. Get a good night's sleep. Start fresh in the morning.'

'How about you? Aren't you tired, too?'

'Me? Haven't you heard? I'm Superwoman. Besides, I don't have a wife to go home to.' She leaned back. 'Sometimes I think,' she said, stretching and yawning, 'that that's what I really need. A wife.'

'And kiddies?'

'Maybe someday. What brings you back to Happy Valley?'

'Work, I guess. Plus, at the moment, I don't have any-one to go home to either. Casey's at Sunday River with a friend. Kyra's decided to wait out the murder at her own place.'

'How come?'

'Apparently I'm not much fun to be around when there's a killer on the loose.'

Maggie smiled. 'She may have something there. Any-way, I'm glad you're here. I was going to call you. Found out some stuff you'll need to know, and I didn't want to interrupt you at Wolfe's.'

'Okay. You want some coffee first?' he asked. 'I can put on a fresh pot.'

'Nah, I don't think so.'

'I'll make you some anyway. That way you won't be stealing most of mine.'

He walked down to the small kitchen alcove at the end of the hall just across from the conference room. Maggie followed and watched as he poured out the dregs of the old pot made hours ago and now as thick as sludge. He tossed the grounds and washed out the pot. Then he poured in cold water and measured out coffee into a fresh filter. He could feel her presence behind him, leaning against the wall.

'Never thought of you as being domestic,' she said.

He smiled. 'Oh yeah,' he said, 'a real homeboy.' He flipped the switch on the Mr Coffee. The machine started making gurgling noises. He turned. She stood in the shadows watching him, her long body nearly as tall as his own, less than two feet away. He caught her scent. Eau de cop? No. Something sexier. A lot sexier.

'It's not a good idea,' she said.

'What isn't?'

'What you're thinking.'

He smiled. The Maggie radar. Always on target. 'You're right,' he said. 'It's not. As you once noted yourself, I'm taken.'

'Yes. You are.'

'I'm sorry,' he said.

'Don't be. Kyra's a terrific woman.' The Mr Coffee made hissing noises indicating the brewing cycle was finished. 'Why don't you pour us some coffee?'

They went into the conference room, flipped on the bright overhead fluorescents, and sat at opposite ends of the long table.

'Alright,' he said, 'now what is it you think I should know about?'

'I'm pretty sure Barker's been eavesdropping on Goff's apartment. At least an audio bug. I think video as well.'

'Hidden cameras?'

'Knowing the guy, yes. He's the perfect peeping-tom type. Horny. Afraid of women. Afraid of rejection. Probably been ignored or dumped on by every woman who ever laid eyes on him. Then Goff turns up. She's at work all day, and he has a key to her apartment. How could he resist?'

'What are you basing this on?'

'I brought Barker in for an interview. Sat him down. He couldn't take his eyes off my chest.'

McCabe smiled. 'It's a very nice chest.'

'Try to restrain yourself. Anyway, between Andy sneaking peeks, I managed to wheedle out of him that the photographer of the shots on Lainie's wall was Nancy Chu.'

'Of the 3R Chus?'

'Yes.'

'Is Chu a professional photographer?'

'No. She's a software engineer. Says photography's her hobby but she's passionate about it.'

'She's also talented.'

'Yes, she is. Apparently Chu and Lainie became friendly about a year ago. She told Lainie about her interest in photography. Lainie asked to see her work. She showed her the industrial shots. Lainie bought the six that are hanging in the apartment. Then she asked Nancy if she'd be interested in photographing her in the nude. Nancy told me she always wanted to try figure work. Lainie made a gorgeous model. So Nancy said sure.'

'How does Barker know Chu took the shots?'

'How indeed? The sixty-four-thousand-dollar question. I had Chu in for an interview right after Barker left. She's positive Lainie wouldn't have told him. She only posed on the condition that Chu keep it all absolutely confidential. She also went to some lengths to make sure her face was hidden in the nude shots. Plus, Andy himself told me, more than once, Lainie never said a word to him about the photographs.'

'Chu didn't let it slip somehow?'

'She says not. She said yes, she took the pictures at Lainie's request, but no, she never said anything to Barker or anyone else about it. In fact, Chu is sure she never even mentioned her interest in photography to Barker. She finds the guy creepy and doesn't talk to him. Never talks about personal things. She won't let him into her apartment unless her husband is there.'

'Did he ever see similar pix hanging in the Chus' apartment?'

'There aren't any nudes. Chu said she does have a couple of the industrial shots hanging there, but they're not signed, and she insists there's no way Barker would know she took them.'

'Where were the two of them when Goff asked her to take the photos?'

'In Goff's apartment.'

'Did you ask Barker how he knew Nancy Chu took the pictures?'

'No. I didn't want to tip him off about what I suspected about hidden mikes or cameras.'

'What do you think Barker was doing last night when I caught him with his flashlight and tool belt?'

'I think he went up to Goff's to remove his cameras and mikes before we found them.'

'Anything else?'

'Yes. I did a little digging and discovered Andy used to work for a specialty electronics outfit. His job was doing high-end video installations. Getting the right stuff and putting it in would have been right up his alley.'

'Jacobi didn't sweep the place for bugs or hidden cameras last night?'

'Nope. We never thought about it.'

'So, assuming Barker records what he sees, he may have some pictures of whoever it was who tossed Lainie's apartment.'

'Yeah. Among other things.'

'And if there are videos, they're in his apartment?'

'I would think so.'

'Did you get some people over to sweep Goff's apartment for the equipment?'

'No. I want to wait until we have a warrant to search his place as well. If he knows we found the cameras, he'll destroy any videos he has hidden away in a New York minute.'

'Wouldn't he have destroyed them already?'

'I don't think so. If he has videos of Lainie, I think they'll be precious to him. He won't want to get rid of them. Especially now that she's dead. He'll just hide them away really well. Still, I have a uniform watching the apartment for any late-night visits to the dump. Or anywhere else, for that matter.'

'You requested a search warrant?'

'Judge Krickstein has the affidavit now. Said he wanted to sleep on it but he'd get back to me first thing in the morning.'

'Okay,' said McCabe. 'Anything else I should know about?'

Maggie slid a black-and-white photo across the table. 'Kyle Lanahan,' she said. 'The hot-dog man. Tasco brought him in for a chat.'

McCabe looked down at a mug shot of a good-looking man in his mid- to late forties. Gray hair. Straight features. Probably a real ladies' man. 'Anything?'

'Nah, I don't think so. That pic's about five years old. He did a little time for burglary. Now he sells hot dogs for a living and presumably coke. Both kinds. Anyway, he's got airtight alibis for both the twenty-third and last Tuesday. Tommy doesn't think he's our guy. Neither do I.'

McCabe nodded. 'Okay. What else?'

'Sturgis talked to the cleaning crew. Three men. Three women. All Muslim. He needed an interpreter to help with some of them.'

'How'd he do?'

'So-so. Five out of the six gave us nothing. Number six tried to be helpful. She's a Somali woman named' – she checked her notes, then read out the name slowly – 'Magol Gutaale Abtidoon. Ms Abtidoon said she noticed someone coming in with them wearing a heavy coat with a hood on his head. All she could see of him was his glasses. Heavy black frames, she said.'

'Kelly wears glasses like that.'

'He didn't have any on in the party photo.'

'He did when I spoke to him. Let's show Ms Abitoon some pictures of Kelly plus some other men with black glasses. Maybe something will click.'

'Okay. How'd you do with Dr Wolfe?'

'It was an interesting conversation. He said she has no friends he's aware of. Has no idea where she might be hiding. He thought she might have gone to Sanctuary House. Thinks we ought to search the place. I don't think so. Kelly said she wasn't there. I don't think he was lying, because too many people would have seen her there.'

'Anything else?'

'Yeah. He wondered if Abby might not have killed Goff herself.'

Maggie frowned, considering the possibility just as McCabe had earlier. After a minute she said, 'I don't think so.'

'I didn't either. Let's hear your reasoning.'

'Okay, Abby's schizophrenic, and yes, schizophrenics do sometimes go off the deep end, but there's no way Abby would have done it the way it was done. A neat little hole carefully placed in the back of the neck? Carting the victim back and forth to the mainland on the ferry? Leaving notes from Amos in her mouth? No way. Forget it.'

'Great minds think alike. I didn't give Wolfe all those details, but if I did, I think even he would agree.'

'Is that it?'

'No.' McCabe slid the photo from the party down the table to her. 'See that tall guy in the middle?'

'What about him?'

'That's Todd Markham. According to Wolfe, Goff knew him well enough to hit him up for a big donation to Sanctuary House just before Christmas. Goff and Kelly closed the deal.'

'How does Wolfe know about it?'

'He's on the Sanctuary House board. So was Goff.'

'How big was the donation?'

'Ten thousand dollars big.'

'Not bad.'

'Not bad at all.'

'You suppose she was sleeping with Markham, too?'

'It occurred to me. She was killed in Markham's house.'

'Well, I know Markham's not the killer. His story checks out six ways to Sunday.'

'You're sure?'

'I'm sure. Both his clients separately confirmed they had dinner with him in Chicago Tuesday night. Markham paid for the meal with his American Express Platinum card, and AmEx has a record of the charge. Later, at exactly 11:17 P.M. Central time, 12:17 Eastern, about the time Abby Quinn was running away from her monster and forty-five minutes or so before she woke up Bowman, Markham ordered a nightcap in the hotel bar. A Macallan single malt, by the way, which cost him fifteen bucks plus tip. You have expensive tastes, McCabe.'

'Just an educated palate.'

They both sat silently for a moment, weighing the possibilities. 'On the other hand, Markham did tell you, did he not, that Isabella sometimes comes up to Harts Island in the winter when he's away on business?'

'Yes, he did. And if he *was* sleeping with Goff –'

'And gave ten thousand dollars to Sanctuary House in consideration of that relationship –'

'And Isabella found out about it –'

'Could the seventh person on the Monument Square video have been a woman?'

'Possible. Of course, Abby told Bowman she saw a man.'

'Yes, but Abby hallucinates. We both know that.'

'Okay. Let's get the Markhams up here for prints, DNA, and a discussion.'

McCabe waited while Maggie made the call.

Twenty-Five

Murder/suicide seemed the simplest solution. Quick. Clean. Easy. Two fat birds with one deadly stone. The cops'd buy it. Why wouldn't they? A pair of crazies. One known to be suicidal, under enormous stress, and, as it turned out, carrying a loaded gun. How would the papers report it? SCHIZOPHRENIC WOMAN SLAYS FRIEND, TURNS GUN ON SELF? Yes, that sounded good. In the darkness of the living room, the rest of the story played out in the killer's mind.

Following an anonymous tip phoned in to the Press Herald *early this morning, police went to an apartment at 131 Summer Street in Portland, where they found the bodies of two women, Leanna Barnes, 31, of Portland, an inventory clerk at Seamon's Plumbing Supply in South Portland, and Abigail Quinn, 25, of Harts Island. Ms Quinn worked as a waitress at the Crow's Nest Restaurant on the island.*

In a late-morning press conference, Portland police chief Thomas A. Shockley told reporters that Ms Barnes's body was found in the apartment's lone bedroom lying on the bed. She had been fatally shot with a .22 caliber pistol, possibly while sleeping. Ms Quinn's body was found next to her. According to Chief Shockley, Ms Quinn apparently shot Ms Barnes twice and then took her own life with a single shot to the head, fired from the same weapon. He said evidence technicians had found gunshot residue both on Ms Quinn's hand and on her head. 'That pretty well seals it,' said Shockley.

The weapon used in the shootings was registered to Ms Quinn's late father, Earl Quinn, a Harts Island lobsterman who passed away in 2002.

Detective Sergeant Michael McCabe, head of the Portland Police Department's Crimes Against People unit, told the Press Herald police had been looking for Ms Quinn as a material witness in the earlier slaying of Portland attorney Elaine Goff, whose body was found Friday night on the Portland Fish Pier. Asked by reporters if Ms Quinn was considered a suspect in the Goff murder, Sergeant McCabe would only say, 'We're considering that possibility.'

The two victims, both of whom were diagnosed as schizophrenic, met while they were patients at Winter Haven Hospital, a psychiatric facility in Gorham. Ms Barnes was released from the hospital eighteen months ago in June of 2005. Ms Quinn was released two months later. She lived for six months at Sanctuary House, a shelter for runaway teens in Portland, before returning to her mother's house on Harts Island early last year. According to Dr Richard Wolfe, a psychiatrist on the staff of Winter Haven, Ms Quinn had attempted suicide twice in the past. 'However,' he added, 'we all thought Abby was doing well lately. This tragedy comes as a terrible shock to everybody at Winter Haven who worked with either of these two patients.' Dr Wolfe continued treating Ms Quinn after her release from Winter Haven at his office on Union Wharf in Portland. Asked if he had any warning that Ms Quinn posed a threat either to herself or anyone else, Dr Wolfe replied, 'Not to others, no. Abby tried suicide in the past, so I knew that would always be a danger for her, but we had no inkling she represented a danger to anyone else.' When asked if he thought Ms Quinn might be the killer of Portland attorney Elaine Goff, Dr Wolfe simply replied, 'No comment.'

Twenty-Six

Maggie dropped McCabe off at his condo on the Eastern Prom around ten thirty. 'Good night,' she said. 'Get some sleep.'

'Good night yourself,' he responded. 'I'll see you in the morning.'

McCabe watched the taillights of her car disappear down the Prom, kind of wishing he'd asked her up for a drink. He didn't go upstairs right away. Instead he dawdled in the parking area, brushing soft snow off the Bird until he couldn't find any more snow to brush. Then he got the mail and looked at that. Bills, circulars, and Casey's report card. He thought about walking down the hill to Tallulah's and getting a drink. The noise and warmth of the place seemed appealing. The idea of watching other people having a good time didn't.

Finally he climbed the three flights to the empty apartment, flipped on a single lamp, and put the bills on the desk, the circulars in the recycling bin, and the report card, unopened, on Casey's pillow. Their deal on report cards was she got to read them first. Then she showed them to him. There was never anything to hide since she almost always got As.

Still wearing his overcoat, he foraged in the fridge for something to eat. There wasn't a whole lot. Just a couple of boxes of frozen lasagna, some wilted lettuce, most of a loaf of bread. There was also half a container of milk,

Casey's tipple of choice, and half a bottle of Sancerre – Kyra's. He made a mental note to stop at Hannaford's tomorrow and pick up some groceries before Casey got home from Sunday River. The Palfreys would probably leave the mountain when the lifts closed at four. That meant they'd be back in Portland no later than six.

He stuck one of the lasagnas in the microwave, set the timer, hit START. Then he reached down for his crystal glass and poured himself a couple of inches of the Macallan. He walked back into the living room and picked up the landline. The quick beeping of the dial tone indicated messages. The first was from Casey. 'Hi, Dad, it's me. I'll see you tomorrow. The snow was great. The boarding was great. The hot tub was great. I'll be home by six. Love you.' He hit DELETE.

Next Kyra's voice came on. 'I'm just calling to say good night and to tell you that I love you. We'll talk tomorrow.' He played it again.

The third message was from Sandy. 'McCabe, I've tried calling your cell a couple of times, but apparently you're not taking calls from me at the moment. I guess whatever you called about last night wasn't all that important. However, there is something we ought to discuss. Peter and I have been talking. Casey's going to be a sophomore next year, and Peter feels she'll have a better shot of getting into a first-class college from a good prep school than she will from Portland High. Peter's a trustee at Andover, and he thinks he could probably get Casey in as a lower-middler. That's what they call sophomores there . . .'

McCabe hung up the phone before the message finished. He didn't want to hear any more. It wasn't enough that Sandy had abandoned her daughter with about as much thought as a snake shedding its skin. Now she wanted to dump her in some boarding school and take her away from her father as well. Why? So she could tell the other bankers' wives about her beautiful daughter who just happened to be away at a top-notch boarding school? Probably. Well, it wasn't going to happen. McCabe pulled off his coat and tossed it on the couch, found an old Coltrane/Miles Davis collaboration and put it on the machine, and parked himself and his Scotch in the big leather chair in the living room. The one Casey called Dad's chair. He sipped the whisky and regretted Kyra's move back to her place. He wanted to be with her tonight. He didn't want to be thinking about Sandy.

It was funny how his ex-wife never seemed to regret anything. Certainly not any of her extramarital affairs, and there'd been plenty. Kyra once asked him why he hadn't divorced her sooner. The answer was simple. 'Fear of losing Casey,' he told her. 'In most divorce proceedings the mother gets custody. The father gets to visit. I wasn't about to let that happen.'

He could hear Sandy's oh-so-rational arguments even without listening to them. Boarding school would be good for her. Help her grow up. Help her get into Harvard or Yale or whatever Ivy League school Peter, the man who didn't want to raise 'other people's children,' had graduated from. Maybe the saddest part of the whole thing was that Sandy wasn't suggesting private school because she wanted Casey living with her. If she had, she could have proposed sending her to Brearley or Dalton or one of the other hotshot schools in Manhattan. No, Sandy didn't want her daughter back. She just didn't want McCabe to have her either.

He sipped his Scotch and let the familiar music flow over him. He realized the last time he'd listened to it was the night the marriage finally ended. The night Sandy walked out. More accurately, the night he kicked her out. The last night they made love, though by then, of course, love had nothing to do with it, the act having become no more than reflex copulation. Even in the last days of the marriage Sandy knew she could always turn him on, and she loved proving it. He wondered if her efforts were driven by ego or a need to demonstrate her power or maybe she just liked sex.

He smiled bitterly as the memory of that night replayed in his mind. It had been a hot, sticky night in late August, and McCabe and his partner, Dave Hennings, were working late trying to drill confessions out of two seventeen-year-old crackheads who barged into a dry-cleaning store at ten that morning brandishing guns. They ended up killing the owner. It took most of the night, but McCabe had finally gotten the confessions they needed to put the pair away.

McCabe got back to the apartment on West Seventy-first about one fifteen in the morning, hot and tired, his shirt soaking with sweat and sticking to his back under his jacket. Cool air and the unmistakable scent of Sandy in heat hit him smack in the face when he opened the door. The lights were low. The air-conditioning high. Miles and Coltrane were already providing appropriate background music. Sandy was leaning against the wall in the hallway, wearing a sheer silk nightgown, her naked body silhouetted by the light shining from behind the open bedroom door. She'd always been good at provocative lighting. Probably could have made a career of it. McCabe used to joke to himself that what Shakespeare was to tragedy and Michelangelo was to chapel ceilings, Sandy was to sex. A true genius. The real thing. A Hall of Famer.

She led him to the bedroom and helped him take his clothes off. Then she washed his body all over with a cool moist cloth. When that was done, she slipped off her nightgown, knelt down, and took him in her mouth. She brought him almost to the point of climax, then waited a few seconds and did it again. Finally she led him to the bed, climbed on top, and guided him into her. Sex with Sandy was always good. Often it was great. This time was one of the best. Knowing what came next, he wondered if she'd intended it as some kind of farewell gift. Something to remember and regret after she was gone. If so, he supposed it had worked. It was only last night, in Lainie Goff's apartment, that he'd finally broken the spell. At least he hoped he had.

He remembered how, when they were done and he was utterly spent, she slipped out of bed and walked to her dressing table, where she sat, still naked, and examined her face in the mirror. Then she began rubbing some kind of cream into it. Midway through, with streaks of white still showing, she said lightly, almost as an aside, more to her own reflected image than to him, 'Peter Ingram's asked me to marry him.'

McCabe didn't answer. It wasn't unexpected. He didn't really care.

'I've told him yes,' she said.

Still McCabe said nothing. Just waited for the other shoe to drop.

She turned back to the mirror and began rubbing in cream again. 'The wedding will be at Peter's house in East Hampton as soon as the divorce is finalized,' she said, speaking again to his reflected image.

That wasn't the shoe he was waiting for. 'What about Casey?' he finally asked.

'Casey?'

'Yes. You remember Casey? Our daughter? The one who hopefully is asleep on the other side of that wall. What about her?'

Sandy ignored the sarcasm. 'She'll be staying here,' she said. 'With you.' She finally turned and looked at him instead of his image in the mirror. 'I expect you'll be happy about that. She was the only one of us you ever cared about anyway.'

That wasn't entirely true. He had loved Sandy once. Though he couldn't remember exactly why.

'You won't seek custody?' he asked.

'No, McCabe, I won't seek custody. You'll have your little princess all to yourself. Peter has no interest in raising other people's children.'

Other people's children? It was the casualness of the delivery as much as the phrase itself that enraged him. The tossing off of a bit of debris from a life she no longer wanted. Nothing more. McCabe looked at her image in the mirror and realized he had never hated anything as much as he hated Sandy at that moment. He thought about shooting her. It would have been easy enough. His holster and gun were only a few feet away, draped over the chair in the corner along with his clothes. Then he thought about hitting her. How satisfying it would be to feel his fist connect with the middle of her face. Feel her familiar flesh and bone give way, her nose break, her blood spurt out. He closed his eyes. Forced the thoughts of violence away. Sometimes in dreams those feelings had come back, and in dreams he'd often played them out. But that night, five years ago in the apartment on West Seventy-first Street, thanks, perhaps, to his love for Casey, he managed to hold them in check.

'I'll be moving to Peter's place in the morning after Casey's left for school,' she said, her tone again matter-of-fact.

'I don't think so,' he said, his voice flat and angry.

'Oh, yes,' she said, her eyebrows going up as she spoke to emphasize the certainty of the thing. 'It's all arranged.'

He pulled on a pair of boxers and walked over to her dressing table. 'No,' he said, 'what *is* arranged is that you have exactly five minutes to get yourself dressed and out of this apartment.' To emphasize the point he reached across the table and swept all the lotions and creams and tubes of mascara onto the floor with a single swing of his arm.

He saw doubt and, for the first time, maybe a little fear showing on her face.

'You'd better get moving,' he said. 'You're down to four and a half minutes. If you're not out of here by then, I'll toss your naked ass out on the sidewalk and you can walk to Ingram's just the way you are.'

She pulled on a T-shirt, a pair of jeans, and some flip-flops and made it to the elevator just before her time ran out.

Twenty-Seven

He held the gun steady in two gloved hands and sighted his own image in the mirror. An old Ruger Standard .22. Abby's daddy's own gun. Taken from her house, where he'd found it, ready and waiting, fully loaded, the night he killed Goff. The night he realized he'd have to kill Abby as well.

He turned off the lights, walked to the living room window, and looked out on the street below. Empty save for a lone dog walker. A woman. A stranger. He sighted the gun. Slipped off the safety. Slid his finger along the curve of the trigger. He felt a tremor of excitement. His breathing quickened. The power of life and death. He'd never realized how intoxicating it could be.

It was time to go. He closed the blinds, tucked the Ruger under his belt, and checked himself out in the mirror. He put on his glasses with the heavy black frames and smiled and winked. First with one eye. Then the other. Then he went to the closet and put on his heavy coat with the oversized hood. He went out the door and walked to his car.

Twenty-Eight

Even with the covers pulled over her head and her eyes squeezed shut, Abby knew Death was near. She could feel his presence. Smell it. Like ozone in the air before a summer lightning strike. The cold knot of fear she'd been living with since Tuesday had relaxed last night when Leanna opened her arms and welcomed Abby in. Now it was back, bigger and tighter than ever before. Abby reached a hand across the bed, seeking comfort from Leanna's bulk, but, finding none, pulled away. Her friend's body shifted in restless sleep, unaware of the danger lurking close by.

Abby wasn't sure how long she'd been asleep or, for that matter, how long she'd even been here. She remembered arriving with the big guy in the pickup. She thought that was last night. Or, more accurately, early this morning. This morning and not yesterday morning or the morning before. But to be truthful, she really wasn't sure which morning it was.

She remembered the big guy's goofy grin and the microwave containers of Chef Boyardee in his arms. She also remembered the gun under his jacket. Even so, she found herself wishing he were here now. She thought about the card he gave her. JOSEPH L. VODNICK, it said. PORTLAND POLICE DEPARTMENT. There was a phone number. She could call him, except he wasn't at the number. He was up in some dumb-ass lean-to at the bottom of Mt Katahdin. Camping or ice climbing or whatever the hell he was doing on his two days off. When they arrived last night she just wanted him to go away. Hadn't even wanted him to get out of the truck. He insisted on walking her to the door. Said he wanted to make sure her friend was home and she could get in okay. It took a couple of minutes of ringing and banging before Leanna heard them and opened up. All that time they were just standing on the steps looking everywhere else except at each other. Abby was afraid the guy might try to kiss her good night. How goofy was that? He didn't, though. He just reminded her of the card. Told her again to call if she was in any trouble. Then he got back in his truck and left.

Leanna asked who he was.

She looked down at the card. 'Joseph L. Vodnick.'

'Who?'

'Some guy I met at the Mini Mart. He gave me a ride over.'

Leanna pulled Abby inside and shut the door against the still swirling snow.

All Abby remembered after that was taking off her clothes and climbing into the shower and letting hot water course over her until her body was bright pink and all the freeze was out of her bones. After that she checked her Zyprexa. They were all gone. She thought she had some left, but she didn't. Must have been taking more than she thought. Or maybe she dropped some out there in the storm last time she opened the bottle. Maybe it didn't matter. They didn't seem to be helping a whole lot anyway. Leanna gave her a couple of pills from her own stash. Blue ones. Not Zyprexa. Something else. Leanna said the pills would help her sleep, and, boy, did they ever – but now she was wide awake and Death was coming.

The smell had become stronger, and Abby wondered if he was in the room. She pulled back the sheet and blanket enough to allow one eye to peer out of her warm cocoon. Enough dim light from the winter moon filtered through the gauzy curtains to make out the shapes of things. But not enough to penetrate the shadows where she knew Death would hide. She scanned the wall and corners on this side of the room. She saw nothing. She knew she'd have to pull the blankets all the way off her head and sit up if she was going to look over Leanna's body and check the other side. She had to do it, she told herself. The only alternative was to lie here and wait for him to stick his knife into the back of her neck. She remembered how the woman at the Markhams' house dropped. A puppet with her strings cut.

Abby pushed the image away. She wasn't ready for Death. Not today. Maybe not ever. She pulled herself into a sitting position. Leanna's breathing continued slow and steady. She looked across. Nothing there either. Just a chair piled high with clothes. A table that was really a box with a cloth thrown over it and a lamp on top. He wasn't there. Still the smell lingered.

The insistent ringing of the phone woke McCabe from his fitful sleep. Why didn't the damned thing stop ringing? He glanced at caller ID. J. VODNICK. He pressed TALK. 'This is McCabe.'

Too late. Vodnick had hung up. McCabe debated whether to call him back or not. It wasn't much of a debate. If Joe Vodnick was calling his cell, it had to have something to do with the case. He called.

'Sergeant, this is Officer Vodnick. Joe Vodnick? From last night at the pier?'

'I remember, Joe. What's up?'

'It's about that girl. That woman you guys put out the ATL on.'

McCabe sat up, instantly alert. 'Yeah? What about her?'

'Well, I didn't see the ATL when it came out because I went off duty at midnight Friday.'

'Okay. Keep going.'

'I'm up at Katahdin. I've got a couple of days off, and I'm doing a little ice climbing and winter camping.'

'Get to the point, Joe.'

'I think I saw her. I think I know where she is.'

'Katahdin? You saw her at Katahdin? You sure it's her?'

'No. Not at Katahdin. Let me back up. I was just talking to a pal of mine in Community Policing? My girl-friend, actually. She saw the ATL and was telling me about it. From what she said I'm pretty sure it's the woman I saw —'

'Joe, Joe, slow down,' McCabe interrupted. 'Just tell me where you saw this woman and why you think she's our witness.'

'I dropped her off about five this morning at 131 Summer Street.'

'In Portland?'

'Yeah. In Portland. She seemed disturbed, and she fits

the description of the woman in the ATL. Right age. Right hair color. Right clothes.'

'Did you get her name?'

'Just her first name.'

'Which is?'

'Abby. She told me her name was Abby.'

Twenty-Nine

Abby looked around the room for a weapon. She didn't see anything. She knew she could find something in the kitchen, but she didn't want to go to the kitchen. Death might be waiting for her between here and there. So she looked harder and found something she thought might do. In a corner propped against a wall where she hadn't noticed it just a minute ago was Uncle Willis's old wooden tennis racket. Least it looked like Willis's racket. Most of its strings still broken just the way she remembered it.

She slipped out of bed, lifting the hem of Leanna's big flannel nightgown and gathering it around her so she wouldn't trip, and went to the corner, where she examined the racket more closely. Looked just the same. She picked it up, took a practice swing or two. It felt just the same. She heard the Voices cackling quietly. She swung harder. The Voices cackled louder. She didn't care. Maybe Willis's racket wasn't a frying pan, but the sonofabitch Death would sure as hell feel it if she whacked him in the balls with it. She cackled back at the Voices, but that didn't shut them up. She swung the racket as hard as she could. Forehand. Backhand. Once. Twice. Again. Again. She sailed across the room, holding up the hem of the nightgown with her left hand and swinging Willis's racket with her right. The Voices cackled louder. Suddenly Death was there in the room. Now in front of her. Now behind. She whirled and swung. The side of the racket connected with his head. She whirled and swung again. This time he went down. Just as he had on the ice. She stood over him and swung again. Chopping down at his head as if she were splitting logs for the stove. Wham! She chopped and kept chopping. He was spurting blood. Wham! More blood. Wham! Wham! Wham! Stupid nightgown with its stupid pink flowers kept getting in the way, but she kept swinging anyway. Swinging and swinging. Clubbing Death to death. Clubbing him into a bloody, bloodied pulp. The Voices were screaming. She'd never heard them sound so fucking happy before.

'Abby, what in hell are you doing?' Leanna. Not the Voices. She didn't want to listen to Leanna now. Not yet. Not when one more swing would finish the fucker off! Wham! The racket exploded against the side of his head.

Leanna leapt from the bed and threw her arms around Abby. Squeezed and held her tight. Abby struggled to break free of the grip. Together they toppled, a flanneled flowery mass, with little pink ribbons at their necks and wrists, down onto the bed.

'Let me go!' Abby shrieked, struggling against the grip of Leanna's arms. 'Let me swing! Let me swing! Let me finish the fucker off!'

Abby screamed and writhed and squirmed. Leanna pushed herself into Abby, clamping her arms by her sides. Abby felt the racket slip from her hand. 'My racket,' Abby screamed. 'I dropped my racket!'

'There is no racket.'

'There is, too. It's Uncle Willis's racket.'

'There is no racket.'

'Yes! There! Is!'

'I can't see it.'

'You're a big fat lying fuck.'

'I'm big and I'm fat, but I'm not lying. I can't see it.'

Abby lay still in the dark with Leanna lying on top of her. She was quiet now. The Voices still chattered, but she didn't listen. Tears poured from her eyes. Sometimes, she thought, Leanna was just like Wolfe. Just like the rest of them. If anyone should know there really was a racket even if she couldn't see it, it was Leanna, because she was crazy, too.

Finally Leanna loosened her grip. Abby didn't move. Leanna rolled off. When everything was quiet, when the Voices finally shut up, Abby reached one arm down to the floor and picked up Uncle Willis's racket from where she'd dropped it. She pulled herself up into a sitting position with her back against the wall. She tucked her knees up under the nightgown and laid the racket across them. She did wonder how the racket got here. She hadn't seen it in years and was pretty sure she hadn't brought it over from the island. But Abby had years of experience of things happening she didn't understand or remember, so she didn't question it further.

She thought about Uncle Willis. He was her mother's older brother, and he saw things and heard voices no else could see or hear just like she did. Abby knew, because she'd read up on it, that schizophrenia has a genetic component, that it sometimes runs in families, so she supposed that's where hers came from. Uncle Willis. Crazy Willis people called him, usually behind his back but sometimes right to his face, which Abby thought was mean. But he didn't seem to mind or really even notice. What Willis mostly saw when he was having one of his 'attacks,' as Gracie called them, was bats. Furry little black bats flying at his face and wanting to bite him. Nobody else saw them. Just Willis. He was forever swatting at them, and swearing at them right out on the street. Calling them furry little fuckers and dirty black bastards. All Gracie would say was 'Dammit, Willis, don't talk that way around Abby.'

Didn't stop him, though.

Willis hadn't always had the racket. He found it in the island dump and brought it home, about a year before he killed himself. He couldn't have been happier. Gave him something to swat the bats with. Didn't bother him that the racket had almost no strings left. He swatted anyway. 'Gotta work on that forehand, Willis,' some of the drunks outside the Legion hall on summer nights would shout as Willis walked by swatting at the bats. 'Gotta work on that serve.'

Uncle Willis never answered them. He just looked confused and kept on swatting. Which is what he did right up until the day when Abby was eight and she opened her mother's closet door and found Willis hanging inside. The wooden racket was on the floor under him. Abby didn't scream when she found him. She'd seen enough dead things to know Willis was dead. She touched him once. The only thing she could remember thinking was *I guess the bats won't be bothering him anymore.*

Abby hadn't seen the racket since. She thought her mother had taken it back to the dump along with the rest of Willis's stuff. She sighed a long sigh and wondered if Death really was dead. She could still smell him. Even closer than before. She grasped the taped handle and flicked the racket back and forth with her wrist. She could hear the drunks at the Legion laughing at her. Or maybe it was the Voices. 'Gotta work on that forehand, Abby. Gotta work on that serve.' She felt tears running down the sides of her cheeks. She heard a banging on the door.

Thirty

McCabe drove the Bird and beat Maggie to 131 Summer Street by less than ten seconds. She pulled up right behind him. He was still wearing the clothes he'd worn all day. Maggie had on sweats, sneakers, a windbreaker, and a black watch cap, her shield pinned to the outside. Her holster and weapon were strapped around her waist. They looked at the house. A small wood-frame two-unit badly in need of TLC. Both doors had black numbers painted on them. Number 1 on the left. Number 2 on the right. Apartment 1 lay dark and empty, an APARTMENT FOR RENT sign taped to the window. Number 2 was clearly occupied. A dim light shone through the curtains, and the door was open a crack, a sliver of light shining through it as well. Maybe Abby had peeked out the door and seen them coming and then run off, failing to close it completely.

'I'll take the front,' McCabe said. 'You go around back and pick our girl up if she tries to slip out that way.'

Maggie nodded and headed down the driveway, running in a low crouch. McCabe gave her a minute to get in position and then started up the concrete walk toward the front. About halfway to the house he heard a woman scream. There was a shout of 'Fuck' and then a loud pop. All in quick succession. McCabe recognized the pop. A. 22 handgun. Maybe with a suppressor. More likely not.

He took the three stairs to the porch in a single leap and hit the cheap hollow-core door low and at full speed, the force of his body shattering the wood. A chain latch and screws flew in front of him as he rolled into a dimly lit room, sweeping his .45 in an arc in front of him. Across the room he saw a figure dressed in blue disappearing through the wide-open back door.

'Police! Freeze!' he shouted. The figure kept going.

'Police! Freeze!' Maggie's voice echoed his own, from the backyard.

To his left, a woman wearing a flannel nightgown writhed on the floor. Blood gushed in spurts from a wound in her neck. Not Abby. Someone bigger, fatter, older. She looked like someone dying.

'Freeze!' he heard Maggie shout again. 'Flat on your face! Hands behind your head!'

In a desperate attempt to stanch the woman's bleeding, McCabe yanked up the hem of her nightgown, rolled the soft cotton into a kind of bandage, and pressed it into the wound on her neck. But it didn't do much good. There was too much blood, and it kept coming. Deep red spread across the makeshift bandage. The woman's eyes were open. She blinked. Gurgled a word. 'Ellie.' Her name? 'Ellie,' she gurgled again. Her eyes began to glaze over.

From outside he heard two pops followed by the deeper boom of Maggie's .45. Shit. He thought she had the bastard. He raced for the open back door onto a small deck, leapt through, and heard another pop. Then nothing. Below to his left he saw Maggie. She was on her knees, her two hands still shakily holding her .45 in front of her, trying to aim at the fleeing figure. McCabe calculated the distance and direction to the target, aimed, and fired. The man kept running. McCabe knelt. Using the deck rail as a platform, he aimed again into the darkness. Then he stopped. He could no longer see who he was shooting at, and there were innocent civilians out there. Sleeping in their bedrooms. Walking on the street. An errant slug could easily hit one of them. He couldn't risk that. Even if it meant letting the bastard get away.

He holstered his weapon and ran down the steps. Maggie was lying in the snow at the bottom. He could see a small red circle slowly expand across the right side of her sweatshirt just above the black of her holster. Her .45 was still in her two hands. She was trying to sit up. Cupping the back of her head in one hand, he took her weapon, engaged the safety, and stuffed it in his coat pocket. Then he eased her down on her back, her head on the snow. Keeping his own .45 pointed in the direction of the shooter, he took out his cell and hit PPD911. That number took him straight through to Department Dispatch. Maggie looked up at him, conscious but in obvious pain. She tried to smile. 'This is McCabe.' He spoke fast. 'Detective and civilian down. Both gunshot wounds. One thirty-one Summer Street. That's one three one Summer. Civilian a possible 10–49. Send two ambulances and alert all units. Male suspect fleeing on foot, south from location toward Commercial Street. Tall. Dressed in a dark hooded coat.'

'Wearing glasses,' Maggie croaked.

'Anything else?' McCabe asked her.

She shook her head. 'It was dark. He had the hood up. All I saw was his glasses. Black frames.'

'Wearing glasses, black frames,' McCabe repeated. 'Suspect is armed. Consider extremely dangerous.'

He pulled up her sweatshirt to look at the wound. There was a small red and black hole in the right side of her abdomen. About what you'd expect with a .22. Not a lot of blood. It didn't look lethal, but you never knew. If the bullet hit an organ she could be in trouble. He wondered if there was an exit wound on the other side. He didn't want to roll her over to look.

'Gotta go,' he said. 'I'll be back.' He ran up the stairs.

The voice from Dispatch came back on. 'Ambulance en route. All units alerted. We'll be right there.'

The living-room floor was covered in blood. Ellie, if that was the woman's name, was dead. Her eyes were open but empty. He knelt by her side and wrapped two fingers around her wrist to feel for a pulse. Nothing. He unrolled the bloody nightgown from around her neck and covered her nakedness. There was no further need for bandages.

He had to find Quinn if she was still here, still alive. It was a small apartment. Living room. Kitchen. A single bedroom. A small bath. 'Abby!' he called out. 'This is the police. We're here to help you.'

He listened. No answer. Leading with his .45, he moved into the bedroom. Dim light shone through the curtains. An unmade king-sized bed. A chair. A lamp. No Quinn. He moved to the closet door, stood to one side, whipped it open. Abby wasn't there either. He called again. 'Abby Quinn! This is the police. Come out!' Still no answer. Either she was in the bathroom or she was gone again. He moved to the bathroom door. Outside he could hear sirens. Shouts. The sound of running feet. Red flashing lights bounced against the living-room walls.

He threw open the bathroom door and stepped in. Heard a whimper from behind the shower curtain. He pulled it open. There was Abby, standing in the tub wearing a clone of the flannel nightgown Ellie had on. At least two sizes too big. Her eyes were tightly shut, her two hands together, one atop the other, as if she were clutching something.

'It's alright, Abby,' he said. 'I'm the police.'

She opened her eyes wide, looked at him. An expression of baffled terror crossed her face. She drew her two arms back to the left, twisted her body a little in the same direction. She swung her two hands forward hard. An almost perfect pantomime of a two-handed backhand, grunting like Serena Williams in a nightgown. Except Abby's hands held no racket.

She started screaming and swinging her arms. She fell forward. He caught her. He wrapped his arms around her body and held her tight in a straitjacket hug like he would a child having an uncontrollable tantrum. She writhed and fought and screamed, her eyes wide with horror. He barely managed to hold on. 'It's alright, Abby,' he tried saying, but his voice was drowned out by her screams. She tried head-butting him, but she missed. An EMT rushed into the bathroom.

'Keep holding her!' he shouted. McCabe held on. Barely. Out of the corner of his eye he could see the man push up Abby's sleeve and shoot something in a hypodermic into her arm. She kept screaming and writhing for a minute or so longer, but then her body began to relax. Still he held on. Her screaming stopped. Abby laid her head against McCabe's shoulder and just continued crying. When she was finally quiet, two EMTs came in, strapped her onto a gurney, and walked her out to an ambulance.

'McCabe?' said a man's voice.

It was T. Ly, the same cop who'd driven him to the Fish Pier. Hard to believe that was less than thirty-six hours ago.

'How's Maggie?' he asked. Outside he could see the flashing blue lights of half a dozen police cars and the red ones of two ambulances.

'Okay, I think. Medic says they can't be sure till they get her into the ER, but he thinks she'll be fine. Says the bullet didn't seem to hit anything vital.'

McCabe nodded and walked outside. He called Terri Mirabito at home. Woke her up. She said she'd be right there. Next he called 109 and told them to see if they could find an evidence tech who wasn't out on Harts Island with Jacobi.

Maggie was still conscious as they carried her to the second ambulance. He smiled at her. She smiled back, but her smile turned to a wince as they loaded her in. They shut the doors, and he watched it drive away.

Thirty-One

Two A.M. It looked like a busy night at Cumberland Medical Center. McCabe supposed the combination of a Saturday night and warmer temperatures was luring people out of their houses and into trouble. He stood inside the entrance to the ER looking for someone who could tell him where he could find Maggie. No one seemed to be manning the reception desk. He looked through tight knots of people, the overflow from the waiting area. A teenaged boy moaned nearby. He finally spotted a woman in a white coat, kneeling down and taking information from a dirty-looking man who lay stretched out across three plastic chairs in the waiting area. He looked like he'd come out on the wrong end of a bar fight. McCabe headed toward her, squeezing past a couple in their eighties who sat quietly side by side, holding hands, her head on his shoulder, her eyes red as if she'd been crying. Next to them a three-year-old child was howling in his mother's arms.

'I'm looking for Detective Margaret Savage,' McCabe said, holding up his shield to the woman in white.

'Who?' She looked confused.

'Savage. Margaret Savage. Portland PD.'

'Wait over there,' she said, pointing him toward a counter with nobody behind it.

'That's the gunshot wound, right?' A male voice. One of the EMTs from Summer Street. 'She's in Trauma

Three. Right over there.' The guy pointed. McCabe nodded his thanks and started across the open space in that direction.

'Hey, you can't go in there.' A nurse rushed after him. McCabe ignored her. One of the hospital security guards followed.

'Hey,' she shouted again. McCabe held up his gold shield and pointed it in their direction and kept going. They didn't follow.

He spotted Maggie lying on a gurney surrounded by seven or eight people, all in scrubs, all moving fast. They were, in turn, surrounded by an array of screens and monitors. A couple of the machines were making beeping noises. Two IVs were hooked into Maggie's neck. Two more into her arms. Someone, probably a resident judging by his age, was moving a small white wand around Maggie's abdomen a couple of inches below her navel and watching a screen on what McCabe was pretty sure was an ultrasound machine. Near the wand on Maggie's right side, he could see a small, ugly red and black hole where the bullet went in just above her hipbone. A blanket covered her body below the wound.

Doctors and nurses were calling out information to each other.

'Airway clear.'

'BP 145 over 90.'

'Pulse 105.'

Maggie spotted him and tried to roll her eyes in a kind of 'how dumb is this?' gesture. A wave of pain must have hit her pretty much at the same time, because her expression changed to a tight grimace. He spotted her clothes, cut from her body and lying in a heap on the floor. He still had her gun, but her empty holster was perched on top of the heap, her badge wallet on top of that. He walked to the pile and picked them up.

The team leader, a blonde woman about forty, approached him.

'I'm Dr Herrold,' she said. 'Emergency attending. Are you McCabe?'

'Yes.'

She accepted his ID and appeared to examine it carefully. 'Good. She's been asking for you. You'll need to sign a confirmation that you've taken charge of Detective Savage's belongings. We'll put the rest of her things in a bag, and you can take those as well.'

He tilted his head toward Maggie. 'She's gonna be okay, right?'

'I think she'll be fine. The bullet appears to have torn some muscle, but it didn't hit anything vital.'

He tilted his head at the young man with the wand. 'What's he doing?'

'Finishing up what's called a FAST exam. Using ultrasound to make sure there's no abdominal hemorrhaging that could cause problems.'

'Pelvic view clear,' the man with the wand told Herrold.

'That's the last quadrant. Your colleague was lucky,' Dr Herrold said to McCabe. 'A couple of inches either way and she would have been in trouble. As it was, the bullet seems to have skimmed the muscle fascia at the top of the pelvic rim and then angled down. There's an exit wound at the top of her butt on the right side.'

'Great. A scarred ass. Just what I need.' Maggie looked

pale, and her eyes were still closed, but hearing her wise-crack made him feel better.

'Do you have the bullet?' McCabe asked. 'We'll need it for forensics.'

'Sorry, we can't help you with that. We don't have it. Bullet tore through her sweats. I suspect your people will find it on the ground somewhere near where she was hit. I don't think it would have gone very far.'

'Did you catch the bastard yet?' It was Maggie again. Her eyes were still closed, her voice weak.

'Not yet.'

'But you do have Quinn?'

'Yes. She's here as well,' said McCabe. 'Somewhere.' Cumberland Medical Center was a big place.

'Are you talking about the woman who came in at the same time as your detective?' asked Herrold.

'Yeah. Do you know where she is?'

'Yes. There was no physical injury, but she's heavily sedated. We sent her up to the psychiatric unit on four.'

A nurse handed McCabe a big paper bag. He removed Maggie's keys from the pocket of her jeans and stuffed the rest of her things into the bag. 'When can I have her back?' McCabe asked Herrold, nodding his head at Maggie.

'We'll keep her overnight. Put her on antibiotics and Percocet for the pain. She'll hurt for a while, probably be limping around for a week or so, but she ought to be out of here tomorrow.'

'I've got your keys,' he told Maggie. 'I'll go over to your place and get you some clothes and things.'

'Do me a favor.'

'What?'

'Have Kyra do it.'

'Why?'

'Why? Because I don't trust you, that's why.'

McCabe told her to get some rest and tucked the brown paper bag under his arm. He found the right elevator and headed up to Cumberland Medical Center's small psychiatric unit on the fourth floor.

He was intercepted by a young resident who told him Quinn was no longer there. 'We gave her some antipsychotics and transferred her over to Winter Haven.'

'On whose orders?'

'Mine.'

'Why?'

'This is a very small unit. We have almost no room here. They're much better equipped to handle someone with her history there.'

McCabe thanked the young man and took the elevator to one. He left the hospital the same way he'd come in. The old couple was still holding hands, and the homeless guy was still lying across the plastic chairs. He was snoring loudly.

Thirty-Two

Flashing blue lights still surrounded 131 Summer Street when McCabe pulled up in the Bird. News vans from all four of Portland's network affiliates were lined up behind the police units. Tom Shockley's black Chevy Suburban was parked to one side. Bill Fortier's brand-new Impala, its vanity plates reading looey, was tucked in right behind. McCabe got out. Wasn't much for him to do, so he just leaned against the Bird's driver's side door and watched the goings-on. Eddie Fraser wandered over and leaned alongside. Eddie pulled out a pack of Marlboros, lit one, and blew a long stream of smoke into the night air.

'Hey, Mike,' said Fraser after a bit.

'Hello, Eddie. Thought you quit smoking.'

'I did. For nearly a whole week. Want one?'

'Don't tempt me.'

'Enjoying your weekend?'

'Peachy, thanks. How about yourself?'

'Oh yeah, great. Excitement is what I live for. How's Mag?'

'Well, aside from being pissed off about having a bullet hole going in her hip and coming out on her butt, she appears to be fine. Ought to be out of Cumberland tomorrow. What's going on here?'

'Chris Beneman's inside doing his thing. The GO's itching to get on the air.'

Beneman was a senior evidence technician. Had to be the last one the department had available.

'Jacobi and Tasco still out on Harts?'

'They were as of half an hour ago.'

'We ID the dead woman yet?'

'Yeah. A friend of Quinn's from Winter Haven. Her only friend, according to the people I talked to at the hospital.'

'Patient or staff?'

'Patient. Another schizo. Name's Leanna Barnes. It's her apartment.'

'Leanna, huh?' So she hadn't been telling him that her name was Ellie. She must have been telling him something else. Like who shot her. Not Ellie. Kelly. The man with the black-framed glasses. McCabe pushed his tongue up against his top row of teeth to make an 'ell' sound. He then released it and pushed out air for the 'eee' at the end. But if you wanted a 'kuh' sound at the beginning of the word, you had to make it at the back of your throat. Something you wouldn't be able to do if a bullet had just blasted your throat all to hell. The killer was John Kelly. For McCabe, that pretty much sealed it. Father Jack. The guy who studied the Old Testament prophets. The guy McCabe's gut had told him hadn't done it. *The minute anyone starts thinking they know who or what John Kelly is*, Wolfe had told him, *it's time to think again*. McCabe's gut had got it wrong. It was time to think again. He told Eddie to find John Kelly and bring him in.

'What if he says no?'

'Arrest him.'

'Okay,' said Eddie, stubbing out his cigarette. 'Where you gonna be?'

'Me? I'm going back to Harts Island.'

Thirty-Three

Tom Tasco waited till McCabe'd jumped from the rear deck of the *Francis R. Mangini* onto the dock before he started talking. 'Goff's prints are all over Kelly's cottage,' Tasco said as they started up the ramp. 'Specially the bedroom. Also some hairs that might be hers. Sonofabitch must have kept her there for a few days at least before moving her to the Markhams'.'

'Any other prints aside from hers?'

'Lots of Kelly's. Plus a few smudges and smears belonging to person or persons unknown. How's Maggie?'

'She'll have a sore hip and butt for a while. Otherwise, she's fine.'

The black-and-white Explorer was, once again, waiting at the top of the ramp. Bowman was behind the wheel, this time in uniform. Tasco climbed in back, leaving the passenger seat for McCabe.

'Hello, Scotty, how're you doing?'

Bowman grunted something unintelligible, pulled a U-turn, and took off up Welch Street away from the landing. McCabe sat silently, watching the dark, empty island streets flow by. At least it wasn't snowing, and the air was a lot warmer. The cops in the elevator must have been right about the January thaw. McCabe tried to force his overtired brain cells back onto the issues at hand.

Okay, he was pretty sure Kelly was guilty, but he wasn't at all sure he could prove it. Not to a jury. Not if Father Jack got himself a smart defense lawyer. Goff's prints provided hard evidence that she had been in Kelly's house, but they didn't prove Kelly killed her. Leanna Barnes's dying words wouldn't help that much either. *You heard her say what, Detective?* Ellie. *She said Ellie? Not Kelly?* That's right. Ellie. Not quite the right name, gurgled and garbled by a dying woman who couldn't herself testify. Sure, he could explain how Leanna's wound prevented her from forming the letter *K* in the back of her torn-apart throat, but his assumption that she was really trying to say Kelly would be dismissed as pure conjecture. No. Burt Lund would need more.

There was Kelly's paper on the Old Testament prophets. That'd help. If they found it. Even if they did, though, he didn't think it would be enough to convict. Even if the Amos quote was right on the front page, underlined and circled in red, some slick lawyer could make the case that anybody might have known that Old Testament quote. Anybody could have broken into Kelly's house and found Kelly's old grad school paper.

Then there was Abby. Even if hypnosis helped her identify Kelly as the killer, no jury in the world would convict on testimony from a schizophrenic witness. A schizophrenic witness who, according to her own psychiatrist, could have been off her meds. As for the other witnesses, both Maggie and Magol Gutaale Abtidoon could only testify that the bad guy wore a heavy coat and glasses with black frames.

Finally there was the not insignificant issue of motive. Goff's insurance policy might work for a jury, but he was sure a lawyer would try to pooh-pooh it as a gift to a worthy charity and not something that could be used to enrich an individual. Especially one who had deliberately chosen a life of relative poverty so he could, in turn, help others.

What else was there? McCabe knew firsthand Kelly was volatile. Given to easy anger. But this, the lawyers would eagerly point out, wasn't a killing committed in a rage. It was too planned. Too choreographed. Plus, Kelly was gay, so why'd he keep her alive so long? Not for sex, unless he swung both ways. Possible, but not convincing.

About ten minutes out from the landing, Bowman left the paved road and bumped the Explorer onto a circuitous pattern of dirt trails, going from one to another until, after another ten minutes or so, they came to a small clearing. He pulled in behind Jacobi's crime scene van. McCabe could see some lights about a hundred yards ahead. They climbed out.

'That's Kelly's cottage, if you want to call it that,' said Bowman. 'More of a shack really. We go the rest of the way on foot.'

Directly in front of him was a small wooded area about fifty feet wide. Beyond that lay a snowy and possibly rocky field.

'There's sort of a path,' said Bowman, 'but there's lots of icy ledge between here and there. The ice is covered by mushy snow, so you'll have to walk carefully.' He shined his flashlight on McCabe's city shoes and smirked. 'You may have some trouble walking in those. You're sure as hell gonna get wet feet.'

'I'll live with it.'

'Might even break an ankle.' Bowman smiled as if he thought that was worth hoping for.

'I'll be fine.'

'Suit yourself.' Bowman handed McCabe a flashlight. Tasco already had one. 'I'll go first. Watch my feet and step where I step. I'll let you know if there's anything treacherous coming up.'

The January sun wouldn't be up for another couple of hours, and there was no moon. 'Place was built about a hundred years ago,' Bowman said as they started down the path. 'House is cantilevered out over a cliff maybe fifty feet above the ocean. Nothing but rocks and breakers below. An old set of wooden stairs to the side over there takes you down to the beach. Hell of a view from the house, but it beats me how it's stood up to the nor'easters all these years. I would've guessed the storms that blow in here would've knocked it to hell and gone long ago, but there it is.'

McCabe followed Bowman and, as instructed, walked in his tracks. Tasco brought up the rear. He felt wet snow slipping into his shoes. Within seconds his socks and feet were soaked. There was no way he was going to complain about it. He'd sooner get frostbite, even lose a toe or two, than give an asshole like Bowman the satisfaction of hearing him whine. It took ten more minutes of careful foot placement to traverse the hundred yards to the house. McCabe slipped a couple of times and landed on his ass once. He got up and kept going.

Bowman pushed the door open. In the dim light of a single lamp, McCabe saw Bill Jacobi, seated at a small wooden table, systematically leafing through piles of paper files taken from a cardboard moving carton set in front of him. Neater piles, already examined and sorted, were arranged on the far end of the table. Two more cartons were on the floor.

Jacobi looked up. 'Okay to come in,' he said. 'We're finished in here except for this stuff.'

McCabe entered and looked around. The place was about as different from the Markhams' as two structures described as island cottages could be.

'Where are your guys?' McCabe asked.

'Out searching the property with a few of the locals. Kelly's got about five acres here. Doubt they'll find much, but hey, you don't know if you don't look.'

Bowman left to join the searchers. Tasco sat down next to Jacobi. McCabe slipped off his shoes and explored the space. The room they were in was a small combo kitchen and living room. Beat-up furniture. Appliances that reminded McCabe of what his parents had in the Bronx thirty years ago, and his parents' stuff was old then. One door led to a small bedroom that was pretty much filled by a double bed with a bare mattress, a small painted bureau, and one bedside table. On the table was an alarm clock, digital numbers flashing as if it hadn't been reset after a power cut. A couple of books. A telephone. He pulled open one of the drawers in the bureau. Nothing. Not even a pair of dry socks. Books were piled everywhere on the floor. He saw no obvious signs of Lainie having been in residence.

A second door led to a bathroom. A sink. A cheap metal shower stall. He turned the tap. No water. Turned off for the winter. What did Lainie drink if this was her prison? Where did she wash? Using the toilet wouldn't have been a problem. The seat was set above a hole hanging out over the sea. Probably illegal these days. And, no doubt, a little cool on the ass.

McCabe came back into the main room and sat with the others. He rubbed each set of toes in turn, trying to get the circulation going in them again. He'd read you can always tell when you've got frostbite because you can't feel the pain anymore. If that was right he was okay. His toes hurt like hell.

'You guys been here a while?' he asked.

'Pretty much all day.' Tasco looked at his watch. 'And all night.'

'Find anything other than the fingerprints?'

'Yeah,' said Jacobi. 'Lot of DNA sources. Hairs in the bed. A couple long and brown like Goff's. What looks like dried semen stains on the sheets.'

'Where are the sheets?'

'Packed up and on their way to Augusta. Some dirty cups and silverware that were in the sink. Also en route. May have traces of DNA. There're cold ashes in the woodstove. Can't tell how long ago the last fire was. We'll sift through them in case Kelly tried burning something incriminating.'

'Anything else?'

'The phone's connected,' said Tasco. 'Dial tone's beeping like there's a voice mail message on it.'

'You haven't listened to it?'

'Can't. Not till we get Kelly's password. One oh nine is supposed to be checking with Verizon. I would've thought we'd have something by now.'

'Can I help with the files?'

'Sure. Just wear these and don't smear.' Jacobi tossed him a pair of gloves. 'I'll want to check all this stuff for prints later.' Looked like a big job.

The boxes contained a potpourri of Kelly's life. Letters, photos, postcards from vacationing friends. Also a lot of notes and papers from college and seminary. A number of photos showed a younger Kelly with the same young man. Teddy Childs? Or maybe an earlier partner. In a couple he was dressed as a priest, but mostly not. One photo showed a young Kelly with an older woman who stared at the camera with the same intense blue eyes. Presumably his mother.

Jacobi and the two detectives kept at it for an hour, none of them speaking, each of them glancing at each piece of paper, then placing it in one of several neat piles arranged by type of document. The room was silent save for the sound of men breathing, hands shuffling paper, and an occasional creak from the house moving on its precarious foundation. McCabe imagined the whole thing tumbling off the cliff and into the ocean with the three of them still in it. *Wynken, Blynken, and Nod one night sailed off in a wooden shoe.* There was no wind. No roar from the dead-calm sea. Not even the ticking of a clock. Just the creaks.

'This what you're looking for?' The sudden sound of Jacobi's voice made McCabe jump. Jacobi was holding out a spiral-bound booklet with a clear plastic cover. McCabe took it. The first page contained only title, author, and date. '*An Examination of the Prophetic Tradition in the Old Testament.* John Kelly, TOR. May 2, 1994.'

He opened it and began reading. At the top of page 21 he found exactly what he was looking for. An italicized quote, *All the sinners of my people shall die by the sword, which say, The evil shall not overtake nor prevent us.* Beneath it was what appeared to be a lengthy and scholarly discussion of how and why a vengeful God would deal with those who ignored his precepts. McCabe stared at the quote. Seeing it on paper seemed to seal the deal. Kelly was guilty. McCabe just needed a motive and some hard evidence that would convince a jury. Jacobi got up from his chair and stood looking over McCabe's shoulder.

'So Kelly's your pither, huh?'

'Looks that way.'

The quiet in the room was broken by the William Tell Overture, the part that used to be the theme music from *The Lone Ranger* on TV. Tasco hit a button on his phone. The music stopped. 'Tasco,' he said. 'Yeah? Okay. Good. Let me write that down.' He removed a small notebook and pen from his coat pocket and made a notation. 'Thanks, Andrea. Yeah, you, too.' He looked at McCabe. 'That was Verizon.'

'Kelly's password?'

'Yup.'

'What is it?'

'Bunch of numbers.' He read from the note. '726288279.'

'It spells "sanctuary."'

'What?'

'The numbers. They spell out the word 'sanctuary' on a telephone keypad. Should've guessed that one an hour ago. I must be losing it.'

They went into the bedroom. McCabe picked up the receiver and dialed the number for Verizon voice mail. 'John Kelly,' said a male voice.

Then a computerized female voice came on. 'Please enter your password.'

McCabe entered the letters S-A-N-C-T-U-A-R-Y.

'You have one new message. To listen to your messages now, press one.'

McCabe pressed one.

'First new message. From unknown caller. Received Tuesday, December twentieth, at 6:44 P.M.'

'I know what you've been doing, you asshole, and you're not going to get away with it. We need to talk. And don't try ignoring me. I'll try your other line.' McCabe realized he'd never heard Lainie Goff's voice before. Still, he was sure it was her.

'To hear the message again, press one.'

He pressed one. 'I know what you've been doing, you asshole, and you're not going to get away with it. We need to talk. And don't try ignoring me. I'll try your other line.' *I know what you've been doing, you asshole.* What exactly *was* Kelly doing? Was it the motive McCabe was searching for? He handed the phone to Tasco and let him listen.

The front door opened and closed. Bowman's voice called out, 'Hey! McCabe! Where are you?'

'In here.'

Bowman appeared in the door of the bedroom. 'Get your coats on,' he said. 'You guys better come see what we found.'

*

It was still dark, and McCabe didn't see it at first. Not until Bowman positioned the beam of his flashlight right on the spot. A human hand, sticking up out of melting snow and attached to about six inches of skinny arm that was covered in a solid mass of blue tattoos. Young and almost certainly male. Both hand and arm looked frozen. The same waxy sheen he'd seen on Lainie Goff's body. McCabe looked around to position himself. They were standing in a wooded area a couple of hundred feet southwest of the house. 'This still Kelly's property?' he asked.

'Yeah,' said Bowman. 'It goes back another fifty feet about to that big pine tree over there.'

Two of Jacobi's techs, Jeff Feeney and Carla Morrisey, had already started stringing yellow crime scene tape in a wide perimeter around the spot, shooing away a couple of the local searchers. They retreated to the far side of the tape.

I know what you've been doing, you asshole, and you're not going to get away with it. Goff's accusation played over and over in McCabe's head. Was this what Kelly was doing? Abusing teenaged boys from Sanctuary House? Just like the priest who had abused him? Had Goff found out about it and accused him? Had he killed Goff, and this boy as well, to keep her from going public? To keep her from calling the cops and, in the process, destroying him and his life's work, Sanctuary House? McCabe shined his own light on the hand and arm sticking out of the snow. He was sure he'd found a motive that, for John Kelly, would have been far more powerful than mere money.

When the area was circled in tape, Feeney and Morrisey hauled a small generator and a couple of powerful floods out of the back of their van. Feeney began setting them up on top of steel tripods. Morrisey unrolled heavy black cable from the generator to the lights. She plugged it in and flicked a switch, and suddenly the burial site was lit up like center field at Yankee Stadium.

McCabe called Terri Mirabito at home again.

'Jesus, McCabe, don't you ever sleep? What is it now?'

'We found another body.'

'You've got to be kidding me.'

'Frozen.'

'Pithed?'

'Don't know yet.' McCabe watched as Feeney began shooting the crime scene photos with a high-end digital camera. Morrisey was taking measurements to precisely position the spot where they found the arm on a location diagram. 'All we can see so far is an arm. Looks like a boy's. The rest of the body, assuming there is a rest of the body, is still buried in a couple of feet of snow and ice. If the weather hadn't warmed up and melted a bunch, we wouldn't have found it at all.'

'Okay. I'm getting dressed. Where do I go this time?'

'Head on down to Casco Bay Lines. I'll make sure the fireboat's waiting for you.'

'Harts Island?'

'Yeah. There'll be a car waiting on this side. I'm calling Fortier, too, so don't take off without him.'

It was nearly six o'clock, and Fortier was already awake sipping coffee. He said he'd throw some clothes on and be at the dock in fifteen minutes. Before he hung up McCabe asked him to bring along some dry socks and, if he had them, an extra pair of waterproof boots, size eleven or thereabouts, and, oh yeah, if he didn't mind terribly, maybe a hair dryer. Fortier said he'd see what he could rustle up.

By the time all the crime scene photos were shot and the measurements taken, a thin strip of orange was beginning to appear over a mostly green and gray eastern horizon. Feeney and Morrisey had started gently digging away the snow from around the arm. They worked carefully, like archeologists uncovering a precious artifact. McCabe looked up and saw Terri trudging through the snow toward him, carrying her little black doctor's bag. Fortier walked behind her, holding a white shopping bag with MACY's printed on both sides. He handed the bag to McCabe, who took it and headed for the cottage, forcing himself not to look back at the smirk he was sure was planted on Bowman's face.

Inside the white bag McCabe found a pair of dark blue crew socks rolled in a ball, a pair of size eleven L.L. Bean trademark boots – green rubber on the bottom, tan leather on top – and a small portable hair dryer. He located an electric outlet, one of only two in the room, and dragged over a wooden chair. He removed his shoes and socks. His toes were totally numb, but they didn't look as frozen as the kid's arm. He took that as a good sign. He plugged in the dryer and started blowing warm air over his feet. It didn't feel good. After only a few seconds his toes started hurting like a bitch. He wondered if PPD regs said anything about a detective's fitness for duty if he happened to be missing a toe or two. It was time, he told himself, to start dressing properly for Maine winters. Manhattan was a long time ago and a long way away.

*

It took about half an hour of careful scraping before the frozen corpse of a teenaged boy began to emerge. He was lying on one side and was naked except for the tattoos that covered both arms and the rows of silver rings that were pierced into the skin above his right eye and along the curve of his lower lip. Even in death he had the sweet angelic face of a child, one that reminded McCabe of the face of Edward Mullaney, the abused altar boy he'd known so many years ago. The altar boy who was now a convicted pedophile and rapist. And so the cycle of sin continues, McCabe mused to himself, transmitted like a virus from abuser to abused, down through the generations and back again.

Judging by the layers of crusting ice around his body, McCabe figured the boy had been buried three snowfalls ago. He stood between Fortier and Terri and watched the techs take pictures of the uncovered corpse. 'We've managed to move Goff's limbs enough to straighten her out,' Terri said.

'And?'

'I think she was sexually tortured. There are burn marks in and around the opening of her vagina.'

McCabe closed his eyes and sighed deeply, wondering why Kelly had had to do that. It was so hard to think of the man as a sadist. *The minute anyone starts thinking they know who or what John Kelly is, it's time to think again.*

'What about the bruising we saw in the trunk of the car?'

'My guess is those bruises are old. She probably fought back when he grabbed her. Then he drugged her and kept her drugged, except maybe for the torture sessions. I have a hunch when we finally get the tox reports, we'll find she was heavily sedated at the time of death.'

'Anything else?'

'No. Nothing under her nails, and other than the burns, the body is as clean as a whistle. I think he may have bathed her just before he killed her.'

Maybe that's why he took her to Markham's house, thought McCabe. No heat or water here. Plenty of both there – and, as Markham himself said, half the island knew where the key was hidden.

When the techs had finished, Terri knelt down next to the body in the hole they'd made and began her preliminary examination with gloved hands. 'Yep. He's been pithed, alright,' she said. 'There's also considerable bruising and what looks like bleeding and torn skin around the rectum.'

'Rough sex?'

'I don't know. Maybe. Either that or . . .'

Terri paused. She didn't look happy.

'Or what?'

'I think our friend may have enjoyed pushing sharp objects into places they didn't belong.'

McCabe winced again. Lainie Goff's words came screaming back to him one more time. *I know what you've been doing, you asshole, and you're not going to get away with it.* Unfortunately, Kelly got her before she got him. At least she was right about one thing. He wasn't going to get away with it.

Thirty-Four

At exactly 8:30 A.M. Sunday, McCabe dropped Maggie's keys off with Kyra. Half an hour later he strode into 109. In spite of the fact that he'd had about six hours' sleep in the last forty-eight, he felt good. Better than good. Thanks to the adrenaline rush of uncovering Lainie Goff's killer, combined with four large cups of coffee, he felt locked and loaded. Primed for confrontation. Ready to rock and roll. Coffee number five was warming his hand. Tanzanian Peaberry Fair Trade Dark Roast from the Coffee by Design on India Street.

A handwritten note from Shockley greeted him at his desk. *Come see me ASAP. I'm in my office. P.S. Congratulations!!!*

McCabe headed down the hall for the chief's office on the southeast corner of the floor. He could hear the reporters buzzing from fifty feet away. He spotted Shockley standing at the door, jacket off, tie loosened, arms folded, sleeves rolled up. A textbook image of the hard-charging leader who'd been up all night leading his troops in the apprehension of a vicious killer.

At the moment the GO had the ear of Luke McGuire of the *Press Herald.* The rest of the sizable room was crammed with just about every other crime reporter in the state plus a few stringers from the Boston and New York papers. McCabe scanned the room and found Shockley's girlfriend, Josie Tenant. She was in the corner writing some notes, no doubt preparing to broadcast good news to the world as soon as Shockley gave the go sign. Cameras were pointed toward Shockley's desk, awaiting the chief's reassuring message to an anxious and waiting city.

'Mike! Come on in.' The chief leapt up, grabbed his elbow, and steered him through the throng to his desk. He smiled expansively. 'Thought I'd make the announcement from right here in my office. Kind of give the viewers an inside look at the department. What d'ya think? Nice touch, huh?'

It wasn't exactly the way it was supposed to be done. That's what the pressroom on the ground floor was for. McCabe knew Shockley didn't care. He probably figured announcing Kelly's arrest from his office, perhaps sitting casually on the corner of his desk, would let the public know that they could credit him personally with catching the bad guy.

McCabe didn't care about that either. With Kelly in custody and Quinn safely in Winter Haven, today was a good day, and Shockley's bullshit couldn't screw it up. After all the darkness, the sun was finally beginning to shine. They'd caught Lainie Goff's killer less than sixty hours after finding her body at the end of the Fish Pier. Maggie was okay and getting out of the hospital. Casey was coming home. And, best of all, so was Kyra. They'd have a good dinner. They'd make love. Maybe he'd get a little sleep – and he wouldn't have any ugly dreams about his ex-wife.

'Sure, Chief, that's great. You enjoy yourself. Just do me a favor. Let me see what I can get out of Kelly before you make any major announcements.'

'Hold on, McCabe,' Shockley said in a lower, more private voice. 'We need a conviction on this.' The smile was gone. 'Are you telling me you're not sure you've got enough?'

'Just let me interview him.'

'What more do you need?'

'A confession would help. We're also waiting on DNA results from Augusta. Joe Pines promised the matches for this morning. The last thing you need is to make a big announcement and then have to take it back.'

'Alright.' Shockley sighed. 'For now, I'll just say we're talking to "a person of interest." That'll hold 'em for a while. Just do me a favor. Don't wait too long.'

McCabe headed out into the corridor. 'Good morning, ladies and gentlemen.' He could hear Shockley's voice behind him, the man's trademark smile in the delivery. 'This morning, as you may have guessed, I've got some very good news . . .'

On the monitor in Fortier's office, McCabe watched Kelly sitting alone in the small interview room. He didn't look happy. 'Did you have to cuff him?'

'Yeah. I think he might have gotten violent if I didn't,' said Brian Cleary, 'and then I would have had to get violent back.' Cleary grinned. 'And I know how you hate that.'

'He say anything?'

'Not yet,' said Eddie Fraser. 'Other than to tell us several times we were assholes. He's just sitting there seething.'

'Ask for a lawyer?'

'Again, not yet.'

Even on the monitor, McCabe could feel anger radiating off the man in waves. He stared at the image, trying to square Kelly's hot temper with the cool, methodical MO of Lainie Goff's murderer. He was sure Kelly was capable of killing Goff. He was just surprised at the way he went about it. The whole scene at the Fish Pier didn't feel right. It was too showy. On the other hand, maybe he was reading the guy wrong. *The minute anyone starts thinking . . .* Wolfe's words played in his head again. Maybe that was it. Maybe he'd better think again.

Before entering the room, McCabe unbuckled his holster and weapon and handed them to Fraser. He'd decided to remove Kelly's cuffs, and he knew Kyra would be really pissed if he let a prisoner shoot him with his own gun. Probably never agree to marry him.

'Hello, John,' McCabe said in a cheerful voice. 'Sorry about the restraints.'

Kelly looked up. His blue, nearly violet eyes bore into McCabe for a few seconds. Then he turned away.

'I can remove the cuffs if you like.'

No response.

'You've just got to promise you're not going to get crazy on me or anything.'

Kelly looked down. Closed his eyes. Took some deep breaths. McCabe could see his jaw muscles working as if he were clenching his teeth. Finally he looked up. 'Okay.'

'Okay what?'

'Unlock the cuffs. I won't beat you up.'

McCabe smiled. 'Good. My girlfriend will be glad to hear that.'

He went behind Kelly's chair and freed his arms. Then he walked around to the other side of the table and sat.

Kelly stretched his arms, rubbed his wrists, then clasped his hands on the table like a student in Catholic school waiting for the teacher. Neither of them said anything. They just sat there looking at each other for a while.

McCabe spoke first. 'We searched your cabin.'

'Yes. I know. I gave you permission. Remember?' There was still an edge in his voice.

'We found the quote.'

'Good for you.'

'The one from the Book of Amos. It was in the paper you wrote. The one from grad school.'

Kelly shrugged. 'Okay.'

'Oh, by the way. We also found the boy.'

He saw a flicker of doubt in Kelly's eyes. Then it disappeared. 'What boy?'

'The one outside your cabin.'

'I don't know who or what you're talking about.'

'He was only about fourteen or so, wasn't he?'

'I still don't know what you're talking about.'

'The boy you sexually abused? Then killed. Then buried in the snow. At your place? On Harts Island. You did a hell of a job, John. What did you stick up his rear end? The same knife you used to kill Goff?'

Kelly stared at him with a puzzled expression. He looked like he was trying to figure something out. McCabe guessed it was probably how he was gonna get himself out of this one.

'Why did you have to kill him, John? Was it because he told Goff what you were doing? So you had to get rid of both of them? Because they both knew? Is that what it was?'

Kelly remained silent.

'When was it you brought him out there? To your cabin, I mean?'

Kelly looked up. 'I haven't been to Harts Island in months.'

'Where were you about one o'clock this morning?'

'I told your buddies. I was home. Asleep.'

'In your apartment?'

'Yes.'

'With your partner?'

'Yes.'

'How do you know Leanna Barnes?'

'I don't know any Leanna Barnes.'

'That's funny. I've got a couple of witnesses who say they saw you at her apartment around one this morning.' Not exactly true, but not exactly untrue if you counted Barnes saying the word 'Ellie' and Maggie seeing a man in glasses with heavy black frames.

'They're wrong.'

'They swear it was you.'

'I told you. They're wrong. I don't know any Leanna Barnes. I don't know where her apartment is.'

'They say you shot her.'

'They're even more wrong. I never shot anybody in my life.'

'You've hit people.'

'Yeah. With my fists, and usually when they deserved it.

I've never even fired a gun. I wouldn't know how to hold one.'

McCabe looked at Kelly and decided to try a different tack. 'The good thing, John, is it looks like Barnes is going to be okay. Be able to testify in court. So you'll only be up on two counts of murder, not three,' he said carefully, watching Kelly's eyes for a reaction. He didn't see one. 'Amazing the gun didn't do more damage.'

'I'm glad to hear that.'

'Yeah. She'll be right as rain in no time. Be able to tell the jury how it was you who shot her.'

'You're lying.'

'You mean you thought Leanna was dead? Is that what I'm lying about?'

'I don't know any Leanna. I've never been to her apartment, and what you're lying about is the whole thing.'

'Yeah? You're saying maybe the witnesses got it wrong?'

'I'm saying you're lying.'

Kelly's hands were clenched tightly together, the knuckles white. He was barely holding it together. He was talking, though. At least for the moment.

'You know your place on the island?'

Kelly didn't answer. Just looked at him.

'Was the boy we found the first one you killed out there? Or were there others? You ever bring any other boys out there? You know, for a little fun and games? You must have known a lot of little lost boys, didn't you, John? Just like Peter Pan. Runaways who wouldn't be missed. No matter what you did to them. Is that why you started Sanctuary House? So you'd have your own little magnet to draw them right in. As many as you wanted. Whenever you wanted. A real treasure trove, wasn't it? And if they disappeared or turned up dead, hey, who was going to miss them? They were runaways. Nobody at home waiting up or worrying about kids like them, was there, John? Except of course for you. Come in, come in, said the spider to the fly.'

Kelly hung his head and clenched his teeth. Then he looked up. He spoke quietly and slowly. 'I have devoted my entire life to protecting kids. To helping them. Not to abusing them. Or killing them. That is the covenant I made with God. That is the covenant I have honored. And God knows, even if you don't, that is the simple truth.'

'Really? When was the last time you were out there on Harts Island?'

'I already told you.'

'Oh yeah? I don't remember. Tell me again.'

'I don't use the place in winter. I haven't been there since, I don't know . . . I think Teddy and I went out the weekend before Thanksgiving.'

'You sure you haven't been out there more recently? Say in December? After it started getting cold and the ground froze too hard to dig.'

McCabe slipped two of the crime scene photos of the boy, lying in the snow dead and frozen, across the table. 'Like maybe for a little recreational outing?'

'Oh, sweet Jesus.' Kelly stared at the pictures, one in each hand, looking first at one, then the other.

'You do know this boy, don't you, John?' McCabe dropped the teasing tone. His voice was hard now. Threatening. 'Well, don't you?'

No answer.

'Answer the question, goddammit, Kelly. You do know this boy, don't you?'

'Yes.'

'And how exactly is it that you know him?' McCabe was standing now. He spat the words out, leaning in across the table, his face inches from Kelly's.

Kelly looked up. His face was pale. He spoke softly. 'He lived at Sanctuary House.'

'Really? Well, then, I guess you must know his name.'

'Callie Connor.'

'Callie?'

'Short for Calvin.'

'You last saw Calvin when?'

'I don't know. Sometime before Christmas.'

'Is that when you took him to the island? For . . . what was that phrase again? A recreational outing?'

'No.'

'Maybe one that included a little fucking?'

'No.'

'And stabbing?'

'No.'

'And burying his naked body in the snow? With his ass all cut up and bruised from what you did to him?'

'No!' Kelly screamed. 'No! No! No! No!'

When Kelly stopped, he looked at the pictures again, eyes blinking, tears forming.

'And maybe Lainie Goff found out about it? Didn't she? So you had to kill her, too? Isn't that what happened? Isn't that what you did?'

Kelly looked up, silent.

'Goddammit, answer me!' McCabe shouted, slamming his open palm down on the table so hard the empty file flew up.

Kelly didn't answer.

McCabe sat back down, and his voice dropped from a shout to just above a whisper. 'Isn't that what really happened, John? You killed this boy. You killed him because you were abusing him, and he told Lainie about it, and she called you and threatened you. She wasn't about to let you get away with it, was she, John? So you had to kill her, too. To keep her from telling people. Isn't that right, Father Jack? To keep her from telling people like me? Isn't that what really happened?'

'I've never killed anyone.'

'You know what I still don't get? What I still don't get is why you left Lainie's body out there on the Fish Pier with that note stuffed in her mouth. Amos. Chapter nine. Verse ten. Right where you knew we'd find it and connect it to you. You remember the words, don't you, John? *All the sinners of my people shall die by the sword, which say, The evil shall not overtake nor prevent us.* Did you do that because you knew Lainie wasn't someone who could just disappear like Calvin Connor did? People would miss her. People would look for her. Powerful people with powerful connections. So you stuck her out there and tried to make it look like some religious whacko did her in?'

Kelly folded his arms on the table and dropped his head on them.

'Might have worked, too, Jack, except you made one mistake. You didn't destroy that book in your bookcase at Sanctuary House. The one on Old Testament prophets.

You didn't destroy your old college paper either. I don't know why that was. Was it because you thought the guys in blue suits – isn't that what you called us, Jack? The guys in blue suits? Was it because you thought we just wouldn't be smart enough to put two and two together?'

'I never killed anyone,' Kelly said, his voice muffled by his arms.

'Or maybe, Jack' – McCabe leaned in again, his face just inches from Kelly's – 'maybe you left her there with the note in her mouth and the book still on your shelf so we *would* find you and put a stop to the evil things you were doing. To put an end to your guilt? Is that what it was, Jack? Is that what you wanted? *All the sinners of my people shall die by the sword.* All the sinners, Jack. Including you. Except we don't have the death penalty here in Maine. So you'll either have to live with your guilt – or confess it.'

McCabe lowered his voice so that it was barely more than a whisper. 'Is that what you want, Jack? To put an end to your guilt? If it is, we can help you with that. All you've got to do is confess your sins. Tell us what you did to Calvin Connor. Tell us what you did to Lainie Goff. Come on, do it, Jack. You know what comes next. First there's confession. Then there's absolution. Forgive me, Father, for I have sinned. Come on, Jack, say it. Forgive me, Father, for I have sinned. Then tell me how you killed Callie Connor and then, when she found out, how you killed Lainie Goff.'

'Fuck you, you stupid bastard,' Kelly screamed. 'I never killed anyone!'

After that McCabe sat back in his chair. He didn't say anything for a minute.

'Well, if you didn't kill them, who did?'

'What?'

'Somebody must have killed them.'

'Yes. Somebody else.'

'Oh, really? Well, then, if that's the case, maybe you'd be good enough to explain how it happened we found this on your phone?' He raised his left hand in a silent signal to Cleary in Fortier's office.

Lainie Goff's voice filled the small room. 'I know what you've been doing, you asshole, and you're not going to get away with it. We need to talk.'

'You found that? On my phone?'

'Yes.'

'Which phone?'

'On Harts Island. In your cabin. What do you think about that?'

Kelly shook his head and shrugged his shoulders more or less at the same time. 'What I think is, I think I need to call a lawyer.'

'Well, that's your privilege, Jack. There's only one small problem I can see.'

'What?'

'You told me your lawyer was Lainie Goff, and I'm sorry, Jack, but I don't think she's taking any calls at the moment.'

Thirty-Five

'Nice job, McCabe. You did good.' Maggie was standing with the aid of a cane and leaning against the wall behind Cleary and Fraser in Bill Fortier's office. The monitor was still turned on, showing an empty interview room.

'Not so good. I didn't get a confession. And you know what else?'

'What?'

'I walked out of there with this crappy feeling that he may not be our guy.'

'You've gotta be kidding,' said Fraser. 'We've got evidence up the wazoo.'

'Yeah, we do,' said McCabe. 'Most of it circumstantial.'

'McCabe,' said Maggie, 'I saw the sonofabitch with my own eyes. He fired a gun at me.'

'What you said, and I quote, was "It was dark. He had his hood up. All I saw was his glasses. Black frames."'

'That's right. Glasses. Black frames. Just like he's wearing now.'

'Lots of people wear glasses with black frames.'

'Maybe so, but most of those people don't have quotes from the Book of Amos sitting in a box in their island hideaways. Or a murdered boy buried in the snow in their backyards. Or incriminating phone messages. McCabe, what the hell more do you want?'

'I don't know. For starters, I guess I want to see the DNA results, which we don't have yet.'

'We'll have reads on the semen stains any minute now,' said Eddie Fraser. 'Tasco told Joe Pines to make them top priority.'

'What are you doing here, anyway?' McCabe asked Maggie. 'Why aren't you still in the hospital?'

'Well, you see, Sergeant McCabe, nobody's ever shot me before. So let's just say I bullied my doc into letting me go. Like I told him, this time it's personal.'

'This time it's personal?' McCabe smiled. 'You said that?'

'Yeah.'

'Great line. Advertising theme for *Jaws: The Revenge*. Also known as *Jaws 4*. It was the best single thing about one of the worst movies ever made. I was at NYU when it came out – 1987.'

Maggie sighed. 'Listen, McCabe, at the moment, I've got a sore ass and a short temper, and I'm in no mood for Trivial Pursuit.'

'Sorry.'

'Why don't you think he did it?'

'I didn't say I didn't think he did it. I said I had a feeling. I wasn't sure.'

Cleary cocked his head. 'Y'know, boss, that ain't the song you were singing when you told us to bring him in.'

'I know.'

'You know, McCabe, the GO's in there right now,' said Maggie, 'just itching to tell the world about Kelly's arrest. Personally, having just listened to your little tête-à-tête with Kelly, I think he should.'

'I don't think so.'

'Okay, what's your problem? Why, suddenly, aren't you sure?' Maggie winced as she spoke. 'Sorry. This sucker hurts.' She flipped open a prescription bottle of pills and dry-swallowed one. 'Percocet. I'm popping them like M&Ms.'

'Should you even be walking around?'

'Yeah, the doc said it was good for me.' She shifted position to relieve pressure on her right leg. 'Anyway, you were going to expound on your theory of Kelly's possible innocence.'

McCabe moved behind Bill Fortier's desk and sat. 'A couple of things bother me about Kelly being the bad guy. Obviously, the MO's one of them. The whole scene at the Fish Pier was pure show biz. It was too cute by half. It still doesn't seem to be the kind of thing Kelly would do.'

'You explained it pretty well in the interview room. Convinced me. Besides, people sometimes act out of character.'

'Yes, they do,' McCabe admitted, 'and maybe that's what's going on here.'

'You said there were two reasons. What's the other?'

'The phone message. There was something we left off when we let Kelly listen to it in there just now. Something I didn't think about till that very minute.'

'What?'

'According to the Verizon computer voice, the call was received on Tuesday, December twentieth, at 6:44 P.M. The whole message says, "I know what you've been doing, you asshole, and you're not going to get away with it. We

370

need to talk. And don't try ignoring me. I'll try your other line."'

'Yeah, so?'

'"I'll try your other line"? That means she called the island number first. Why? Kelly says he hardly ever uses the place in winter.'

'Maybe Lainie didn't know that. Or maybe he told her he would be there that particular day,' said Maggie.

'Maybe, but why would he be? It was a Tuesday, and on Tuesday nights Kelly's usually working at Sanctuary House. I think Lainie would have known that and called him there first. Or called his cell phone. The island phone should have been the last place she called, not the first.'

'It should be easy to check if he was at Sanctuary House that Tuesday,' said Fraser. 'Also easy to check his cell messages.'

'I agree. Let's do it. However, I've also got a small problem with the rest of the message. The first time we listened to her say, "I know what you've been doing, you asshole, and you're not going to get away with it," we were at Kelly's cottage. Ten minutes later we find the boy's frozen and sexually assaulted body on the edge of the property. It was only natural to assume that abusing Callie Connor was what Lainie meant by "I know what you've been doing."'

'It was – and it is. We were right. It fits,' said Maggie.

'Why? Because Kelly's gay?'

'No. Not just that. You told me Kelly was abused himself when he was a kid. We both know most adult abusers were abused themselves as children. Besides, whether it was the first number she called or the last, the simple fact is that Lainie's message was on Kelly's phone.'

'Yeah, but you know what suddenly struck me while we were playing it for him?'

'No, but I have a feeling you're going to tell me.'

'It struck me that maybe it wasn't Lainie who left it there.'

'What do you mean? We know it was Lainie. It's her voice.'

'Yes, it's her voice – but what if she originally left the message on somebody else's voice mail or message machine and not on Kelly's? Now let's suppose that person – whoever he was – decided to kill Goff to keep her from revealing what she knew. Let's further suppose that that person – whoever he was – decided to frame Kelly for Goff's murder. Wouldn't it be a good idea for that person to re-record Lainie's original message onto Kelly's island voice mail? Easy enough to do. Especially since she never called him by name. Just called him "you asshole." Re-recording it onto the island phone instead of his cell or Sanctuary House phone is a brilliant move because Kelly never uses the place this time of year and almost certainly won't check or erase the message before we hear it.'

Maggie nodded thoughtfully. 'Interesting. He re-records the message where he knows we're bound to search,' said Maggie, 'where he knows we'll find the quote from Amos and where he knows we'll find the boy's body.'

'Sounds like you're agreeing with McCabe,' Fraser said to Maggie, 'that Kelly's not the killer.'

'Well, I'm agreeing with McCabe that he *might* not be the killer. I'm not totally convinced yet one way or the other.'

McCabe got up and moved to the window. He stood looking out, watching the light Sunday morning traffic flow by on Franklin Arterial.

'What's that twisted brain of yours thinking about now?' asked Maggie.

'I was just wondering exactly what Lainie was referring to when she said "I know what you've been doing."'

Maggie shrugged. 'Presumably to the fact that Kelly – or possibly the real killer – was sexually abusing Callie Connor.'

McCabe turned and looked at her. 'How would Lainie have known about that?'

'I don't know,' said Maggie.

'Kelly wouldn't have told her if it *was* him. Neither would some other so-called real killer. So who did?'

'Connor lived at Sanctuary House. Lainie worked with the kids there. Maybe he told her himself.'

'Maybe. But Lainie only worked with the girls.'

'He still could have told her. Or he may have told one of the girls.'

'Again, maybe. But here's another thought. What if the real killer was abusing one or more of the kids, but it wasn't Callie Connor he was abusing. In fact, what if it wasn't a boy at all. What if the real killer isn't gay but heterosexual and the person he was abusing was a girl. Or maybe girls plural.'

'That makes no sense, McCabe. If Lainie was confronting him about abusing a girl, why would he kill Connor and not the girl?'

'It does make sense if his goal is to make us think John Kelly, the gay ex-priest who was abused as a child, is the murderer. If he was using Connor's death as nothing more than another piece of carefully orchestrated misdirection to push the investigation in Kelly's direction.'

'Then he would have also had to kill the girl who told Lainie,' said Cleary.

'Yes, he would. Or girls. Plural.'

'If he did,' said Maggie, 'their bodies may not be as easy to find as Connor's was.'

'You guys are blowing my mind,' said Fraser. 'As of now this is all pure conjecture. And, if you'll pardon my French, maybe pure bullshit. As of now all the evidence for all the killings still points straight to John Kelly.'

Fortier's phone rang. Cleary picked it up. 'Lieutenant Fortier's office. Cleary speaking. Hey, Joe.' Pause. 'Really?' Pause. 'Interesting.' Pause. 'You're sure the final reads will back up the prelims? Okay. Yeah, I'll let 'em know.' Cleary hung up. 'Well Sergeant, I hate to throw a monkey wrench into your Sherlock Holmes conjectures, but –'

'But Pines says the semen on Kelly's sheets came from the kid?' asked McCabe.

'Yeah, some of it did. But not all of it. Some of it came from Kelly himself. None of it comes from some unknown mystery killer. Does that convince you Kelly's the guy?'

'I don't know. Maybe it's Kelly. Maybe not.'

'If not Kelly,' asked Maggie, 'then who?'

'I don't know, but there are two people who might be able to tell us.'

'Yes.' Maggie nodded. 'Unfortunately, at the moment, Abby can't and Barker won't.'

'Did you ever get the search warrant for Barker's place?'

'Krickstein signed it this morning. Said we could pick it up anytime.'

'Good. Let's pay Andy a little visit. Would you like me to get you a wheelchair?'

'You mean like Ironside?'

'Sort of. Except you're way better looking than Raymond Burr.'

'I don't know. He was cute in an ugly sort of way. Anyway, I'd rather hobble. It hurts too much to sit down.'

'After Barker, let's see if we can get some answers from Abby Quinn.' McCabe picked up the phone and called Wolfe's office. There was no answer, but he left a message saying Abby was at Winter Haven and it was time to try hypnotherapy as they'd discussed. The sooner the better.

On the way out they could still hear Shockley bragging to whoever was still listening about great police work.

Thirty-Six

At exactly 10:32 A.M. four PPD vehicles pulled up around the corner from 342 Brackett Street. Uniformed cops emerged from two black-and-white units and slipped around the back and sides of the building to keep Andy Barker from sneaking out. When they were in position, McCabe and Maggie, along with evidence techs Bill Jacobi, Jeff Feeney, and Carla Morrisey, entered the building. Jacobi and Feeney lugged two silver-colored metal suitcases filled with electronic equipment up to the second floor. Maggie limped up behind them, and they all waited silently on the landing. Downstairs McCabe knocked on the door to apartment 1F. 'Barker?' he called out.

There was no answer, but McCabe could hear the sound of someone shuffling around inside.

He knocked again. 'Andrew Barker? This is the police. Please open the door now.'

He heard more scurrying on the other side.

'Mr Barker. We have a warrant to search your apartment. If you don't open the door now, I'll be forced to have it removed.'

Another few seconds passed. The door opened an inch or two, a gold-colored security chain stretched across the opening. Barker peered out. 'You again. Why won't you people leave me alone? What do you want now?'

McCabe held up a sheet of paper. 'I have a warrant

signed by Judge Harold Krickstein of the district court authorizing a search of your premises. Please open the door now.'

'What if I say no?'

'Trust me, Mr Barker, I don't think you want to do that.'

There was a moment's further hesitation; then Barker slipped off the chain and opened the door. He was unshaven and wearing a dark blue terrycloth bathrobe. Probably had nothing on underneath. Skinny white legs wearing black ankle socks protruded from under the robe. From upstairs, McCabe could hear Maggie and the three techs unlocking Goff's apartment and going in.

Barker frowned at the sound. 'Who's that up there?'

McCabe ignored the question and moved past Barker into the room. A wave of hot air hit him. It had to be over eighty degrees, and the place stank of sweat, garbage, and dirty laundry.

Barker eyed McCabe warily. 'Who's upstairs?'

'Move away from the door, Mr Barker,' said McCabe. 'Come in and close it.'

Barker didn't argue. McCabe looked around. Almost every surface was covered with something. Clothing, videos, and magazines. A fifty-two-inch flat-screen TV dominated one wall. A single La-Z-Boy recliner covered in stained brown corduroy faced the screen; a copy of a publication called *Boobz* lay open on the seat, its cover graced by a naked woman with the biggest breasts McCabe had ever seen. Behind the recliner were a couple more chairs and an old-fashioned couch covered in a brown gingham check.

'Who's upstairs?' Barker asked again.

McCabe pointed to the gingham couch. 'Sit over there, Andy. We need to talk.'

Barker sat. McCabe stood over him and showed him a piece of paper. 'This is a warrant to search your apartment.'

'I know. You told me. So what are they doing upstairs?'

'Detective Savage and a team of police technicians are sweeping apartment 2F for hidden cameras and microphones, Andy. The ones you used to spy on Elaine Goff.'

Barker started to rise, his face red with rage. 'They can't . . . What the hell?'

McCabe pushed him gently back down. 'I think you better stay right where you are, little Andy-Man, and tell me all about your video collection.'

Barker's rage turned to fear. His eyes started blinking rapidly, perhaps uncontrollably. His hands were shaking. 'I have no idea what you're talking about.'

'Oh, sure you do, Andy. The spycam videos you took of Lainie. You liked watching her, didn't you, Andy? Better looking than those gals in *Boobz* magazine, don't you think? Y'know, I can just see you now, sitting there in your La-Z-Boy getting off on watching Lainie when she didn't know you were looking. What did you like best? Watching her getting undressed? Or maybe taking a bath? Or maybe your best fun was watching her have sex with somebody? You watched it all, didn't you? Right there on your super duper fifty-two-inch high-definition plasma TV. Or is it an LCD? I always get them mixed up.'

Barker just kept blinking.

'In fact, you're a regular little Peeping Andy, aren't you?'

Barker closed his eyes and began repeating his mantra. 'I have the right to remain silent —'

'Andy, Andy.' McCabe held up a hand like a traffic cop stopping a line of cars. 'Please don't start that again. We all know that song.'

'I have the right to remain silent,' Barker began again. 'Anything I say can and will be used against me in a court of law. I have the right to have an attorney present during questioning –'

'Yes, you do, Andy, but hold on. When you hear what I have to offer, maybe you won't want to remain silent.'

Barker just looked at him.

McCabe's cell rang. 'Yes? Yes. Good. Thank you.'

He put the phone away and turned back to Barker. 'That was the folks upstairs. They found your cameras hidden in the old ceiling light fixtures. One in the bedroom. One in the bathroom. One in the living room.' McCabe looked at his watch. 'Took them about ten minutes start to finish. They're just double-checking now to make sure there aren't any more.'

Barker took a deep breath and looked toward the TV. 'What do you want?'

'Now, since you wouldn't want all that good stuff you were watching to go to waste, my guess is you were recording videos. My other guess is you have them right here in this apartment.'

McCabe paused for a response. There was none, so he continued. 'Since we have this search warrant, we can rip this place apart until we find your stash, wherever it is, and then go back to Middle Street and sit there watching your dirty movies till we find what we're looking for. Then again that seems like a lot of unnecessary work, don't you think, Andy, when you can just point us to the right ones?'

'What are you looking for?'

'The video of the guy who searched Lainie's apartment Friday night before I got there. Plus any other video that shows her talking to a man, maybe the same man, either in person or over the phone.'

'What do I get out of it?'

'You hand them over and you get charged with a Violation of Privacy. A Class D offense. Max sentence only one year, which you'd probably serve in the county jail and not state prison. In fact, if you have a clean record and no priors, you might get off with no jail time at all. Just probation.'

'What if I don't hand them over?'

'That becomes what I call helping the bad guys and what the Maine statutes call Hindering Apprehension. A Class B crime. Up to ten years in the state prison. Even without priors, you'll do at least four. And it's hard time, Andy. In a place where a cute little fella like you might not do very well. So it's no jail time if you help. Four to ten if you don't. Sounds like a good deal to me, but it's your call. Take it or leave it.'

'Can I think about it?'

'Sure. You've got one minute.'

'Can I get it in writing?'

'It already is in writing. Just check the Maine statutes. Violation of Privacy versus Hindering Apprehension.'

'Do I get to keep my other videos?'

'You mean of Lainie?'

'Yes.'

McCabe did his best to keep a straight face. Who was this goofball? 'No, I'm afraid not.'

Barker sighed, got up, and walked to a DVD machine on a table next to the television. He took one video off the top. Then he hit POWER, pressed EJECT, and took out a second disk. He handed both to McCabe. 'I think these are what you're looking for.'

'Where are the rest of them?'

'Back of the closet. There's a false panel. It slips right out. You just have to find the latch. There's a box in there. That's where I keep them.'

Thirty-Seven

Word of the spycams spread fast. By the time McCabe and Maggie walked in with the box of videos, the conference room was full, everyone gathered and waiting. All of McCabe's detectives plus Starbucks and Bill Fortier. Even Shockley was there, seated at the head of the table, impatience written all over his face.

Maggie found a chair between Fortier and Tasco. Sturgis slid a foam rubber seat cushion across the table. 'Here you go, Savage. I heard you weren't as much of a hard-ass as I thought. I figured this might help.'

'Why, thank you, Carl,' said Maggie, slipping the cushion under her. 'How very thoughtful of you.'

McCabe waited for them to settle, then ran through the two-minute drill on what he hoped to find on the two disks they were about to watch. Brian Cleary volunteered to review the rest of Barker's stash. On the house. No overtime. McCabe declined. Maggie rolled her eyes. Shockley glared.

'Can we get moving here, people?' asked McCabe. 'The clock is ticking.'

The two disks Barker had handed McCabe were differentiated by a letter code and dates handwritten across the top in red marker. Seemed Barker was an organized guy. One was marked *LR-1/3/07*. That would have been last Tuesday. The day of Lainie's death. The other read *LR-*

12/20/06. Two weeks earlier. He figured *LR* stood for living room as opposed to bedroom or bathroom. Jacobi told him Barker's spycams were motion activated. That was good. There'd be no need to waste time looking at nothing happening.

McCabe slid the disk from January third into the machine and hit PLAY. The room went quiet. No gossip. No cracking jokes. Nobody nibbled on a sandwich or even sipped a cup of coffee. At first all they could see was a blank screen, then black, then a flash of white, then a view of Goff's living room as the apartment door swung open, activating the camera. A shaft of light from the hallway hit the Angela Adams rug, the glass coffee table, the white chairs and couch. A fish-eye view looking down from the ceiling. The time code read *2:33:19 AM 1/03/07.* The middle of the night. Or, more accurately, very early morning, the Tuesday of the murder. A dark figure entered, dressed in a dark hooded coat. The same kind of coat they'd seen fleeing Leanna Barnes's apartment. It was impossible to tell whether the figure inside the coat was John Kelly or someone else. All they could see was a hood pulled up over the head and a pair of shoulders. The intruder turned, closed the door. The image went black, then lightened as the lens automatically adjusted to the ambient light entering through the windows.

The intruder turned on a flashlight and scanned the beam around the room, the lens once again adjusting the aperture to available light. He went through the living room and disappeared into the hall between the kitchen and bedroom, making sure, McCabe guessed, that the place was empty. Ten seconds later he was back.

'Alright, you're alone,' McCabe murmured to the figure on the screen. 'Now take off the hood and show us who you are.'

Almost as if reacting to the request, the guy reached up, put a hand on the dark cowl, and held it there.

'C'mon, baby, just pull it off.'

The guy paused. There wasn't a sound in the conference room. They were all holding their breath. The intruder dropped his hand.

There were moans and grumbling from around the table.

Still hooded, the intruder walked to the bookcase on the right side of the room. He shined the light at the top shelf. The camera angle was down and at his back, and you couldn't see a damned thing except the coat and hood and the flashlight beam running along the row of books. The light stopped at one of the books. Then another. Then it went back to the first and stayed there. He reached up and pulled it down from the shelf. It was an oversized volume, maybe an art or travel book. He set the flashlight carefully on one of the lower shelves and rotated his body to the right. A thin sliver of face became visible. But not enough. You could tell he was a white guy, but that was it. He stood there, angling the book so the light was pointed directly at the pages. Happily, so was the spycam.

They watched him riffle through the pages until he found what he was looking for. A nine-by-twelve orange envelope. He removed the envelope, closed the book, returned it to its space on the top shelf. He turned the envelope in his gloved hands. Once. Twice. He paused.

McCabe could make out something written in the

upper left-hand corner, where a return address would go. He froze the image, then moved ahead one frame at a time, but it was impossible to read what the words said. Palmer Milliken? Maybe. Maybe Starbucks could enlarge it and play with the focus so they could read it. Maybe not. McCabe hit play again. The guy turned the envelope over again. Probably debating whether to open it here and now or wait till later. Apparently here and now won, because he removed the leather glove from his right hand and slid a bare finger under the seal. He reached inside and pulled out what looked like a stack of black-and-white photographs. McCabe again froze the image and advanced the frames one by one. He couldn't tell what the pictures were of. Again he'd have to depend on Starbucks to manipulate the images. The intruder slid the pictures back in the envelope and folded it lengthwise and pushed it into his coat pocket, not seeming to care if he bent the pictures. The pictures must have been what he was looking for, because he took his flashlight, headed for the door, and left. The time code read *2:36:15*. He'd been in the apartment less than three minutes. He'd turned out no drawers. Dumped nothing on the floor. McCabe was certain it wasn't the same guy who tossed the apartment night before last. This guy had found what he wanted. That guy hadn't. McCabe fast-forwarded through the rest of the disk. It was empty. He hit eject, and it slid out.

'What the hell was that all about?' asked Shockley. 'Is that your murderer?'

'I'm sure it was,' said McCabe. 'Unfortunately, we still don't know if it was Kelly or someone else.'

'Oh, for Christ's sake McCabe, every piece of evidence

we've got points to Kelly. Even the DNA says it's him. I say we arraign the sonofabitch and stop screwing around watching TV shows.'

'Let's just see what's on the next disk.'

He inserted the disk marked *LR-12/20/06*. The camera turned on when the top of Lainie Goff's head entered frame. Same fish-eye view as before. The time code read *12/20/06. 8:34:44*. Seventy-two hours before her abduction. Two weeks to the day before her death. Lainie turned on a table lamp, the sudden light creating a white flash in the upper corner of the frame. There was a knocking sound. She crossed the room, opened the door a crack, and peered out.

She said something to whoever was on the other side of the door. A male voice said something back. Both voices too far from the mike to make out what was being said. The male voice spoke again. Lainie seemed to hesitate, as if debating whether or not to let him in. She apparently decided she would and opened the door all the way. If she knew he was a killer, why would she do that?

The guy was wearing the same dark hooded coat as before, only this time the hood was down. Now you could see the top of his head but not his face. Still, it was enough to tell them it wasn't John Kelly. This guy had neatly cut gray hair, parted on the left and combed across to the right. It looked like Henry Ogden's hair. Like Wallace Stevens Albright's hair. Even kind of like Kyle Lanahan's, only a little shorter. In fact, it could have been any number of parties both known and unknown. Mr Gray Hair looked nervously around the room, then moved to the white couch and sat down. He was sitting almost directly under the lens, head down. Lainie sat across from him in one of the white chairs.

'You enjoy inflicting pain, don't you?' she asked. 'Especially on girls who are young and defenseless.' McCabe could hear better now. Not great but better. Her voice was distorted, and when she had her head down you could barely make out the words. Barker was obviously more interested in the quality of the video than the audio. Maggie and McCabe exchanged glances, a silent communication perfectly clear to both of them.

'I don't know what you're talking about,' the man answered. At least that's what McCabe thought he said. He hoped Starbucks could improve the sound.

'Yes, you do, you bastard. There's proof. There are pictures.'

'What kind of pictures?'

'Dirty pictures.'

'How could there be pictures?'

'Remote control mini camera. Amazing technology. Fit right inside her box of Camels. She just pointed it at the bed. Shoots in low light. Any light. Almost undetectable. Of course, you were so into your fun and games you never would have noticed anyway.'

A deep sigh was audible even on the lousy mike. 'I need to see them,' he said.

'No. They're in a safe place.'

Not safe enough, thought McCabe. Not safe at all, stuck in some book in her bookcase. She should have known that wasn't safe. Goddammit, she would have known that. She couldn't have been that careless. Maybe she hadn't been. He hit STOP, and the image froze.

'What are you doing now?' asked Shockley.

'Making a phone call.'

'Right now?'

'Yes. Right now.' He punched in Janie Archer's cell number. This time she answered.

'What we talked about is cool?' he said.

'McCabe?' said Archer.

'We found your message on Lainie's cell phone. When you thought she was in Aruba. You said, "What we talked about is cool."'

'Yeah. I guess. So?'

'What was cool?'

'She sent me an envelope. FedExed it the day before she was supposed to leave. She asked me to put it in a safe place.'

'Why didn't you tell me this Friday night?'

'I don't know. I was kinda wasted Friday. I didn't think about it.'

'Have you opened it?'

'No. I was gonna look at it tomorrow. Then, if it seemed pertinent, call you.'

'Why not look today?'

'I can't. Today's Sunday. It's in my safe deposit box. You know, like Lainie said? A safe place?'

'What bank?'

'Chase.'

'What branch?'

'Around the corner from here. First Ave and Seventy-second Street.'

'Where are you now?'

'Home. My apartment. East Seventy-first. Between First and York.'

'Alright. Stay there. I'm going to call a friend of mine on the NYPD. Lieutenant Art Astarita. He may be able to get you into the bank today. If he can, he'll call you back, and you and he can go there together.'

Archer agreed to stay put. McCabe called Astarita, who said he'd try to track down the branch manager and see what they could do. McCabe gave Astarita Janie Archer's number. Then he hit PLAY. The video picked up where it left off.

'But you've seen them?' asked the man.

'Oh, yes. I've seen them.'

'Graphic, I suppose.'

'Extremely graphic. Disgusting, in fact.'

'There's nothing illegal. The girl was sixteen. The age of consent.'

'Some of the others weren't.'

'You know about the others?'

'Yes. She told me.'

'But you don't have pictures of the others, do you? Or any other kind of proof.'

Lainie said nothing.

'Where are the pictures?'

'I told you. In a safe place.'

The man got up and walked around the room, head down, face away from the camera. If they were going to arrest, if they were going to convict, they needed to see his face.

The man sat down again. 'You're bluffing. There are no pictures.'

'You think so?' Now there was a hard, mocking tone to Lainie's voice. 'Then call my bluff.'

The man hesitated as if he were thinking about doing just that. 'Alright. What do you want?' he finally asked.

'I want you to leave Portland. I want you to leave Maine. I want you to have nothing more to do with kids, girls, boys, anyone, wherever you go. And wherever it is you do go, trust me, I'll be watching. I'll know.'

'If I ignore you?'

'Unfortunately, I don't think I have enough to send you to jail. As you said, she's sixteen.'

McCabe wondered if the girl they were talking about was Tara, the one with the fluffy white jacket on the porch at Sanctuary House. Kelly said she was sixteen. He could ask her. If she was still alive. If the guy hadn't killed her like he killed Lainie Goff. And Callie Connor. And Leanna Barnes. McCabe wondered how long the list of victims might be. He took a deep breath and held it.

'So what will you do?' the man asked.

'You know, it's funny,' Lainie said. 'I've been dealing with self-righteous, hypocritical creeps like you all my life. My mother was married to one.'

Scratch Albright, thought McCabe.

'What I only recently realized is that what you fear most is exposure. You know that, and now I know that. So here's the deal. You disappear like I said, and I'll keep the pictures to myself.'

'If I don't?'

'Then you'll be famous. I'll publish them everywhere I can. On the Internet. In the newspapers. Maybe even *Dateline* will be interested. I'm a damned good lawyer, and if I bend my mind to it I may even figure out a way to send you to prison after all.'

'I'm not going to prison, and you're not going to publish anything.'

'No. Because you're going to go away quietly. Knowing your type, practically nothing would be as painful to you as public humiliation. I'm leaving Saturday for two weeks' vacation. When I get back I expect you to be gone. I also expect you to let me know where you are and what you're doing. If both those things don't happen, I go public. Now get out of here before I puke. You're stinking up my apartment.'

The guy made a guttural sound. Somewhere between a sigh and a moan. Barely loud enough to be picked up by Andy Barker's lousy mike. He closed his eyes. Laid his head back on the back of the chair. And there he was.

McCabe froze the frame and stared at the image. It wasn't full face, and the lighting was bad. But it was enough. McCabe knew they had to find Richard Wolfe and find him fast. He just hoped they weren't too late.

Thirty-Eight

McCabe called Winter Haven. Abby Quinn was in a room on the third floor. Room 317 North. He told the operator to connect him with the unit nursing station.

While the phone rang on the other end, he scribbled Wolfe's home and office addresses and all three of his phone numbers. 'Call in an ATL,' McCabe said, handing the note to Fraser. 'He drives a black Lexus IS 350.' McCabe closed his eyes, reconstructing the precise image of the car parked by the building on Union Wharf. 'Maine plates. 4351LN. He's probably still got the .22, and remember, he's already killed three people. Right now he doesn't know we know it's him, but once he figures it out, he'll have nothing to lose.' Fraser nodded and picked up the conference room phone.

The nursing station phone was still ringing. McCabe handed Maggie another Post-it. 'Here's his cell. See if the Call Center can triangulate current location.'

'If he's got it turned on,' she said. 'He's not dumb.'

'Like I said, he doesn't know anything about Andy Barker's videos. Doesn't know we're after him.' She took the Post-it and flipped open her cell.

'Three North. Amanda Moehler.' The voice of a middle-aged woman. Probably an experienced nurse. That was good.

'Ms. Moehler. This is Detective McCabe. Portland police. I need you to check on your patient Abby Quinn.'

'What? Why?' Moehler sounded puzzled. 'She's fine. She's resting. We just gave her –'

'Ms. Moehler, please. Quinn may be in danger.' McCabe spoke quietly but added an unmistakable urgency to his voice. 'Please go to room 317 right now and check on Abby Quinn.'

There was a moment's hesitation on the other end of the line; then Moehler said, 'Hold on.'

Thirty seconds later she was back on the line. 'She's not there. I don't understand how she could've just disa –'

McCabe cut her off. 'Have you seen Dr Wolfe?'

'Yes. He was with her about an hour ago, but he left. I haven't seen him since.'

Shit. A whole hour since Wolfe had left. And McCabe himself had told the bastard to try hypnotherapy. Abby could be anywhere wandering around in a hypnotic trance. Even worse, she could be with Wolfe. 'Ms. Moehler,' McCabe said, 'transfer me to hospital security now.'

While he waited for Security to answer, he told Cleary to get Gorham PD on the phone. Chief John Sax.

'Winter Haven Security. Garth Andersen speaking.'

'Andersen, this is Sergeant Michael McCabe, Portland PD.'

'How can I help you?'

'I need you to organize an immediate search of the building and the grounds.'

'Alright. Who or what am I looking for?'

'A patient named Abby Quinn. Brought in last night. Female schizophrenic. Twenty-five years old. Reddish brown hair. She may be wearing civilian clothes, and she may be with Dr Richard Wolfe.'

'Wolfe? I know Wolfe. I can just page him.'

'Don't do that. Tell your people not to say anything to Wolfe.' The last thing McCabe needed was some unarmed security guard alerting Wolfe they were after him and getting his ass shot off in the process. 'Just find Quinn and take her into custody. If Wolfe's with her, tell him you're under orders and call us immediately. If he objects, don't interfere. Just keep an eye on him and call me.' He gave Andersen his number. 'Gorham police will be there to back you up in a few minutes.'

'I'll need some kind of authorization on this.'

'Call Portland PD. Chief Shockley's office.' McCabe looked over at Shockley. 'He'll confirm what I've told you.'

Shockley went back to his office to take the call.

'I've got Chief Sax from Gorham on line one.' Cleary held out the phone. McCabe took it.

'Hey, McCabe, John Sax here.'

'John, we need your help,' said McCabe. He gave Sax a quick rundown on the situation. Sax said he'd scramble all available units and head them to the hospital. He'd go over there himself and take over from Security.

'Tell your people to be careful, John,' said McCabe. 'Wolfe's armed and very dangerous. He doesn't know we're after him yet. Let's keep it that way as long as we can. We'll e-mail you photos of both Quinn and Wolfe.'

He nodded at Starbucks, who nodded back and left to make it happen.

He looked around the table. 'Tom, you and Carl get over to Sanctuary House and turn the place upside down. If Wolfe doesn't have her, Quinn may be hiding there.'

The conference room phone rang. Fraser picked it up, then held it out to McCabe. 'It's Nurse Moehler from Winter Haven.'

'Yes, what is it?' asked McCabe.

'I just found some things in Quinn's room that may be important.'

'Go ahead.'

'Her hospital gown was balled up next to the toilet. She didn't have any other clothes when she came in last night, and nobody's been to see her. Dr Wolfe must have brought her some clothes.'

'Anything else?'

'Yes. A note. On the table next to her bed.' He could hear Moehler take a deep breath. 'She may be suicidal.'

'What's it say?'

'It's kind of, I don't know, a poem or something.'

'What's it say?'

Moehler began reading.

> *I smell Death all around me.*
> *My beginning and my end.*
> *I'll go back to my heart*
> *where I first saw his blue, blue eyes.*
> *I long to embrace Death again.*
> *For the very first time.*

'That's it?'

'That's it.'

He didn't know if Abby wrote poetry. But he hoped she did. Because if she didn't, Richard Wolfe did, and that was bad news. *I long to embrace Death again.* 'Let's go, Tonto,' he said, pulling Maggie out of her chair. 'We're out of here.'

'Where to?'

'Harts Island.' On the way out he asked Cleary to make sure the *Mangini* was waiting for them.

McCabe drove. Lights. No siren. They were at the pier in less than two minutes. Maggie was on the line to the Harts Island cop shop when they climbed aboard. A cop named Bob Fane took the call.

She put Fane on speaker and told him to get a search party together. Quinn was on her way back to the island. Probably suicidal. 'You guys need to check any and all boats coming in. Not just the ferries but lobster boats, fishing boats. Anything that floats. She's already tried jumping from the rocks twice. She may try again.'

'Jesus, Mag, there are a hundred places on this island she could jump from.'

'Well, round up as many people as you can and check them all. Also check her house. If you find her, hold her. If she's with a man, it'll be Richard Wolfe. Arrest him – but be careful. He's armed and definitely dangerous.'

'Got it.'

'One more thing. McCabe and I are on the *Mangini* now. Should be on the island in five to seven. We're heading to Kelly's. We need wheels.'

'Tell the skipper to drop you at the sailing club dock. That's closer to Kelly's than the landing. Someone will meet you there with a four-by.'

Maggie's last call was to Casco Bay Lines. She left word for the ferry crews to be on the lookout for Abby Quinn and for Richard Wolfe.

Thirty-Nine

Harts Island, Maine

An attractive woman in her forties with short blond hair and a trim figure was leaning on a Ford F-150 pickup when the *Mangini* pulled in.

'Hi, I'm Lori Sparks.' McCabe recognized the name as the owner of the Crow's Nest. 'Bob Fane said you guys needed wheels.' She waved at the truck. 'Keys are in the ignition. Just leave it outside the Nest when you're done.'

They thanked her and climbed in.

'Hope you find her,' Sparks shouted as they pulled out. 'She's a good kid. She deserves a break.'

McCabe drove as fast as the twisty and narrow island lanes would allow. He felt certain Quinn was here on Harts Island, certain she was at Kelly's. *Back to my heart. Where I first saw his blue, blue eyes.* Casco Bay and the Portland skyline flashed by to their left. The distinctive shapes of office buildings and the twin spires of the Observatory and the Catholic Cathedral of the Immaculate Conception stood out, graceful silhouettes against an orange Hollywood sunset. Portland's native son director, John Ford, would've loved it. At the end of the paved road McCabe bumped the big Ford onto the same rutted dirt trail he'd followed last night, the truck nearly too wide for the space. Maggie tilted her body to avoid putting weight on the exit wound. The bumps hurt.

'Just a couple of minutes more,' said McCabe.

His phone vibrated. Art Astarita in New York. McCabe stopped to take the call.

'We're in the bank,' said Astarita. 'Archer's just opening her box now.' Pause. 'Okay, we've got the envelope. We're opening it.'

McCabe resisted the urge to tell Astarita to hurry.

'Jesus, McCabe, you got some real cuties up there in Portland. This stuff's gross. Some older guy doing weird shit to a girl who looks like she's about twelve. Bondage. Maybe torture.'

'She's supposed to be sixteen.'

'Sure as hell doesn't look it.'

'Can you see the guy's face?'

'Yeah. Front face. Side face. Everything else, too. I'll e-mail you the stack soon as I get 'em scanned. You got a real charmer there. Hope you cut his balls off.'

McCabe thanked him, the gratitude genuine, the circle closed. Would the photos be enough to send Wolfe to prison? Lainie didn't think so, but that was before she was murdered.

He pulled the truck into the turnaround. No other vehicles. If Abby was here, she hadn't driven. If Wolfe was here, he hadn't either. They could see no signs of life by the shack. Maybe McCabe was wrong about the poem. Maybe they were somewhere else.

They moved silently through the woods, Maggie using the cane for balance and to probe the snow in front of her. The last thing she needed was to fall on her ass. They stopped where the clearing began, maybe a hundred feet from the house. They could see Abby now, standing alone, with her back to them on the edge of the cliff. She was looking down at the rocks below, bare feet toeing the icy edge of a large overhanging rock that jutted out into open space. It made a nearly perfect diving platform. There was no sign of Richard Wolfe.

Abby was dressed in a floaty white summer dress. The kind of thing she might have worn for her high school graduation. Portland High. Class of '99. Incongruous both for the season and the place. Her hands were down at her sides. It looked like she was holding something. Whatever it was was lost within the soft folds of fabric that swayed in rhythm with the wind that blew in from the sea. Abby's reddish brown hair was pinned back, a garland of white flowers arranged in a band across the top of her head. No, it wasn't her graduation, McCabe decided. Abby was dressed for a wedding. A bride awaiting her groom's arrival. *I long to embrace Death again. For the very first time.* All that was missing was a bouquet and a veil. The wind was picking up now, and, January thaw or not, McCabe figured she had to be freezing. He wondered if just seeing them approach would be enough to cause her to jump.

'Keep an eye on our friend,' he said to Maggie. 'I'm going to check out the cottage.' He slipped his .45 from its holster and into the deep pocket of his coat and started toward the house. He moved across the open clearing as fast and silently as he could, Bill Fortier's L.L. Bean boots giving him better, though not perfect, traction on the icy ledge.

He reached the cottage and pushed himself up against

one wall. He peered through the window. The main room looked dark and empty. He pushed in through the front door. Nothing.

'Richard? Are you here?' He kept his voice friendly, collegial.

No answer. He quickly checked the other rooms. Nothing. Through the window he could see Abby still perched on her rock. Maggie had moved closer. She was now only about fifty feet away.

Suddenly there was movement at the end of the cliff, and Richard Wolfe's head appeared above the rocks, followed by his shoulders. Wolfe was climbing up the rickety wooden steps that rose from the rocky beach below. He was still wearing the same dark hooded coat as before, but in the warmer air the hood was down. Wolfe walked toward Maggie. If he still had the .22 it wasn't in his hand. McCabe drew the .45 from his pocket. He felt his cell phone vibrate. Caller ID said M. SAVAGE. He knew it wasn't because Maggie wanted to talk to him. She was just telling him to stay put and listen in. He put the phone to his ear and watched through the window.

'You must be Dr Wolfe?' Maggie said when he was about five feet away.

'Yes. Who are you, and what are you doing here?'

'I'm with the police,' she said. 'Detective Margaret Savage, Portland PD.' She held up her badge wallet. He glanced at it. 'We've been looking for Abby.'

Maybe it was because she heard her name or perhaps because she simply sensed their presence behind her, but Abby turned and looked. First at Wolfe. Then at Maggie. McCabe could see her eyes, but in the failing light of a late

January afternoon it was hard to tell if what he saw in them was madness or merely despair. Behind her, weather clouds were closing in. The wind was rising. Waves of white fabric rippled against a darkening sky. He still couldn't see what was in her hand.

'Abby, my name is Margaret Savage,' Maggie called to her. 'I'm a friend. I'm here to help you. I'd like you please to step away from the edge.'

Abby seemed nervous, distracted. McCabe wasn't sure she had even heard Maggie's calm request. Perhaps with the wind blowing she was too far away. Maggie probed the snow in front of her with her cane, making sure her next step, if she took one, would find firm footing. 'I'm coming to talk to you,' she called.

'I wouldn't go any closer,' Wolfe said. 'She'll jump, you know. I've been trying to get her to step in from the edge for nearly an hour now. Without success. If you go any closer, I think she'll go over.'

McCabe thought about pulling the window up a couple of inches and using the sill as a firing platform. A tough shot from this distance. Too easy to miss. Besides, the shot might cause Abby to jump. No, it wasn't a good idea.

'I can try talking her out of it,' he heard Maggie say to Wolfe. She was keeping her voice too low for Abby to hear. She took another step toward Abby and then another. At the same time, she began moving sideways, crossing in front of Wolfe to his other side, forcing him to turn away from the cottage in order to watch her. Forcing him to keep his back to McCabe.

'Where are you going?' Wolfe asked. 'What are you doing?' There was anxiety in his voice now.

'I need to get closer or she won't hear me,' said Maggie, her tone calm, matter-of-fact.

McCabe slipped out the cottage door as she spoke.

'Talking her down won't work if I have to shout,' Maggie continued.

'It won't work anyway,' said Wolfe. 'I want you to go away. Abby doesn't know you. She knows me. I'm her doctor. She trusts me. Just leave, and I'll get her to come in.'

McCabe flipped the phone off and stuck it in his pocket. He was close enough now to hear without it.

'Did you hypnotize her?' Maggie asked.

'Yes, I hypnotized her.'

'How'd it work?'

Wolfe didn't hear McCabe approaching. Now less than ten feet from Wolfe's back. Too close to miss. Maggie didn't alert Wolfe by glancing up.

'She went under quite easily. In fact, she's still in a hypnotic trance. She'll do anything I ask.'

'Really? Anything?'

'Yes.'

'Including asking her to walk in from the edge of that cliff?' asked Maggie.

'Yes,' said Wolfe.

'Well, why is it you're not doing that?' asked McCabe.

Wolfe turned. His eyes widened at the sight of the .45 leveled at his chest.

'Is it because you want her to jump?'

'What on earth are you talking about?'

'There were hidden cameras in Goff's apartment the night she told you about the pictures. You know, the dirty pictures. We have the whole conversation on video. We know it was you. You're under arrest.'

If Wolfe was surprised he didn't show it. A thin, ugly smile passed his lips. 'There's only one problem with that,' he said. 'You were right a minute ago. I do want her to jump. And all I have to do to make it happen is say one word . . . let's call it the magic word . . . and, poof, over she goes.'

McCabe didn't know whether Wolfe was bluffing. Maybe there was a magic word, maybe there wasn't. He considered his options. One was simply pulling the trigger. That would end it – but the shot might also drive Abby over the edge. An unacceptable risk.

Out of the corner of his eye he could see Abby turn back and look the other way, down at the rocks and at the sea below. Then she turned her gaze back to the three of them. Was she in a hypnotic trance? McCabe didn't know. All he saw on her face was fear. Afraid to move forward to her death. Afraid to move back toward them.

'I have a question for you, Richard,' said McCabe. 'If Detective Savage and I do what you ask and leave, what happens next? You take Abby with you as your hostage?'

'That's my plan, yes. Plan B, actually. My backup. My dinghy's on the beach at the bottom of the stairs. My boat's anchored nearby. You leave. Abby and I sail away. When I feel it's safe, I'll drop her off on the coast. If you or the Coast Guard or some down-market Galahad in a lobster boat follows me . . .' Wolfe shrugged.

'You'll say your magic word, and she'll jump overboard.'

Wolf smiled. 'No, actually, at that point, I'll just shoot

her. I keep a small revolver on board. A Smith & Wesson Airweight .38.'

McCabe was familiar with the Airweight. It was light. Easily concealed. Deadly at close quarters.

'Out of curiosity, Richard, what was Plan A?'

'Oh, Plan A was much simpler. There would have been no video. Kelly would have gone to jail for the murder.'

'Murders plural.'

'Yes, murders plural. Abby, not needed as a hostage, would have jumped off the cliff, her third and final try at suicide tragically successful. I would have sailed back to my office in Portland. And, of course, we all would have mourned her loss in the morning.'

'Why did she have to die?' asked Maggie. 'She couldn't describe what you looked like.'

'There was no guarantee of that. Her memory might have come back at any time.'

It was a no go. McCabe knew that if Abby got on Wolfe's boat, he would kill her as soon as he didn't need her anymore. Again he considered his options. Shooting the bastard was still number one. He couldn't think of a second.

'One last question, Richard.'

'Before you go?'

'Yes. Before we go.' He leveled the .45 at Wolfe's throat. Where Wolfe's magic word would come from. If there really was a magic word. 'It's sort of a physics question. You know, like the ones we had in high school. If train A leaves station B at forty miles an hour. That sort of thing.'

Wolfe stared at McCabe and then at the gun and said nothing.

'Want to know what my question is, Richard? It's kind of an important one.'

Still Wolfe said nothing.

'My question is, if the bullet in the chamber of my gun leaves the barrel at exactly the same instant you start to shout your magic word, will you be dead before or after the word leaves your mouth?'

'You're bluffing.'

'I don't think so.'

'That would be murder.'

It was McCabe's turn to smile. 'No. Murder is what you do, Dr Wolfe. What I do is called justifiable use of force against a killer threatening a hostage.'

'McCabe,' said Maggie.

'What?' he answered, his eyes still glued to Wolfe.

'She's off the cliff. She's walking this way.'

McCabe glanced quickly to his right. Abby was heading toward them through the snow. Her feet were bare. Her hands still hung by her sides.

'Well,' said McCabe, 'it seems Abby has solved our hostage crisis. That makes everything much simpler. I want you facedown on the ground with your hands behind your back.'

Wolfe didn't move.

'Now, Richard. Otherwise I may shoot you just for the hell of it. You know the headline. "Perpetrator shot and killed resisting arrest."'

When Quinn was about ten feet from Wolfe, she stopped. 'You're Death,' she said. 'You have to die.'

She raised a small shiny revolver. Wolfe's Airweight .38.

'Abby! No!' Maggie leapt, hitting Quinn's legs just as

she fired, knocking both knees out from under her and the gun from her hand. The bullet went wide. Wolfe and Maggie dove for the gun. Wolfe won.

He scooped up the revolver and, in one swift motion, rolled to his feet behind Abby. He wrapped an arm around her neck, pulling her in and pushing the short barrel of the Airweight against her throat.

She struggled to get away, but he was too strong, his grip too tight. He started pulling her back, one step at a time, looking first left at McCabe, then right at Maggie.

McCabe and Maggie followed his retreat, McCabe circling left toward the wooden stairs, Maggie circling to the right. Both working to create a wider angle that would give at least one of them a clear shot at Wolfe without hitting Abby. Wolfe looked from one side to the other. Then he looked at the stairs. McCabe was standing in front of them, blocking his escape.

'Out of the way,' Wolfe shouted, 'or she's dead.'

'You'll be dead, too, Richard. Death all around.'

Without warning, Abby wrenched her body violently forward and down, screaming, 'Shut up! Shut up! I won't listen to you anymore!'

Suddenly exposed, Wolfe fired at McCabe at precisely the same instant that McCabe fired back. McCabe was a better shot. The big .45 a better gun. McCabe's bullet struck Wolfe high on the chest, driving him back. Maggie's bullet hit his back a fraction of a second later, four inches lower. The impact of their two shots drove him backward over the edge of the cliff. He didn't scream as he fell. McCabe figured that was because he was already dead.

'Tell them to shut up,' Abby shrieked. 'Tell them I won't listen to them anymore. I won't listen.'

She tucked herself into a fetal position and wept. Maggie sat down in the snow next to her and gently stroked her back. McCabe peered over the cliff through the growing darkness. He saw a retreating wave pull Wolfe's body away from the rocks and out into the frigid water. If the bullets hadn't killed him, surely the fall had. If not the fall, then surely the icy cold January seas. Any way you cut it, it was over.

'He was Death. He had to die,' Abby told Maggie between sobs. 'He had to die.'

McCabe called for the fireboat and an ambulance to meet them on the other side. They were taking Abby to Winter Haven. He hoped she wouldn't have to be there long. But there was no way of knowing.

Forty

Maggie and McCabe returned to 109. The photographs from New York were waiting for them in McCabe's e-mail in-box. They both peered at the screen and flipped through them one at a time. There were six in all, and Lainie was right. All six were both graphic and disgusting.

For what it was worth, the girl in the photos wasn't Tara. It was someone who looked much younger with a thin, barely developed body. She may have been sixteen, but, as Astarita said, she looked more like twelve.

'I'm glad he's dead,' said Maggie, staring at the screen.

'That's the first time I've ever heard you say that.'

'I only wish we could have made it more painful.' She turned away from the images and went back to her desk. 'Maybe we'll find her alive,' she said as she eased herself down in her chair. 'Maybe she managed to get away.'

'Yeah, maybe,' said McCabe. 'You never know.'

They both knew they were blowing smoke. The odds of Wolfe's having let the girl live when he'd killed all the others were next to zero. Even now, teams of cops equipped with ground-penetrating radar and a couple of cadaver dogs were out searching John Kelly's five-acre property. If they didn't find her there, they'd extend the search to the rest of the island. But the truth was, her body could be almost anywhere. The girl didn't fit into Wolfe's scheme to frame John Kelly, and like Maggie said, Maine was a big state.

'I guess Kelly will be able to tell us who she is,' he said. 'Maybe help us find her.' The District Attorney's office had authorized the ex-priest's release less than an hour earlier. He was probably already home.

McCabe shut down his computer, stuffed a couple of files in his bottom drawer, and stood up from his desk. 'Why don't you go home?' he said to Maggie. 'You've got to be at least as tired as I am. Maybe more. I don't have the benefit of two bullet holes in me. Tom or Brian can go over the pictures with Kelly.'

'You go,' she said. 'Don't you remember what I told you last night? I'm Superwoman. Besides, I'd like to finish this up myself.'

McCabe called Kyra from the car. Told her it was over. Told her he was back. She was in her studio, she said, putting the finishing touches on a new painting. She told him she'd be home in an hour.

'Wagging your tail and happy as a clam?'

'Absolutely. I'll stop at Hannaford's on the way for some groceries. Somehow, I have a feeling you guys could use a decent meal.'

The lights were on in the apartment when McCabe pulled into his place on the Eastern Prom. He climbed the stairs to the third floor and unlocked the door.

'Hello,' he called. There was no answer. He tried again. 'Anybody home?'

Still no answer. He headed for Casey's room. She should have been here by now.

She was. Sitting on her bed, back resting against the headboard, *Harry Potter and the Half-Blood Prince* propped on her knees. Ear buds in her ears. He studied her face, serious and intent on the story.

'Haven't you read that before?' he shouted to be heard over the music.

'I'm reading it again,' she said. Her eyes remained glued to the book.

'Can I come in and maybe get a "hello, I missed you, and I'm glad to see you" kiss?'

'In a minute ... just let me finish this chapter. Just another . . .' She flipped the pages. 'Three more pages.'

'Oh no!' He threw a hand over his heart, 'Rejected again.'

Apparently she didn't find that funny, 'cause she didn't laugh. 'Just a couple of minutes, okay?' she said.

'Okay.' He went to the kitchen and poured a couple of inches of the Macallan into the cut crystal glass, came back to her room, and eased himself down onto the dark wood floor, resting his back against the door of her closet. He sipped the Scotch and studied her face. She was growing up fast, starting to look even more like Sandy than she had as a little girl. A lot more, he realized now, than Lainie Goff ever had. She had the same mouth and nose. The same silky dark hair. The same startling blue eyes. The same perfect skin. Fourteen years old and not even the trace of a zit. She was facing the blessing and the curse of being a drop-dead beautiful woman. Just like Sandy. But, thank God, that's where the resemblance ended.

Inside, Casey was totally different. She was bright and funny and giving in a way that Sandy never was, and she had a silly sense of humor that was totally a McCabe gene. She'd taken the best of both her parents. There was going to be no stopping this kid.

'There,' she said, marking her place and closing the book. She got up and walked to where he was sitting, opened her arms wide, closed her eyes, and squeezed her lips in an exaggerated pucker. 'Get up,' she said. 'You may welcome me home.'

'Not sure I want to now,' he said, looking up. 'You blew your chances.' He took another sip of his Scotch.

'Well, then pooh on you.' She turned away and headed for the kitchen. 'By the way, there's nothing to eat,' she called back. 'Just a dead lasagna that looks like it's been in the microwave since before I was born.'

He got up and followed. 'Hey!' he called after her.

'Hey, what.'

'Hey, pooh on you, too,' he said, wrapping his arms around her slender body. They gave each other a long, hard squeeze.

'Kyra's picking up some food,' he said, releasing her. 'She'll be here in an hour.'

She flopped down on the couch. He sat in Dad's chair.

'How was the boarding?'

'Awesome except for the tow lines. We got a ton of snow Friday night.'

'I heard.'

'Saturday and today were both gorgeous. You and Kyra should have come. You would have loved it.'

'I'm sure. How was your report card?'

'Good.'

'Can I see it?'

'Sure.' She went back to her room and returned with the card. Four As and one B. He wanted to ask her about going away to school without biasing her by telling her it was Sandy's idea. He didn't think it would be anything she'd want to do. Still, he needed to be sure.

'Have you thought any more about where you want to go to college?' he asked.

'I don't know. Orono, I guess. Or maybe USM. Then I could live at home.'

'How about Harvard? Or Yale?'

'Yeah, right,' she snorted. 'Nobody gets in there.'

'Somebody must. They have a whole bunch of students at both places. Grades like these, you could be one of them.'

'I doubt it.'

'You could if you went to a good boarding school first.'

'Boarding school?' She looked at him as if he'd suggested taking classes on Mars. 'Where did that come from?'

'Just a thought.'

'Not a very good one. I don't want to go to boarding school. We can't afford it, anyway. You're always saying you can't even pay the bills we already have.'

'They have scholarships,' he said. 'You might get one.' If she decided she did want to go away to school, there was no way he'd let Peter Ingram pay for it. She was his daughter. Not Ingram's.

Her eyes narrowed. Her version of his Clint Eastwood squint. 'I don't want to go to boarding school, and I don't know why you're even bringing it up. You sound like you want to get rid of me or something. Like Mom did.'

He went over and sat near her on the edge of the couch. 'No, I don't want to get rid of you, and no, I don't want you to go to boarding school. In fact, I'd hate it if you weren't here.'

'Then what'd you bring it up for?'

'It's something your mother suggested, and I just needed to be sure it wasn't something you wanted to do before I told her no way.'

'No way.'

'Okay. Good. No way it is, then.'

'Besides, like I told you before, I want to be a cop. Like you.'

The family business. He smiled to himself. Would it suck in yet another generation of McCabes? It hadn't missed a single one since his great-grandfather joined the force in New York back in the 1890s. How long could they keep the string going? How long did they want to?

'I don't think I need to go to Harvard to do that.'

'No, but you do need to go to college before you decide.'

'Orono's fine.'

'It's better than fine. It's a good school.'

He hugged her again. They heard the front door open and close. Kyra appeared carrying a bag of groceries. 'Hello. Could I have one, too? A hug, I mean?'

He took the shopping bag and put it on the floor and wrapped his arms around both his women. 'Welcome home,' he said.

'It's good to be home,' said Kyra. 'In fact, I don't think I'll be leaving again.'

'Not even if I have another murder?'

'Not even.'

He looked in the bags. 'What's for dinner?' he asked.

'Chicken Saltimbocca,' she said. 'Sautéed chicken breasts topped with prosciutto and melted mozzarella cheese in a butter and wine sauce.' Kyra was at least as good a cook as she was an artist. Whatever she made would be delicious. 'I'll start it now.'

'I'll help you,' said Casey. 'Okay?'

Kyra looked surprised. 'Okay.' She'd never asked before. 'Of course.'

McCabe poured Kyra a glass of Sancerre, then hauled himself up on the kitchen stool, sipped his Scotch, and watched them work.

A couple of minutes later, the doorbell rang. He debated whether or not to answer it, but then it rang again, and so he did. John Kelly was on the other side.

'Hello, John.'

'I stopped by police headquarters. Detective Savage told me I'd find you here.'

'What can I do for you?'

'I saw the pictures.'

'I'm sorry we had to put you through that.'

'Yes. Me, too. Her name was Kimberly Watkins. She was one of Lainie's girls. She disappeared from Sanctuary House just before Christmas.'

'You didn't report it?'

'No. I didn't think much of it. Kids take off all the time.

She's from a town called Mapleton up near Presque Isle. I thought maybe she went back for the holidays. Even the runaways get sentimental sometimes.'

'Well, maybe she did.'

'Yeah, maybe. But I doubt it. So do you.'

McCabe nodded. 'Yes, I do. Anyway, what can I do for you?'

'Nothing really. I just wanted to thank you.'

Thank him? McCabe had spent over an hour verbally beating this guy over the head and he wanted to thank him. 'Thank me? For what exactly?'

'For digging deeper. For not accepting the easy answers. From me or anyone else. For stopping that bastard.'

McCabe shrugged. 'It's my job. I do it the best I can.'

'A lot of cops wouldn't have bothered. You did. I wanted to thank you for that.'

'You're welcome. Would you like to come in? Join me for a Scotch?'

'Thanks, no.'

'Or some Irish? I've got a bottle of Black Bush around here somewhere. My brother sent it. Wanted to prove the Irish make whisky as good as the Scots any day.'

'Some other time, maybe. Teddy's waiting for me downstairs in the car. You go on back to your family.' He held out his hand. McCabe shook it. Kelly left.

McCabe returned to the kitchen and climbed back up on the stool.

'Who was that?' asked Casey.

'One of the suspects in my murder case.'

'I assume it was one who didn't do it,' said Kyra.

'Yes, it was. I was wondering,' he said, 'do you think, after dinner, you might be able to borrow the keys to the gallery?'

'I don't know. I can call Gloria and ask. Why? What do you have in mind?'

'I thought maybe, after dinner, we all ought to stop by and take a look. I understand they're showing some new work by a major Maine artist. I heard she was really good.'

Kyra smiled. 'Yeah, I heard that, too. I'll see what I can do.'

JAMES HAYMAN

THE CUTTING

He is stealing the hearts of beautiful young women . . .

Portland, Maine. A missing high-school athlete's mutilated body is found in a scrap metal yard. Her heart has been surgically removed. The same day a young businesswoman is abducted . . .

Former NYPD detective Michael McCabe believes both crimes are the work of one man. A killer with surgical expertise who is targeting young women. Now McCabe and his team face a race against time to rescue the missing woman and unmask this sadistic killer - before it is too late.

'An engrossing account of a deviously motivated psychopathic serial killer'
Booklist

'A clever and suspenseful thriller' *Boston Globe*

'A thriller of a thriller!' Tess Gerritsen

He just wanted a decent book to read ...

Not too much to ask, is it? It was in 1935 when Allen Lane, Managing Director of Bodley Head Publishers, stood on a platform at Exeter railway station looking for something good to read on his journey back to London. His choice was limited to popular magazines and poor-quality paperbacks – the same choice faced every day by the vast majority of readers, few of whom could afford hardbacks. Lane's disappointment and subsequent anger at the range of books generally available led him to found a company – and change the world.

'We believed in the existence in this country of a vast reading public for intelligent books at a low price, and staked everything on it'
Sir Allen Lane, 1902–1970, founder of Penguin Books

The quality paperback had arrived – and not just in bookshops. Lane was adamant that his Penguins should appear in chain stores and tobacconists, and should cost no more than a packet of cigarettes.

Reading habits (and cigarette prices) have changed since 1935, but Penguin still believes in publishing the best books for everybody to enjoy. We still believe that good design costs no more than bad design, and we still believe that quality books published passionately and responsibly make the world a better place.

So wherever you see the little bird – whether it's on a piece of prize-winning literary fiction or a celebrity autobiography, political tour de force or historical masterpiece, a serial-killer thriller, reference book, world classic or a piece of pure escapism – you can bet that it represents the very best that the genre has to offer.

Whatever you like to read – trust Penguin.